HIS PRINCESS OF CONVENIENCE

BY
REBECCA WINTERS

MILLS &
BOON

First Published in Great Britain 2016
By Mills & Boon, an imprint of HarperCollins*Publishers*
1 London Bridge Street, London, SE1 9GF

© 2016 Harlequin Books S.A.

Special thanks and acknowledgement are given to Rebecca Winters for her contribution to The Vineyards of Calanetti series.

ISBN: 978-0-263-91952-3

23-0116

Our policy is to use papers that are natural, renewable and recyclable products and made from wood grown in sustainable forests. The logging and manufacturing processes conform to the legal environmental regulations of the country of origin.

Printed and bound in Spain
by CPI, Barcelona

The Vineyards of Calanetti

Saying "I do" under the Tuscan sun...

Deep in the Tuscan countryside nestles
the picturesque village of Monte Calanetti.
Famed for its world-renowned vineyards, the
village is also home to the crumbling but beautiful
Palazzo di Comparino. It's been empty for months,
but rumours of a new owner are spreading like
wildfire... and that's before the village is chosen
as the setting for the royal wedding of the year!

It's going to be a roller coaster of a year,
but will wedding bells ring out in
Monte Calanetti for anyone else?

Find out in this fabulously heart-warming,
uplifting and thrillingly romantic new eight-book
continuity from Mills & Boon Romance!

A Bride for the Italian Boss by Susan Meier

Return of the Italian Tycoon by Jennifer Faye

Reunited by a Baby Secret by Michelle Douglas

Soldier, Hero... Husband? by Cara Colter

His Lost-and-Found Bride by Scarlet Wilson

The Best Man & The Wedding Planner
by Teresa Carpenter

His Princess of Convenience by Rebecca Winters

Saved by the CEO by **Barbara Wallace**
Available February 2016

Rebecca Winters, whose family of four children has now swelled to include five beautiful grandchildren, lives in Salt Lake City, Utah, in the land of the Rocky Mountains. With canyons and high alpine meadows full of wildflowers, she never runs out of places to explore. They, plus her favorite vacation spots in Europe, often end up as backgrounds for her romance novels, because writing is her passion, along with her family and church.

Rebecca loves to hear from readers. If you wish to email her, please visit her website, www.cleanromances.com.

This book is dedicated to every woman
who was once a little girl with a dream to be a princess.

CHAPTER ONE

August, Monte Calanetti, Italy

THE FLOOR-LENGTH MIRROR reflected a princess bride whose flowing white wedding dress, with the heavy intricate beading, followed the lines of her slender rounded figure to perfection. It probably weighed thirty pounds, but her five-foot-nine height helped her to carry it off with a regal air.

The delicate tiara with sapphires, the something-borrowed, something-blue gift from the queen, Christina's soon-to-be mother-in-law, held the lace mantilla made by the nuns. The lace overlying her red-gold hair, to the satin slippers on her feet, formed a whole that looked…pretty.

"I actually feel like a bride." Her breath caught. "That can't be me!" she whispered to herself. Her very recent makeover was nothing short of miraculous.

Christina Rose, soon-to-be bride of Crown Prince Antonio de L'Accardi of Halencia, turned to one side, then the other, as past memories of being called an ugly duckling, the chubby one, filled her mind.

From adolescence until the ripe old age of twenty-eight, she'd had to live with those unflattering remarks muttered by the people around her. Not that she really heard people say those things once she'd grown up and had been spending her time doing charity work on behalf of her prominent family. But she knew it was what people were thinking.

In truth her own parents were the ones who'd scarred her. They'd left her with nannies from the time she was born. And as she'd grown, her father had constantly belittled her with hurtful barbs by comparing her unfavorably to her friends. "Why is our daughter so dumpy?" she'd once heard him say. "Why didn't we get a boy?" They'd picked out the name Christopher, but had to change it to Christina when she was born.

His unkind remarks during those impressionable years had been wounds that struck deep, especially considering that Christina's mother had been a former supermodel.

Christina didn't know how her father could have said such cruel things to his daughter when she had loved both her parents so much and desperately wanted their approval. Between her unattractive brownish-red hair she'd always worn in a ponytail, to her teeth that had needed straightening, she'd been an embarrassment to her parents, who moved in the highest of political and social circles in Halencia.

In order to keep her out of sight, they'd sent their overweight daughter to boarding school in Montreux, Switzerland, where forty-five girls from affluent, titled families were sent from countries around the world.

Her pain at having to live away year after year until she turned eighteen had been her deepest sorrow. Christina was a poor reflection on her parents, whose world revolved around impressing other important people in the upper echelons of society, including the favor of the royal family of Halencia. Her father particularly didn't want her around when they were entertaining important dignitaries, which was most of the time.

If it hadn't been for Elena, the daughter of Halencia's royal family attending the French-speaking boarding school who'd become her closest friend, Christina didn't know how she would have survived her time there. With both of them being from Italian-speaking Halencia, their nationality and own dialect had immediately created a bond between the two women.

Though Elena bore the title of Princess Elena de L'Accardi, she'd never used it at school or behaved as if she were better than Christina. If anything, she was a free spirit, on the wild side, and good-looking like her older brother, the handsome Crown Prince Antonio de L'Accardi, who was the heartthrob of Halencia, beloved by the people. He'd had a hold on Christina's heart from the first moment she met him.

Elena never worried about breaking a few rules, like meeting a boyfriend at the local ice-skating rink in Montreux without their headmistress finding out. And worse, sneaking out to his nearby boarding school and going rowing on the lake at midnight, or sneaking her out for a joyride to Geneva in the Lamborghini his wealthy parents had bought him.

Christina had loved being with Elena and secretly wished she could be outgoing and confident like her dear friend. When the royal family went on their many vacations, Christina missed Elena terribly. It was during those times that Christina developed a close friendship with the quiet-spoken Marusha from Kenya.

Marusha was the daughter of the chief of the westernized Kikuyu tribe who'd sent his daughter to be educated in Switzerland. Marusha suffered from homesickness and she and Christina had comforted each other. Their long talks had prompted Christina to fly to Kenya after she turned eighteen and Marusha prevailed on her father to open doors for Christina to do charity work there.

Once she'd established a foundation in Halencia to deal with the business side, Christina stationed herself in Africa and lost herself in giving help to others. She knew she was better off being far away from home where she couldn't be hurt by her parents' dissatisfaction with her.

Caught up in those crippling thoughts, Christina was startled to hear a knock on the door off the main hallway.

"Mi scusi," sounded a deep male voice she hadn't heard since his phone call two months ago. "I'm looking for Christina Rose. Is she in here?"

What was Antonio doing up here outside the doors of the bridal suite?

In a state of absolute panic, Christina ran behind the screen to hide. She'd come up here to be alone and make sure her wedding finery fit and looked right. For him to see her like this before the ceremony would be worse than bad luck!

Her heart pounded so hard she was afraid he could hear it through the doors. Trying to disguise her voice to a lower pitch, she said, "Christina isn't here, *signor*."

"I think she is," he teased. "I think it's you playing a game with me."

Heat filled her cheeks. He'd found her out. "Well, you can't come in!"

"Now, *that's* the Christina I remember. Still modest and afraid of your own shadow. What a way to greet your intended beloved."

"Go away, Antonio. You should be at the chapel."

"Is that all you have to say after I've flown thousands of miles to be with my fiancée?"

The large four-carat diamond ring set in antique gold belonging to the L'Accardi royal family had been given to her at their engagement four years ago. Though she'd gone through the sham ritual for the most worthy reason, it had been a personal horror for Christina.

But when her parents had acted overjoyed that she'd snagged the crown prince, she felt she'd gotten their attention at last. Becoming a royal princess had made them look more favorably at her, and that had helped her enter into the final wedding preparations with growing excitement.

The minute Antonio had flown back to the States, she put the ring in a vault for safekeeping. To damage it out in Africa would be unthinkable. She'd only gotten it out to wear on the few times they were together in Halencia. Now it was hidden in her purse.

Christina had never felt like a fiancée, royal or otherwise. She knew Antonio had been dreading this union as much as she had, but he was too honorable for his own good. Therefore Christina had to follow through on the bargain they'd made for Elena's sake.

"I didn't really believe this day would come."

He'd stayed away in San Francisco on business. The press followed his every move and knew he'd only been with her a handful of times since the engagement. He'd flown home long enough to be seen with her at the palace when she flew in from Africa. They came together in order to perpetuate the myth that they were in love and looking forward to their wedding day.

"San Francisco is a long way from Halencia, Christina, but I should have made time before."

"I know you've been married to your financial interests in Silicon Valley. No fiancée can compete with that." Not when she knew he'd been with beautiful women who were flattered by his attention and couldn't care less that he was engaged.

"You want to marry a successful husband, right? We had an agreement for Elena's sake."

He was right, of course, and it had been a secret between her and Antonio. But no one knew how Christina had pulled off such an improbable coup. The press had dubbed her the Cinderella Bride.

"I know, Antonio, and I plan to honor it. But not one second before I have to go downstairs to the chapel. Don't you have something else to do?"

"I'm doing it right now. Do you mind if I put a little

gift on the bed for you?" He'd said it kindly. "I promise I won't look at you and I'll hurry back out."

"What gift? I don't want anything." She knew she sounded ungracious, but she couldn't help it. She'd never been so nervous in her life!

"It's your family brooch, the one that a Rose bride wears at her wedding to bring her marriage luck. One of the stones had come loose, so I had it repaired for you to wear and couldn't get it back to you until today."

The brooch?

Christina had heard the story behind the brooch all her life. It was supposed to bring luck, but she thought it had been lost a long time ago. She'd asked her wedding planner, Lindsay, to try and track it down for her, but to no avail. Her father's aunt Sofia certainly hadn't whispered a word about it during all the wedding preparations. Why hadn't she given it to Christina herself? Furthermore how did Antonio get hold of it?

"Thank you for bringing it to me," she said in a subdued voice. "It means a lot." In fact, more than he could know. A special talisman to bring her luck handed down in the Rose family. Now she felt ready.

"It was important to me that you have it. I want this day to be perfect for you."

She was thrilled by the gesture and heard the door open. If all he had to do was put it on the bed, she should be hearing the doors closing any second now.

"Are you still holding your breath waiting for me to go away, *bellissima*?"

Bellissima. Christina was not beautiful, but the way

he said it made her feel beautiful, and today was her wedding day. She imagined he was trying to win her around with all the ways he knew how. She had no doubts he knew every one of them and more.

He laughed. "I'm still waiting, but we don't need to worry, Christina. After all, this isn't a real marriage."

She took a deep breath, realizing he was teasing her. "Well, considering that this isn't going to be a real marriage, then I'd say we need all the luck we can get, so please leave before even the ceremony itself is jinxed by your presence here."

"A moment, *per favore*. It's a lovely bridal chamber. The balcony off this suite shows the whole walled village of Monte Calanetti—it's very picturesque. I do believe you have a romantic heart to have chosen the Palazzo di Comparino for our wedding to take place. All nestled and secluded in this place amongst the vineyards rippling over the Tuscan countryside. I couldn't imagine a more perfect setting to celebrate our nuptials."

"After living near the vineyards of the Napa Valley in California all these years, I doubt a spot like this holds much enchantment for you. I guess I should be thanking you for letting our wedding take place here instead of the cathedral in Voti. Now, will you please go so I can finish getting ready?"

Christina was still her vulnerable self. Antonio stopped the teasing for a minute. "If it's any solace to you, I'm sorry for the position I've put you in."

After a long silence she said in a defeated tone,

"Don't worry about it." He heard a sadness in her voice. "To be honest, it isn't as if I've had any other offers."

Her comment revealed a little of her conflict, the same conflict torturing him. There was a part of him that wanted to be crazy in love. If only he'd been an ordinary man like his best man, Zach, who could marry the woman who'd captured his heart. To choose a bride his heart wanted had never been a possibility.

When he thought about Christina, he realized she was having similar feelings that increased his guilt, but he couldn't dwell on that right now. It was too late for regrets. They would be married within the hour and he intended to be a good husband to her.

"Just remember we're doing this for Elena," he reminded her, hoping it would help her spirits. "She'll be up in a minute to escort you to the chapel." His eyes closed tightly for a moment. "Would it help if I told you I admire you more than any other woman I know?" It was the truth.

"Actually it wouldn't," she came back. "Thousands of women have entered into political unions disguised as marriage. We thought our engagement wouldn't last long. I thought that after four years you would fly to Africa and tell me in person we didn't have to go through with it."

"I'm afraid that wasn't our destiny, Christina. Everything has escalated out of control, the paparazzi have driven things to a higher pitch. Father's chief assistant, Guido, had me on the phone, urging me to marry you as soon as possible. The people are fed up with my parents. They want our marriage to take place for the good of the monarchy, reminding me of the danger of an abolished royal family if we wait."

"I know. That's because they want you for their king, and you need a queen. I understand that, but I'd rather you didn't start using meaningless platitudes with me."

"I was complimenting you," he asserted.

"I'm glad we could help preserve Elena's reputation along with your family's, but I don't want compliments. Your sister is doing much better these days and has a boyfriend who treats her well. Let's be happy for that and avoid any unnecessary pretense."

Antonio had come to the bridal suite already deeply immersed in troubled thoughts about their forthcoming marriage. Her last remark only added to his anxiety. He put the small velvet-lined box at the foot of the bed. After closing the doors quietly behind him, he left the bridal suite and walked down the corridor to the staircase of the three-storied palazzo.

Zach, his best friend, would be waiting for him in the bedroom just off the staircase of the second floor. By now some hundred and fifty guests had arrived for the ceremony, including his parents and their entourage. The small wedding Christina wanted had grown to royal proportions. It had been inevitable.

Antonio had met Christina when he went to Switzerland many times to visit his younger sister at boarding school. She always asked if her roommate, Christina, could come along with them when they went out for *fondue au fromage* or took the ferry to see the sights around Lake Geneva.

Though Antonio thought of Christina as his sister's pudgy friend, he'd found her sensible and soft-spoken, and probably the sweetest girl he'd ever met. That favorable impression of her grew deep roots when she'd phoned him in the middle of the night about Elena four years ago.

His sister had needed help because she and her loser addict boyfriend had been hauled off to jail on drug possession. Her boyfriend had been arrested and charged. What if Elena was next to be tainted with a jail record?

The paparazzi would have blown his sister's mistake into a royal scandal that would do great damage to the already damaged royal family. Antonio's parents hadn't been in favor with the country for a long time and were constantly being criticized in the press for their profligate ways.

In order to keep Elena's latest scandalous affair out of the news, Antonio had to think of something quick to take the onus off his wayward younger sister. Thankful beyond words for Christina's swift intervention with that phone call, he was able to turn things around and had talked her into entering into a mock engagement with him to create a new piece of news.

If the press focused on his stunning announcement, it would take up column space and deflect the paparazzi's interest in his sister's scandal, thus saving Elena's poor reputation and the family from further scrutiny and ruin.

After some persuasion Christina had agreed to fly to Halencia and become his fiancée because she loved

Elena and had believed the engagement wouldn't last long. They'd be able to go their own separate ways at some future date. Or so Antonio had thought…

But once he'd leaked the news of their engagement to the press and it had gone public, everything changed. Elena's problems with the paparazzi went away like magic. Even more startling, the news of his engagement to the unknown Christina Rose grew legs.

The country approved of the Cinderella fiancée doing charity work in Kenya, whom he'd plucked out of obscurity. Immediately there was a demand for a royal wedding to become front and center. Guido was insistent on it happening immediately.

Antonio understood why. The royal approval ratings had dropped to an all-time low. In particular, his and Elena's philandering parents drew criticism with their string of affairs. There were accusations of them dipping into the royal coffers to fund their extravagant lifestyle. To his chagrin, Elena was also becoming infamous for her wild party ways and uncontrolled spending habits.

The press had been calling for the king and queen to step down. It was the will of the people that the monarchy be turned into a republic. Or…put Antonio on the throne.

A lot had gone wrong with his family while Antonio was pursuing his studies and business interests in the US. To his amazement, the separation that had distanced him from all this scandal had endeared him further to his subjects, who saw him as the one person to save the royal dynasty! Christina's hope that

there wouldn't be a wedding was dashed. So was his…
Guido's phone calls to him had changed everything.

And had made him feel trapped.

Once Antonio reached the second floor of the palazzo, he entered the bedroom designated as the groom's changing room.

"There you are!" Zach declared with relief. "You have a letter from your father." He handed him an envelope.

Antonio opened it and after reading it, he put the note back in the envelope and slid it in his trouser pocket. What were his parents up to now, spending the taxpayers' money on a honeymoon he hadn't asked for? He couldn't say no, but this was the last time public money would be spent on private, privileged citizens of the royal family.

"It's getting late," Zach reminded him. "You have to finish getting ready now. Lindsay has the wedding planned down to the second."

Antonio looked at his best man through veiled eyes. "I had to deliver the brooch to Christina so she could pin it on her wedding dress before the ceremony."

"How did that go?"

"She was hiding behind a screen and told me to leave." Considering the fact that she'd been forced to go through with this marriage they hadn't planned on, he shouldn't have been surprised she sounded so upset.

"That was wedding nerves. Christina was a sweetheart when Lindsay and I met with her for her fittings," Zach said, helping him on with the midnight blue royal dress uniform jacket.

After their unexpected exchange upstairs, Antonio didn't exactly agree with his friend. "She's not happy about this wedding going ahead."

Zach attached the royal blue sash over his left shoulder to his right hip, signaling his rank as crown prince. "She's a big girl, Antonio. No matter how much she cares for Elena, she wouldn't have agreed to an engagement with you if deep down she hadn't wanted to. Christina doesn't strike me as a woman who would bow out on a commitment once she'd given her word."

Antonio grimaced. "She wouldn't," he admitted, "but she would have had every right. When I was talking to her upstairs, I heard a mournful sound in her voice. She thought our engagement would have ended before now and she wouldn't have to go through with a real wedding." He'd felt her pain. From here on out he'd do everything he could to make her happy.

"You both underestimated the will of the people who want you to be their ruler."

His jaw hardened. "But she didn't ask for this." He had a gut feeling there was trouble ahead.

"So use that genius brain of yours and look at your wedding as new territory. Think of it the way you do with every challenge you face at work. Think it and rethink it until it comes out right."

"Thanks for the advice, Zach."

His friend meant well, but Antonio couldn't treat it as he would a business problem. Christina wasn't a problem. She was a flesh-and-blood human being who'd sacrificed everything for her friend Elena. That kind of loyalty was so rare, Antonio was humbled by it. His concern was to be worthy of the woman whose selflessness had catapulted her to the highest rank in the kingdom.

Zach gazed at him with compassion. "Are you all right?"

He sucked in his breath. "I'm going to have to be. Because of you, I was able to give Christina that brooch. I can't thank you enough for getting it from Sofia."

"You know I'd do anything for you."

A knock on the outer door caused both of them to look around. "Tonio—" his sister called out, using her nickname for him. "It's time. You should be out at the chapel."

"I know. I'll be right there."

"I hope you know how much I love you, brother dear."

"I love you too, Elena."

"Please be happy. You're marrying the sweetest girl in the whole world."

"You don't have to remind me of that." He'd put Christina on a pedestal since she agreed to their engagement. But he'd heard another side come out of her in the bridal suite.

"Lindsay says you two have to hurry!"

Zach's wife had planned this wedding down to the smallest detail. The schedule called for a four-thirty ceremony to avoid the heat of the day. He checked his watch. In the next fifteen minutes Christina would walk down the aisle and become his unhappy bride.

"We're coming," Zach answered for them.

Antonio glanced at Zach. "This is it."

"You look magnificent, Your Highness."

"I wish I felt magnificent. Let's go."

Christina heard Elena's tap on the door of the suite. "Come in."

Her friend hurried in, wearing a stunning blush-colored chiffon gown. On her stylishly cut dark blond hair she wore a tiara. "You look like the princess of every little girl's dreams," Christina cried softly.

"So do you. The tiara Mother gave you looks like it was made for you." Elena walked all the way around her, looking her up and down. "Guess what? This afternoon all eyes are going to be on you, *chère soeur*." They would be sisters in a few minutes. Tears smarted Christina's eyes. "Oh, la-la, la-la," she said. "My brother will be speechless when he sees you at the altar. Your hair, it's like red gold."

"I just had some highlights put in."

"And you got your teeth straightened. How come you didn't do it a lot earlier in your life?"

"Probably reverse snobbery. Everyone thought I looked pathetic, so why not maintain the image? I knew it irked my parents. It upset me that they couldn't accept me for myself. But when the wedding date was announced, I realized I would have to be an ambassador of sorts.

"Antonio deserves the best, so I knew I had to do something about myself and dress the right way. Until a month ago, I never spent money on clothes. It seemed such an extravagance when there are so many people in the world who don't have enough to eat. Elegant high fashion wouldn't have changed the way I looked."

"Oh, Christina." Elena shook her head sadly. "I always thought you were pretty, but now you're an absolute knockout! If all the girls at our boarding school could see you, they'd eat their hearts out."

Christina's cheeks went hot with embarrassment. "Don't be silly."

"I'm being truthful. You've lost weight since the last time I saw you. Your figure is gorgeous. With your height, the kind I wish I had, that tiara gives you the elegance of a young queen. I'm not kidding. Lindsay found you the perfect gown and I love the interlocking hearts of your brooch. Is there anything more beautiful than diamonds?"

"It's been in the Rose family for years and supposed to bring luck. Antonio brought it to the room earlier. Do you think I pinned it in the right place?"

"It's right above your heart where it should be. You look as pure and perfect as I know you are."

She averted her eyes. "You know I'm not either of those things."

"I know how much your parents have hurt you, but you *can't* let that ruin your opinion of yourself. One day they'll realize you're the jewel in their crown. Today my brother is going to see you as his prize jewel. I've never told you this before, but all the time we were in Switzerland together, I had the secret hope he would end up marrying you one day."

I had the same hope, Christina admitted to herself, but she'd never confess it to anyone, not even Elena.

"The day I met you at school, you became the sister I never had and you never judged me. That has never changed. After we left school, our friendship has meant more to me than you will ever know."

"I feel the same," Christina said with a tremor in her voice.

"That awful night I phoned you when Rolfe was arrested for drugs, I knew I could count on you to help me. I believe it's destiny you contacted Tonio. Now you're about to become his bride to save my reputation." Her eyes glistened with tears. "You have to promise me you'll be happy, Christina. Tonio's the best if you'll give him a chance."

Christina reached for Elena's hands. "I know he's the best because he was always kind to me when we were in Montreux. And because of his sacrifice for you, that takes brotherly love and goodness to a whole new level. He honors his family and his heritage. Who couldn't admire him?"

"But I want you to learn to *love* him!" Her eyes begged.

"You're talking a different kind of love." After he'd phoned to tell her the date they were going to be married, she was forced to accept her fate. "I haven't dated much, Elena. I did spend time with one doctor in Africa. But when I got engaged to Antonio, that ended any possibility of a relationship with him or any man, let alone potential love."

In a way, her engagement had helped her to hide

from love for fear that she would never be good enough for anyone. If she wasn't good enough for her parents, why would she be good enough for any man?

Still, her parents had been overjoyed with the engagement, which made her happy. And Christina had adored Antonio in secret for years, not only for the way he loved Elena, but for his hard-work ethic. In Christina's new position as his wife, the number of people she'd be able to help with her charities would be vastly increased. Was it worth giving up on the possibility of true love?

Christina had never felt worthy of love and so had never been hopeful of meeting "the one." At the end of the day she'd reconciled herself to this marriage.

"Can you honestly tell me you're not excited about your wedding night?"

"Oh, Elena—you're such a romantic and I know you feel guilty about what's happening, but don't let that worry you. Yes, I'm excited, but mostly I'm nervous. Antonio and I have never spent time alone together. You know what I mean. But Antonio has been with other women both before and probably after our engagement. My eyes are wide-open where he is concerned. After the women he has been with, I'm afraid I'm not going to compare."

A stricken look entered Elena's eyes. "Don't you dare say that! And don't think about any of his past relationships. He knew they would never amount to anything, and today he's marrying *you*."

"I know, but it's still hard to believe." Christina stared at her friend. "I wasn't convinced Antonio planned to go through with our nuptials. You can't imagine my surprise when he finally called me and said I needed to start making the wedding plans with Lindsay."

"He meant it, Christina. I know he got engaged to you to save my skin, but he could have chosen any number of eligible royal hopefuls. Why do *you* think he chose you?"

"I was…convenient."

"That's not the answer and you know it. There was something deeper inside that drove him to choose you. I think you need to think about that as you walk down the aisle toward him today looking like any man's dream. If you don't believe me, take one more look in the mirror."

"You're very sweet."

"It's true. Tonio came to Switzerland a lot during our days at boarding school. He liked you right off and enjoyed your company. He trusts you."

"But he's not in love with me."

"Give him a chance and he *will* fall in love with you. *I've* always loved you and feel all the more indebted to you for the sacrifice *you're* making to save me and our family from scandal. Will you promise me one thing?"

"If I can."

"Pretend that today you're going to get married to the man you've always loved and who has always loved you."

I have always loved him…from a distance. There was no pretense on Christina's part.

Elena rushed over to her and they hugged.

"What's wrong, Elena? Are those tears?"

"I just don't want anything to go wrong. This wedding is all my fault. I'll pray for you and Antonio to be happy."

Christina took a big breath, sensing that deep down Elena was really worried. Why? What wasn't she telling her, unless her guilt was working overtime?

"It'll be fine, Elena." She'd made up her mind about that. Today was her wedding day and she was living her fantasy of marrying the prince of her dreams. For once in her life she planned to enjoy herself. She could do it. She'd seen herself in the mirror and felt confident to be his bride.

"You'd better start working on it right now," Elena warned. "Otherwise you're going to give everyone a heart attack if you don't make an appearance in the chapel in the next minute."

"I'm ready."

"I love you, Christina."

"The feeling's mutual. You have to know that by now."

Elena blew her a kiss. "I do."

Together they walked down the stairs to the foyer of the palazzo and out the main entrance to the courtyard. The chapel faced the palazzo across the way with a beautiful fountain in the center. Lindsay was waiting for them inside the church doors of the foyer with their flowers.

She let out a gasp when she saw Christina. "You're perfect! Better than anything I'd imagined. So perfect, in fact, I can't believe my eyes."

Christina smiled at Zach's wife. "You outdid your-self, Lindsay. All the credit goes to you. This dress is divine."

Louisa, the owner of the palazzo, hurried toward her. "You're the most stunning bride I've ever seen."

"Thank you, Louisa. You look lovely too. I'm in-debted to you for your generosity in letting us be married here. The Palazzo di Comparino is the most ideal setting for a wedding in all of Tuscany."

"It's been an honor for me. I told Prince Antonio the same thing."

Louisa had given Christina a tour of the newly reno-vated chapel yesterday. She'd met the elderly priest who would be marrying them. While he walked with her in private, they chatted about the renovations.

She'd been utterly enchanted with the fabulous un-earthed fresco of the Madonna and child now protected by glass. The charming chapel had an intimacy and spiritual essence. It thrilled her to know she'd be tak-ing her vows in here. She intended to make this the perfect wedding day.

"Everyone is inside waiting," Lindsay whispered. "Here's your bouquet, Christina."

"Oh—these white roses are exquisite."

"Just like you. And here's your bouquet, Elena." Lindsay had matched the flowers to the soft blush of her gown. "Zach will hand you the ring to give Anto-nio when the time comes during the ceremony. As we rehearsed, once you hear the organ, you and your father will enter the chapel with Elena five paces behind you.

The king and queen are seated on the right side with their retinue. Your family and friends are on the left."

Christina looked around. "Where's my father?"

"I'm right behind you."

As she turned, her heart thudded mostly in fear in case she saw rejection in his dark gray eyes. He had a patrician, distinguished aura and was immaculately dressed. His gaze studied her features for a moment. "I'm glad to see you've changed for the better. Today the Rose family can be proud of you."

"You look very handsome too, Father."

"Christina?" Lindsay reminded her. "Take your father's arm."

The organist had started playing Wagner's "Wedding March." There'd probably never been this many people inside. Her joy was almost full.

She clung to her father as they slowly made their way down the aisle of the ornate interior. The only eyes she searched for were her mother's, wanting her approbation. Her mother, who was in her midfifties, was still a beautiful brunette woman and the envy of many.

Just once Christina hoped to find a loving smile meant for her alone. As she passed the pew, she made eye contact with her. A proud smile broke out on her mother's perfectly made-up face. That acknowledgment made Christina feel as if she were floating as she walked toward her prince.

She focused her attention on the two men standing at the altar before the priest. Zach, as best man, stood several inches taller than the crown prince, who was six foot one, according to Elena. They were watching her progress.

A slight gasp escaped her lips when she looked into the startling blue eyes of the man she was about to pledge her life to. It had been several months since the last time she saw him at the palace. His visit had been brief.

In full dark blue ceremonial dress, Antonio looked so splendid she was shaken by her reaction to him. His light brown hair, smart and thick, was tipped with highlights from the sun, reflecting a healthy sheen. With such a lean, fit body, he was the epitome of a royal prince every little girl dreamed of marrying one day.

How incredible that Christina was about to become his wife. *If I were the type, I'd pass out at the feet of the most desirable man in all Halencia. But I'm not going to make any mistakes today. This is my wedding day. I love it already.*

Caught up in all the wedding preparations, she felt that she *was* his beautiful bride and she intended to be the woman he was excited to marry. Her teenage dream had come true. The only thing more she could ask of this day was that the fantasy would last forever.

CHAPTER TWO

MAYBE ANTONIO'S EYES were playing tricks on him. The
stunning woman walking on the arm of her father with
the grace of a queen had to be Christina, but it was a
Christina he'd never seen or imagined.

When did the brownish-red hair, which he remembered she'd worn in a ponytail, turn out to be a spun
red gold?

Had her body ever looked like an hourglass before
now?

The lace veil against her smooth olive skin provided
a foil for her finely arched dark eyebrows. Because of
the light coming through the stained glass windows, her
crystalline gray eyes had taken on a silvery cast. Her red
mouth had a passionate flare he'd never even noticed.

His gaze fell lower to the brooch she'd pinned to the
beaded bodice of her wedding dress. The diamonds
sparkled in the light with every breath she took.

Elena approached her side to take the bouquet
from her. When Christina smiled at his sister, Antonio caught its full effect and was blindsided by the
change in her.

While he'd been talking to her earlier in the bridal suite, parts of her sounded like the woman he'd gotten engaged to four years ago. But she wasn't the same person on the outside. It threw him so completely that he felt a nudge from Zach to pay attention to the priest.

"Your Highness?" he whispered. "If you will take your bride-to-be by the hand."

Antonio reached for her right hand. Her cool, dry grip was decisive. If she was suffering wedding nerves, it didn't show. He didn't know if he was disappointed by her demeanor, which seemed unflappable.

In a voice loud enough to fill the interior, the priest began. "Welcome, all of you. Today we are gathered here for one of the happiest occasions in all human life, to celebrate before God the marriage of a man and woman who love each other. Marriage is a most honorable estate, created and instituted by God, signifying unto us the mystical union that also exists between Christ and the Church. So too may this marriage be adorned by true and abiding love. Let us pray."

Antonio bowed his head, but his burden of guilt over compelling Christina to follow through with this marriage weighed heavily on him. As Zach had reminded him, she'd entered into this union of her own free will because of her love for Elena, but the words *may this marriage be adorned by true and abiding love* pierced him to the core of his being.

In the past four years he'd done nothing to show her love. The only thing true about this marriage was their love for Elena, and on his part the need to preserve the monarchy. But at this moment Antonio made up his mind that their love for his sister would be the foundation upon which they built a life together.

Antonio's absence from her life except for those four quick visits had made certain she had no anticipation of love to come. To his surprise she sounded happy as she repeated the marriage covenant. He hadn't expected that.

When it was his turn to recite his vows, he felt the deep solemnity of the moment and said them with fervency.

"Who holds the rings?"

"I do," Zach responded.

"Grant that the love which the bride and groom have for each other now may always be an eternal round. Antonio? Take the ring and put it on Christina's finger saying, 'With this ring, I thee wed.'"

She presented her left hand while he repeated the words. Her hand trembled a little as he slid the wedding band next to the diamond from the royal family treasury he'd given her four years earlier. So she wasn't quite as composed as he'd thought, but it didn't make him feel any better. If anything, he felt worse because he'd done nothing to ease her into this union and lamented his selfishness.

Now it was her turn to present him with his ring. She took it and placed it on Antonio's finger. His new bride was suddenly so composed that again he marveled. "With this ring, I thee wed," she said in a steady voice.

They were married.

The deed was done.

"Antonio and Christina, as the two of you have

joined this marriage uniting as husband and wife, and as you this day affirm your faith and love for each other, I would ask that you always remember to cherish each other as special and unique individuals, that you respect the thoughts, ideas and suggestions of one another.

"Be able to forgive, do not hold grudges, and live each day that you may share it together. From this day forward you shall be each other's home, comfort and refuge, your marriage strengthened by your love and respect."

Antonio's shame increased. *I've shown her no respect.*

"You may now kiss your bride."

When Antonio turned to her, he saw a look of consternation in her eyes. *Oh, Christina. What have I done to you? You're so good. So sweet.* His eyes focused on her lovely mouth before he grasped her upper arms gently and kissed her.

Not only her lips but her whole body trembled. Her fragrance assailed him. He deepened the kiss, wanting her to know he planned to make their marriage work. Whether she was putting on a show for everyone, or responding instinctively to new emotions bombarding her as they were him, he didn't know. But she kissed him back and he found himself wanting it to go on and on.

The priest cleared his throat, prompting Antonio to lift his mouth from hers. A subtle blush had entered her cheeks. He removed his hands.

"Antonio and Christina, if you'll turn around."

When they'd done his bidding, he said in a loud voice, "May I present Crown Prince Antonio de L'Accardi and his royal bride, Princess Christina Rose. Allow them to walk down the aisle to the foyer of the chapel, where you can mingle outside."

Elena came forward to give Christina her bouquet, and then the organist played the wedding march. Taking a deep breath, Antonio grasped her free hand, still feeling the tingly effect of her warm, generous mouth on his. He guided her to the first pew where his parents were seated and stopped long enough for both of them to bow to the king and queen of Halencia.

To show Christina's parents his respect, he escorted her across the aisle to their pew to acknowledge them. He gave her a sideward glance. Her eyes glistened with unshed tears. He didn't know what that was about.

How could you know when you haven't spent any real time getting to know her?

More upset with himself and even more shaken by their kiss, he walked her slowly down the aisle. He darted her another glance, but this time she was smiling at everyone. She was so gracious it impressed the hell out of him. She could have been born to royalty.

He'd honored Christina's wishes by letting her plan the wedding here instead of the fourteenth-century cathedral in Voti. She'd insisted on a simple ceremony. If there'd been any royal formality or long traditional ceremony, she wouldn't have agreed. Antonio had been so thankful she hadn't backed out that he'd fallen in with her every wish.

In private he'd asked his parents to take a backseat

so this could be Christina's day. She was beloved of the people, but she couldn't have abided all the pomp and circumstance. Since his parents were resigned to their fate to put Antonio on the throne, they'd acceded to his wishes. He'd even heard them say they were relishing the idea of retirement and looking forward to more freedom in the future.

At his engagement four years ago, Antonio had vowed to sacrifice his personal freedom and return from California to take the throne at a later date with Christina at his side. He'd felt a strong loyalty to his country and had always been conscious of his royal duty. But he'd only been prepared to marry her on *his* terms, and hadn't considered her fears.

There were going to be a lot of changes after his coronation in another week. He had a raft of constitutional issues that would put the royal family in a figurehead role, with specific duties. There would be a much reduced civil list, no hangers-on supported by the state; all personal belongings and lifestyle choices and holidays would be paid for by personal business interests rather than the state.

The areas of change went on and on, which was why the monarchy had been on the brink of disaster. This marriage would hopefully turn the tide of criticism. Christina's values of hard work and true charity resonated with the people. Her example of selflessness was the big reason they'd embraced Antonio as their soon-to-be king. Antonio still had to prove himself equal to the task. And much more, like becoming the husband Christina deserved.

He walked her outside and across the courtyard to the terrace bedecked in flowers at the side of the palazzo. A small orchestra was playing a waltz at one end of the terrace with an area reserved for dancing. Hundreds of tiny lights strewn among the trees and flowers made it look like a true fairyland and had created a heavenly fragrance. The grand serving table with its fountain and flowers was surrounded by exquisitely set tables, an enchanting sight he'd always remember.

The late-afternoon Tuscan sunshine shone down on them. The picturesque setting and vineyard had an indescribable beauty, yet all he could see for the moment was the stunning bride draped in alençon lace, still clinging to his hand. Antonio swallowed hard.

She's my wife! She's the woman I promised to love and cherish.

Suddenly he seemed to see a whole new world ahead of them, uncharted as yet. Her faith in their marriage made him open his eyes to new possibilities. This was their wedding day. He wanted it to be wonderful for both of them. After their kiss at the altar, he was eager to feel her in his arms.

"Christina? Look this way."

She was so dazed by what had happened at the end of the ceremony that she was hardly aware of the photographers brought in to make a record of their wedding day. When Antonio had deepened their kiss, she felt a charge of energy run through her body like a current of electricity. She could still feel his compelling mouth on hers.

Maybe this was how every bride felt when kissed on her wedding day. But Antonio wasn't just any man. He was her husband, for better or worse.

Before everyone could crowd around to congratulate them, Antonio pulled her close. "Do you mind if we talk to our guests later? I'd like to dance with you first," he said in his deep voice.

Her heart thumped hard before she looked at him. "I'd love it."

His hot blue eyes played over her features. "Let me put your bouquet on this table."

After he laid it down, Christina felt his arm go around her waist. The contact reminded her of the kiss they'd shared at the altar. She hadn't been the same since and was more aware of him than ever as he led her to the dance area.

She couldn't help thinking back to the time she'd been at boarding school. Never in her wildest imagination would she have believed she'd eventually become the wife of Elena's dashing older brother. This moment was surreal.

As he drew her into his arms she said, "You need to know I haven't done much dancing in my life."

He held her closer. "Didn't they teach you to dance at boarding school?"

"Are you kidding? Whatever you think goes on at boarding school simply doesn't happen. We were all a bunch of girls who'd rather be home. We all had a case of homesickness and waited for the letters that didn't arrive. We ate, studied and slept four to a room in an old freezing-cold chateau. You don't even want to know how frigid the water closet could be."

He laughed out loud, causing everyone to look at them.

"Once a week we were allowed to go to town with the chaperone. She chose the places we could visit. Elena managed to scout out the dancing places we weren't supposed to visit, then dragged me with her where we met guys who flocked around her."

"Sounds like my sister."

"She taught me the meaning of *fun*. The rest of the time we went to a symphony or an opera, and other times we went to a play, always on a bus. I liked the plays, especially one adapted from Colette's writings about a dog and cat."

Antonio started moving them around the terrace decorated with urns of flowers. "Tell me about them," he whispered against her hot cheek. His warm breath sent little tingles of delight through her body.

"Elena and I bought the books and studied the lines to help us with our French. Both animals loved their master and mistress. Their battles were outrageous and hilarious."

"You'll have to lend me the book to read."

"Anytime. Wouldn't it be fun if animals really could talk? I used to love the *Doctor Doolittle* books as a child. When I first got to Africa, I thought I really had arrived in Jollijinki Land."

He lips twitched and he held her a little tighter, but her gown provided a natural buffer. "I have a feeling you could entertain me forever."

She moved her head so she could look into his eyes. Marrying Antonio felt right. She felt like a princess. The feeling was magical. She was living her fantasy and never wanted it to end. Her parents were proud of her today. Everything was getting better with them. "This is a new experience for both of us, Antonio. Forever sounds like a long time. Let's just take it one step at a time."

His lips brushed hers unexpectedly, creating havoc with her emotions. "One step at a time it is. Since everyone is watching us, let's put on a show, shall we?"

She smiled at him. "I thought we'd already been doing that."

"They haven't seen anything yet."

Her adrenaline gushed as he waltzed them around the terrace. It didn't surprise her that he knew what he was doing. She followed his lead as he dipped her several times, causing people to clap. Dancing with him like this was a heady experience she hadn't anticipated. He must have been enjoying it too, because one dance turned into another.

"This is fun," he murmured against her lips. "Your idea for having our wedding here at the palazzo has turned out to be sensational. I remember once when the three of us climbed into the mountains above the vineyards lining Lake Geneva and came to an old farmhouse that had been turned into a quaint inn.

"You said it was your favorite place and went there often on your hikes and bicycle rides with Elena for fondue bourguignonne. I think you must have had it in mind when you chose the Palazzo di Comparino for our wedding. I see similarities."

Her head tilted back in surprise. "I can't believe you remembered that hike, let alone made the association with this place."

His gaze played over her features. "I've remembered all our outings. The truth is, I found you and my sister more entertaining than most of my friends, with the exception of Zach." His comment made her smile.

"When I did fly to Switzerland, I came because I wanted to. Being with you two was like taking a breath of fresh air and kept me grounded. I've never told you this, but I was always relieved to know you were there to help temper my sister. She's always had trouble with boundaries."

"And I was the insipid, boring tagalong, afraid to break out of my shell, right?"

He frowned. When he did that, he looked older and quite fierce. "You were shy, but amazingly kind to my sister. Even when she got herself into impossible situations you never judged her."

"You were kind to me too by including me. Remember the day we visited the Chateau de Chillon? We'd climbed up on the ramparts and I was taking a picture when I dropped my camera by mistake and it fell into the lake several hundred feet below."

"You should have seen the tragic look on your face," he teased.

"I was so upset, but you turned everything around when you bought me a new one just like it and gave it to me before you left us at the school." She felt her eyes smart. "That was the kindest thing anyone had ever done for me."

"Then we're even because Elena needed a constant friend like you and you were there for her in her darkest hours. You have no idea what that meant to me. I knew I could always count on you. I wish I could say the same for our parents. They've been so caught up in a lifestyle that has cost them the confidence of the people that they've neglected Elena, who needed a strong hand."

Christina sucked in her breath. "I needed her friendship too."

"Elena told me you had problems with your parents."

"Yes, but I don't want to talk about them right now. We were talking about your sister. She's so sweet. Elena cared about me when no one else did. She made me believe in myself."

"The two of you have an unbreakable bond. Otherwise you wouldn't have stayed close over all these years. You don't know how lucky you are. How rare that is."

"According to Elena, you have that kind of relationship with Zach."

He nodded. "But I didn't have a friend like you while I was at boarding school and college. It wasn't until I moved to San Francisco. If you want to know a secret, I envied you and Elena."

She heard a loneliness in his admission that went deep. "Because you're the prince, it was probably hard for you to confide in someone else during those early years. With you being expected to rule one day, you had to watch every step."

Antonio stopped dancing and grasped her hands in both of his. "You understand so much about me, Christina." His blue eyes had darkened with emotion. "But you paid a price by agreeing to get engaged to me."

Giddy with happiness she said, "What price is that when I'm having the wedding of my dreams?"

Her thoughts flew back to their engagement. The king and queen had thrown the supposedly happy couple a huge, glossy engagement party, but it had been the worst night of Christina's life. To have to be on show, self-consciously standing next to the most gorgeous man she'd ever known, she'd never felt so unglamorous in her life. Especially when she knew her parents considered her a failure.

Yet they'd acted thrilled over the engagement and made such a fuss over her that it made her happy that they showed her that kind of attention. She'd been starved for it. But once she saw the photos, she'd been unable to bear the sight of herself looking so dull and plump. But that was a long time ago and she refused to dwell on it.

The guests had been going through the buffet line before finding their seats at individual linen-covered tables with baskets of creamy roses and sunflowers. Christina had to admit the estate and grounds looked beautiful. A fountain modeled after the one in the courtyard of a draped nymph holding a shell formed the centerpiece. Everything looked right out of a dream-world, including the beautifully dressed people.

Antonio drew her even closer as they walked past the guests to get their food. He handed her a plate and they moved back and forth, choosing a delicious tidbit here and there. But she was too happy and stimulated to sit down to a big meal with him at a table reserved for them alone.

Several of the guests had started to dance. Among them Louisa, who was being partnered by Nico. According to Louisa, the two of them weren't on the best of terms, but the way he was looking at her right now, Christina got the feeling they had a strong attraction. Well, well. It appeared the festive party mood had infected everyone.

Antonio finished what was on his plate. Since hers was empty, he put them both on the table. When he looked at her she was filled with strong emotion and said, "Today I'm so happy to be your wife, Antonio. I mean that with all my heart."

"Christina," he said in a husky voice, squeezing her hand. "Because of your sacrifice for me—for the country—I trust you with my life." He said it like a vow and kissed her fingers in a gesture so intimate in front of the wedding guests that she made up her mind to be the best wife possible.

Just then Louisa happened to pass by her. "You look radiant," she whispered.

Christina was still reacting to Antonio's gesture as well as his words. "So did you out there dancing with Nico."

"Who knew he could waltz?"

Her comment made Christina chuckle. Antonio

smiled at her. "I want to dance the whole evening away with you, but I think we need to say something to our parents."

They walked hand in hand toward the king and queen and they all chatted for a moment. Christina's parents were seated by them. While Antonio was still talking with his parents for a minute, her mother, dressed in an oyster silk suit, got up from the table to greet Christina with a peck on the cheek.

Though Christina had known this began as a publicity stunt, she'd tried to win her parents' affection. Four years later she was still trying and had hopes that her marriage to the future king had softened their opinion of her.

Her mother stared into her eyes. "You look lovely, Christina. I do believe that tint on your hair was the right shade."

A compliment from her mother meant everything. "I'm glad you like it."

"It's a good thing Lindsay planned everything else, including your new royal wardrobe. You'll always want to look perfect for Antonio."

"I plan to try."

"I know you will. Certainly today you've succeeded." Her voice halted for a minute before she added, "You've never looked so attractive."

Christina's eyes moistened. She couldn't believe her mother was actually paying her another compliment. In fact, she sensed her mother wanted to say more but held back.

"*Grazie*, Mama," she said in a tremulous voice, and kissed her mother's cheek.

Marusha stood nearby. Christina hugged her. She'd flown in for the wedding. Her family would be coming for the coronation. For this ceremony, only their closest friends and relatives made up the intimate gathering.

Next came Christina's great-aunt Sofia. "You look enchanting." The older woman embraced her. "Working in Africa has made all the difference in you," she said quietly. "You have a queenly aura that comes naturally to you."

Christina craved her aunt's warmth and hugged her extra hard. "I'm thrilled to be wearing the brooch." She was glad Antonio had sneaked up to the bridal chamber to give it to her.

"It suits you. I'm so proud of you I could burst."

"Don't do that!" she said as they broke into gentle laughter.

"I've been watching your handsome husband. He's hardly taken his eyes off you since we came outside." Her brown gaze conveyed her sincerity. "I can see why. You're a vision, and you're going to help Prince Antonio transform our country into its former glory. I feel it in these old bones. I have the suspicion that you didn't need the brooch to bring you good luck. You and your prince are special, you know?"

No, Christina *didn't* know, but she loved her aunt for saying so. "I love you."

Her great-aunt kissed her on the cheek before Elena rushed in to hug her hard. "Ooh—you're the most gorgeous bride I ever saw. I do believe you've knocked the socks off Tonio. All the time he's been talking to the parents, he's had his eye on you."

Sofia had said the same thing. From the mouths of two witnesses…

"The two of you looked so happy out there it seemed like you were sharing some great secret. By the way, in passing I heard your mother tell your aunt Sofia that she'd never been so proud of you."

"Thank you for telling me. Things seem to be better with Mother," she whispered. "It is a beautiful wedding, isn't it?"

"It's fabulous, and you know why? Because you're Tonio's wife and will make him a better man than he already is. Meeting you was the best thing that ever happened to me. He's going to feel the same way once he gets to really know you the way I do."

Tears glistened on Christina's eyelashes. She hugged her again. "We're true sisters now," she whispered.

CHAPTER THREE

"YOUR HIGHNESS, THE photographer is waiting for you and your bride to cut the wedding cake."

Antonio switched his gaze to Zach, but his mind and thoughts had been concentrated on Christina and it took a moment for him to get back to the present. "Thanks, Zach. We're coming."

"I hope you love wedding cake," she whispered as they made their way to the round table holding the fabulous three-tiered cake.

He flashed her a quick smile. "Is this the moment you're going to get your revenge on me for past misdeeds?"

"If you're referring to the chocolate you fed me full of cherry cordial that dripped down my blouse on one of our outings, I wouldn't be surprised." The impish look in her beautiful gray eyes was so unexpected that his heart skipped a beat.

"Be gentle," he begged, putting his arms around her from behind to help her make the first cut with the knife. Another chuckle escaped her lips. With great care she picked up the first piece and turned to him, waving it in the air as if trying to decide how to feed it to him. This produced laughter from the guests.

"Just take your best shot, whatever you have in mind."

"So I *do* have you a little bit worried."

"Please, Christina."

"I tell you what. I'll have a napkin ready." She plucked one off the table. "Now open sesame."

He closed his eyes and obeyed her command.

"You have to keep your eyes open, coward," she said in a low teasing voice.

"I can't do both," he teased back.

"Then I'll eat it instead."

Shocked by her response, he opened his eyes only to be fed the cake, part of which fell onto his chin into the napkin she held for him. The wedding guests laughed and clapped their hands. Of course everything had been caught by the videographer.

Christina cleaned him up nicely, then kissed his chin. "Thanks for being a good sport, Your Highness."

"Don't call me that."

She looked surprised. "No?"

"Not ever."

She flashed him a smile. "Are we having our first fight?"

Her question caught him off guard. Before he could respond, Lindsay came up to Christina with her bridal bouquet. "When you're ready to leave the party, you can toss it behind you."

"Thank you, Lindsay. All your planning has made

this the most beautiful wedding party in the world. I've never been happier."

"You look radiant, Christina." She gave her a hug, and Antonio saw his wife whisper something to her in private.

"It's already being taken care of," Lindsay whispered back, but Antonio read her lips.

Intrigued, he couldn't wait to get his bride alone, but no one was ready to leave the reception yet and Zach had snatched her away to dance. He decided now was the time to dance with his mother, then his mother-in-law.

The queen gave him a hug before he danced her around the terrace. "You're going to have to keep an eye on that one," she said, eyeing Christina, who was still whirling around with Zach. "She isn't quite as docile as I remember."

"She's her own person," Antonio replied with the sudden thrilling realization that his new bride might mean more to him than he could have imagined.

"Indeed she is. You both look perfectly marvelous together. She's changed so much since the engagement that I hardly recognize her. You have no idea how glad I am that you've come home for good to settle down. A man needs marriage, and your marriage is good for the monarchy. I'm very happy with you today."

"Thank you, Mama." Except that marriage hadn't stopped his parents from having their offstage affairs.

He twirled her back to the table and asked Christina's mother to dance. She had been a former fashion model and was still a very attractive woman. But as he gazed at Christina, who was laughing quietly with Zach, he thought she was the *real* beauty. Not only in her appearance, but in her character.

"Are you sorry our daughter wanted the wedding here instead of at the cathedral in Voti?"

"Anything but. Don't you think every woman should be able to have the wedding of her dreams where she wants it?"

"But you're the crown prince."

Antonio smiled at her. "Tonight I'm a new bridegroom and I can't imagine a more perfect setting for Christina and me than this delightful spot in Tuscany."

"Then I'm glad for both of you. You make a stunning pair."

"Grazie."

He could still hear Christina's words when she'd told him what it was like at boarding school. *We were all a bunch of girls who'd rather be home. We all had a case of homesickness and waited for the letters that didn't arrive.* The emptiness in her voice had conveyed pain, even after all these years.

If he didn't do anything else, he would make certain she didn't feel pain because of him. "Did you visit her in Africa?"

"We made it over once and were guests in the palace of Marusha's parents. They're very westernized there."

"Your daughter has made a big contribution. It's no small thing she has done to help those in poverty."

"I'm very proud of her."

He was glad to hear it. On that note he danced her back to the table. After thanking her, he went over to the table where Marusha was seated and asked her to dance with him. The charming woman had come with her husband. He gave her a turn around the terrace.

"You honor me, Your Highness. I'm very happy Christina is your bride. We hope you'll both come to Kenya and stay with us."

"I've always wanted to travel there and promise to visit you when the time is right. You honor us by coming. Christina thinks the world of you and your family."

"We feel the same. Thank you."

Once she was seated, Antonio hurried to find Christina, who was talking to Elena. His sister smiled at him. "It's about time you paid attention to your bride."

"First I want a dance with you, little sister, if it's all right with my wife."

Christina darted him a serious glance. "She's the reason we even know each other. You're welcome to enjoy her for as long as you want."

He knew she meant that and moved Elena around the terrace. She had a gleam in her eye. "Having fun, brother dear? More than you thought?"

"Much more," he confessed.

"Christina has that effect on people. Mother can't get over the change in her. I told her that Christina is like the woman in the stone. All Michelangelo had to do was chip away at the marble until her beauty emerged for all to see."

His sister had just put the right words to his thoughts. "It's a perfect analogy."

She studied his features. "It's growing dark. Are you ready to leave the party?" she asked with a sly smile.

"The truth?"

"Always."

"I feel like I did the first time I had to jump out of a plane during my military service."

Elena chuckled. "Since you survived, I'm not worried."

"In all honesty, I haven't made this easy for Christina by maintaining distance between us over the last four years."

"Don't worry about it. She married you today and I think you've both met your match. I'm so happy for both of you I could burst. Don't let me keep you from whisking your bride away." She kissed his cheek and hurried off.

He was left standing there while her last comment sank in. Antonio hated to admit he felt nervous for what was to come. He'd be taking his wife upstairs to the bridal chamber. This was a new experience for him. Taking a fortifying breath, he made a beeline for Christina, who was talking to more guests.

Lindsay came up to him. "Christina still needs to throw her bridal bouquet to the crowd. If you're ready, take her to the front of the palazzo and I'll make the announcement to the guests to follow you."

"Thank you for all you've done."

"It has been my pleasure."

He kissed her cheek before reaching for his wife. Christina's gaze flicked to his. "What is it?"

"We have one more ritual to perform." He picked up the bridal bouquet. After putting it in her hands, he slid an arm around her slender waist. Her lovely body was a perfect fit for him.

"I already know where I'm going to throw it," she whispered as they left the terrace and walked around to the front entrance of the palazzo.

"So do I," he drawled.

"Antonio?" She eyed him with surprising tenderness. "Thank you for dancing with Marusha. To dance with the future king had to be one of the big highlights of her life."

"I wanted a chance to thank her for coming. She's been your true friend all these years. I have a feeling you two are going to miss each other."

"That's something I want to talk to you about, but we'll discuss it later."

An alarm bell went off in Antonio's head. Did Christina want to go back to Africa? She'd lived a whole period of her life there that he knew nothing about. In fairness, she didn't know details about his former life either. While he stood there filled with new questions that needed answers, the guests had congregated in the courtyard.

Before he knew what she was doing, his wife cleared her throat and faced the crowd. "Antonio and I want to thank you all for coming to share in our beautiful wedding day. I'm one of the lucky girls in the world who actually got to marry a real prince. His kindness to his sister, Princess Elena, my dearest friend, proved his princely worth to me years ago. I can honestly say there's not another man like him, prince or otherwise.

So this is for you, Elena. May you find your own wonderful prince too!"

Christina turned her back to the crowd and threw the bouquet in a southeasterly direction that was no mistake with Elena standing there. It was no accident that everyone made room around his sister so she could catch it. Then a roar of approval and clapping burst from the crowd. Antonio's breath caught. With that speech she'd ensured her place in everyone's heart as their queen-to-be.

Filled with emotion, he put his arm around her shoulders and pressed a kiss to her lips. She kissed him back and it felt convincing, but was this a show for the camera? He'd felt a distinct spark when they kissed at the altar. But if it had only been on his part, he didn't want to believe it right now. Was she nervous too?

Without asking her permission, he grasped her hand and drew her along with him to the inside of the palazzo. He leaned back against the closed door, still holding her hand. Now that the moment was here to be alone with her, he felt slightly breathless. The wedding night was upon them.

"Are you up to climbing to the third floor?"

The bridal suite.

Their bridal suite now. The kiss Antonio had given her in front of the palazzo felt…hungry. In that moment she'd experienced an answering rush of desire that took her by storm. Her fantasy had taken on a new dimension. What was going on with her?

"I think I can about make it," she teased, and started

her ascent. But after a few steps she picked up her gown to give her the freedom to hurry the rest of the way. His footsteps followed, keeping pace with the thundering of her heart.

She almost ran down the hallway to the bridal suite. Before she reached the doors, he caught up to her and picked her up in his arms. "Oh—" she half squealed, surprised her gown didn't hinder him. She knew her husband was strong, but being held close to him like this made her realize what a rock-hard physique he possessed, and he smelled wonderful.

Their faces were only inches apart. He smiled into her eyes. The blue of his irises had a depth of brilliance that ignited every pulse point in her body. "I don't know about you, but I've been looking forward to this all day." He slowly lowered his mouth to hers and began kissing her.

A burst of desire swept through her. Things were moving much faster than she'd anticipated and she found herself kissing him back with an urgency she couldn't seem to suppress. What was happening was perfectly natural for a grown man and woman on their wedding night, but they had come to this marriage as friends from a long time ago. He'd never held her, or danced with her or kissed her, in Switzerland.

When she could take a breath she said, "If you keep this up, our dinner will get cold."

"What dinner?" His gaze was focused on her mouth.

"The one we didn't eat. It's waiting for us out on the terrace of our suite."

"Was that what you were whispering to Lindsay about?"

She nodded.

"I must say I'd much prefer eating with you alone up here. I like the way my wife thinks."

Christina was glad he felt that way, because she needed time to get used to him. A meal would give both of them a chance to unwind while they antici-pated their wedding night. Now that the moment was here, she didn't know what to do and felt so awkward she hoped he couldn't sense it.

Antonio gave her another swift kiss on the lips and managed to open the door. He walked through the foyer of the semidark suite and made it as far as the bed-chamber before putting her down. She eased away far enough to remove the veil and tiara.

He knew she needed some privacy before they did anything else. "I'll be back in a few minutes." He pressed a kiss to her lips. "Don't start dinner with-out me."

"I won't. Your bags should be in the sitting room."

"I'll find them."

Much as he was reluctant to let her go, he needed to make her more comfortable. After giving her upper arms a quick squeeze, he left the bridal chamber for the other part of the suite. Spotting his bags, he went into the bathroom down the hall to freshen up. It was a relief to discard his sash and ceremonial dress jacket. This was a brand-new experience for both of them. To-night he wanted to do everything right for her.

Hoping he'd given her enough time, he left the bathroom and started back to the bridal suite. He'd undone his shirt at the neck and rolled his sleeves up to the elbows.

Against the darkened sky, the candles flickering from the terrace table bathed Christina in soft light. As she leaned over in her exquisite wedding dress to pour their wine, he noticed the glory of her midlength hair where the strands of gold gleamed among the red. It looked so thick and sleek he longed to run his hands through it.

She must have sensed his presence and gave him a sideward glance. Again the candles flickered, turning her eyes to a shimmery silver. His bride had come to this earth with her own unique color scheme, one that resonated with him in ways he hadn't noticed at the age of eighteen. His fifteen-year-old sister and her friend had been too young for him to appreciate the sight he was being treated to tonight.

Between her classic features with those high cheekbones and passionate red mouth, the blood was pounding in his veins. His gaze fell lower to the feminine outline of her body in her gown. While they'd danced, she filled his arms in all the right places and was the perfect height for him.

Her choice of wedding gown had pleased him immensely. She looked demure, but her coloring added the dash of sensuality he'd noticed the first moment he saw her in the chapel.

Christina might not have been aware of it, but he'd

watched the males in the crowd admiring her all evening long.

For the first time he wondered how many men she'd known who'd more than admired her. Though it was a little late to question what her love life had been like prior to the actual preparations for their wedding, he couldn't help but wonder. He felt as if he were swimming in waters over his head.

Her eyes played over him as he moved toward her. He liked the way she was looking at him. When she reached for her wineglass, he picked up his. "This wine comes from the Brunello grapes grown in this vineyard."

Antonio swirled it around in his glass. "That's very fitting. I'm sure it will be delicious. A toast to my wife, who has already made my life infinitely richer by simply agreeing to marry me. *Salud!*" He touched his glass to hers before they both drank some.

She unexpectedly raised her glass again and touched his. "To my husband. You never let your sister down or betrayed her trust. Because of that you've won mine. To you, Antonio. *Salud!* You'll make the finest king our country has ever known."

"If that happens, it's because you're at my side." His throat swelled with emotion, making it difficult to swallow his second taste of the fruity wine.

"Shall we sit down to eat? I'm sure you're as ravenous as I am." She seated herself before he could help her.

They both tucked in to the heavenly food. She ate with an appetite. He liked that. Most women of his acquaintance ate rabbit food—whether to impress him or not—but not Christina. There was nothing fake about her. *That* was what impressed him.

When she lifted her eyes to him he said, "The little speech you gave in front of the palazzo blew me away."

"It did?"

"How could it not? I thought no other man could be luckier than I am to have you for my wife."

"I feel the same way about you."

"Christina—I know I've put you in an impossible situation."

"You don't have to say anything, Antonio. I understand. That's behind us now."

"No, it isn't. Not until I tell you why."

She had hold of her wineglass stem, but she didn't lift it to her lips while she waited for his explanation. Looking at her right now, he didn't think he'd ever seen so beautiful a woman.

"In a word, I was afraid."

Her delicate eyebrows frowned. "Of what?"

"That once I was in Africa where we could really be alone, you might tell me the engagement was off and send me packing."

She sounded aghast and let go of the glass to put a hand to her throat. "I would never have done that to you."

"Then you're a woman in a million. Who else would have sacrificed her personal happiness for the greater good of someone, something else?"

"Our circumstances were very unusual, but I *am* happy."

He shook his head. "You don't need to pretend with me. This is truth time. I did something terribly selfish to ask you to marry me."

A pained look entered her eyes. "Is this your way of telling me you wish we hadn't gone through with the wedding?"

"No, Christina, no—" He reached across the table and grasped both her hands. "I'm just thankful you consented to be my bride. If you'll let me, I'd like us to start over again. Through Elena we've been friends for years, but you and I don't know each other. I want to get to know all about you. What are the things you love to do? What are the things you hope to do?"

Her silvery gaze enveloped him. "Besides grow old with you?"

"Yes. I'd like to learn it all."

"I'm a pretty normal woman, Antonio. I like reading books and eating chocolate. I like spending time with my friends, especially your sister. I love Africa and the time I spent there helping others. But I suppose my greatest wish would be to have a family of my own. When I first visited the Kikuyu villages with all the adorable children, I hungered for a child of my own. How do you feel about children?"

"I want them too, Christina."

"But I want to take care of them myself. Even if I'll be queen, I want to be their mother in the truest sense of the word."

"So you don't want to send them away to boarding school?"

"Why? It doesn't make sense to me that if you have a child, you would send it away as soon as possible."

He released her hands. "You're talking about yourself."

"Yes."

He saw her eyes glaze over.

"I wanted my mother and father during my growing-up years. If you and I have a baby, would you want it to leave us before it was time to let him or her go? Did you like being sent away to boarding school?"

"I didn't have a choice."

"But did you like it?"

"No. I've never admitted that out loud."

"Neither did Elena."

"I know."

"But *we'll* be the parents," Christina said, then added in an anxious tone, "Will our son have a choice? You say you want to know all about me. If you tell me our children will have to leave home before I'm ready to see them go, I couldn't bear it. Why have them at all?"

Antonio got out of the chair and went around to hunker down beside her. He grasped the hand closest to him. "Look at me." She finally did his bidding. "I was wrong not to come to Africa. We did need time to talk about all these things so I could reassure you."

He heard her heavy sigh before she spoke. "I'm sorry I've turned this beautiful night into something else. Forgive me."

"There's nothing to forgive. You have my word that we'll keep any children we have with us for as long as they want to be with us. The only time they'll have a nanny is if you need to attend a royal function with me."

Her eyes lit up again. "Honest? Is that a promise?"

He could deny her nothing. "I swear it."

"Oh, Antonio. You've made me so happy."

To crush her in his arms was all he had on his mind, but he wanted to give her time and feel comfortable with him. "I was afraid you were going to tell me that you wanted to live in Africa part of the year."

"My life is with you, but I'd love it if we took some trips there together one day. Maybe when our children are old enough to enjoy the animal life? But we've been talking about me. What is one of your dreams?"

"I'm a pretty normal man too. I want a family. I want to be a success at what I do. Because I'll be king, I want to change the country's impression of a monarchy that has shown a breakdown in the old values."

"Like what for instance?"

"The excess spending for one. There are so many areas that need change. But I'm boring you."

"Never."

"Spoken like my queen already." He got to his feet and drew her over to the terrace railing with him. He looked out over the peaceful Tuscan landscape. His pulse throbbed with new life. He wasn't the same man who'd slipped the brooch into the bedchamber earlier in the day.

If he had to describe his feelings at this minute, he was excited for what was to come. When he'd anticipated his wedding weeks ago, he didn't count on being thrilled by this woman who surprised him at every turn. He no longer felt trapped.

Things were going so well he didn't dare make the wrong move until she was ready for the physical side of their marriage. For them to get through the wedding without problems when they were virtual strangers led him to believe they could turn their marriage into something strong, maybe even wonderful given enough time.

He already felt strong feelings for her, which surprised him. They'd discussed one crucial element concerning their marriage by talking about the children they would have. But as near to each other as they were physically right now, they were still worlds apart.

"Christina?" He turned to her and cupped her face in his hands. "Tonight I'm happier than any man has a right to be." He lowered his head and closed his mouth over hers. The taste and feel of her set his pulse racing. "You're the most wonderful thing to come into my life."

Antonio pressed kisses over every feature. "I need to get closer to you. Would you like me to undo the buttons at the back of your wedding dress before I change?"

He saw a little nerve jump at the base of her throat. His bride was nervous. That was his fault for not visiting her and letting her get comfortable with him.

"Yes, please."

She turned, reminding him of a modest young maiden. It brought out his tenderest feelings as he began undoing them from the top of her neckline to the bottom, which ran below her waistline. His fingers brushed her warm skin as he set about freeing her trembling body. Never had he enjoyed a task more.

"A-are you finished?" she stammered.

He smiled to himself. "Not quite." When he was done, he lifted her hair and kissed the nape of her neck. Her mane felt like silk. "There. You're free," he whispered, and turned her around. The sleeves and bodice of her gown were loose. All he had to do…

But he didn't dare. "I don't think you have any idea how lovely you are. I want to kiss you, *esposa mia*. Really kiss you." He found her trembling mouth and began to devour her. The few kisses they'd shared up to now bore little resemblance to the desire he felt for her as she responded with growing hunger.

He clasped her against him, feeling her heart thundering into his. Antonio had an almost primitive need to make love to her, but not this stand-up kind of loving. He wanted her in his bed and was so enthralled by her he moaned when she unexpectedly tore her lips from his and eased away from him.

"Christina?" He had to catch his breath. "Have I frightened you?"

"No." She shook her head, clutching her gown to her.

He could tell she was as shocked as he was by what had just happened. He needed to reassure her. "This has been a huge day, especially for you. I'm going to let you go right now. Since we have to be up early to leave on our honeymoon, I'll bid you *buonanotte, bellissima*, and make myself a bed on the couch in the sitting room."

CHAPTER FOUR

CHRISTINA STARED AFTER her new husband, so startled by his sudden departure she could weep. She'd been on fire for him and had been ready to go wherever he led. But in the moment that she'd tried to catch a breath, Antonio left her in a dissatisfied condition.

Was it possible a groom could have nerves like the bride? Confused over what had happened, she blew out the candles and walked to the bedroom. After stepping out of her wedding dress, she laid it over a chair with the veil on top. She put her satin slippers on the floor and placed the tiara on the dresser. They were remnants of the happiest day of her life.

She slipped on a nightgown before brushing her teeth. Then she turned out the lights and got into bed. How could she possibly sleep when her body was throbbing with needs she'd never felt before? He'd awakened a fire in her, but she hadn't known how to handle it when he told her he'd make a bed on the couch for the night. She hadn't had the temerity to go after him.

Sleep must have come, but she awakened early and finished her packing. Making use of the time until

Antonio joined her, she'd touched up her pedicure and manicure. Her nails were done in a two-toned nude shade that matched everything and did justice to her royal antique-gold wedding band and diamond ring.

Since they'd be flying to Paris and would be the target of the paparazzi, Christina had chosen to wear an elegant-looking white two-piece suit from her new royal trousseau. The jacket with sleeves to the elbow fit at the waist. The high neck was half collared and there were pockets on the jacket as well as the skirt. She wore the brooch above the left pocket.

It was the perfect lightweight summery outfit to wear while walking around the City of Lights. Low-heeled off-white pumps and an off-white jacquard de-signed clutch bag with gloves completed her ensemble.

She'd worn her hair parted sideways into a high bun with one loose, hanging side longer than the other. Two white sticks for her hair with pearl tips matched her pearl stud earrings. Christina hadn't worn perfume in Africa in order to avoid attracting insects. Back home now, she used a soap with a delicious flowery scent. Her makeup consisted of a tarte lip tint. She needed no other color.

When she was ready, she walked to the door of the sitting room and knocked. "Antonio? Our breakfast is waiting."

"*Grazie*. I'll be right out." His deep-timbred male voice curled through her. It sounded an octave lower than usual. He must have barely awakened.

She wandered out to the terrace to wait for him. Her eyes filled with the beauty of the Tuscan countryside. The peaceful scene reminded her of a picture in a storybook where the rows of the vineyard formed perfect lines. All around it the gold and green of the landscape undulated off in the distance dotted with a farmhouse here and a red-roofed villa there.

Too bad she felt anything but peaceful inside.

All of a sudden she sensed she wasn't alone and turned to discover a clean-shaven Antonio studying her from the doorway wearing a casual summer suit in a tan color with a cream sport shirt unbuttoned at the throat. With his olive skin and rugged features, he was so gorgeous she couldn't believe she was married to him.

"Buongiorno, esposo mio," she said softly.

His blue gaze roved over her body from her hair to her heels, missing nothing in between. She'd never felt him look at her that way before, as if she were truly desirable. Her legs went weak because she hadn't expected that look after he decided not to sleep with her last night. She honestly didn't know what to expect.

"How are you this morning?" he asked in a husky tone of voice. A small nerve throbbed at the corner of his mouth. What were his emotions after having gone to his own bed last night instead of spending it in hers?

"I'm fine, thank you. I'm excited that we'll be walking along the Champs-élysées later on today. Aren't you?"

A strange smile broke the line of his mouth. "Shall we eat while we talk over our itinerary?" A question instead of an answer. Something was wrong.

He held out a chair for her. When she sat down, his

hands molded to her shoulders for a moment. Warmth from his fingers coiled through her body. "As bewitching as you were to this man's eyes last night, I find the sight of you right now even more beguiling."

Because of the way he'd been looking at her when no one else was around, she believed he'd meant what he just said. But she hadn't been beguiling enough to go to bed with her. She decided to accept the compliment graciously instead of throwing it back in his face.

"Thank you."

"You're welcome." His hands left her shoulders and he took his place across the table from her. They both started eating the rolls and fruit. After drinking some coffee he said, "How did you sleep?"

"The truth?"

"Always."

"Probably as poorly as you. I doubt that couch was long enough to accommodate your feet." She was glad to hear a chuckle come from him. His eyes lit up with amusement. "When everyone sees us, they'll think we're sleep-deprived because of a passion-filled wedding night and they'll be happy to think that a new royal heir could be on the way already. You know that's what's on everyone's mind."

He flashed her a piercing glance through narrowed lids. "But our business is our own."

"Of course."

After eating another roll, he sat back in the chair. "My mother left it to my father to give me some last-minute advice."

That didn't surprise Christina. "What did he have to say?"

"It isn't what they said. It's what they did."

"I'm not following you."

"Read this." He handed her a note from his suit jacket pocket.

She opened it.

Dear Antonio, your mother and I want you to have the perfect honeymoon. We know you wanted to spend a few days touring Paris and the environs before the coronation next week. But we've thought of something much better and it has all been arranged. All you have to do is be ready by eight in the morning. A helicopter will fly you to Genoa, where you'll take the royal jet to a dream spot for your vacation. It's a place neither you nor Christina has been to before. As always we remain your devoted parents.

They weren't going to Paris?

Her pulse raced. She'd thought there would be so much to do there and they'd have time to get to know each other while seeing the sights. Just what kind of dream vacation did his parents have in mind?

To be gone for a whole week together alone— It worried her that in a week's time he might find out she was unlovable. That old fear never quite went away.

What was Antonio's reaction to the news? Christina's first impulse was to tell him she didn't want to go on any dream vacation. But she couldn't refuse to do the first thing he was asking of her, especially when it was a wedding present from the king and queen themselves.

"I can hear every thought running through your head, Christina. The look in your eyes is all I need to see to know this is the last thing you expected or wanted. If it's any help, it's a surprise to me too. The idea of our honeymoon being scripted by my parents at the taxpayers' expense is typical of the lavish way they've lived their lives and expected me to do the same. If you still want to go to Paris, that's what we'll do."

"And hurt your parents?" It took a courageous man to say that to her. She was touched that he would put her feelings first. Her watch said it was almost eight now. "No, Antonio. We have the rest of our lives to plan our own vacations when we can get away. I don't want us to start off our marriage by alienating your parents. What difference does it make where we go?"

Something flickered in the recesses of his eyes. "Thank you for saying that. I like it that my new bride is adaptable and sensitive enough not to hurt their feelings. Have you done all your packing?"

"Yes." It was a good thing Elena had done some shopping with her and had insisted on her buying a couple of bikinis. "You never know when you need beachwear," her friend had confided. Maybe Elena had known about the location of the vacation spot her parents had planned for them and wanted Christina prepared for any eventuality. "How about you, Antonio?"

"I'm ready as I ever will be."

"Then I'll freshen up and meet you downstairs." She got up from the table and hurried into the bathroom for one last look in the mirror. After applying a new coat of lipstick, she walked into the bedroom and noticed her suitcase was missing. She could count on Lindsay and Louisa to make certain her wedding things were packed and returned to the royal palace in Voti.

All she needed was her purse and gloves. When she left the bridal suite and started down the stairs, she discovered Antonio waiting for her in the foyer of the palazzo.

He stood there looking tall and heartbreakingly handsome. His brilliant blue gaze swept over her in a way that sent her pulse racing. "Will you accuse me of using a platitude to tell you how beautiful you look this morning?"

"Even with bags under my eyes from lack of sleep?" But she smiled as she said it.

"Even then," he murmured. A tiny smile lifted one corner of his lips. "As you said earlier, any onlookers will speculate on the reason why and consider me the luckiest of men."

She took the last step, bringing her closer. "You're good, Antonio. I'll give you that."

He cocked his head. "What do you mean?"

"I think you know. Aren't you afraid all these compliments are going to turn my head?"

The smile disappeared. "If you want to know the truth, I'm afraid they won't."

While she stood there confused again and wondering how much truth was behind his statement, Guido, his father's chief of staff, opened the doors. "Your Highness? Princess Christina?"

Guido had addressed her as *Princess*. She'd better get used to the title, but the appellation was still foreign to her.

"If you're both ready, your cases are stowed in the limousine. Your helicopter is waiting in Monte Calanetti to fly you to Genoa."

"*Grazie*, Guido. We're coming."

She preceded Antonio out to the smoked-glass black limousine with the royal crest on the hood ornament. Guido held the rear door open for her so she could climb in, then shut the door. Antonio went around the other side and got in, shutting the door behind him. He slid close to her while they both attached their seat belts.

"This is nice," he murmured, and grasped her hand. "I'm excited to be going off on a trip with my new wife. I only wish I knew where."

She glanced at him out of the corner of her eye. "Your sister may have given me a hint, but I didn't realize it at the time."

"What did she say?"

"She made sure I bought some bathing suits when we went shopping. Did you pack one?"

"I'm sure mine is in my case somewhere."

"Do you think Hawaii or the Caribbean? I've never been to either destination."

"I have." He released her hand long enough to pull the note from his pocket. "According to this, it's someplace where neither of us has been before."

"That's right. I forgot."

"Our parents probably collaborated. It ought to be interesting."

"I agree. From what Elena has told me, you've been all over the world."

He smiled. "Let's put it this way. I've traveled over many countries without ever landing."

Christina returned his smile. She'd taken many helicopter trips with Marusha into the more inaccessible areas of Kenya's forested interior, so she was no stranger to the sensation of liftoff or landing. Before she knew it, they'd arrived on the outskirts of the village where their helicopter was waiting.

Antonio helped her out of the limo into one of the rear seats of the helicopter. He climbed in next to her while Guido placed their cases inside, then got in the copilot's seat for the short flight to Genoa. Passing over the Tuscan countryside was a constant delight.

Once they boarded the royal jet with its insignia in huge gold lettering, Christina was introduced to the pilot and copilot before being given a tour. She was struck by the staggering opulence inside and out. To her mind, the platinum curving couches, mirrored ceilings and ornate bathroom were out-of-this-world outrageous.

With an office, a gourmet kitchen and two bedrooms, all extravagant to the point of being ridiculous, she imagined the plane that contained a cockpit meant for the emperor of the universe must have cost in the region of millions upon millions of dollars.

Antonio must have been watching her, because he

said in a quiet voice, "Is there any question in your mind why our country is outraged by the unnecessary spending of my own parents? Papa bought this off an oil-rich sheik. When I'm king, I have every intention of selling it to the highest bidder and using the money to bolster Halencia's economy and put more funds in your charity foundation."

When she thought of the relief that money could bring to the Kikuyu people, she wanted to throw her arms around his neck in joy, but she didn't dare with Guido and the steward in hearing distance.

After they sat down on one of the couches, Guido made a surprising announcement. "This is where I leave you, Your Highnesses. When you reach your destination, you'll be met and taken to your vacation paradise. After the plane lands, you'll be flown in a helicopter to your own private paradise. There'll be no phone, television or internet service there."

What?

While she sat there stunned, she could tell by the lines around his mouth that Antonio wasn't amused either. "Guido? You've gotten us this far, but I refuse to travel any farther until you tell me where we're going."

"I suppose it couldn't hurt to say that you'll be arriving on the other side of the world in approximately twenty-one hours from now."

"That's not much help," Antonio said in a clipped voice.

"I'm only following the king's orders. Is there anything I can do for you before I leave?"

Antonio turned to her. "How about you, Christina?"

She had compassion for Guido, who was loyal to his king first. "I don't need anything. Thank you for everything you've done."

"You're welcome. Enjoy your honeymoon." He bowed to Antonio before leaving the plane.

In a few minutes the engines screamed to life and the fasten-seat-belts sign flashed on. Before long the jet headed into the sun. Once they'd achieved cruising speed, they got up from the couch and moved to sit in the lavish dining area where the steward served them a fabulous lunch.

"Don't be upset with Guido. It's obvious your parents' big surprise is important to him and to them."

One eyebrow lifted. "Twenty-one hours one way takes a lot of fuel. Round-trip means thousands more dollars being paid out from the public coffers. It isn't right."

She sat back while she sipped her coffee. "I agree, and I admire your desire to change the dynamics of the L'Accardi family's spending habits. But for now, why don't we decide to be Jack and Jill, two normal people who got married on a whim, and have just been given a windfall from their oil-rich uncle in Texas who wants to make us happy."

"Oil?"

"Why not? When we return to civilization, that's the time to start trimming the budget."

When she didn't think it was possible, he chuckled. "Jack and Jill, eh?"

She nodded. "One of the American girls from Texas

at the boarding school had the name Jill, and her brother's name was Jack."

By now his eyes were smiling. "I'll go along with that idea. What do you say we go to one of the bedrooms and watch a movie where we can be comfortable?"

Each bedroom had a built-in theater. She wiped her mouth with a napkin. "I'll find my suitcase and change my clothes."

He reached across the table and grasped her hand. "I'm sorry you're not able to show off that lovely white outfit in Paris."

A warm smile broke out on her face. "Don't be." She wouldn't forget the way he'd stared at her when he walked out on the terrace earlier that morning. Christina had seen a glint of genuine male appreciation in his eyes that brought her great pleasure. "We'll do Paris one of these days."

Feeling his gaze on her retreating back, she walked through the compartment and found the bedroom where both their cases had been placed. She took hers and crossed the hall into the other bedroom.

After putting it on the queen-size bed, she found a pair of lightweight pants in dusky blue and a filmy long-sleeved shirt with a floral pattern of light and dark blues combined with pink. It draped beautifully against her body to the hips.

The white suit went in the closet before she slipped into her casual clothes and put on bone-colored leather sandals. After removing the pearl tipped sticks from her hair, she exchanged the pearl studs for gold earrings mounted with star-shaped blue sapphire stones. As she was applying a fresh coat of lipstick, she heard a knock on the door.

"Antonio?"

He opened it but didn't enter. "Come on over to the other bedroom when you're ready."

Her heart started to thud. "I'll be there in a minute."

Antonio had changed into jeans and a sport shirt. Normally he would have put on the bottoms of a pair of sweats and nothing else for the twenty-one-hour flight. But out of consideration for Christina, he needed to make his way carefully for this journey into the unknown. Their honeymoon was in the process of becoming a fait accompli.

He'd experienced two heart attacks already: one at the altar when his fiancée appeared in her white wedding dress and lace veil. The other attack happened this morning when he first saw her on the terrace ready for their trip to Paris wearing a stunning white outfit. When he heard her call out his name just now, he should have known to brace himself for the third attack.

"Enter if you dare," he teased. Antonio had stretched out on the bed with his head and back propped against the headboard using a pillow for a buffer.

"Ready or not," she countered, and came into the room. The incredibly beautiful woman dressed in blue appeared, and the sight almost caused him to drop the remote. With her shiny hair, she lit up any room she entered. How could he have ignored her for so long?

The few phone calls and visits to her had been made out of duty. The busy life he'd been leading in California had included hard work *and* one certain woman when he had the time.

Thoughts of his future marriage for the good of the country had only played on the edge of his consciousness, as did the woman who'd been thousands of miles away in Kenya. He couldn't go back and fix things, but he could shower her with attention now. They didn't know each other well yet, but had made a start last night when their passion ignited.

Antonio recognized that he needed to treat her the way he would any beautiful woman he'd just met and wanted to get to know much better. He patted her side of the bed. "Come and join me. We have a choice of five films without my having to move from this spot."

She laughed and pulled a pillow out from under the quilt. The next thing he knew she'd thrown it at the foot of the bed and lain down on her stomach so she could watch the screen located on the other side of the bedroom. "Why don't you start the one you'd like to see without telling me what it is?" she said over her shoulder.

Christina made an amazing sight with those long legs lying enticingly close to him. "What if you don't like it?"

"I like all kinds of movies and will watch it because I want to know what makes my husband tick."

His heart skipped a beat. "You took the words out of my mouth." He clicked to the disk featuring a Neapolitan Mafia gangster film. "I only saw part of this when it first came out."

"I'm sure I haven't seen it. Italian films are hard to come by when you're out in the bush. This is fun!"

He found it more than fun to be watching it with the woman he'd just married. She made the usual moans and groans throughout. When it concluded she turned on her side and propped her head to look back at him. "I heard that the Camorra Mafia from Naples was the inspiration for that film. Were there really a hundred gangs, do you think?"

"I do."

"Did any cross the water into our country?"

"Three families that we know of."

"Do they still exist?"

"Yes, but were given Halencian citizenship at a time when our borders were more porous. They're no longer a problem. What I'm concerned about is creating high-tech jobs. Tourism and agriculture alone aren't going to sustain our growing population. I have many plans and have been laying the groundwork to establish software companies and a robotics plant, all of which can operate here to build Halencian industry."

"So *that's* what you've been doing in San Francisco all these years. No wonder you didn't come home often."

"Are you accusing me of being a workaholic?"

Her eyelids narrowed. "Are you?"

"I make time to play."

"Since I won't be able to go to sleep for a long time, what can I do for you, my husband?"

"How about reading to me?"

The question pleased her no end. "You'd like that?"

"I saw a book in your suitcase. Have you read it already?"

"I'm in the middle of it."

"What's it called?"

"*Cry, the Beloved Country* by Alan Paton. He wrote about South Africa and the breakdown of the tribal system. It's not the part of Africa I know, but it's so wonderful I'm compelled to finish the book."

"I never got around to reading it," he said.

"Tell you what. I'll read you the blurb on the flyleaf. If it interests you, I'll read from the beginning until you fall asleep."

"I'm surprised you don't carry a Kindle with you. Aren't physical books heavy to carry when traveling?"

"They can be, but I really like to hold a book in my hands. They're like an old friend I can see peeking at me from the bookshelf, teasing me to come and read again."

"I've decided you're a Renaissance woman, Christina."

"That's a curious word."

"It really describes you. You're a very intelligent woman. I see in you a revival of vigor and an interest in life that escapes most people. You're more intriguing than you know."

If she was intriguing, that was something. "When did you discover that?" she asked without looking at him.

"It happened when you were just fifteen. I drove

you and Elena to an old monastery in the woods above Lake Geneva. When we went inside, you were able to translate all the Latin inscriptions in those glass cases. I detested Latin and at eighteen I still needed a tutor for it. To hear you translating for us, I was so stunned at your expertise, it left me close to speechless. Do you remember that time?"

He remembered that? It caused her pulse to pick up speed. "Yes. I was showing off to you so you wouldn't think that your sister was spending time with a complete numbskull. My mother hated it that I was such a bookworm and would rather read than go to tea with a bunch of girls who only talked about boys and clothes."

"This conversation is getting interesting. When *did* you first become interested in boys?"

"Actually I was crazy about them at a very early age." Pictures of Prince Antonio and Princess Elena were constantly in the news. From the time she was about eight, she always liked to see photos of the famous brother and sister in the newspaper accompanying their family on a ski trip or some such thing.

He was the country's darling. By the time she met him in person, she'd already developed a crush on him that only grew after being with him. Of course all the silliness ended when she left Montreux and had new experiences in Africa. Once in a while she and Marusha would see him in the news, but until Elena's brush with the law he'd been as distant to her as another galaxy.

Antonio broke into laughter. "The secret life of Christina Rose. How scandalous."

She chuckled. "Marusha had plenty to tell me about tribal mating rituals of the Kikuyu. In fact, she kept me and Elena royally entertained most nights after lights went out. We'd stay up half the night talking. She had a crush on this security guard who was guarding a VIP at the Montreux Palace Hotel.

"You know how beautiful Marusha is. Well, we'd walk past him and she'd say things to him to capture his interest. He never spoke, but his eyes always watched her. He was tall, maybe six foot five, and he kept his arms folded. He was the most impressive figure I ever saw and I think he was the reason she could handle being in Montreux when she'd rather be home in Africa."

Laughter continued to rumble out of Antonio.

"Your sister had other interests. There was a drummer in the band that played at this one disco we were ordered not to visit. He was crazy about her and kept making dates with her. She only kept one of them. It was through him she met other guys, the kind she finally ended up with who got thrown in jail for drugs."

"Let's be thankful she has grown up now, but don't stop talking," Antonio murmured. "I could listen to you all night. What masculine interest did *you* have?"

Christina didn't dare tell him that there was no male to match Antonio. His image was the one she'd always carried in the back of her mind. "Oh… I always loved men in the old Italian movies. You know, Franco Nero, Marcello Mastroianni, Vittorio De Sica."

"No Halencian actors?"

"No. I've liked a couple of British actors too. Rufus

Sewell...*ooh-la-la*." She grinned. "Now, there is a male to die for! So, which actress did it for you?"

"That would be difficult to answer."

"You don't play fair. You manage to get a lot of information out of me, but I ask you one question and suddenly you play possum."

"What does that mean?"

"It means you play dead like a possum when you don't want to reveal yourself. The possum does it for protection. It's a very funny American expression and it describes you right now. What are you hiding from? Is the truth too scary for you?"

"Have a heart, Christina. I'm not nearly so terrible a womanizer as some of the tabloids have made me out to be. They're mostly lies."

"That's all right. You just keep telling yourself that. When I married you I forgave you for everything. But I've talked your ear off, so excuse me for a minute."

She hurried into the other bedroom and grabbed the book from the table, and then she returned to Antonio. "Are you still in the mood to be read to, or are you ready to confess your sins?"

"Yes and no."

He was hilarious.

"All right, then. Here's the quote from it. 'Cry, the beloved country, for the unborn child that is the inheritor of our fear.'" She read the rest.

A long silence ensued before Antonio murmured, "That's very moving. Tell me something honestly. Are you going to miss Africa too much?"

"What do you mean?"

"You've spent ten years of your life there. So many memories and friends you've made."

"Well, I'm hoping that from time to time I'll be able to fly to Nairobi to keep watch over the foundation, which I plan to continue with your permission."

"There's no question about that."

Good. "But our marriage is my first priority, and your needs come first and always will with me."

"You're wonderful, Christina, but that isn't what I asked, exactly. Did you leave your heart there?"

"Certainly a part of it, but I could ask you the same thing. Do you feel a strong tug when you think of San Francisco and the years you spent there?"

"I'd be a liar if I didn't say yes."

"I didn't expect you to say anything else. As for me, I've decided I have two homes. One there, where I've always been comfortable, and now the new one with you. I see them both being compatible. When you long for San Francisco and want to do business there, I'll understand."

"You'd love it there. I want to take you with me and show you around."

He couldn't have said anything to thrill her more. "And maybe you can fly to Africa with me for a little break from royal business."

"We'll make it happen."

She studied him for a long time. "Is there a woman you had to leave who's missing you right now? Maybe I should rephrase that. Is there someone you're missing horribly?"

Antonio should have seen these questions coming,

particularly since he hadn't slept with her last night. "I haven't been a monk. What about you?"

A quick smile appeared. Her appeal was growing on him like mad. "I'm no nun."

For some odd reason he didn't like hearing that.

You hypocrite, Antonio. Did you want a bride as pure as the driven snow? Did you really expect her to give up men while she waited four years for you to decide when to claim her for your wife?

"Who was he?" His parents' affairs had jaded him.

"A doctor who'd come to Kenya to perform plastic surgery on some of the native children. Once I came back to Africa with the engagement ring on my finger, he left for England three days later."

"I kept you waiting four years," Antonio muttered in self-disgust.

A frown marred her features. "Antonio, none of that matters. I'm your wife! But you still haven't answered my question. Is there a woman who became of vital importance to you before you had to fly home to get married?"

He got off the bed. "The only woman of importance was one I got involved with before our engagement, Christina."

"Then you've known her a long time. If there'd been no engagement, would you have married her?"

"That's hard to say. I might have if I'd decided to turn my back on my family and wanted to stay in California for the rest of my life. But when your call came telling me about Elena's problems and I talked to her, I realized how binding those family ties really are right from the cradle."

"I know that all too well," she whispered. Christina had obviously been talking about the relationship with her parents.

"The accident of my being born to a king and queen set me on a particular path. To marry a foreigner and deviate from it might bring me short-term pleasure. But I feared I'd end up living a lifetime of regret."

She shook her head. "How hard for both of you."

Her sincerity rang so true he felt it reach his bones. "Though I continued to see her after the engagement party, nothing was the same because we knew there would have to be an end. We soon said goodbye to each other.

"In a way it was a relief because to go on seeing her would not only have made a travesty of our engagement, but the situation was totally unfair to her and you. My sources at the palace confirmed that the country was suffering and there were plans afoot to abolish the monarchy. I knew it was only a matter of time before—"

"Before you had to come home and marry me to save the throne," she broke in. "I get it."

"Christina—" He approached her and grasped her hands. "Do you think it's possible for us to forget the past? You know what I mean. When I said my vows in the chapel, I meant what I said. I will love you and honor you all the days of my life. Can you still make that same commitment to me after knowing what I've told you?"

Her marvelous eyes filled with tears. "Oh, Antonio, I want you to know that when I made my vows at the altar, I was running on faith. Now that faith has been strengthened by what you've just admitted to me. If we have total honesty between us, then there's nothing to prevent us from trying to make this marriage work. You've always been the most handsome man I've ever known, so my attraction to you isn't a problem."

He kissed her fingers. "Can you forgive me for staying away from you before the wedding?"

"We've already had this discussion."

He slid his hands to her upper arms. "No woman but an angel like you would have sacrificed everything to enter into an engagement that didn't consider your own personal feelings in any way, shape or form. Forgive me, Christina. I don't like the man I was. I can only hope to become the man you're happy to be married to."

Her eyes roved over his features. "I liked the man you were. That man loved his sister enough to save her and their family from horrible embarrassment and scandal. She wasn't just any sister. She was the princess of Halencia, my friend. I loved you for loving her enough to help her.

"You have no idea what she did for me. She was the only person in my world besides my great-aunt Sofia who was good to me. Elena was the person I cried to every time I was hurt by my parents, especially my father, who wished I'd been born a boy." The tears trickled down her flushed cheeks.

Antonio sucked in his breath. "*Grazie a Dio*, you're

exactly who you are." He started kissing the tears away.
When he reached her mouth he couldn't stop himself
from covering it with his own. The taste of her excited him. Without her wedding dress on, he could
draw her close and feel the contours of her beautiful
body through the thin fabric of her shirt. Her fragrance
worked like an aphrodisiac on his senses, which had
come alive.

"Bellissima."

CHAPTER FIVE

THE FIRST TIME Christina had heard Antonio use the word *bellissima*, he'd said it in a teasing jest outside the door of the bridal suite. Just now he'd said it because she could sense his physical desire for her. After last night, there was no mistaking their attraction to each other. But she needed to use her head and not get swept away by passion until they'd spent more time together.

He'd wanted to put off making love to her last night. She was glad of it now. They did need more time to explore each other's minds first. Antonio might have walked away from the love of his life in San Francisco, but that didn't mean the memories didn't linger.

Christina could make love with him and pretend all was well, but she knew that until she held a place in his heart, then making love wouldn't have the same meaning for either of them. She wanted their first time to happen when it was right.

As soon as he lifted his mouth, she eased out of his arms. Avoiding his gaze she said, "I'm going to freshen up before dinner. Where do you want to eat?"

"How about the other bedroom? There'll be other

films to pick from. Your choice. I'll tell the steward to bring it in ten minutes."

"Good. After our fabulous lunch, I can't believe I'm hungry again."

When he didn't respond, she left him to use the restroom. Some strands of her hair had come loose. It was smarter to just undo it and brush it out. Before he brought their dinner, she pulled out the pillows and propped them against the headboard. After taking off her sandals, she reached for the remote and got up on the bed. Before long Antonio walked in carrying a tray.

"Put it here between us." She patted the center of the bed.

"The steward still won't breathe a word of where we're going." He put the tray down. Sandwiches and salad.

"Loyal to the end." She smiled at him. "In the meantime this looks good."

"I think so too." He joined her on the bed and they began to eat.

"Do you mind if we talk? We haven't discussed how we're going to live. In the fairy tales the prince takes his bride to his kingdom and they live happily ever after, but we never get to see *how* they live."

He smiled. "I have my own home in one wing of the palace. Our bedroom and living room overlook the Mediterranean. It's totally private and will be our home. My office is on the main floor adjoining my father's. My parents have their own suite. You've already visited Elena in her suite, which is in the other wing. But we're far enough apart to lead separate lives."

She poured them both more coffee, then sat back to drink hers. "Is it going to feel terribly strange bringing a wife into your world?"

He finished off the rest of his sandwich. "I thought it would. In fact, I couldn't comprehend it. But after being with you, I'll feel strange if you're not with me. I've discovered that I've slipped into the husband role faster than I would have thought and I'm enjoying every minute of it."

Christina studied him for a moment. "Today I feel like we're beginning to get to know each other and aren't afraid to be ourselves. That was my greatest fear, that you'd be different from the man I knew as Elena's brother. I've worried that in living with the man you've become, I'd feel invisible walls that kept us strangers. But I don't feel that way at all when I'm around you."

"That's good to hear. I have no idea if I'm easy to live with, Christina, and beg your forgiveness ahead of time."

A gentle laugh escaped her lips. "That goes for me too. So far I have no complaints. I hope you don't mind if I ask you a few more questions."

"Why would I mind? This is all new. You can ask me anything."

She put down her empty coffee cup. "Is Guido going to be your chief of staff when you take over?"

"At first, yes. But he's been loyal to my father for years and when he sees how I intend to rule the country, he may have trouble supporting me."

As he was lying in bed, he'd worried about how everything would go while he was away on his honeymoon. If something went wrong before the coronation, he wouldn't be there to smooth things over. His father's note said no phone, no TV or internet while they were on vacation. He'd never been without those things and couldn't comprehend it at the time.

"*I'll* support you, Antonio. I believe in the changes you're going to make."

He heard the fervor in her voice and smiled at her. She was too good to be true. "If things get bad, how would you like to be my new chief of staff?"

Christina broke into laughter. "Now, there's a thought. The media will claim that Princess Christina is running the show."

"Better you than anyone else I can think of. But seriously, let's not worry about the future of the monarchy today. Look—" He sat forward. "I know everything will be strange at first."

"Elena said your mother has her own personal maid. I don't want one, Antonio. I find it absurd to ask someone to fetch and carry when I'm perfectly capable of doing those things myself. And I'd like to cook for you, go shopping at the markets. I can balance homemaking with the time spent at the charity foundation office in town."

The more she talked, the more he liked the sound of it. "We're on the same wavelength. All the years I lived in the States I did most things myself and prefer it, so I get where you're coming from. We'll make this work."

Her silvery eyes glistened with unshed tears. "Thank you for being so understanding." When she spoke, her heart was in her eyes and it touched a part of his soul.

"Thank *you* for marrying me." He meant it with all his heart.

A shadow crossed over her face. "Antonio—if I'd told you I didn't want to get married when you called, what do you think you would have done?"

"I don't know. What saddens me is that you weren't sure I'd follow through and marry you. Christina, I swear not to do anything consciously to hurt you or bring you grief. Do you believe that?"

"Of course I do," she answered in a trembling voice. "Now I'll stop pestering you and hand you the remote. Here are half a dozen movies. Choose whichever one you want. I'm loving this.

"When we get back to Halencia, I'm afraid everything will change. Elena told me your father's daily schedule is horrendous, so I consider this time precious to have you all to myself. Tomorrow we'll reach our destination, so I'm taking advantage of the time to talk to you."

"You've always been so easy to be with, Christina. You still are." More than ever… He clicked the remote and flipped slowly through the titles so she could have time to choose.

"Stop!" she cried out. "*The African Queen* in Italian? Half of that film was filmed in the Congo!"

Antonio grinned. "I never saw it."

"I bet we have Elena to thank for this one." She smiled. "Trust her to find me a film I'd enjoy. Do you mind if we watch it?"

"Not at all. It will give me a feel for where you've lived and worked all these years."

"I never worked in the Congo. The Kikuyu tribe lives on the central highlands, but it doesn't matter. The part in the Congo is authentic. Just don't forget it's an old, old movie, Antonio."

He flashed her a smile that turned her heart over. "I like old if it's good."

"This is good. I promise."

Christina settled back to watch the film while she finished her sandwich. She could tell Antonio liked it. He kept asking questions as if he was truly interested. Maybe he was. But if she continued to wonder when his reactions were natural or made up to please her every time he spoke, their marriage didn't have a hope of succeeding.

"The actress is a redhead like you."

"The poor thing. She probably suffered a lot as a child."

"She became a movie star, Christina. It obviously didn't hurt her."

He lay back on the bed and slid his hand into her hair splayed on the pillow. He lifted some strands in his fingers. "I love your hair. It gleams like red gold and smells like citrus."

"My shampoo is called Lemon Orange Peel. When I'm in Africa I have to use a shampoo with no scent so the tsetse flies and mosquitoes won't zero in on me."

"You'd be a target all right. Do you love it there so much?"

"Yes."

"You're wonderful, you know that?"

Her eyes filled with telltale moisture.

His hand moved to her face. He traced the outline of her jaw with his fingers. "You have flawless skin and a mouth I need to kiss again." Without asking her permission his lips brushed hers over and over until he coaxed them apart and began drinking deeply.

A moan escaped her throat as she felt herself falling under his spell. He rolled her into his rock-hard body. A myriad of sensations attacked her as she felt him rub her back, urging her closer. With every stroke, her body continued to melt as the heat started building inside her, making her feverish. Antonio was taking her to a place she'd never been before.

She wasn't cognizant of the fasten-seat-belt sign flashing until the captain's voice came over the intercom. "We've started to experience turbulence. For your safety, you need to come forward and sit until we get through this."

On a groan Antonio released her, much more in control than she was. "Come on. Let's go." He got off the bed and helped her to her feet.

She couldn't believe how bumpy it had become and clung to him while they made their way out of the bedroom and down the hallway to the couches. Christina had so much trouble fastening her seat belt that Antonio did it for her and then fastened his own.

"It's going to be all right." He reached for her hand.

The incident didn't last long. When the sign went off, she undid her seat belt and got up before Antonio did. "It's late. If you don't mind, I'm going to get ready for bed. Last night I hardly slept and now I'm exhausted."

After he undid his seat belt, he stood up. "You go ahead. I'm going to have a chat with the captain and will see you in the morning." He put a hand behind her head and pressed a firm kiss to her mouth before releasing her. "Get a good sleep."

"You too," she whispered before walking back to the bedroom she'd just left. Her legs felt like mush, but this had nothing to do with the bumpy flight. The kiss he'd just given her was able to reduce her to a trembling bride. A little while ago she'd experienced the kind of passion that would have rendered her witless and breathless given another minute in his arms.

Frightened because she'd almost lost control, she showered and got ready for bed. Once under the covers she had a talk with herself. It *was* too soon in their marriage for the physical side to take over. She didn't doubt Antonio's intentions. He was doing his best to be a considerate husband. There was nothing wrong with that, not at all. But she wanted to know his possession and realized this was what she got for entering into a marriage of convenience.

I don't want to be his convenient bride.

Christina wanted him to make love to her because he was in love with her and couldn't live without her. She wanted Antonio in every way a woman wanted her husband. From the age of fifteen she'd been attracted to him. All it had taken was that kiss at the altar to turn her inside out.

What have you done to me, Antonio?

She closed her eyes, reeling from that torturous question until she fell into oblivion. The next time she was aware of her surroundings, her watch indicated she'd slept ten hours. All in all, they'd been flying twenty hours with refueling stops she hadn't been aware of. That meant they were close to their unknown destination.

If Antonio had come to her in the night, she didn't know about it. Chances were he'd been exhausted too and needed sleep as much as she did. She threw off the covers and went to the bathroom to brush her teeth and arrange her hair back in a French twist.

The more she thought about it, the more she believed they were flying to a beach vacation. After some deliberation, she chose to put on a pair of white pants and toned it with a filmy white top of aqua swirls that looked like sea spray. The short sleeves and round neck made it summery. Once she'd put on lipstick, she packed her bag so it would be ready to carry off the jet.

Antonio must have had the same thoughts, because when she walked through the plane to the dining area, she discovered him dressed in white pants and a white crew-neck shirt with navy blue trim. His virility took her breath.

As she approached, he broke off talking to the steward. "I was just about to come and wake you for breakfast. We'll be landing pretty soon. I've been told we don't want to miss the view before we touch down."

"That sounds exciting. How did you sleep?" She sat down at one of the tables.

He took his place opposite her. "I don't think as well as you."

"I'm sorry."

"Don't be. I'm a restless sleeper when I travel. When we touched down to refuel, I got out of the jet to stretch my legs. I peeked in on you to see if you wanted some exercise too, but you were out like a light."

She felt Antonio's admiring gaze before the steward served them another delicious meal that started off with several types of chilled melon balls in a mint juice. "Mmm. This is awesome."

"I agree," he said, still eyeing her face and hair over his cup of cappuccino until she felt a fluttery sensation in her chest.

They ate healthy servings of eggs, bread and jam. If she ate like this for every meal, she'd quickly put on the weight she'd slowly lost over the past year.

The steward came to their table. "The pilot will be addressing you in a minute. When you're through eating, please take your seats in the front section. He'll start the descent, allowing you a bird's-eye view."

"Thank you," Antonio said, exchanging a silent glance with her. By tacit agreement, they got up from the table and walked forward to one of the couches, where they sat together and buckled up.

In a minute the fasten-seat-belt sign flashed and they heard the captain over the intercom. "Your Highness? Princess Christina? It's eleven a.m. Tahitian time."

"Tahiti—" she blurted in delight, provoking a smile from Antonio who reached for her hand.

"We'll be landing at the airport built on the island next to Bora Bora. From there you'll be taken by helicopter to a nearby island that is yours exclusively for the next four days. The sight you're about to see is one of the most glorious in the world. Start watching out the windows."

Christina felt the plane begin to descend. Pretty soon she saw a sight that was out of this world. The captain said, "Bora Bora has been described as an emerald set in a sea of turquoise blue with a surrounding necklace of translucent white water."

"Incredible!" she and Antonio cried at the same time.

"There are dark green islands farther out in the lagoon that face the mountain. This lagoon is three times the size of the land mass."

"Oh, I can't believe this beauty is real." She shook her head. "No wonder sailors from long ago dreamed of reaching Bora Bora."

"To the southeast you'll see a coral garden with waters swimming with manta rays, barracudas and sharks. You can watch them at their feeding time."

She turned to her husband. "I'm not sorry your parents gave us this beautiful gift, Antonio. They couldn't have planned a more glorious honeymoon retreat for us."

"You're right." He squeezed her hand.

The jet circled lower and before long they touched down. Antonio undid both their seat belts. "I'll grab our suitcases. What else?"

"My white purse on the dresser."

He nodded. "I'll be right back." His excitement matched hers. They'd come to paradise and couldn't wait to get out in it.

She walked toward the galley to thank the steward.

"It's been my pleasure, Princess."

Antonio caught up to her with her purse. The steward carried their cases to the entrance of the jet where their pilot was waiting. He shook his hand. "Thank you for a flawless flight."

"It has been an honor for me to serve you and the princess. There's a helicopter waiting to fly you to your private resort where every need will be met. In four days I'll be here to fly you back to Halencia. Enjoy your honeymoon."

She left the jet with Antonio following her and made her way to the helicopter. The pilot, an islander, greeted them warmly and explained they'd be flying to one of those dark green islands in the distance.

Christina sat in one of the backseats. The second Antonio joined her and buckled up, the rotors screamed to life and they lifted off, flying low over the aquamarine water. The pilot spoke to them over the mic.

"Welcome to Tahiti. The resort has heard that the future king and queen of Halencia are our guests. Word has come that you are much beloved, Princess. No one else will disturb your vacation, but you have a staff to wait on you. Ask for anything."

"Thank you."

When she looked back at Antonio, he was staring at her. "Do you know everyone who meets you is so charmed by you that you have them eating out of your hand? I noticed it as we were walking down the aisle after the ceremony. All eyes and smiles were focused on you."

A blush seeped into her cheeks. "A bride is always the center of attention at a wedding. It's the way of things."

"But my bride is exceptional and loved by the people already. If I'm to gain any credibility with the country when I'm king, it will be because of you."

"Thank you, but you don't need to say things like that to me."

"Yes, I do." The sincerity in his voice convinced her.

Before she knew it, the pilot set down the helicopter on a stretch of the purest white beach she'd ever seen. Another man in shorts and T-shirt was there to take their bags.

"Welcome to Bora Bora, Your Highnesses. I'm Manu and will be serving you. If you want anything, it will be at your disposal. With the powerboat you can go where you wish to fish, scuba dive, hike. Anything you want."

They shook his hand and followed him to their resort. It turned out to be a massive island bungalow of traditional Polynesian design with a vaulted ceiling situated on stilts over their private lagoon of turquoise water. As they walked inside, the living room looked like a sumptuous palace suite with windows on all sides and glass floors throughout to watch the fish.

There were windows on all sides and two different sundecks facing Bora Bora with platforms so they could step off directly into the lagoon.

Outside were oversize chairs and more glass floor panels. Manu showed them the dining room and kitchen with a refrigerator stocked with snacks and drinks. "There's food here to enjoy inside or to make a picnic. The spacious bathroom has two tubs and walk-in showers."

They followed him to the fabulous bedroom, also with a vaulted ceiling, where he put down their cases. Then he showed them out to one of the platforms. "The powerboat is ready and filled to capacity to take you where you want. Come with me to the other platform."

They followed him. "You have your own two-seater kayak, snorkeling equipment, rubber rafts, whatever you want including towels and sunscreen. The lagoon water is eighty degrees and the nighttime temperature is the same."

Warmer than a bathtub?

Christina marveled that everything you could ever want had been provided. She thanked Elena silently for taking her to buy some swimming suits.

"I'll be the person waiting on you. Pick up the phone to order your food or when you need clothes washed or ironed. There's one in the living room and another one in the bedroom. There's no internet, no television. If there's an emergency, you call me on the house phone and I'll take care of it. Can I answer any questions?"

"Not right now." Antonio shook his hand. "Thank you, Manu."

After the islander disappeared, she looked around in wonder. "All of this just for us?" she murmured to her husband. "Only a king could afford to pay the re-sort enough money to keep the world away."

He chuckled and turned to her. "What do you want to do first?"

"Let's unpack and then go for a swim. That water is calling to me."

Antonio couldn't help but admit that this had to be the ultimate getaway. His parents had gone over-the-top on this one, but he'd promised Christina they'd enjoy this outrageous luxury and not count the cost.

It didn't take long to put their things in closets and drawers. Then she disappeared in the bathroom. While she was out of sight he changed into his boxer-style black bathing trunks. Wanting to create a mood, he went into the living room and searched in the entertainment center for the radio.

When he turned it on, he got Tahitian music, exactly what he wanted. There was a switch that said Outside. He flipped it and suddenly they were surrounded with island music that no doubt could be heard out on the beach.

A smiling Christina came hurrying in wearing a lacy peach-colored beach robe over what looked like a darker peach bikini. Her gorgeous long legs took his breath away. "That's such romantic music, I think I'm dreaming all this."

"Fun, isn't it? Let's go try out the water."

He opened the door that led to the platform off the living room. She leaned over the railing to look down at the water. "It's clear as crystal." When she reached the edge of the platform, she removed her beach coat and put it over the railing.

"Wait, Christina. You need some sunscreen or you'll pick up a bad sunburn."

"You're right."

"I'll get it." He went over to the basket and brought it to her. "I'll put some on your back and shoulders."

She turned her back toward him without hesitation. Her skin felt like satin and he loved rubbing the cream over her. The legitimate excuse to touch her made him wish he didn't have to stop. Summoning all the self-control he could muster, he handed her the tube so she could do the rest herself.

"Thank you," she said in a shaky voice. "Now it's my turn to put some on you, although you're already tanned."

He longed to feel her hands on him. His pulse throbbed as he felt her spread the cream over his shoulders and back. After putting the tube on the railing, she jumped in the shallow water and shrieked with joy.

"Oh, Antonio— This is divine!" She splashed the water with her hands and laughed in delight before lying back while her legs did the work of keeping her afloat.

One look at her and he couldn't reach her soon enough. Bathtub was right. The temperature here stayed around eighty day and night. He swam up next to her, infected by her sounds of excitement. With the Polynesian music filling the air, they were like children who'd discovered the fount of pure pleasure.

Together they moved out deeper into the blue lagoon. He swam under and around her. The glimpses of her exquisitely molded body set his heart pounding.

"Look at that darling little sea turtle!"

Spectacular as it was, he would rather look at her. As they trod water, they caught sight of other types of small fish including a clown fish with orange and white stripes. One discovery turned into another. They played and darted through the water for several hours, concocting silly games to identify the fish they saw. Her prowess as a swimmer was going to make this the adventure of a lifetime.

Since there was no one else around, Antonio felt as if they were the last two people on earth...or the first. Adam and Eve?

He loved the idea of it, loved being with her like this where her guard was down. Her sense of fun was already making this trip unforgettable. "What do you say we go back and drink something icy cold while we sunbathe on the lounge chairs?"

"That sounds perfect. I'll race you back."

Together they did the crawl. He slowed his pace to stay even with her. When they reached the platform he climbed up first, then helped her. She put on her beach robe and headed for one of the loungers.

"I'll order some drinks and be right back."

"No alcohol for me. Even a little wine can give me a headache."

"Did you suffer from one on our wedding night?"

"No, because I only sipped a little, but I know to be careful."

That was something he didn't know. He rarely drank himself and was pleased to learn she didn't care about it. His parents constantly overindulged.

A few minutes later and Manu appeared with two frosted glasses of juice topped with a flower.

"I could get used to this in a hurry," Christina commented after they'd given him their order for dinner and were alone again. Antonio handed her some of the brochures from the table in the living room. He looked over one, but would study the rest of them later. Right now he was content to study her and look at the white clouds moving slowly across the sky.

He finished his drink. "It'll be several hours before dinner, but it's already late in the day. How would you like to go exploring in the powerboat? We'll follow the directions in that brochure and make our plans for tomorrow."

"That's exactly what I want to do. While we were descending in the plane, I longed to spend more time just to get acquainted with this glorious place."

A few minutes later they undid the ropes and Antonio idled them out into the lagoon. He reached into one of the lockers. "Here—put this lifesaving belt on." He handed it to her.

"But the water isn't that deep."

"It doesn't matter. If we got into trouble, you'd be glad of it."

"I'll wear it if you wear one too."

"Nag, nag." But he smiled as he put one on.

"Now that I think about it, can you imagine the media storm if we had an accident and word got out that the future king and queen of Halencia had almost drowned because they hadn't been wearing preservers? People would wonder what kind of ruler they had."

He chuckled. "Point taken. It would never do."

Off Point Matira they came across a group of huge manta rays. There were spotted and gray rays. Antonio swam near their boat while they watched in fascination.

"We should be marine biologists," she exclaimed. "Just think, we could come out to places like this and spend all day long for weeks on end."

Antonio nodded. "Being out here, you can understand the appeal for that kind of work. Are you interested in watching the locals feed the sharks? We're not far from there."

"I guess it's safe or they wouldn't advertise it, but I think I'll want to stay in the boat."

He drove them to the spot where the local divers stood chest deep in the water. Four-and five-foot sharks circled around them to get their food.

"That's scary to me," Christina said. "I've changed my mind about being a biologist."

"Instead you'd rather be in Kenya where you can be dragged off by a lion."

"No—" She grinned at him.

For their last destination they took off and headed for the coral garden, an underwater park southwest of Bora Bora Island. For an hour they were spellbound by the amount of colorful fish and coral. Like an excited child she squealed over the varieties.

"I'm going to take a quick dip before we head back."

Antonio couldn't have stopped her. She was too anxious to get closer. Off came her belt and she lowered herself in the water. The sight of her going underwater made him nervous. He watched her like a hawk.

To his relief she came back up a few minutes later, but she looked distressed.

"I stepped on something, but I don't know what."

Diavolo. "Does it sting?"

"No. It's just kind of sore on the pad of my foot."

Antonio leaned over and helped her into the boat. He set her down on the banquette so he could inspect it. "You made contact with a sea urchin, but luckily I only see two spines." *Thank heaven.* "They'll need to come out. Keep your leg on the banquette and I'll get us back home." He wrapped the life belt around her, kissed her lips and got behind the wheel.

"Do you think it's serious?"

"No. I once got a whole foot full of them, but I was fine. Still, we'll ask the doctor to check you."

"Oh no—I didn't mean for this to happen."

"Accidents can happen anytime in the water, as you reminded me."

The sky was darkening fast. He was glad when they reached their island. After tying up the boat, he undid the life belts and carried her from the deck into their bedroom.

After setting her down on top of the bed, he phoned Manu and asked for a doctor to come. "I'll get you some ibuprofen after we've talked to the doctor."

"Will you carry me to the bathroom? I need to get out of my suit and into a robe."

"Of course." He lifted her in his arms once more and let her hang on to him while he reached for her robe hanging on the door. "Can I help you?"

"I'll be all right." He waited until she said she was

ready, and then he carried her back to the bed. In another moment he heard Manu's voice coming from the main entrance. "The doctor is here."

"Will you show him into the bedroom, Manu?"

Within seconds the two men came in. "Princess Christina? This is Dr. Ulani."

He brought his bag with him. "Thank you for coming, Doctor. As you can see, my wife stepped on a sea urchin. She's in pain."

"Hush, Antonio. It's not that bad at all. More of a discomfort."

The native doctor smiled. "Accidents like this happen every day, even to someone like Your Highness. Let me check your foot. I'll try not to add to your pain."

Antonio placed a chair for him to sit while he worked on her. Relieved as he was that she was getting medical attention, it suddenly hit him how frightened he'd been when she first surfaced. In very little time she'd become so important to him that he couldn't bear the thought of anything truly serious being wrong with her.

The doctor opened his bag and proceeded to get rid of the two spines. He put ointment on the sores and a dressing. "You'll be fine tomorrow. Just make sure you wear some kind of shoe in the water if you're not snorkeling with fins. I'll give you a tablet for you to sleep that will kill the pain. Tomorrow if you're still too sore, take some ibuprofen."

"Thank you so much. It feels better already."

"It's a privilege to help you, Princess." When he'd finished, he stood up. "Take care, now."

"I'll make sure of it," Antonio muttered. He shouldn't have let her slip into the water like that. The action had caught him off guard.

"Here's the pill. Tomorrow you can take off the dressing."

Antonio walked him out to the living room. "I can't tell you how grateful I am you came."

"It is my pleasure to wait on the future king and queen of Halencia. Our people are aware of your presence here and they are delighted. Don't hesitate to get hold of me through Manu if you are alarmed by anything."

Manu stood by. "You want your dinner in the bedroom, Your Highness?"

"Yes. Thank you. Will you bring a glass of water so she can take her medicine?"

He nodded and hurried to the kitchen. Antonio headed back to the bedroom. "Christina? It's my fault you got hurt this evening."

"Nonsense. I wasn't thinking. When I saw those fish, I just had to get in closer."

"Please tell me you'll give me a heads-up next time before you do a disappearing act."

His mermaid was resting against the headboard with a sore foot. "I'm sorry to be the one at fault for not having the sense to get in the water prepared. But, Antonio, you don't have to try to be perfect with someone as imperfect as I am. I did a stupid thing, but the situation really is funny, don't you think? Your parents planning for every contingency to bring us joy? And I blew it. At least for tonight. Now you have to give me my medicine and be stuck with your ball and chain until morning."

"Don't say that! Not ever! I don't feel that way about you and never could. Promise me!" He sounded truly upset.

"I promise," she said as Manu appeared with their dinner. Antonio thanked him and put the tray of food on the side of the bed next to her. He handed her the glass of water and the pill. "Take this first."

After she did his bidding, he sat in the chair the doctor had used and they ate their dinner. He heard her sigh.

"It's another beautiful night, so balmy. I'd wanted to go walking on the beach with you."

"We'll do that tomorrow night. For now, you need to try and fall asleep."

"You won't leave me?" Her eyes beseeched him.

"As if I would," he murmured, experiencing a hard tug of emotion. It came to him that his new wife had become of vital importance to him. "I'll join you as soon as I change out of my swimming suit."

"Good. Don't be long."

Christina, Christina.

He put the tray on the table and went into the bathroom to change. After putting on a robe, he turned out the lights, then got into bed beside her. The pill must have been powerful, because her eyelids were drooping. Antonio rolled her into him and she let out a deep sigh. Soon she was asleep. Before long, oblivion took over.

Around six in the morning he felt the bed move. She'd gotten up to use the bathroom.

He eyed her through sleep-filled eyes. When she returned he said, "How's the pain?"

"There's hardly any at all. I can walk fine as long as I'm careful."

"That's wonderful news. Come back to bed and rest that foot some more. It's still early."

CHAPTER SIX

CHRISTINA EYED HER HUSBAND, who'd kept a vigil over her all night. She got back in bed, lying on her side so she could watch him sleep. He was such a gorgeous man. Dawn was sneaking into the bedroom with the morning breeze. Through the open windows she could see the unique shape of the mountains on Bora Bora. If she could be anywhere in the world, she wanted to be right here with the man she'd married.

When next she came awake, she found herself the object of Antonio's blue gaze. She propped her head up with her hand. "How long have you been awake?"

"Long enough to watch my lovely wife. You've been sleeping so peacefully."

Without hesitation he leaned over to kiss her. "Good morning, *esposa mia*. I dreamed about kissing you all night long."

"I had the same dream."

Before she could blink he put his arm around her and kissed her deeply, not letting her go until she had to breathe.

He sighed. "I needed that."

"I'm pretty sure you need something else after taking care of me all night. I'll ring Manu to bring our breakfast tray." She reached for the phone and put in their order. After hanging up, she turned to her husband.

"How did you know?"

"That you're starving?" she quipped. "I'm hungry too."

He raised himself up and leaned over her. "You have no idea how beautiful you are, do you? I could eat you up."

But at that moment Manu appeared at the door. "Shall I put your breakfast on the table?"

"No, Manu," Antonio said. "I think we'll have it right here in bed."

The other man smiled and set it on the end of the bed before making a discreet departure.

She smiled at her husband. "We're spoiled rotten. You know that."

He moved to put the tray between them. Christina propped her head with a couple of pillows and bit into a croissant. "If the famous French impressionist Gauguin were here to paint us, he'd entitle it *Petit Déjeuner au Lit Tahitien*."

His lips twitched. "Breakfast in a Tahitian bed is far too mundane. I think a more appropriate title would be *Le Mari Amoureux*."

The Amorous Husband? Christina laughed to cover the quiver that ran through her. She'd forgotten he'd attended a French/Swiss boarding school too and was fluent in French besides Halencian, Italian, English and Spanish.

"What do you want to do today?"

"I'm up for anything."

"Honestly?"

"My foot doesn't hurt and I don't want us to miss out on anything while we're here. We don't have that much time before we have to go back."

"I don't want to go back."

Her pulse raced. "Neither do I."

"What do you say we take out the kayak and just paddle around for fun?"

"That sounds perfect. I'll get my suit on and wear a T-shirt so I don't pick up any more sun on my shoulders." With a kiss to his jaw, she slid out of bed. "I'll be back in a minute."

He'd been worried about that. The need to touch her was growing. A bad case of sunburn could make her feel miserable for several days. Relieved that her foot was healing well, he got excited to think about spending another glorious day with her. It was pure selfishness on his part to want her able to do everything with him waking or sleeping.

There was only one bed, but a number of couches. He had no intention of sleeping on a couch or a sun lounger tonight. He wanted his wife in that oversize bed clinging to him while the scented breeze from Bora Bora wafted through their bedroom.

"Antonio? I'm ready when you are."

He looked up to see her standing there with a white T-shirt pulled over her suit. "I'm glad you're wearing your tennis shoes."

There was no doubt his bride had one of the most

beautiful faces and bodies he'd ever seen, starting with her glorious hair. She'd fastened it on top with a clip. He wanted to reach up and pull her down to him, but right now it was important they keep having fun while breaking down walls.

Levering himself out of bed, he hurried to the bathroom to put on his trunks. Then he joined her at the edge of the platform. The Sevylor inflatable plastic kayak had been secured to the post with cords. Once they were undone he reached down to hand her a belt life preserver. While she put hers on, he fastened his.

"I'll go first." After getting in the front seat, he held out his hands to her and eased her into the backseat.

"Ooh—" She laughed. "It's tippy. I'm used to a canoe."

"You'll soon get the hang of it."

They unloosened their oars and started paddling. He led them around in circles to get her used to the motion. Over his shoulder he said, "According to the brochure, there's no surf here because of the reef across the lagoon. When you're ready, we'll head out to that other island in the distance."

"I can see you're an old pro at this."

"During my boarding school days in Lausanne, some friends that my parents didn't approve of flew home with me on breaks. We'd go kayaking around Halencia on weekends. But as you know, the Mediterranean can be choppy when the wind comes up. This lagoon is like glass in comparison."

They started paddling together and headed out. "I

wonder if I ever saw you out there during the few times I came home from boarding school."

"I've been wondering the same thing myself. Do you believe in destiny, Christina?"

"To be honest, until I received the phone call from you that we were really getting married, I believed that I was meant to—" She broke off abruptly. "Oh, it doesn't matter what I believed."

He stopped paddling and turned to look at her. "Tell me. I want to know."

She shook her head. "If I told you, you'd see me as a pitiful creature who feels sorry for herself."

"You're anything but pitiful. I want to know what you were going to say."

Christina rested her oar. She cast her gaze toward Bora Bora. "My parents didn't want me, Antonio. They really didn't. The only genuine love I felt came from my great-aunt Sofia, but I wasn't her daughter and didn't see her very often.

"I believed it was my lot always to live on the outside of their lives. This became evident when they didn't put up a fuss about my working in Africa. I was crushed when they sounded happy about my doing charity work there. They didn't miss me, not at all. Marusha's parents have been more like parents to me than anyone."

Her suffering had to be infinite. "That's tragic about your parents."

"I was afraid you'd say that, but I don't want you to feel sorry for me. They were warmer to me at the wedding, especially Mother. You asked for the truth and I've told you. As for believing in destiny, despite my pain, I was happy with my life in Africa and decided I'd probably live there forever. The ability to help other people brought me a lot of peace I hadn't known before."

"Until I turned your world upside down," he bit out in self-deprecation.

"It wasn't just you, Antonio. Elena had already become family to me. When she got into real trouble, I felt her pain. Like you, she led a life of isolation being royal. I can understand why she took up with guys from my world. In your own way, you and Elena have led a life of loneliness. It's a strange world you two inhabit and always will be. But I was lucky enough to be the friend Elena let in. If I could have had a sister, I would have wanted her."

"You're very perceptive, Christina. I originally went to San Francisco to learn business. It was there I worked with normal people. Zach became a true friend and I enjoyed it so much I didn't want to go home. My parents' lifestyle was a personal embarrassment to me. But when I heard of the trouble Elena was in, I couldn't turn my back on her. Forgive me for using you."

"By phoning you, I used you too," Christina came back. "Did you really have a choice to do anything but try to draw the paparazzi's attention away from her? I was the perfect person to help. After all, we were an unlikely threesome, yet no one knew me or knew about me. What I want to know is, why didn't you break off our engagement a few years later and ask the woman you loved to marry you?"

His jaw hardened. "I wouldn't have done that to you."

"You see what I mean?"

Her sad smile pierced him.

"You tried to be like everyone else, but in the end, the prince in you dominated your will. The princess in Elena let you fall on your sword because you were both born to royalty and knew your duty. She wanted you to be king one day.

"Before I phoned you, did you know she wanted to admit everything to the police and take the blame so there'd be no reflection on you or your family? But I wouldn't let her. I told her I was going to phone you because I knew you could fix things and you found a way."

"Which involved you." His voice throbbed. His emotions hovered near the surface. "Let me ask you a question. Why didn't you tell me to go to hell when I called you to give you the wedding date? You would have had every right."

She breathed in deeply. "Because your royal dust had blown on me years before. I'm not a Halencian for nothing. My country means everything to me. The engagement we entered into was very bizarre, but it made a strange kind of sense. In fact, the only kind of sense that would satisfy the people.

"I'm positive it would have been hard for them to accept your marriage to a woman from a different nationality as you pointed out. But if you'd wanted it badly enough, you could have made it happen."

He eyed her for a moment. "When it came down to

it, I didn't want her badly enough to break my commitment to you."

"Thank you for saying that. I want you to know I'm not sorry, Antonio."

His heart skipped a beat. "Do you honestly mean it? Even though it meant ending an important relationship with the doctor you met in Kenya?"

"It wasn't that important. I didn't want to break my commitment to you either. You and Elena have trod a treacherous path all your lives. You always will because you were born to the House of L'Accardi.

"Elena and I were friends from the age of fifteen. I knew her sorrows. She bore mine. Her greatest fear was that you might end up living in California one day and giving up the throne so she would have to be queen. That was one of her greatest nightmares."

Good heavens. So much had gone on that he hadn't known about behind the scenes because of his selfishness in pursuing his own dream. "I didn't realize…"

"How could you if she never said anything? At our reception, Elena acted so happy we got married that she could hardly contain herself." Even though there was still something she seemed to be holding back.

"Her happiness went much deeper than that because it meant she wasn't going to lose the best friend she's ever had."

Christina flashed a full, radiant smile at him, stunning him. "Now she's got both of us and our threesome can go on forever."

Forever.

* * *

Antonio turned around and started paddling again. There'd been a time when the thought of being married forever stuck in his throat. But no longer. When they returned to the hut, Manu had served their dinner on the deck.

"Tonight you are eating freshly caught mahimahi with coconut rice and mango salsa."

"It looks fantastic, Manu."

After he left them alone Christina said, "They've gone all out for us. Now I know the true meaning of being treated like a king."

His blue eyes glinted with amusement as they sat down to eat.

Christina took her first bite. "The fish is out of this world."

"This is Bora Bora mahimahi," he quipped. "We won't be getting anything this good in Halencia. If I could put off the coronation for a while, I'd like us to stay here for a month at least! I'm thinking our first-year anniversary. What do you say?"

"But we'll fly commercial. And we'll stay in a little bungalow over the water and play tourist like everyone else."

"And climb the mountain and scuba dive. Have you ever been?"

"No."

"Then you've got to take lessons. I'll go with you."

"You mean you'll take time out of your busy day?"

"You'll need a buddy. I don't want anyone else buddying up with *my* wife."

The possessive tone in his voice thrilled her.

Once dinner was over Christina showered and washed her hair. After toweling it, she used the blow dryer until it swished against her shoulders. She put on a pale lemon-colored nightgown. Her skin had picked up some sun, adding color to her complexion. To her relief her injury was barely noticeable.

Her lamp was the only light on in the room. There were more brochures for her to read on the side table, but she wasn't ready for bed yet. Antonio had turned on more romantic music. The thought of him made her heart thump out of control. She'd just spent the most heavenly day of her life with the man who was now her husband.

Before long he came into the bedroom wearing a robe. Without a shirt he had an amazing male physique with a dusting of dark hair on his chest. Her mouth went dry just looking at him. When he came closer, she could smell the soap he'd used in the shower. "The night is calling to us. Let's go out on the deck. I want to dance with you."

He grasped her hand and they walked out into the balmy night. Christina gasped softly to see millions of stars overhead. "Antonio—have you ever seen the heavens this alive? I just saw a shooting star."

"We don't need a telescope when the universe seems so close. It's even in your eyes. They are shimmering like newly minted silver. Combined with the red gold of your hair, you're an amazing sight. A new heavenly body to light up this unforgettable night."

His words overwhelmed her before he wrapped his

arms around her and started dancing with her. Not the kind of dancing they did at the reception. This was slow dancing. She melted into him. The night had seduced her. There was a fragrance in the air from the flowers on the deck that intoxicated her. Being held against his hard body like this was pure revelation.

Her womanhood had come alive in his arms. She liked being taller because their bodies fit together. He'd buried his face in her hair. She could feel the warmth of his breath, tantalizing her because she longed to feel his mouth on hers. On their wedding night she'd thought the fantasy was over. How could she have known they would come to this paradise where she was finding rapture beyond her dreams?

"Give me your mouth, Christina," he murmured. "I'm aching for you."

She had the same ache and lifted her head. Their mouths met and they kissed for a long time, giving and taking, back and forth. She clung to him, needing the pleasure he gave her with every caress of his hands roaming over her back. When he moved his mouth lower, she moaned as he slowly kissed her neck and throat. Everywhere his lips touched, it brought heat that spread through her body like fire.

Without her realizing it, he'd danced them back inside. Then he swept her into his arms and followed her down on the bed. "I could eat you alive," he whispered against her lips, and once again Christina was consumed by his kiss, hot with desire. A *husband's* desire. She hadn't known it could be like this.

"*Bellissima?* Tell me something. Have you ever been to bed with a man?"

The question jolted her. "No. Does my inexperience show so much?"

"Not at all. But I worried that if I'm the first man to make love to you, then I don't want to rush you into anything. You're so sweet, Christina. I didn't need Elena to tell me just how sweet you really are. I want our first time to be everything for you."

"Everything has been perfect so far," she whispered, fearing something had to be lacking in her for him to bring it up. When he didn't say anything, she eased away a little, but he drew her to him with her back resting against his chest.

"I'm glad, but I want to give you time to get used to me. Until you're truly ready, let's simply hold each other tonight. If I'd gone to Africa to see you, this is what we would have done. We have the rest of our lives and don't need to be in a hurry." He kissed her neck. "This is heavenly, you know? You smell and feel divine to me."

To be held in his arms was heavenly, but little did he know she *was* ready! Though she loved him for trying to make their first time perfect, she was dying inside. Still, by his determination to ease her into marriage, it showed a tender side of his nature that proved what a wonderful man she'd married. How many men would care enough about their brides' feelings to go to these lengths?

"This has been my idea of heaven, Antonio. I can't wait until tomorrow." Maybe tomorrow night he'd realize she didn't want to wait a second longer.

When she awakened the next morning, she discovered her husband fast asleep. They'd slept late. Christina slid out of bed without disturbing him and rushed into the kitchen to phone Manu and order breakfast. Then she showered to get ready for the day.

With that accomplished she put on another bikini. This one had an apple-green flutter top. Both she and Elena had loved the crocheted look of the top and bottom overlying a white lining. It was more modest than many of the suits.

Since they'd probably be out in the water most of the day, she decided the best thing to do with her hair was to sweep it on top and secure it with her tortoiseshell clip. She removed her gold studs and put on a pair of tiny earrings the shape of half-moons in a green that matched her bikini.

Before going in to Antonio, she threw on a lacy white beach jacket that fell to just below her thighs. Now she was ready to greet her husband. But when she entered the bedroom, he'd turned onto his stomach and was still out for the count. Only a sheet covered his lower half. What a fabulous-looking man! She was still pinching herself to believe he was her husband.

He would need a shave, but she loved the shadow on his hard jaw. He looks were so arresting that his state of dress or his grooming didn't matter. She'd loved the handsome eighteen-year-old prince. But over the years he'd grown into a breathtaking man no woman could be immune to.

While she sat feasting her eyes on him, she heard sounds coming from the kitchen. She got up from the side of the bed and went back to bring him their breakfast tray. She brought it in and put it on the end of the bed.

The aroma of the coffee must have awakened him. He turned on his side and opened his eyes. Between the dark fringe of his lashes, their brilliant blue color stole her breath. Antonio raised himself up on one elbow. "Well, what do we have here? Could it be the nymph from the fountain holding the seashell?"

She loved the imagery. He'd noticed the fountain sculpture in the courtyard in front of the palazzo. "Yes, sire." His eyes darkened with emotion. "I'm here with your breakfast. Your wife told me you would awaken with a huge appetite."

"My wife told you that? Her exact words?"

"I never lie."

"Then will you tell her that spending the day with her yesterday was more than wonderful? But I'll tell her just how wonderful when we're alone again today. Those will be words for her ears only."

Christina couldn't prevent the blush that rose into her cheeks. "I'll be happy to do that after I've served you your breakfast." She got up and put the tray in front of him. "Do you wish me to leave? You have only to command me."

"Then I command you to bring that chair over to the side of the bed and we'll enjoy this food together."

She smiled secretly and moved it next to the bed. "Your wife won't mind?"

He flicked her an all-encompassing gaze. "She might. A woman serving me breakfast who looks as gorgeous as you might worry, so I think we'll keep this moment to ourselves. How does that sound to you?"

She reached for a roll and bit into it. "You flatter me, sire."

"I haven't even started. That's quite an outfit you're wearing."

Christina drank some orange juice and reached for a strip of bacon. "You like it?"

"I can't keep my eyes off you. Do you serve all the men like that?"

"What men? You're the only one on this whole island."

He ate his food in record time. "That's good because if I found out otherwise, I'd have to confine you to a room in the palace where I have the only key."

Their conversation was getting sillier and sillier, but she loved it. She loved *him*.

"What are your plans for today, sire?"

"This and that."

"Does your wife know about that?"

His eyes narrowed on her mouth. "She'll find out."

"I see." Her heart jumped. "Well, if you've finished your breakfast, I'll take the tray back to the kitchen."

"*Grazie.* When you see her, tell her I want her to come to me. *Now.* I don't like to be kept waiting."

She trembled as she reached for the tray. "*Si*, Your Highness."

The second his wife left the bedroom on those long, shapely legs, Antonio headed for the shower and freshened up. Since she'd already put on her bikini, he pulled on a fresh pair of white bathing trunks. When he'd told her last night he could eat her alive, he hadn't been kidding.

"*Ciao*, Antonio." She was looking at one of the brochures while waiting for him.

"I understood you wanted to see me?" Her smile curved so seductively he wanted to throw her on the bed and stay there all day, but he resisted the urge. She was a fetching siren. Who would have guessed?

"How would you like to go to the nearby island with the waterfall? Manu says it's a short hike, but worth it if you're wearing tennis shoes."

"I love hikes. I did it all over Switzerland and Kenya."

She was amazing. "Manu told me it's off-limits to everyone else while we're here on our honeymoon."

Her eyes lit up. "A whole island to ourselves? Let's do it! I'll pack us some food so we don't have to come back for dinner."

"Why not pack enough food in case we want to stay there overnight?"

"You mean sleep by the waterfall?"

He smiled at her. It was all he could think about. "Why not? Haven't you ever wondered what it would be like to be Tarzan and Jane?"

She chuckled in response. "Yes. Many times."

"We'll take the speedboat."

With their day decided, they packed things in the backpacks supplied by the resort, including light blankets, food and water. Antonio rang Manu to let him know where they were going. Then they left their retreat and took off for one of the dark green islands they could see in the distance that was taller than the others.

"The lagoon never changes, Antonio. It's like eternal beauty all the time. I've never been this excited to do anything."

She was reading his mind. They skimmed across the gorgeous blue water before reaching the white beach. Once they'd drunk some bottled water, they headed for the trail Manu said would be visible. Sure enough, they found it and started up the incline.

"The vegetation is so lush!" she exclaimed.

"Our own rain forest." Their gazes clung before they got going on their trek. It took them less time to reach their destination than to have kayaked over there. Flowers grew in abundance. They spotted terns and swallows. The water came down in a stream, small at first, then widening before they reached the waterfall itself.

"Oh, Antonio—it reminds me of a waterfall scene in an old movie I once saw, but I think it was filmed in Hawaii."

"This is as primitive as it gets." He helped her off with her pack and gave her a long kiss. Then he removed his.

"Isn't that spray marvelous? Look up there. If we can get on those rocks, we can ride the water down to the pool," she said.

"Let me test the depth of it first." He walked over to the edge and waded in the swirling water. He discovered that after a few steps there was a drop-off, but when he swam underwater he found it was only about twenty feet deep. When he emerged, he waved to her. "Come on in. It's safe but a little cooler than the lagoon. Keep your tennis shoes on."

For several hours they played in the water like children. Eventually they climbed up the side to reach the spot where the water from the mountain poured over the top of the rocks. He turned to his wife. "Shall we do it?"

"Yes."

"Scared?"

"Terrified."

"Take my hand."

Together they moved onto the slippery rocks and before long the strength of the waterfall washed over them, plunging them down into the pool. Christina came up laughing. "Oh, Antonio—talk about a rush! This just couldn't be real."

He swam to her and kissed her over and over again while keeping them afloat. "We've found paradise, *innamorata*. How about one more jump, and then we'll make camp for the night?"

Once again they hiked up the side to the top. Before they went out on the rocks, he plucked a white flower with a gardenia scent, growing on a nearby vine. He tucked it behind her ear. "Now you're my Polynesian princess."

Her eyes wandered over him. "I don't ever want to go home."

"Then we won't." He grabbed her hand and they inched their way onto the rocks until the force of the water took them over the edge. It was like free-falling into space until the water caught them and brought them to the surface.

Together they swam to the edge of the pool where they'd left their packs. He helped her out of the water and they proceeded to set up camp. After they'd made their bed, they put out the food. The exertion had made them hungry. They sat across from each other and ate to their hearts' content.

He finally stretched. "I've never felt so good, never tasted food so good, never been with anyone I enjoyed more. In truth, I've never been this happy in my life."

"I feel the same way," she responded. "I want it to last, but I know it's not going to."

He shook his head. "Shh. Don't spoil this heavenly evening. We have two more days and nights ahead of us."

"You're right."

"You've lost your gardenia. I'm going to pick another one." He got up and walked a ways until he found one. When he returned, he hunkered down next to her and put it behind her ear. "This is how I'm always going to remember you."

Antonio couldn't wait to get close to her again and cleaned up their picnic. When everything had been put away, she started to leave, but he caught her by the ankle. "Stay with me."

"I was just going to get out of my bathing suit."

"But I want to hold you first." He pulled her down and rolled onto his side so he could look at her. "I've been waiting all day for tonight to come."

"So have I." Her voice throbbed.

He pulled her into him and claimed her luscious mouth that had given him a heart attack last night. "You could have no idea how much I want you. Love me, Christina. I need you."

"Would it shock you if I told I wanted you to love me on our wedding night?" she admitted against his throat.

He let out a slight groan. "Why didn't you tell me?"

"I was afraid you would think I was too eager. I decided you needed time."

Laughter broke from him. When he looked down at her, those fabulous silvery eyes were smiling. "I think that from here on out we each need to stop worrying about what the other one is thinking, and do more doing."

"I couldn't agree more. You drove me crazy on the way over in the jet."

"Maybe that was a good thing," he teased, kissing every feature on her face.

"It was painful!"

"Tesora mia," he cried in a husky voice before starting to devour her. "I love your honesty. Come here to me."

Christina melted in his arms and kissed him with the kind of passion he'd never imagined to find in this marriage. His heart jumped to realize he had such a loving, demonstrative wife.

CHAPTER SEVEN

ANTONIO HAD CALLED her his treasure. Christina felt cherished and desirable. His hunger aroused her to the depth of her being. This was her husband bringing her to life, shocking her, thrilling her as they found new ways to worship each other with their bodies.

His long legs trapped hers. "Why did I wait four years?"

She couldn't have answered him if she'd wanted to. Enthralled by the things he was doing to her, Christina was too consumed by her own hunger for him. Like the spiral constellations lighting the canopy above, he sent her spiraling into another realm of existence. Throughout the hours of the night they loved fully until they finally fell asleep, only temporarily sated.

After their passion-filled night of ecstasy, she couldn't believe they were still on earth. During the night he'd swept her to a different place, so intimate she'd wanted to stay on that sphere of euphoria forever.

She lay there wondering if last night's lovemaking had resulted in a baby. Stranger things had happened to other women. She suddenly realized that she wanted his baby so badly she could hardly stand it.

Heat washed over her to remember what had happened between them last night. Christina wasn't sorry that he hadn't made love to her at first. Far from it. Last night had been magical.

Taking great care not to wake her husband *and* lover, she lay there looking at him. The sun was already high in the morning sky. They'd slept in late again, but it didn't matter.

Oh, Antonio—I love you so much, you have no idea.

Antonio heard his wife sigh and glanced at her in sleep. She was the most unselfish lover he could ever have imagined. Last night she'd made him feel totally alive. Whole. When had he ever felt like this? Long after the stars had come out, they'd made love again and early this morning, again. He'd found paradise with her.

The next time he had cognizance of his surroundings, the sun was high in the sky. His wife lay on her side facing him. For a while he lay there studying her, then got to his feet and took a dip in the pool before pulling on his bathing trunks. He opened the backpack to get out some rolls and fruit. They'd need more food to stay on this island. He drank half a bottle of water while he ate.

She must have heard him and opened her eyes. "Oh—you're up!"

"Just barely. Loving you has given me a ferocious appetite."

She laughed. "I'm getting up, but you'll have to turn your head."

"Why?" he teased.

Christina blushed beautifully. "You know why."

"I'm your husband."

"I know, but—"

"All right. I'll close my eyes, but I'll give you to the count of ten to reach the water before I open them again."

"Antonio—" she squealed.

"One, two." He could hear the blanket rustle before she got up. A second later he heard water splashing and turned to watch her treading water. "You see? You made it."

"If you'll please put my bikini near the water and turn around, I'll get dressed."

Antonio's deep laughter resounded through the forest. She could feel it reverberate inside her. "Anything to oblige." He did her bidding. "I hate to tell you this, but the water is so transparent I can see you perfectly."

"You're no gentleman to say that to me."

"Is that what you thought I was?" he mocked before turning his back.

She climbed out and dressed as fast as she could. When she reached him, he crushed her in his arms and gave her a kiss to die for. Then he handed her food and drink.

"Thank you."

"You're welcome."

"I wish we could stay here longer. Last night—" Her voice caught.

Their eyes met. "Last night will be burned in my memory forever, *tesora*."

"Mine too." She finished eating and started putting everything in their packs.

He worked with her. "Are you about ready?"

"Yes."

After slipping on their tennis shoes, they started down the trail to the beach. In some parts she walked behind him, enjoying the play of muscle across his back and shoulders. Antonio had great legs for a man. In fact, there wasn't a part of him that wasn't perfect.

They reached the boat and loaded it. Christina helped him push it into the water, and then he helped ease her up and in before he took his place at the front. Before they took off across the lagoon, he looked back at her. As far as he could see, they were the only people out on this part of the lagoon.

"What do you want to do after we get back to the hut?" he called over his shoulder.

"I'd love to go to that coral sea garden and do some more snorkeling."

"That makes two of us. When in our lives will we ever have a chance to see fish like this up close?"

"Probably never. I'm still pinching myself to believe there's a spot like this on earth."

"We'll eat a meal and then go out for the rest of the day. Do you know what?"

"What?"

"You're more fun than any of my friends."

"Thank you."

"I mean it. I don't know anyone, male or female, who loves what I love and can do everything with me and keep up."

"I'm afraid I didn't turn out to be like my social-ite parents."

"Thank heaven!"

Those two words warmed her heart all the way back to their island. After putting things away, they sat down to a meal, then went back out to the deck. Antonio covered her in sunscreen. His touch made her knees buckle. "Shall we stay in bed the rest of the day instead?"

Christina could hardly talk. "I'd love it, but our time here is so short, we need to take advantage of it." She couldn't believe she'd worried that in a week Antonio might be bored with her. Maybe it was because all the time they'd spent together in Switzerland had prepared her to be more comfortable with him where everything felt so natural.

"Just remember we'll have all night," he whispered against her neck. His breath sent tendrils of delight through her system. While she was still trying to re-cover, he got out the snorkels and fins. Once again they got into the boat and went looking for fish. The lagoon was home to so many species they had the time of their lives viewing everything.

She lost track of the time. So did Antonio. It wasn't until they suffered hunger pains that she realized it was time to go in. When they returned to the island and were tying up the boat, Manu was there to greet them.

"You two must have had a good day to be out so long."

Christina smiled at him. "Every day is a good day here." But she sensed he had something else on his mind. So did Antonio.

"What's wrong, Manu?"

"There was a call from the palace in Halencia. You are to call your sister as soon as you can. You can use the phone here and I'll put it through for you."

Both Christina and Antonio exchanged worried glances. Any number of things could be wrong for her to interrupt their honeymoon. "Thank you. I'll do it as soon as we're finished here."

"Your dinner is in the kitchen when you want to eat."

"You're terrific, Manu," she said.

After he disappeared, Antonio helped her out of the boat and they put their gear away. Already there was a change in her husband. Lines darkened his features, making him look older. They'd had an unforgettable night of loving and had been so carefree she could have cried to see that anxious look cross over his face.

Together they walked inside the bedroom of the hut, both of them still wearing their bathing suits. He turned to her. "I'm going to put on a robe, then make the call."

While he went into the bathroom to change, she pulled out some underwear and dressed in a pair of tan shorts and a cream top. Then she hung her bikini over the outside rail to dry, all the time frightened something serious had happened back home. An accident, or worse?

Antonio came out of the bathroom and walked over to the side of the bed to the phone. She sat down next to him. He put the phone on speaker and grasped her hand while he waited for Manu to connect the call.

"Tonio?"

"Elena?" His heart was racing. "What's wrong?"

"I'm so sorry to bother you on your honeymoon, but—"

"Is anyone ill?"

"No, no. Everyone's fine, but there's something you need to know. I hope you're sitting down to hear this."

Antonio looked at his wife, anxious for what was coming. "Go ahead."

"I—I have to give you some background first," she stammered. "You know that guy Rolfe? The drug addict I wish I'd never met?"

He sucked in his breath. "Yes?"

"Last week he was arrested on heavier drug charges. He called me from the jail and told me that if I didn't help him out of the new charges, he'd tell the press everything about what happened when he was jailed the first time."

"What?" he and Christina cried out at the same time. His thoughts were reeling.

"I thought he was high on drugs when he called me and I hung up on him. But he phoned me on the morning you were getting married and threatened me again. I told him there wasn't anything I could do. He hung up on me telling me I'd be sorry.

"Oh, Tonio—he leaked the news about your fake engagement to the press. It's all over the media that you thought up the bogus alliance with Christina to get me out of trouble with the police. He claimed I used drugs too and should have been jailed along with him.

"It's gone viral too. The internet is alive with rumours that you were having an affair in California while Christina was in Africa having an affair with the doctor. He made it all up, but it's done its damage.

"Marusha phoned me and told me she and her family are sick about this and want to know what they can do to stop it getting any worse. I don't know what to do.

"The palace is in an uproar. Both sets of parents are beside themselves. Guido's trying to help everything by preparing a new list of princesses. In case you can somehow salvage your reputation and get your marriage annulled, you'll have a list of royal hopefuls to choose from. I'm fighting for you, Tonio, but I can't do it alone."

Pain ripped him apart. His arm went around his wife. He could only imagine how Christina was feeling right now.

"I heard Father give immediate orders for the jet to be flown to Tahiti to bring you home. It's on its way now and will arrive at the airport at six in the morning Tahitian time. You need to be ready with a plan and come home as quickly as you can to help sort out this disaster, because that's what it is!

"There's a groundswell from people who don't believe you should be crowned because of the lie. I've been labeled a drug addict and am the result of my parents who aren't worthy of ruling the country. The people are afraid the lack of integrity on both your part and Christina's has compromised everything.

"If feelings reach tipping point, the people could withdraw their support for the monarchy and this could be the end of it. The coronation has been called off until further notice."

"No," Christina cried out.

"Oh, Christina, I didn't know you were listening. Let's face it. I'm the one responsible for all this. I'm the reason any of this has happened and I feel so horrible about it I want to die. I never realized how vindictive Rolfe could be. How cruel and heartless after what you did to get him a light sentence. I spent time with him when I was at my most rebellious and wasn't careful with the information I let out without realizing it. You and Christina have every right to hate me."

"Of course we don't hate you," he ground out. "For now you'll just have to hang on until we get back to Halencia. Trust me. We're going to sort this out. I'll talk to you tomorrow in person. And, Elena, never forget that we love you."

Christina had buried her face in her hands. *"Bellissima—"* He took her in his arms.

Hearing that word applied to her produced a groan from her. She was so horrified over the news she felt physically ill and couldn't form words.

His body stiffened. "I wondered what form of chicanery has been underfoot while we were on our honeymoon. It's what I expected. I just didn't know in the exact manner it would explode. Christina? Look at me."

She tried, but his image was blurry.

"I know this has come as a shock, but we're going to get through this because there's been total honesty between us, *grazie a Dio*. Remember Elena needs our protection more than ever. She's very fragile right now."

"You're right. I knew there was something wrong when she kept saying she hoped we'd be happy. Throughout our wedding she was terrified and had to keep all that bottled up inside. The poor thing."

He kissed her lips. "I'll make arrangements for the helicopter to be here at five a.m. Then you and I are going to have a long, serious talk."

His composure under these precarious circumstances was nothing short of miraculous. The affairs of the kingdom were falling apart, yet his mastery in dealing with it was a revelation. As far as she was concerned, this was Antonio's finest hour.

Whether she ever became queen or not, she would act like one right now because Antonio had never needed her help more to present a unified front. She knew deep down he wanted to be king in order to save his country from possible ruin. More than anything, Christina wanted that for him, whatever it took.

She grabbed two bottles of water from the refrigerator and hurried through the hut to their bedroom. While she waited for him to come, she started the packing for both of them. Five o'clock would be here soon enough. They needed to be ready to leave.

Christina lifted her head when he came into the bedroom with their dinner tray. "Did you get through to Manu?"

He nodded. "Everything is set. Since you've packed the bags, we can eat." He put it on the bed. "Come on."

She took a shaky breath. "I—I couldn't."

"You have to. I don't want my wife getting sick on me. We're on our honeymoon and I intend to enjoy it for the next six hours."

Christina actually laughed despite her agony.

Together they got on the bed and ate. When they'd finished eating, he got up to put the tray on the table. "Excuse me a moment. I'll be right back."

She wondered what he was doing until she heard Tahitian music from the radio piped into their room. Once he reappeared, he turned off the lamps and crawled onto the bed beside her.

"This music is enchanting, isn't it?" she said.

"I love it. Come here to me," he whispered. "I need you."

The blood pounded in her ears before she moved into his arms. "What are we going to do, Antonio?"

"We're going to stay just like this."

"You know what I mean."

"Yes, but there's nothing to do about anything until we reach Halenica, so you're stuck with me."

"That's no penance. You smell wonderful."

"So you've noticed."

She swallowed hard. "I notice everything."

"So do I. You're a warrior under that fiery mane."

"What a compliment."

"It is, because you're going to be queen and now I know you have the steel to help me. Any other woman would have gone into hysterics a little while ago. Not you."

She smiled in secret pleasure. "You wouldn't let me. That's the sign of a great king."

"The priest's words never had as much meaning to me until now."

"Which words were those?"

"The part where he said 'From this day forward you shall be each other's home, comfort and refuge.' Whatever we have to face when we get back home, Christina, I'm not worried because you've become my refuge in a very short time."

Tears stung her eyelids. He kissed them. "I didn't mean to make you cry."

"It's the good kind. When I'm happy, I often cry."

"I saw tears when you looked at your parents in the chapel. What was going on in your mind?"

"That I didn't always want to be a disappointment to them. Now that there's a national scandal, they'll consider that I've hit rock bottom."

"If they can't see beyond the end of their noses and recognize a hatchet job of major proportions, how sad for them. But I couldn't be happier that you turned out just the way you are. My one regret is that we're going to have to leave our paradise far too soon. I've had you all to myself since the wedding ceremony and I love the privacy so much I'm loath to give it up."

"I feel the same. We've been living most people's fantasy."

He suddenly held her tighter and burrowed his face in her neck. "I want this fantasy to go on and on." The longing in his voice echoed the desire of her heart. "I want you to know I'll treasure this time together for the rest of my life."

"I've loved every second of it too. Isn't this place wonderful?"

"Yes, but it would be a waste without the right person along. We'll come back again one day and spend time over at the coral garden. We'll do a lot of things, but right now I just want to make love to you."

Once again the age-old ritual began. This time Christina took the initiative to show her husband how much she loved him. She loved him in every atom of her body and poured out her feelings, wanting to take away any pain he was feeling tonight. At one point he pulled her on top of him. It was heaven to cover his face with kisses and play with his hair. He was such a beautiful man, there were no words.

"Christina? We only have a few hours before we have to return to Halencia and deal with the mess. If I'd known it was going to happen, I would have insisted we get married sooner and enjoy a month's honeymoon at least. Now it's too late for that."

But before their wedding, neither of them had a clue that they would come to care for each other in so short a time. Christina was positive that flare of desire she'd felt when he kissed her at the altar had been unexpected for him too.

"Are you happy?" His voice sounded anxious. "Because I want you to be happy."

She heard the longing and drew in a breath. "I'm happier right now than I've ever been in my life."

"*Grazie a Dio*, because I am too. I hope our daughter has red hair like her mother."

"Would you mind if our son has red hair instead?"

"Your hair is glorious. Why would I mind?"

"Mother wanted to turn me into a brunette."

"It's a good thing you didn't listen to her. When the time came, I wanted you for my bride."

Yes. And he wound up with Christina to save his sister from disgrace. And now that the news had leaked, it was a national scandal, but he didn't seem worried.

Their trust was on solid ground. More than ever she understood the deeper words of the priest. *Be able to forgive, do not hold grudges, and live each day that you may share it together. From this day forward you shall be each other's home, comfort and refuge, your marriage strengthened by your love and respect.*

So far they'd shared each incredible day together. Their nights had been euphoric. This bedroom had become their home and refuge. She'd been able to comfort him in a way she wouldn't have imagined. Living with Antonio was already changing her life and it frightened her that the happiness she was experiencing might be taken away from her after they returned home.

The next morning they awakened for breakfast. It had arrived with a newspaper. He pored over it.

Her heart thudded. "Anything to report about us?"

"There's a photo of me taken at the airport. No matter how hard my father tried, the word still got out. But so far Manu has managed to keep our exact location a secret. He's worth every Eurodollar he's being paid."

"Do you think your father will be upset?"

"Yes." He flicked her a searching glance. "Are you in with me?"

"All the way. You know that."

He put the newspaper down and moved himself away from the table. "Come out on the deck with me. I crave a walk along the beach with you before it rains."

Her husband reached for her hand as they stepped down to the edge of the water and started walking. "With Bora Bora appearing and disappearing mystically through the clouds this morning, it looks surreal, Antonio. I feel like we're in some primordial world. The air is so balmy it's unreal."

After they'd gone a ways, he stopped and grasped her arms so she faced him. "You're so lovely *you* seem unreal. I need to know if I'm with a phantom wife." In the next breath he lowered his mouth to hers and gave her the husband's kiss she'd been dying for. Fire licked through her veins as she was caught up in his embrace. She knew he had to be in pain, but the way he was kissing her had her senses reeling.

Their bodies clung. She could feel the powerful muscles in his legs and melted against him. He released her mouth long enough to kiss her face and neck. His hands plunged into her hair before he kissed her throat, in fact, all the area of skin exposed by the sundress she was wearing home.

"Touch me," he whispered in a ragged voice.

Succumbing to his entreaty, she wrapped her arms

around his waist and heard his moan of pleasure as his mouth began devouring hers. The rain had started and was so ethereal in nature it felt more like a mist, adding to the rapture building inside her. Antonio was doing the most amazing things to her with his hands and mouth.

Too soon Manu arrived to tell them the helicopter had arrived. It was time to go.

CHAPTER EIGHT

THIRTY HOURS LATER the royal jet landed at Voti International Airport, where a helicopter was waiting to fly them to the palace. To their relief, no press was allowed on the tarmac.

During the times throughout the flight while Christina napped, Antonio had talked with his sister at length to get her to stop blaming herself. During the night his wife had been restless and couldn't sleep. They were flying home to a hornet's nest. She was holding her own, but he knew the emotions of his brave, beautiful wife were in turmoil.

At one o'clock that afternoon the helicopter landed on the back lawn of the palace closed to the public. He helped her down and they hurried toward the south entrance with several staff members bringing their luggage.

They rushed up the grand staircase to the second floor of the east wing. When he reached the doors of his apartment, he picked her up again like a bride.

"Antonio—" She hid her head against his shoulder. "We've already done this once."

"I don't care. I might feel like doing it every time we come in." Before she could say another word, he silenced her with a kiss because he couldn't help himself. She'd become the drug in his system. Her response electrified him. At this point he needed to be with her inside their home away from the world and make love to his wife.

After managing to open one of the two tall, palatial doors, he swept her through the apartment to the bedroom and followed her down on the bed. The staff knew better than to do anything but place the suitcases inside the main doors and leave them alone.

"Welcome to my world, Christina de L'Accardi. Besides family, you're the first and only woman I've ever brought here. It's always been a lonely place for me. Now it's going to be our home." It was liberating to crush her against him. One kiss turned into another. She wanted him as much as he wanted her.

Like clockwork both his cell phone and room phone started ringing. He moaned aloud before continuing to kiss her, but the ringing persisted until she tore her lips from his. "Of course everyone knows we're back, Antonio," she said out of breath. "You at least have to say hello."

"That's all I'll say." He sat up and reached for the bedside phone first, impatient because of the interruption of civilization. Being away from technology for a few days had been the best thing that could have happened to them. *"Pronto—"*

"Come sta, figlio mio?"

He looked at his wife, whose silvery eyes fastened on him still had the glaze of desire burning in their depths. His fingers ran over her lips. "Christina and I have been to heaven thanks to your generosity, Papa. But we were called back to earth too soon."

"I'm thrilled you've had a wonderful time, but now we must talk."

"Not now, Papa. My wife and I need the rest of this day together."

"But there's a crisis."

His muscles clenched. "So I've been informed, but nothing's more important than my time with her. I promise I'll take care of things starting tomorrow. Give my love to Mama. *Ciao.*"

Christina chuckled. "You'll have to answer your cell phone or it will never stop." Letting out another sound of frustration, he reached in his pants pocket and pulled it out. When he saw the caller ID, he didn't mind answering.

"Zach!"

"I'm glad you answered. Where are you?" His friend sounded more than anxious.

He smiled down at Christina. "We've just entered our humble home after being flown to paradise and back." She kissed his fingers.

"I've never thought of Paris as paradise."

"No. Bora Bora. A surprise wedding gift from my parents. You should take Lindsay there. You'd never want to come back."

"Antonio? Is this really you? You sound strange, like you're on something."

He grinned. "I've been drugged all right." A laugh came out of his wife. "Listen, I'll call you tomorrow."

"But you've got problems, buddy. Big problems."

"My other half is going to help me solve them."

"But she's part of the problem, if you get my meaning," Zach said, lowering his voice.

"You've got that wrong. She's the solution, but I appreciate your concern. You're the best friend a man ever had next to his wife. *Ciao*."

No sooner had he hung up to indulge himself with his beautiful bride than Christina's cell phone rang. She had to get off the bed for the purse she'd accidentally dropped on the inlaid wooden flooring while her husband was carrying her.

She didn't need to look at the caller ID to know who it was. Might as well get this over now. *"Pronto?"*

"Christina?" Her mother sounded mournful rather than angry. "Is it true that you had an affair while you were engaged to Antonio?"

She held her breath. "If I tell you that was a lie, would you believe me?"

"Yes."

"Would Father?"

"I—I can't speak for him. What are you going to do?"

Her mother sounded as though she really cared. "It's up to Antonio."

"Just remember I'm here for you if you need me."

For her mother to say that was astounding to Christina. "Thank you, Mama. We'll talk later."

Antonio's arms were locked around her from behind. But for once she didn't feel like crawling into a dark hole never to come out again. She turned to Antonio. "Mother just gave me her support."

"It's about time, but don't forget you've got me now."

"I know." She lifted her mouth to kiss him, but there was a knocking on the outer doors, loud enough to reach their ears in the bedroom. "Tonio? It's me," Elena cried. "Can I come in? It's an emergency!"

"Tell her to come," Christina urged him. "She's been waiting for us."

He gave her another hug before they both hurried through the apartment to greet his sister.

When he opened the door, they barely recognized Elena, who'd been crying for so long her blue eyes were puffy and her face had gone splotchy. "I'm so glad you're home." She threw herself into Antonio's arms and sobbed.

Christina closed the door and the three of them went into the living room. When he let her go, she turned to Christina. As they hugged, his sister had another explosion of tears.

"Elena—it's going to be all right. Come and sit down on the couch." She drew her by the hand. Antonio sat in the love seat near them.

She brushed the tears from her cheeks. "I have something to tell both of you. Marusha and I have had a long talk. Her husband found out through another doctor that before Roger left Africa, he got drunk and told things to the doctor that were supposed to be kept quiet. But the other doctor was unscrupulous and leaked it to the news."

Christina shook her head. "I should never have gone out with him."

Antonio stood up. "If we all keep blaming ourselves for everything, nothing will be accomplished. What's done is done."

"There's more," Elena admitted.

He took a deep breath. "Go on."

"I broke down and told our parents why you and Christina got engaged. I also told them Christina had never slept with that doctor. It was pure fabrication."

"It's all right, Elena. The truth will free all of us."

His wife was so right!

He'd already known that Christina hadn't given herself to the doctor. Antonio had been stunned at the time and overjoyed.

"They think you're both so noble," Elena kept on. "Our parents are prepared to do anything to help you. But as you know, they've lost Guido's respect and he has powerful friends in the council who are ready to abolish the monarchy altogether. Some of the others wanting to keep the monarchy alive have prevailed on the archbishop to grant an annulment so you can re-marry. There's a list of titled women they're vetting now with Princess Gemma at the top."

Filled with joy that Christina was his wife, Antonio stopped pacing. "No. That isn't going to happen. I've got plans, ideas to build the economy. Christina and I plan to enlarge the African charity to make it far-reaching. I have a new jobs initiative to help us become a leader in technology. Scandal has rocked this nation for years, but we'll weather it. We have to."

Elena stared at him as if she'd never seen him before.

His wife got up from the couch and stood in front of him, wearing the same white suit she'd worn on the plane to Tahiti. *"We will."*

Two beautiful words from the mouth of the woman he couldn't imagine living without. He kissed her in front of his sister before walking over to Elena and pulling her to her feet. "I'm glad the truth is out, all of it." He gave her a hug. "Everything is going to work out."

"It's got to, because I love you two so much."

Antonio looked at his clever, adorable wife. She was so remarkable he couldn't believe he was lucky enough to be married to her.

He brushed his sister's cheek with his finger. "So, what is the latest between you and Enzio?"

"We're good."

"Just good."

"Um, very good."

"I'm glad to hear it."

"But you don't need to hear about my love life right now. I'm going to leave you to your privacy and will talk to you later."

They both hugged her before she hurried out of the apartment. He put his arm around Christina's waist and walked her back to the bedroom. "Before we do anything else, I need to take another look at your foot. Why don't you get undressed first? I want to make certain it is healing properly."

"This is almost like déjà vu."

While she started to take off her top and pants, her phone rang again. She'd left it on the end of the bed. "Let me get this first." The caller ID said it was her great-aunt calling.

She clicked on. "Sofia?"

"Welcome home, darling. How was your trip?"

"Heavenly."

"But you've come home to a viper's nest. I know something that you don't and I'm calling to warn you."

Antonio came to stand next to her.

She gripped the phone harder. "What is it?"

"I've spent part of the day with your parents. Your father has left for the palace to talk to you. I tried in my own way to ask him to wait until tomorrow, but you know how he is."

Yes… Christina knew exactly.

"For once in your life, darling, stand up to him and don't let him bully you. He's like his father and grand-father, born mean-spirited."

This conversation meant her father was furious. "He's a hard man to confront because he doesn't have a soft side."

"Unfortunately your mother has always been too afraid of him to intercede for you."

Her eyes filmed over. "I always had you, Aunt Sofia."

"And you've been one of my greatest joys."

"Thank you for alerting me."

"If there's anything I can do…"

Christina turned to Antonio. "My husband and I are prepared to face whatever is coming. I love you so much for caring. Talk to you again soon." She clicked off.

"What's going on?" he murmured.

"My father is on his way over to talk to me."

"I won't leave you alone with him."

She loved Antonio for saying that. "Knowing his style of quick attack, he won't be here long. Do you mind if we talk in the living room?"

"Of course not. This is our home. You can have anyone you want here, anytime."

"Thank you." She rose on tiptoe and kissed him.

"I'll go downstairs to my office and talk to my executive assistant. If you need me, I'll be here in an instant." She nodded. He put on a fresh sport shirt and left the apartment. Antonio was far too handsome for his own good.

This was her first chance to walk around her new home. The palace was a magnificent structure. Antonio's apartment was bigger than any home she'd ever been in. Already she knew her favorite place would be the terrace overlooking the water.

To think Antonio had been born here and had lived here until he was old enough to be sent away to schools and college. There was so much to learn about him as a child as well as an adult, but she couldn't concentrate when she knew her father would be coming any minute.

The phone on the bedside table rang. She walked over to pick it up. "Yes?"

"Princess Christina? This is the office calling. Your father is here to speak to you."

"Can you send him to our apartment?"

"Si, signora."

"Grazie."

"Prego."

Five minutes later she heard the knock on the door and opened it to see her father standing there. "Come into the living room, Papa."

He looked around while he followed her, but he didn't take a seat when she suggested it.

"Where's your husband?"

"In his office downstairs."

"What I have to say won't take long."

It never does.

His eyes glittered with anger. "If you want to do one thing to restore the name Rose in people's estimation, you'll leave Antonio for the good of the monarchy."

"I thought you wanted a king for a son-in-law."

He stared at her. "Not when his queen dishonored him by being with another man during the engagement. The people will forgive him, but they'll never forgive you."

She lifted her chin. "I didn't dishonor him. Is that all you came to say?"

His lips thinned. "Use the one shred of decency left in you to allow Antonio to rule with the right queen at his side. He may stand by you now, but in time doubts will creep in, and doubt can ruin a marriage faster than anything else. Let him marry Princess Gemma."

"Antonio didn't want her the first time around. He chose me."

Her father's cheeks grew ruddy. "The archbishop

will sanction a divorce since the marriage was fraudulent and your behavior during the engagement has painted you an immoral woman. You have one more opportunity in your life to right a tremendous wrong. Then public sentiment will end up being kind to you."

"So if I do that and bow out of his life, will you forgive me for being born a woman instead of a man and be kind to me?"

"The one has nothing to do with the other."

Her breath caught. "You mean that no matter what I do, there can be no forgiveness from you in this life?"

"You always were a difficult child."

She stiffened and fought her tears. "I'm your daughter. Yours and Mother's. I wanted your love. I wanted your acceptance. I tried everything under the sun to be the child you could love."

"We gave you everything, didn't we?" He turned to leave.

"Papa—"

Halfway out the door he said, "Has he told you he loves you? Because if he hasn't, then you need to do the right thing. If you don't know what is in Antonio's heart, why take the risk?"

Beyond tears, she walked out to the terrace, clutching her arms to her waist. The warning phone call from her aunt Sofia hadn't helped. She'd been thrown into a black void. Antonio had never said he loved her. She hadn't expected him to love her, but that was before they'd gone to Tahiti together and she'd found rapture with him.

If she truly didn't know what was in Antonio's

heart, then was it a risk to stay in the marriage as her father said?

After standing there for a while, she went back to the bedroom and called the palace switchboard. "Would you connect me with the palace press secretary please?"

"*Si.*"

In a minute a male voice came on the line.

"This is Princess Christina. I have a statement to come out on the evening news. I'll have it sent to your office by messenger. If you value your job, you'll tell no one. I mean, not a single soul."

"*Capisco*, Princess."

She hung up and went into the den, where she wrote out what she wanted to say. It didn't take long. After putting the note in an envelope and sealing it, she phoned the charity foundation in Voti. Arianna, the manager, answered the phone. Thank heaven she was still there.

"Christina? I can't believe you're calling. I thought you were on your honeymoon."

"We're back. I need a favor from you. A big one. Can you stop what you're doing right now and drive to the west gate of the palace?"

"Well, yes."

"I'll be waiting. This is an emergency."

"I'll be there in five minutes."

"Bless you."

She hung up and started throwing the things she'd need for overnight in her large tote bag. There was always money in her bank account and she had her passport. Without stopping to think, she left the apartment and hurried down the long hall of the west wing to the staircase.

When she reached the main doors, she stopped to talk to one of the guards. "Would you see that the palace press secretary receives this immediately?"

"Of course."

"Thank you."

Then she passed through the doors to the outside where another guard was on duty. "If the prince wonders where I am, tell him that an emergency came up at the charity foundation in town. One of my head people is picking me up so we can deal with it. I'll phone the prince later, but he's in meetings right now and can't be disturbed."

"*Capisco.*"

So far, so good. She rushed outside and waited under the portico until she saw Arianna's red Fiat. Christiana hurried around the passenger side and got in. "You are an angel, Arianna, and I'll give you a giant bonus."

"Where do you want to go?"

"Back to the foundation." She put on her sunglasses. It only took a few minutes to reach the building. "Why don't you go on home? I'll be working late and will lock up again."

"All right."

"This is for your trouble." She handed her a hundred Eurodollars and got out of the car. When her friend drove off smiling, Christina hailed a taxi and asked to be driven to the ferry terminal. There were ferries leaving on the hour for Genoa during the summer.

She paid the driver, then hurried inside and bought

a ticket. Within twenty minutes she walked onto the
ferry and sat on a bench as it made its way to the port
in Genoa. From there she transferred to the train station and caught the next train going to Monte Calanetti
via Siena. So far no one had recognized her because
pictures of her wedding to Antonio hadn't been given
to the press.

When it pulled in to the station, she phoned Louisa.

"Dear friend?" she said when Louisa answered.

"Christina?"

"Yes. I'm in Monte Calanetti. Do you have room
for a visitor?"

"Did I just hear you correctly?"

"Yes."

"Of course I have room!" No doubt Louisa figured
correctly that there'd been trouble since their flight
back from Tahiti. "You can stay in the bridal suite for
as long as you want."

"Thank you from the bottom of my heart. I'll be
there soon and tell you everything."

As the taxi drove her to the Palazzo di Comparino,
she turned off her phone. No one knew where she'd
gone and that was the way she wanted things to stay.

Antonio had spent more time in his office than he'd
meant to. He'd given Christina as much time as she
needed to be with her father. After taking care of some
business matters, he hurried to his wing of the palace.
He planned to order a special dinner for them and eat
out on the terrace. Having to come home early had
robbed them of another precious night in Bora Bora,

but tonight he intended to make up for everything. The need to make love to his wife was all he could think about.

"Christina?" There was no answer. He walked through to their bedroom. She wasn't there. Maybe she'd gone exploring, but she hadn't left a note. It was possible that after being with her father she'd gone to visit Elena. He phoned his sister. "Does Christina happen to be with you?"

"No."

"Hmm. I was doing a little business, but she's not here."

"She loves the outdoors. Maybe she took a walk outside to the kennel. That's what we usually do when she visits me. You know how much she adores animals."

"Thanks for the tip."

He put through a call to the kennel, but no one had seen her.

Angry with himself for not putting a security detail on her first thing, he phoned the head of palace security. "Alonzo? I'm looking for Princess Christina. Find out where she is and let me know ASAP. I want surveillance on her twenty-four-seven starting now."

"Yes, Your Highness."

He put off ordering dinner and hurried downstairs to the palace's main office. "Did anyone here see Princess Christina's father arrive?"

One of them nodded. "The princess asked that he be shown to your apartment. About twenty minutes later he passed by the office and left the grounds in a limousine."

More than frustrated at this point, Antonio headed for Alonzo's office. "Any news about her yet?"

Alonzo shook his head. "We're still vetting everyone on the force. Some of them went off shift at five o'clock and we're still trying to reach them for information."

He frowned. She wouldn't have gone to his parents' apartment, would she? He called them on the chance that she was there for some reason. But they had nothing to tell him.

Definitely worried now, he put through a call to Christina's parents. He should have tried there first. Her father got on the other extension. "Your Highness?"

"I'm looking for my wife. If you have any idea where she is, I'd like you to tell me now. The last anyone saw of her was you."

"You mean she's missing?"

His anger was approaching flash point. "What did you say to her?"

"The only thing a good father could say to his daughter. Do the right thing."

Antonio saw red. He clicked off and spun around in fury. It was almost nine o'clock. Could she have flown to Nairobi without telling him?

Frantic, he asked Alonzo for his men to check the airport to see if she'd flown out. Within a few minutes the news came back that she hadn't boarded any planes going anywhere.

"Hold on, Antonio. There's another report coming in. The guard at the west gate saw her leave the palace grounds in a red Fiat before he went off duty just before five. He had no idea you were looking for her. She told him she was going to the charity foundation to take care of an emergency and didn't want you to worry."

His hands balled into fists. "Find out if she's still there! We need to call all the girls working there to find out who drove the Fiat."

Before long the report came back that the building was closed for the night. No sign of Princess Christina anywhere. In another minute they had a woman on the line. Antonio took the call. "Arianna?"

"Your Highness. I didn't realize you were looking for her. When I dropped her off in front of the building, she said she was going to work in there for a while and that I should go home."

"So you have no idea where she went, or if she even went inside."

"No. I'm so sorry."

"What state was she in?"

"She definitely had an agenda and asked me to hurry, but that's all."

"Thank you, Arianna."

He handed the phone back to Alonzo.

Where are you, Christina. What did your father say to turn you inside out?

While he stayed there in agony, wondering where to turn next, the press secretary, Alonzo, came hurrying into the office. "Your Highness?"

Antonio turned to him. "Do you have news about the princess?"

His face had gone white. "I do. She told me if I

said anything I'd lose my job, but I can't let you suffer like this."

"What do you know?"

"She handed me an envelope and wanted the television anchor to read her statement during the ten o'clock news."

"She *what*?"

He nodded. "It'll be on every network in five minutes in every country in the world."

Alonzo turned on the big-screen television in his office. Antonio felt so gutted he started to weave.

"Better sit down, Your Highness."

"I'll be all right." His heart plummeted to his feet as he saw the words *breaking news* flash across the screen.

Suddenly the female news anchor appeared. "There's huge news breaking from the royal palace in Voti, Halencia, tonight, threatening to rock the already shaky monarchy decimated by scandal. It is struggling to stay alive in a nation so divided that one wonders what the ultimate outcome will be.

"I have in front of me a statement that Princess Christina, recently married in a private ceremony to Crown Prince Antonio de L'Accardi, has asked the press to read. These are her words and I quote. 'Dear citizens of Halencia. It is with the greatest sadness that I, Princess Christina de L'Accardi, am removing myself from the royal family to end the bitter conflict. I confess that although my relationship with Prince Antonio started out as a publicity stunt for reasons I don't intend to go into, I want everyone to know I love my new husband with every fiber of my being. A man with his integrity doesn't come along every day, or even in a lifetime. I knew him when we were both teenagers. Even then he showed a love and loyalty to his country that put others to shame. I want everyone to know he's the light of my life and my one true love. But I'm sorry that it isn't enough for the people of Halencia.'"

Christina...his heart cried.

"Wow! How's that for a heartfelt confession from the 'Cinderella Bride' as the nation has called her? Her charity in Africa has gained international attention. I have to admit I'm moved by her sacrifice and graciousness. That doesn't happen to me very often. Stay tuned for news coming from the palace as the fallout from her surprising statement is felt throughout the country and the world.

"There's no word from the prince or his family about this shocking development. You'll have to stayed tuned when more news will be forthcoming."

The television was shut off. Alonzo eyed Antonio with concern. "We'll find her. Just give us time."

"Thank you, Alonzo." But he knew the damage had been done when her father talked to her. He'd done such an expert job of destroying her that Antonio doubted Christina might ever come out of hiding.

As he left the office and started up the staircase for his apartment on legs that felt like lead, his phone started ringing. He looked down. Good old faithful Zach. He clicked on.

"Antonio?"

"*Si?*"

"What a hell of a mess."

"That doesn't even begin to cover it," he half groaned.

CHAPTER NINE

September, Voti, Halencia

AFTER HIS SPEECH, Antonio stood before the divided government assembly to answer questions.

"With all due respect, Your Highness, Princess Christina has graciously stepped aside to appease those voices who still want you to rule, but with someone more befitting to be your consort. Why won't you listen to reason?"

His anger was acute. "What princess on your short list has devoted half her life to charity and worked among the poverty-stricken in Africa with no thought for herself? What princess would willingly give up the title of queen in order not to stand in the way of her husband?"

The room grew quiet.

"My wife hasn't made excuses or defended herself, so I'll do it for her. This so-called affair of hers was in truth a friendship, nothing more, but trust evil to find its way to do its dirty work. She remained true to our engagement. So I'll say it again. If I can't rule with Christina at my side, then I have no desire to rule. Therefore I've given orders that there'll be no coronation."

A loud roar of dissent from that part of the council loyal to him and the crown got to their feet, but he was deaf to their cries.

"But, Your Highness—"

Antonio ignored the minister of finance, his good friend, who was calling to him and stormed out of the council meeting. He walked out of chambers and headed straight for his office down the hall of the palace.

"Roberto?" he barked.

"Your Highness?" His assistant's head came up.

"Call the press secretary and ask him to come in here right away. No one is to disturb us, do you understand?"

"Si." He picked up the phone immediately.

Antonio went into his private suite and slammed the door, but he was too full of adrenaline to sit. With Christina's stunning press statement read over the airwaves three weeks ago, plus her disappearance that had come close to destroying him, the joy he'd experienced on his honeymoon had vanished. He felt as if he'd been shoved down a pit and was falling deeper and deeper with no end in sight.

Within a few hours of searching for her that night, Alonzo's security people had tracked his wife to the Palazzo di Comparino. Apparently Louisa had taken her in. His clever, resourceful wife had made her getaway so fast by car, taxi, ferry and train that it had knocked the foundation from under him.

There'd been no word from her for the past desolate three weeks, but he hadn't expected any. Her father had made certain of that. With her press statement ringing out over the land, she would never come to him now. Meanwhile, Antonio had made a firm decision. He'd meant what he'd just said before the council. If he didn't have her at his side, he didn't want to be king at all.

For the first time in his life he was doing what he wanted, and he wanted Christina. No amount of argument could persuade him to change his mind. Being reminded by Guido that Christina had decided to sacrifice her own heart for Antonio's reputation and the country had only made him fall harder for his wife, if that was possible.

Roberto buzzed him that the press secretary was outside. Antonio told him to send him in.

When the other man entered the room looking sheepish, Antonio said, "Do you want to redeem yourself?"

"Anything, Your Highness."

"I want you to arrange a press conference for me on the steps of the palace in approximately one hour."

"I'll do it at once, Your Highness."

Louisa had turned the sitting room at the palazzo into a TV room. Christina was grateful, since it was the only way she got information from the outside world. The rest of the times she took long walks and coordinated charity business with the foundations in both Halencia and Nairobi.

Between Marusha and Elena, she was kept apprised of their news. Marusha was pregnant after suffering two miscarriages. Christina couldn't be happier for her. Elena's boyfriend, Enzio, wanted to marry her, but it meant talking to her parents first and she was nervous about that.

Though there was plenty of talk because Louisa had constant visitors, no one mentioned Antonio in her presence. Her aching heart couldn't have handled talking about him. Marusha begged her to come back to Africa. She would always have a home waiting. Christina told her she'd be coming in a few days. She'd outstayed her welcome with Louisa. It was time to go.

This afternoon both love-smitten Daniella and Marianna had come over for an evening with the girls. Christina had the suspicion Louisa was trying to cheer her up. She loved her for it and it was fun for all of them to get together.

Louisa poured wine from the vineyard and showed off her expertise about the vintage. Christina was impressed that she knew so much about it. Nico definitely had something to do with it.

Dinner wouldn't be for another couple of hours. Christina wasn't a wine drinker, but this afternoon was special, so she joined in with the others to take a sip.

Marianna smiled. "Hey, you guys—want to know a little gossip? I overheard Connor and Isabella talking wedding plans with Lindsay."

"I knew it!" Louisa said while everyone cheered. "Oh—it's time for the six o'clock news."

"Do we care?" Daniella interjected.

"I do," Louisa exclaimed. She hurried over to the TV and turned it on. Christina was secretly glad, since it was the only way she had of knowing what was going on at the palace. Her heart was broken for Antonio, who was having to carry on through the fight to determine the destiny of his country.

"*Buonasera.* Tonight we have more breaking news coming from the royal palace in Voti, Halencia. Crown Prince Antonio de L'Accardi has broken his long silence and has prepared a statement, which we will bring to you from the front steps of the royal palace."

The image flashed to a somber Antonio in a dark blue suit who was so gorgeous that Christina feared her heart would give out. The girls grew quiet as all eyes were focused on him.

"Fellow countrymen and women, these have been dark times for the crown and it's time for the conflict to end. I'll be brief. As I told the National Council this morning, I dare any tabloid to come after me or my wife again."

What? Christina shot to her feet.

"I admit that our engagement was originally a strategic move, but having spent time with Christina, I realize what an amazing person she is, how kind, generous and charitable she is, and how lucky this country is to have her as queen! I defy anyone to call our marriage a fake. To me it's the most real and true relationship I've ever had. So I'll tell you what I told the council.

I'm in love with my wife and will *not* be giving her up, even if it means losing the throne!"

Christina was shaking so hard she might have fallen if she'd hadn't been holding on to the chair. The girls stared at her in wonder.

Louisa smiled at her. "Every woman in the world with eyes in her head would love to be in your shoes right now, Christina Rose."

She nodded. "I'd like to be in them too, but he's not here."

Footsteps coming from the hall caused them to turn. Christina came close to fainting when Antonio walked in. "Who says I'm not?"

"Antonio," she gasped. "But you were just on television." He was dressed in a sport shirt and chinos instead of his dark suit.

"That was taped at noon. This afternoon the council reassembled and voted unanimously for our marriage to stand. The coronation will take place in two weeks. Once I was given the news, I flew here in the helicopter. It's standing by for me to take you back to the palace."

By now the girls were on their feet, hugging her and each other for joy.

Christina watched as her husband in all his male glory walked over to her. His brilliant blue eyes blinded her with their heat.

"H-how did you know I was here?"

"Palace security traced you once we heard from the guard that you'd left the grounds with Arianna."

"I thought I was being so careful."

"You were. For a few hours your disappearance gave me a heart attack. Since we'd barely returned from Bora Bora, I hardly think that's fair. Don't you ever do that to me again."

Her love for him was bursting out of her. "I promise."

In front of everyone he picked her up in his arms as he'd done twice before. "Excuse us, ladies. We have very personal matters of state to discuss and must get back to the palace. The limo is waiting for us."

Heat flooded her body as he carried her out of the room and the palazzo. After helping her into the car, he told the driver to head for Monte Calanetti before crushing her in his arms. "You don't have to worry about the state of our marriage, *cara*. I'm madly in love with you and this is a new day."

Christina was euphoric during their flight to Voti. Once they touched ground and were driven to the palace, he swept her along to their home on the second floor. Again he gathered her in his arms and carried her through to their bedroom.

After following her down onto the bed, he began kissing her. They were starving for each other. Christina couldn't get enough of him fast enough. Everything that had kept them apart had been cleared away. She was able to give him all the love she'd stored up in her heart and body.

The next morning she heard a sound of satisfaction as he pulled her on top of him. Their night of lovemaking had appeased them for a little while. She sat up and looked at their clothes strewn all over the floor.

Antonio pulled her back down. "I'm in love with you, Christina. So terribly in love with my red-haired beauty I'll never get over it. You believe me, don't you?"

There was a vulnerability about the question that touched her heart. "I feel your love in every atom of my body, my darling. Is there any doubt how I feel about you after last night? I need you desperately and want your baby."

"Anything to oblige the woman who has made me thankful I was born a man."

"I loved you from the time I was fifteen, but I never dared admit it to myself because—"

Another kiss stifled any words. "We're never going to talk about past sadness. When I called your father to find out what he said to you, he gave me the answer and I had a revelation of what it was like to grow up with him. All we can do is feel sorry for him. I believe your mother has always been afraid of him."

"I know you're right." Just when Christina didn't think she could love him anymore, he said or did something that made her love for him burn hotter. "I can't wait to thank your parents for Bora Bora."

"They've always lived their life over-the-top, but there's one thing they did I'll always be thankful for. They wanted us to find love."

"Yes, darling, and we found it there."

He kissed her neck and shoulders. "I'm the happiest man alive."

"Are you ready for a little more happy news?"

"What?"

"Enzio has asked Elena to marry him."

Antonio grinned. "He's a brave man to want to take her on."

"She's worth the risk. Guess what else? Marusha is expecting a baby." Christina kissed every feature. "I can't wait until we can announce we're having our own baby."

"I'm going to do my best to make that happen. I know now the one thing missing in my life was you and the family we're planning to have. We should have gotten married instead of engaged."

"I think about that too, all the time. But I don't think we were destined to get together until the time was right. We both had work to do first."

Antonio rolled her over and looked down at her. "You're the most beautiful sight this man has ever seen. I love you, *tesoro mio*. Never leave me."

"You *know* why I did."

A pained look entered his eyes. "The last three weeks have been the worst of my entire life."

"For me too. But as you said, no concentrating on past sorrows. We're together now and I'm able to live every day and night with the prince of my heart."

While they were talking, the house phone rang. She eyed her husband. "That's probably Guido wanting to know when you're free to discuss royal business. You better put him out of his misery."

Antonio grinned and picked up. *"Pronto."*

"Your Highness, Princess Christina's mother is asking if she can talk to her daughter in private."

He covered the mouthpiece. "Christina?" Curious,

she looked at him. He stared into her eyes with concern. "Your mother wants to talk to you."

She swallowed nervously. "Is she on the phone?"

"No. It's Guido. What do you want to do?"

"I'll take the call."

He handed her the receiver. "Guido?"

"Your mother asks if she can come to your apartment to talk to you."

She blinked. "Now?"

"She's says it's of vital importance."

"Then have someone show her up."

"Very well."

Antonio had picked up on the conversation. "Are you sure you want to do this?"

"Yes. My mother let me know she's on our side. Why don't you order breakfast while I talk to her in the living room? She won't be here very long, no matter what is on her mind."

He pressed a swift kiss to her lips and did her bidding. As for herself, Christina could have changed into an outfit, but she decided the robe was perfectly presentable. Before long she heard a knock on the main door.

Sucking in her breath, she opened it. Her mother always looked impeccably dressed and coiffed. But Christina knew right away something was wrong when she saw the tears in her eyes. "Come in."

But she just stood there.

"Mother?"

She shook her head. "I thought I could do this, but I can't." She started to turn away.

"Can't do what?" Christina asked, causing her mother to stop.

"Ask your forgiveness, but I don't have the right. I lost the right years ago. I knew your father must have had emotional problems when you were born. He wanted to give you up for adoption because you weren't a boy. I purposely prevented any more pregnancies in case I had another girl."

Christina was aghast at what she was hearing, but it made sense when she considered what her great-aunt Sofia had told her about the Rose men.

"I bargained with him that I wanted to keep you, and he wouldn't be sorry. That's why I kept you away. But you'll never know my shame for what I've done." She hung her head.

"I may have given birth to you, and your father may have provided you with everything, but you didn't have parents who showed you the love and devotion you deserved."

Christina stood there in shock as her mother broke down and sobbed.

"I'll never be forgiven for what I did to you. I don't deserve forgiveness, but you're my sweet, darling girl. I love you, Christina. My pride in you is fierce. Just know that I loved you from the moment you were born and I wanted you to hear it from me. I won't bother you again."

"Mother? Don't say that. I want us to have the relationship we never had. It's never too late," Christina said in a tremulous voice. "What you've told me about Papa changes everything."

Her mother turned to her with a face glistening in tears. "You mean you don't hate me with every fiber of your being? I would, because I'm not the great person you are."

"Oh, Mama—"

Christina reached for her and hugged her until her mother reciprocated. They clung for a long time. With every tear her mother shed, Christina felt herself healing. "We'll invite you over for dinner in a few weeks. I'll be cooking." She kissed her mother on both cheeks. "Dry your tears and I'll see you soon."

"Bless you, *figlia mia*."

On Coronation Day bells rang out through the whole of Voti as Antonio and Christina left the cathedral and climbed into the open carriage. The massive throng roared, "Long live King Antonio and Queen Christina! Long live the monarchy!" They chanted the words over and over as the horses drew the carriage through the street lined with cheering Halencians.

The day had turned out to be glorious. Christina thought her heart was going to burst with happiness. Every few minutes someone called out, "Queen Christina!" When she turned, people were taking pictures.

Antonio sat next to her and squeezed the hand that wasn't waving. "You know what they want, *bellissima*."

She looked back at him. "You mean a kiss? I want it much more." Showing breathtaking initiative that would probably cause her to blush later, she kissed him several times to the joy of the crowds.

The capital city of Halencia teemed with joyful faces and shouts of "Long live the monarchy."

"Your country loves you, darling. You don't know how magnificent you looked when the archbishop put that crown on your head."

"It's a good thing I didn't have to keep wearing it. How does yours feel?"

"I like the tiara. It's light."

"Your hair outshines its gleam."

They were both wearing their wedding clothes. The only thing different was the red sash on Antonio proclaiming him king.

"We made a lot of promises today." She kept waving. So did he.

"Are you worried?"

"No, but the sun is hot," he muttered. Their procession went on for over an hour.

Christina laughed. "I feel it too. But don't worry. We'll make it through and be alone later."

"I can't wait."

Eventually the carriage returned them to the palace. On their way up to the balcony off the second floor, Antonio summoned Guido to bring them a sandwich and a drink. The chief of staff, who'd chosen to stay on with Antonio, looked shocked, but he sent someone for the food.

Antonio whispered in her ear, "Did you see that look he gave us?"

"We're breaking royal protocol, darling."

"We'll be breaking a lot of rules before my reign has come to an end."

She shivered. "Don't talk about that. I can't bear the thought of it."

When the sandwich arrived, they both ate a half and swallowed some water. Feeling slightly more refreshed, they walked out onto the balcony to the roar of the crowd.

To please them her husband kissed her again with so much enthusiasm she actually swayed in his arms. A thunderous roar of satisfaction broke from the enormous throng that filled every square inch of space.

Once the royal photographers had finished taking pictures, Antonio grasped her hand. "Come with me."

"Where are we going?"

"To our home for some R and R until the ball this evening."

"But we're supposed to mingle with all the dignitaries."

"There'll be time for that tonight."

She hurried along with him, out of breath by the time they reached their apartment. When they entered, they discovered a lavish meal laid out for them in the dining room.

"Who arranged for this, darling?" she asked.

"My mother. She said it would be an exhausting day and we'd need it."

"I think she's wonderful."

Once in the bedroom, she removed her tiara and asked him to undo the buttons of her wedding dress. "That didn't take long. You did that so fast I'm afraid you've lost interest already. Last time you took forever."

"I hope it drove you crazy." He bit her earlobe gently when he'd finished. "Did it?"

"I'll never tell."

Antonio caught her to him and rocked her in his arms for a long, long time.

"Your capacity to love is a gift," he whispered against her cheek. "I don't know how I was the one man on earth lucky enough to be loved by you. I'm thankful your mother came to see you on the day we got back from Tuscany. She was able to answer the question that's always been in your heart. The sadness in your eyes has disappeared."

Christina threw her arms around his neck and looked into those blue eyes filled with love for her. "You're right. And now I have one more secret to disclose. You were always the man for me. When you asked me to get engaged, I jumped, *leaped* at the opportunity. To be honest, deep down I was petrified you *would* come to Africa and call it off. So I played it cagey, and it paid off!"

After enjoying a meal, they made love again before it was time to go out to greet their guests and enjoy the royal celebration. Guido looked frantic as they approached the balcony.

"Your Highness, we've been waiting for your appearance to start the fireworks."

Antonio hugged her waist. "We're here now."

No sooner had they stepped out so everyone could see them than a huge roar of excitement from the throng of people filled the air. Suddenly there was a massive fireworks display that lit up the sky, bursting and bursting, illuminating everything. Antonio looked into Christina's eyes. Her heart was bursting with happiness.

"Ti amo, Antonio."

He stared at her. "Darling, you're crying. What's wrong?"

"I'm so happy tonight I can't contain it all."

Giving the crowd what they wanted by kissing her, he whispered, "My beautiful wife. This is only the beginning. *Ti amo, bellissima*. Forever."

* * * * *

Claire felt a hand on her shoulder.

She didn't realize Vic had come out to the barn. His touch triggered her tears. She started sobbing, and before she realized it, he'd pulled her into his arms. They clung to each other, seeking comfort while the tears gushed down her face, wetting his Western shirt.

As his body heaved with unshed tears, tearing her apart, she was aware of the warm smell of the horses combined with the soap he used in the shower. The heady combination plus the feel of his hard body reminded her he was a man as well as her employer. A beautiful man. A loving father. The ultimate protector. The total male. One who was utterly desirable.

Shaken by the feelings coming from deep inside her, she slowly eased herself out of his arms and stepped away. Too many emotions since she'd been hired had been growing and were taking over, surprising her. Overwhelming her. Tonight it was impossible to separate her feelings for Jeremy from the man who'd fathered him.

THE TEXAS RANGER'S NANNY

BY
REBECCA WINTERS

MILLS & BOON

First Published in Great Britain 2016
By Mills & Boon, an imprint of HarperCollins*Publishers*
1 London Bridge Street, London, SE1 9GF

© 2016 Rebecca Winters

ISBN: 978-0-263-91952-3

23-0116

Our policy is to use papers that are natural, renewable and recyclable products and made from wood grown in sustainable forests.The logging and manufacturing processes conform to the legal environmental regulations of the country of origin.

Printed and bound in Spain
by CPI, Barcelona

Rebecca Winters, whose family of four children has now swelled to include five beautiful grandchildren, lives in Salt Lake City, Utah, in the land of the Rocky Mountains. With canyons and high alpine meadows full of wildflowers, she never runs out of places to explore. They, plus her favorite vacation spots in Europe, often end up as backgrounds for her romance novels, because writing is her passion, along with her family and church.

Rebecca loves to hear from readers. If you wish to email her, please visit her website, www.cleanromances.com.

To our wonderful lawmen throughout the country
who lay their lives on the line every day
to keep us all safe.

Chapter One

"There is a storm warning in effect in the Denton area, where two tornadoes have been confirmed this morning. Those driving toward Denton are advised to take shelter beneath an overpass or to abandon their vehicles and find a ditch, if possible, until the storm pas—"

Unable to listen to any more, Texas Ranger Stephen Victorio Malone—better known as Vic—shut off the radio as he drove from his house to headquarters in downtown Austin Monday morning. Though the weather was in the mideighties and had been for the entire month, he broke out in a cold sweat after hearing the warning. He always listened to the news in the car, but any mention of a tornado triggered a response he doubted he would ever overcome.

Three years ago he'd lost his parents and his wife, Laura, in a tornado near his hometown of Blanco, Texas. His initial grief might have passed, but the pain of losing three people he loved at once would stay with him to the end of his life. If it hadn't been for his four-year-old son, Jeremy, who wasn't with the family at the time, he didn't know if he would have survived it.

Austin didn't usually get the tornadoes that other parts of the state experienced. For the first three months after the tragedy, Vic had stayed in Blanco while he put up both his house and his parents' home for sale. During that period, his sister-in-law, Carol, and her husband, Dennis, had helped take care of Jeremy while Vic commuted to work in Austin. Carol and Dennis had two children: Sarah, who was eight, and five-year-old Randy. Randy and Jeremy had become close buddies.

Vic hadn't been prepared for the pushback he got from Jeremy when he told him they were moving to the suburbs of Austin to be closer to his work. But as much as it pained him to tear his son away from his cousin and new best friend, Vic *had* to get on with his life. And so did Jeremy. Austin represented a new beginning for the two of them. He couldn't continue to depend on Laura's sister to be a mother to his son.

The first thing Vic did when they moved was hire a professional cleaning service to clean his new house. That part was easy. The hard part was finding the right nanny for his son. Through an agency he'd found a woman in her early fifties who was a good fit. But after two years she moved to Dallas to be near her older sister. Then Claire Ames, a college student finishing up a master's degree at the University of Texas, came into their lives.

Out of the four women Vic interviewed for the position, Claire was the one Jeremy liked the most. Although he felt a little awkward about it, Vic asked her outright if she was in a relationship with anyone that might interfere with her taking care of his son. Claire assured him there hadn't been anyone since she broke up with her last boyfriend because he didn't like being put off when she had to study. Her explanation convinced Vic to take a chance on her.

Since then everything had been great, but now Vic was faced with the possibility he might lose Claire, as she had just graduated from her master's chemistry program. He and Jeremy had gone to the ceremony on Friday. Claire let Jeremy keep her tassel, which he'd proudly hung from a knob on the chest of drawers in his room.

Now Claire was looking for a full-time position as a chemist. Once she found a job in her field, she'd be leaving them.

Though Jeremy had known that Claire wouldn't always be his nanny, the fact failed to register with his boy. When it came time for her to leave, his son would have a terrible time letting her go. Over the past nine months they'd forged a strong bond. Jeremy was crazy about Claire, who had brought laughter and fun back into the house. Vic couldn't bear the thought of another loss bringing more pain to his son.

Vic's buddies at headquarters knew of his dilemma and encouraged him to pay Claire more money. Maybe she could be bribed into staying another year before leaving to work for some company who knows where. His fear was that she'd be leaving the state. He'd grown used to her presence and couldn't imagine her living so far away. And Jeremy would have a real problem accepting that he might never see her again.

Vic had substantial savings in the bank from the

sale of both homes and his income as a Ranger. And his house in Austin came with enough property to keep his horses there. Money wasn't a problem, and the idea of offering Claire a substantial raise was tempting.

If she didn't get the right job offer soon, he'd discuss with her the option of accepting a raise in her salary to keep her with them a little longer. But to be truthful, the reason he was having such a hard time letting her go wasn't only because of Jeremy. Claire had a fun-loving nature that he liked to be around. They shared the same sense of humor, and she was very respectful of his privacy, which made him feel relaxed around her. You couldn't bottle her positive attributes any more than you could bottle the coppery red-gold color of her hair. That's why he knew he could never replace her.

Selfishly, Vic hoped a great job offer wouldn't come along for at least another year—let alone another man. When he'd hired Claire, she'd told him she didn't have a boyfriend, and as far as he knew, that was still the case. But knowing how hard she'd worked to earn her graduate degree and make a place for herself in the world, made him feel like a terrible person for wanting to hold her back.

AFTER THE HOUSE cleaners left, Claire drove the three blocks to Pinehurst Elementary School to pick up little dark-haired Jeremy. The bell rang at three fifteen, but she always got there early because she didn't want Jeremy to worry. He was usually the first of the kids to run out of the second grade pod. The moment he saw her four-year-old red Honda Civic, he would wave and practically fly to reach the car.

Through school programs and class parties, she'd become acquainted with a lot of the moms who were picking up their kids. She waved to them. They were lined up in their cars all the way down the street. Claire couldn't imagine loving a child of her own more than she loved Jeremy Malone.

With Vic's help she'd learned how to ride a horse. The three of them rode on his property when he was able to get home early from work. Vic's black gelding was named Midnight. Claire rode Marshmallow, the bay Vic's wife once rode. Jeremy had his own pony, Comet. At seven, he was already quite a horseman. He was the cutest, funniest boy she'd ever met, and he had an amazing imagination.

One day quite recently Jeremy told her he was part Apache. She thought he'd made it up because he loved stories about the frontier days. When she told Vic what his son had confided, Vic had let go with a burst of rich laughter. The tough-looking Texas Ranger had another side to him his son brought out. When the man smiled, her insides melted.

His jet black eyes zeroed in on her. "For once that wasn't his imagination, Claire. We have Lipan Apache blood flowing through us. Not a large amount. You know that photograph on the wall in my den?"

"If you mean the one of the Sons of the Forty Texas Rangers surrounding Jack Hayes, Jeremy showed it to me."

"Two of the men were deputized Lipan Apaches

fighting for Texas at Bandera Pass in 1842, and *one* of them is our ancestor through the Malone line. I have a second cousin named Clint who works on the police force. He has a smattering of Apache blood like me and lives in Luckenbach with his wife, Sandra, and family. I occasionally take Jeremy to visit them. We ride and do a little washer pitching."

"Washer pitching?"

"It's like playing a game of horseshoes, Texas style. We'll drive there with the horses when Jeremy's school lets out. After a ride you can try your hand at it."

The explanation fascinated Claire. "I had no idea. From now on I'll try to believe everything your Mini Me tells me."

Vic lifted one black brow. "*Try* has to be the operative word. We could get into a whole lot of trouble if we believed all his tales."

While Claire sat in her car waiting for Jeremy, she couldn't help smiling. That had been the day she forgot she was a nanny. A fluttering had started up in her chest as she sat across the table from Vic, looking at her tall, hard-muscled, thirty-year-old employer. The fluttering had never gone away, but she'd keep it a secret if it killed her. Were he to know how attracted she was to him, he'd fire her on the spot. She'd been hired to take care of his son, not fixate on Jeremy's gorgeous father.

As soon as the bell rang, the doors to the school burst open and children started running out. She was surprised when she didn't see Jeremy right away. Maybe his teacher, Mrs. Rigby, needed to talk to him about something. Claire waited a few minutes before she started to wonder if something could be wrong.

Deciding she'd better check on him, she got out of her car and hurried across the playground to the door leading into the second grade pod. When she peeked inside the classroom, she saw the teacher sitting alone at her desk. No Jeremy. Claire's heart started to thud.

"Mrs. Rigby?"

The older woman lifted her head. "Hi, Claire. If you're looking for Jeremy, he left the second the bell rang."

"But he didn't come out the doors."

"Did you check the office? Maybe he's there for some reason."

"I'll do that."

Claire practically ran down the hall to the main office, but there was no sign of Jeremy. "Have you seen Jeremy Malone since the bell rang?" she asked the secretary. "He's in second grade. Kind of tallish for his age with dark hair and brown eyes?"

"I know who he is, but no, he hasn't been in here."

"Would you call him to the office for me?"

"Sure. I'll do it right now."

The secretary got on the PA system and asked Jeremy Malone to report to the front office. She repeated the request three times. When Jeremy still didn't show up, fear for his well-being cramped Claire's stomach. Where could he be?

"Will you call the security guard and give him a description? Jeremy wore a blue-and-green plaid shirt and jeans today and he has a blue backpack. And can you ask the guard to check with the crossing guards, and look in all the bathrooms, the library, the gym and anywhere else Jeremy might possibly be? I'm worried about him."

While the secretary contacted security, the principal came out of her office. "Is there a problem?"

Claire nodded. "I can't find Jeremy Malone. He didn't come out to the car. I'm going to phone his father and let him know what's happened."

"Maybe you should wait until we've confirmed he hasn't gone home with a friend," the principal suggested.

"No, I have to call him. Jeremy could be in danger."

She'd been around Vic long enough to know that when a person went missing, the first twelve hours were crucial in finding them alive. "Jeremy wouldn't go home with a friend without getting my permission first. We have strict rules about that." Sick to her stomach by now, Claire pulled out her phone and called Vic.

He answered after three rings. "Hi, Claire. What's up?"

"I'm worried about Jeremy."

"What's wrong?" Tension crept into Vic's deep voice.

"I'm here at the school to pick him up, but he never came out. I got here ten minutes before the bell like I always do, but there's been no sign of him. I've checked with his teacher and with the office. They've called his name over the intercom, but he hasn't shown up. The security guard just walked in the door. He's been looking everywhere for him but he's shaking his head."

"I'll be right there. You drive home. Maybe a friend's

mother dropped him off. Call the list of parents we keep by the phone."

"Okay, I will." She hung up and told the principal she was going home to see if Jeremy was there. "Ranger Malone is on his way here."

"Let's hope Jeremy made his way home and is waiting for you."

If he did that, then he'd have left the school through another entrance. Claire hurried out of the building to the car. As she drove to the house, she called out to any kids she could see who were walking home from school. No one had seen Jeremy. Adrenaline caused her heart to pound so hard it was painful.

If anything had happened to Vic's son…

She shouldn't go there, but she couldn't help it. Three years ago Vic had lived through the nightmare of losing his wife and his parents. For him to have to go through his only child's disappearance seemed unimaginably cruel. But her gut told her something bad had happened to Jeremy.

Vic's job as a Texas Ranger made him a target for felons he'd put in prison who were out for revenge. His line of work was terribly dangerous. In fact, when he'd hired Claire, he'd warned her she would have to be extra careful at all times, for her own safety, as well as for Jeremy's.

Jeremy was a very obedient kid. He worshipped his father and told Claire he wanted to be a Texas Ranger like his dad when he grew up. Because of his lively imagination, Jeremy had a spy kit he kept adding to. He'd also come up with a secret password for them to use if either one of them was ever in trouble. *Wolverine*. It was the name of his favorite action figure.

If someone tried to call him on the phone and pretended to be Claire, they had to give him the password. The same held true if someone pretending to be Jeremy called her. The two of them laughed about it when Jeremy came up with the plan, but she wasn't laughing now. If that dear boy wasn't found soon…

Too many negative thoughts ran through her mind as she called the last name on the list of Jeremy's friends. Her heart sank to learn that his friend Nate had been home from school all day with a cold and had no idea where Jeremy could be.

Vic raced to his boss's office. "Captain?"

TJ Horton raised his gray head. "What is it, Vic? You look like you've seen a ghost."

"My son is missing. I don't have a good feeling about this, and I'm headed over to Pinehurst Elementary on Wilson Drive right now. I'm going to treat it as a crime scene and I'll need backup to meet me there. Put a surveillance crew on my house. Claire could be in danger as we speak."

The head of the Rangers nodded. "Kit's in the building. I'll send him over there, too, and I'll tell Dino and Carlos to keep an eye on your nanny."

"Thanks."

Vic rushed out to his gray Chevy Tahoe in the parking area. On his way to the school, Claire phoned to tell him she was at the house, but Jeremy wasn't there.

She'd called the mothers of all the kids he played with, but no one had seen or heard from him.

"Thanks. You stay put, Claire. I'll be in touch soon. Just so you know, we're putting some men outside the house to guard you. They'll be in a surveillance van, so don't be worried when you see an unfamiliar vehicle near the house."

"I won't."

Vic's cold sweat had seeped through his clothes by the time he reached the school. He ran into the main office, where he found the principal telling some other teachers about Jeremy. She turned to him. "Ranger Malone, we're devastated this has happened."

"Me, too. I need a list of all personnel working inside and outside the building with addresses and phone numbers."

"Here's a copy for you," the secretary said and handed the sheet to him.

"Thank you." He turned to the principal again. "Who was on recess duty today? I need to know if there were any strangers on the playground or maintenance workers from the school district."

"I'll get all that information for you right now."

Mrs. Rigby walked over to him. "I'm so sorry," she said.

"It's not your fault. I just want to know if Jeremy was acting any different than usual today."

"No. He's a good student and always well behaved. They were finishing their math when the bell rang. He's almost always the first one out of his desk, and today was no exception. That's all I can tell you."

"Did you have any visitors in your class? Anything different from the normal routine?"

"No. Nothing."

"When he first got to school this morning, he didn't seem upset? It didn't seem as if there could be anything bothering him?"

"No. Today was a very normal day from beginning to end."

Vic sucked in his breath. "Okay. Thank you." He saw his close friend Kit out of the corner of his eye. The other Ranger made a beeline for him. "The crew is already setting up a place in the classroom next door to fingerprint everyone working in the building."

As they spoke, he could hear the principal over the loudspeaker asking all the teachers and staff to come to the office for a police matter.

"Glad you're here, Kit. Claire's phoned all the parents of Jeremy's friends. No one has seen him. Let's scour the second grade pod area first. He was in his seat right up until the bell rang. Whatever happened took place immediately after dismissal."

Directly outside the classroom was a cloakroom where the kids kept their coats and backpacks on hooks and a shelf that ran the length of the wall. With the exception of a Windbreaker on one of the hooks and a baseball cap with a Texas Longhorns logo, neither of which belonged to Jeremy, the cloakroom was empty.

Vic shook his head. "Jeremy wouldn't have come in here after school since he keeps his backpack with him."

From the hallway outside the cloakroom there was a short walk past other classrooms to get to the main hallway. At that point, you could either go left to the office or right to an exit that led to the playground area. En route to the exit, they passed a door that said Custodial Staff.

Vic glanced at Kit. "Are you thinking what I'm thinking?"

"Yup. It's a perfect place to hide or nab a kid walking down the hall."

Vic pulled a pair of plastic gloves from his back pocket and put them on before turning the knob. The door was locked. "I'll call the office to send someone down to open it."

Kit said, "I'll go outside the building to see where it leads. Be right back."

In a minute a custodian who looked to be in his fifties showed up. "I'm Oscar Fyans, the head custodian. How can I help?"

Vic asked him how many custodians worked at the school.

"There are three of us."

"Do you all have your own areas that you're responsible for?"

"Yes. I have the second floor."

"Who's in charge of the first floor?"

"Reba Cowan covers the auditorium, library, the gym, the cafeteria and the grounds. Leroy Bennett covers the first-floor classrooms and bathrooms, but he called in sick this morning, so Reba and I are covering for him."

"How many years have you worked here?"

"Fifteen."

"What about Mrs. Cowan?"

"She's going on thirteen years."

"And Leroy Bennett?"

"He's only been here a couple of months." For some reason that sent up a red flag. "The other custodian retired."

"I see. Have you been in this closet at any time today?"

"No, sir."

"Where's Mrs. Cowan right now?"

"She's in the office with the rest of the staff."

"Will you get her on the phone so I can speak to her?"

"Yes, sir."

Oscar punched in some numbers and after getting Reba on the line, he passed the phone to Vic. "Mrs. Cowan? This is Ranger Malone. As you know, my son Jeremy has been missing since school let out. Have you been over in the second grade pod or the main hallway at any time since school started today?"

"No. I heard Leroy called in sick, so I was going to get to that area after I finished my regular rounds."

"Thank you." He handed the phone back to Oscar. "Is it the rule to keep these storage closets locked?"

"Yes, sir."

"So if Leroy didn't show up today, then to your knowledge this closet hasn't been opened since it was locked last evening."

"That's right. Leroy would have ensured it was locked before leaving the school."

"Will you please put on this glove and unlock the door for me?" Vic pulled another glove from his pocket.

After the custodian put it on, he pulled up his chain of keys from his belt and found the right key. When it clicked, Vic turned the knob and opened the door. He discovered a person could lock the door from the inside.

"Take your time looking around in here, Mr. Fyans. Do you see anything missing?"

The man scratched his head. "Yeah. There should be the big garbage can set on wheels that we roll to the classrooms, but it's not here."

"That's all I need to know. Thank you. Please go to the office and get fingerprinted. I'll take your glove."

"Yes, sir."

Kit rejoined him and Vic told him about the missing garbage can. "You didn't by any chance see a garbage can with wheels while you were outside, did you?"

Kit shook his head. "But there are a couple of maintenance vehicles parked right outside on the playground. I talked to two men who were doing some repair work on the roof. If Jeremy was taken out this exit, another vehicle could have been waiting there for him and no one would have questioned it. I checked for tire marks on the asphalt outside the door and didn't see any. I've put in a call to the school district to find out if a truck is missing."

"Good. Let's search this closet thoroughly."

Kit pulled on his own pair of gloves and started dusting for prints.

"ARE YOU THINKING there could be some connection to the big arrest you made three months ago?"

Vic grimaced because Kit had been reading his

mind. Two months ago Vic had been appointed to the NIGC known as the Indian Gaming Working Group because of that arrest. The group consisted of representatives in the economic crimes unit of graft and corruption. Their work was to identify resources to address the most pressing criminal violations in the area of Indian illegal gambling interests.

After tracking down violations from one of the Indian casinos near Luckenbach, Vic had arrested lobbyist Edgar "Lefty" Quarls for committing conspiracy, fraud and tax evasion. He and his slippery gang of thugs had grossly overbilled their clients and secretly split the multimillion-dollar profits. In one case they orchestrated lobbying against their own clients in order to force them to pay for lobbying services.

At the last report, the tribes were being bilked out of $85 million, but that was only the tip of the iceberg. As one of the key people spearheading the scandal and then being appointed to the NIGC, Vic had no doubts Jeremy had been kidnapped as a personal warning to him to lay off.

This wasn't the case of someone wanting a ransom. Vic didn't have that kind of money. Like Kit, the more he thought about it, the more he was convinced this had to do with his new assignment to the gaming group dedicated to making more arrests.

To take Vic's child from the school in broad daylight smacked of revenge in its most evil form. Lefty had to be involved with someone very high up politically who knew the particulars about Vic's life and hated him enough to hire someone to help pull this off. Why not bribe a janitor?

At the thought of anyone harming Jeremy, searing pain reached his gut, almost cutting off his breathing.

"Your son is tough. We're going to find him, Vic."

He nodded and brushed the tears from his eyes with his shirtsleeve. They checked every inch of the closet for clues that Jeremy had been held there. As far as Vic could tell, there was no sign of a struggle.

After they'd taken half a dozen fingerprints and put them in bags to send to forensics, Vic looked at the yellow bucket wringer in the corner. He walked over and lifted the mop. In the bottom of the bucket he saw a round two-inch button.

He leaned over and picked it up. The second he saw the picture, his heart leaped. "This looks like one of the action hero magnets Jeremy got for Christmas!"

"If that's his, he's left you a clue, Vic. He's not your son for nothing."

"Dear Lord, I hope that's true. It means he was dragged in here and able to get it out of his pocket or backpack before he was taken away." Vic slid the magnet into another baggie.

Kit said, "You drive to the lab quick while I round up the crew. We'll meet you at headquarters. Do you have Jeremy's prints on file?"

"Yes. Last year he wanted to know what it was like when we made an arrest, so I had him fingerprinted at the office to experience the process. I made a copy for him to take home, but his prints are on my computer."

"Then before long you should know if you have a match."

Vic made sure the closet was locked and then hurried outside to his car while Kit took off in the other direction. On the drive to headquarters, he phoned Claire.

"Any news?" she cried. Her question meant his precious son hadn't come home. His heart almost failed him, but he had to focus. Every minute Jeremy was gone, the chances of getting him back alive diminished.

"Claire? Do me a favor? Check on those little two-inch magnets he has in his room with the action figures on them." This was a long shot, but it was imperative he investigate every possible lead. "I think there were eight of them. Let me know if any are missing."

"Just a second. He usually keeps them in the top drawer of his desk."

Thank heaven she knew his son so well. Every second while he waited, visions of what could be happening to Jeremy passed through his mind, torturing him.

"Vic? I found six."

"Do you know which two are missing?"

"Yes. His favorites—Wolverine and Sabretooth. Why do you ask?"

He looked at the face of the magnet through the baggie. "Because I'm holding Wolverine in my hand. I believe he left me a clue in the janitor's closet outside his classroom. I found it in the bottom of the bucket."

"Oh Vic—I *know* he did."

The conviction in her voice sent chills through him. "*How* do you know?"

"Did I ever tell you about the password your son thought up while we were playing spy one day?"

Vic drew in a deep breath. "No. What password?"

In the next minute she explained about their secret code. "He knew exactly what he was doing when he left Wolverine there for you to find. That clever boy. I love him so much. I know you're going to find him," she said with tears in her voice. "I just know it!"

She was a marvel. More than anything on earth he wanted to believe her. He couldn't lose Jeremy. The thought was unfathomable. "You've given me hope, Claire. Thank you. I'm at headquarters now. I'll call you later."

He hung up and, after haphazardly parking his vehicle, hurried through the building to the forensics lab. To Vic's relief the head lab technician was still there. "Stan?"

Before Vic said anything else, the other man rushed over to him with a concerned look on his face. "I heard about your son. What can I do to help?"

His compassion was touching. "We've got more fingerprint samples coming from the staff at the school, but I'd like to find out if Jeremy's fingerprints are on this." He handed him the bag with the magnet. "We found it in the janitor's closet outside Jeremy's classroom. I'll go upstairs and send my son's set of fingerprints to you right now."

"I'll get on it immediately."

Vic raced up the stairs two at a time. Little did he dream that one day those fingerprints he'd taken to satisfy his son's curiosity would be needed.

It didn't take him long to get on his computer and send the vital information to the lab from his personal file. When Vic went back down, he found Kit had arrived with the other bags. "I've got Leroy Bennett's address. When you're ready, I'll drive over to his place with you and we'll find out if he was really sick today."

Vic's teeth ground together. "Yup. Someone had a key to that closet who shouldn't have."

They moved over to the table where Stan was working. He had images of Jeremy's fingerprints up on the screen in front of him. He studied the print that had been taken off the magnet with his magnifying loop. Finally he turned to Vic. "They're a match."

Until Stan gave him the verdict, Vic didn't realize he'd been holding his breath. Kit clamped his hand on Vic's shoulder. "Okay. Now we know where we're going with this."

He nodded. "Let's head upstairs and run Leroy Bennett's name through the IAFIS database. If he has a criminal record, we'll find out. Thanks, Stan."

"We'll do whatever we can down here to help."

Vic hurried back upstairs to his office and typed in Bennett's name on the computer in case he had a police record. Kit stood next to him while they waited to see if anything came up.

"Here we go," Vic muttered.

William Leroy Bennett, 39, Austin, Texas
Six feet
180 pounds
Green eye tattoo above inner wrist of left arm

Two snake tattoos on his chest
A half-moon shaped scar on side of his chin
Dark blond hair short cropped

Arrested in a park in Austin, Texas. He and several other individuals had a confrontation with another group of males. Both sides made derogatory comments. The altercation resulted in a fistfight. Bennett delivered the punch that knocked the victim unconscious. He eventually died. Bennett was determined to suffer from PTSD after a tour of duty in Iraq. After serving two months in prison on a charge of involuntary manslaughter, the charge was dropped and he was released.

Kit frowned. "Look at the date."

"It's close to the date when I made that arrest. He's only been out of prison three months. No arrests since then, but it's too light a sentence," Vic muttered. "The district isn't allowed to hire anyone who's had a prison record, but since the charge was dropped, I guess the rule didn't apply."

"The information on Leroy's school file says he started working for the district a week after his release from prison. Someone higher up had the power to pull strings like that," Kit theorized. "I'll get the full police report on the other men involved in the assault. Maybe the ones causing the confrontation with Leroy work for someone who gives them orders when they want a hit made."

"That's what I'm thinking." Vic got to his feet. "Before the night is over I want to talk to the person at the district who hired him, and find out who put the pressure on him or her. It's time to pay Leroy a visit to find out just how sick he is. Let's go in my car."

"I'll call headquarters right now to get that process started."

It was ten to six when they left the building and drove to the Walnut Creek area known as a hot spot for a large number of auto thefts and larceny. Bennett lived in an older three-story apartment building, in unit 22. Vic parked the car and they entered the main foyer. Several tenants had to have been just getting back from work. They were checking their mailboxes, which were located inside the building.

Vic followed the arrow to Bennett's apartment on the main floor. He knocked on the door. No answer. He tried it again.

Kit grimaced. "We need a warrant."

"Barring that, let's check with that woman across the hall." Vic walked over to the woman who held a sack of groceries in one arm and was in the middle of opening her door. She looked to be in her twenties.

"Ma'am? Can we speak to you for a minute?" He pulled out his ID. "I'm Ranger Malone. This is Ranger Saunders."

She eyed them suspiciously. "What do you want?"

"Can you tell us about the man living in apartment 22? He doesn't seem to be home at the moment."

"I try to avoid him. He's been bugging me to go out with him since I moved in here two months ago. He bragged about being in Iraq."

"Does he ever have friends over?"

"Not that I've noticed." She hunched her shoulders. "He's weird, wanting to show me all his tattoos, you know? I wouldn't be surprised if he's in some kind of trouble."

"When was the last time you saw him?"

"This morning. His parking stall is in the rear near mine. I saw him loading up the back of his truck. I asked him if he was moving out. He just nodded and drove off. I'm glad he's gone and good riddance."

Vic felt as if he'd been stabbed. His only lead already had a ten-hour advantage on him. "Can you describe the truck for us?"

"I don't know models. It was blue and looked old with a bunch of dents."

"Four doors? Two doors?"

"Two doors I think."

"What time was that?"

"Quarter after eight. I have to be to work at eight thirty."

"Thank you for your time."

"Sure."

With that news, the two of them rushed out of the building to Vic's car. "I'll call in for a license plate number. Once it's found I'll ask TJ to send out an Amber Alert. I wouldn't doubt if Leroy was paid off to do his part in the kidnapping, and now he's headed for the border."

Kit nodded. "He must have driven to the school right before the bell and put Jeremy in the garbage bin. All he had to do was put it in the truck parked outside the door and take off with no one being the wiser."

Bile started to rise in Vic's throat. "We've got to find him." He put in a call to the captain. The blood pounded in his temples. Someone had used Leroy to carry out the kidnapping. He could be anywhere in the state by now. If he slipped over the border, it could take a long time to track him down.

When he got off the phone with the captain, Kit looked at him. "As soon as you drop me off at headquarters, I'll ask the boss to get us a warrant to search Leroy's apartment and take a look at his bank and cell phone records.

"Good. Pray we'll come across something that could give us answers. Whoever in Human Resources hired him was taking orders from higher up. I'm hoping we'll catch a break here."

"After we make the search I'll get on the phone and help you talk to the other teachers and school staff who might be able to give us more information about Leroy."

"Claire will help us. We'll call everyone from home with the list the secretary gave me. Someone has to know about his private life and the people he hung out with. I'll call to let her know I'll be home soon." Vic held the steering wheel tighter. "I don't know what I'd do without you, Kit. *Someone has my son—*"

"We're going to find him, Vic."

Chapter Two

After hearing from Vic, Claire hung up and started to fix dinner. She was so horrified over Jeremy's disappearance that she'd lost her appetite. As for his poor father, she knew Vic wouldn't be able to eat, but he needed food in order to keep going. That meant making something light.

Taking stock of the groceries they had, she put together some dinner rolls with ham and cheese. Accompanied by fruit and hot coffee, they would hopefully tempt him. While she listened for Vic's car in the driveway, her mom phoned again to hear if there'd been any word on Jeremy.

"Not yet. Oh, Mom—" Claire broke down in tears. "I couldn't bear if anything happened to him."

"We're all praying he's found soon. Barbara and Kaye have offered to help any way they can."

She loved her sisters. "Tell them thank you."

"You have to have faith that Ranger Malone will find him."

"I do. You don't know how much I love that boy."

"I've known that for a long time."

Of course she did. Claire never stopped talking about him. "This is a nightmare, Mom. Oh—I think I hear Vic now. I'll call you later."

She clicked Off and dashed across the living room to the front door. When she opened it, Vic had just reached the porch. Before walking through the door, he flashed her a look that revealed his terror.

Claire followed him through the house to the kitchen. "What can I do to help?"

He'd gone over to the sink and was drinking water from the tap. The poor man had been gutted. Claire had never felt so helpless. Once he'd washed his hands, he turned to her while he wiped them with a towel. "How are you holding up? I haven't even thanked you for phoning me the moment you knew he'd disappeared."

"I'm all right," she lied. "After all the times we talked about what we should do in situations like this..." She fought the tears stinging her eyelids. "I just never thought..."

"That one would become reality?" he said.

"No."

"Neither did I," he ground out.

She took a deep breath. "Now that it has, I'm here to do anything you need."

"I've got dozens of phone calls to make while I wait to hear from Kit. We've put out an Amber Alert on Jeremy naming Leroy Bennett as his abductor."

"Who is he?"

In the next breath Vic told her all that had happened since he'd driven ninety miles an hour to the school, breaking every law in the process. "He could be any-where, Claire. As for Jeremy…"

"Come and sit down," she urged him. "I'll help you make those calls while we eat." She took the things she'd prepared out of the fridge and put the food on the kitchen table. The coffee was ready. She poured a cup for both of them.

To her relief, he sat down and pulled a folded sheet of paper from his pocket. "This is the list of the school staff. Someone who works there has to have informa-tion that could help us figure out where Leroy might have gone."

"Or know some of his habits," she murmured. "I agree. Why don't you call the names from *A* to *M* and I'll take *N* to *Z*? Just a second. I'll get some paper for us to take notes."

She ran to his office and pulled some sheets from the printer tray. After plucking two pens from his mug that said World's Greatest Dad—the mug she and Jeremy had bought for Vic's Christmas present—she returned and gave him the materials. He was already on the phone.

Claire pulled her phone out of her jeans pocket and got started on her section of the list. As they worked through the list of names, she noted with satisfaction that he automatically reached for a roll. Before long, three of the rolls had disappeared and he'd started on the grapes. She topped up his coffee and finished her section of the list.

But her spirits plummeted when it became clear that no matter how many calls they made, they weren't going to get any pertinent information on Leroy. Everyone said he was a loner. The gym teacher said Leroy had serious social problems, which corroborated what the woman at the apartment building had told Vic.

While Vic was still on the phone, Claire got an idea and phoned Nate's mom. "Sorry to bother you, Ann."

"Not at all. Did you find Jeremy?"

Claire struggled not to break down. "Not yet. We're still looking for him."

"Oh, no…what can I do to help?"

"Would you mind putting Nate on the phone? He and Jeremy are best friends. I'd just like to ask him a few questions without worrying him."

"Of course. I'll get him."

After a few seconds, Nate came on the line. "Hi, Claire." The boy sounded croupier than when she'd spoken with him earlier.

"How are you doing, bud?"

"Not very good."

"I'm sorry. Listen, Nate. I've got something really, really important to ask you. Do you know the custodian who cleans your room at school?"

"Is he the one with the big green eye on his arm?"

Claire swallowed hard. "I didn't know that. Has he ever talked to you?"

"Last Friday he was in the closet in the hall after class. He called out to me and Jeremy."

The admission filled her with alarm. "What did he want?"

"He said he had some neat tattoos to show us."

Her eyes closed tightly. "Had he ever talked to you two before?"

"No."

"What did you say?"

"We both kept walking."

"Good for you. That was exactly the right thing to do. Did you tell your mother?"

"No."

"Why not?"

"I forgot."

Good grief. Jeremy hadn't said anything to Claire or Vic either. She guessed the incident hadn't frightened them. "Thanks for telling me, Nate. I hope you get well soon. May I speak to your mom again?"

"Sure."

While she waited, she looked at Vic, who'd just gotten off the phone. "Nate's mom doesn't know everything that's happened. I think you need to talk to her. Nate just told me something scary. It happened last Friday."

When she related what Nate had told her, Vic reached for the phone and talked to Nate's mom while Claire took the dishes to the sink. After he hung up, he walked over to the stove to pour himself another cup of coffee.

"What made you think to call Nate?"

She turned to him. "Nobody at the school could give me any information. The custodians don't eat in the cafeteria and they don't attend the staff meetings. Leroy was invisible to the teachers I phoned on the list. But none of them had complaints about his work. At that point I figured maybe one of the kids might know something."

He studied her features for a moment. "Since you're

a chemist, I shouldn't be surprised you're a natural born detective. I think you're looking for work in the wrong field."

Claire smiled but let the remark pass.

"That bit of information from Nate about his wanting to show them his tattoos proves that Leroy was getting ready to set things up and had been waiting for the right moment to kidnap Jeremy."

"It was perfect timing. Nate was sick and didn't go to school today. The janitor saw Jeremy was alone and grabbed him. I'm sure that's exactly what happened."

"The kidnapping was no random act. It proves my theory that it was in retaliation for cracking down on the illegal gambling taking place at the Indian gaming casinos."

Claire was certain of it. "Nate says the janitor has a tattoo with a green eye."

"According to the rap sheet on him, he has snake tattoos running down his chest, too."

She shook her head in revulsion. "I take it you didn't learn any helpful information."

"No. So far you're the only person who's given me some clues to work with. If you weren't such a great nanny, you wouldn't have even known where he keeps those little magnets, let alone know the names of them. I'm indebted to you, Claire." His voice throbbed, revealing the depth of his pain.

"It's so little to work with."

"But every tiny scrap of evidence starts to form a pattern." His black eyes took on a savage look as he stared into space. "Frightening, isn't it, that people like

Leroy get into our school system when they have a prison record?"

She let out a gasp. "He was in prison?"

"On an involuntary manslaughter charge. It usually carries a sentence from ten to sixteen months. But he was let out after only serving three. Someone fixed it for him to be released early."

"How could he have gotten a job at the school?"

He raised his eyebrows. "Normally he couldn't, but someone high up the chain who has a vendetta against me made sure his record was expunged so he could be hired."

"Do you have an idea who it could be?"

"I've got a hunch, but it's a big one. Actually, several people come to mind." Politics was a dirty business. He could think of a few names, but they weren't for her ears.

Vic's phone buzzed and he grabbed for it. When he'd hung up, he turned to Claire and said, "Good old TJ. The Amber Alert has gone out with all the information on Jeremy and Leroy, including pictures."

"It's going to work, Vic. Whenever I get an alert on my phone, I'm extra vigilant. Someone out there is going to recognize one of them and call it in to the police."

In profile he looked as stiff as a block of wood. Heartsick, Claire started when her phone rang, too. She clicked On. "Dad?"

"Sweetheart. We were watching TV when the Amber Alert flashed across the screen."

"I know. It's out all over. Keep praying someone's going to have information."

"We're doing that. Are you okay?"

"I will be when Jeremy is home."

"You need to be extra careful."

"I know, but Vic has provided protection for me. Thanks for calling. I'll keep in touch with you. Love you."

She clicked Off and glanced at Vic, who took one phone call after another. He belonged to that special Ranger brotherhood known as the Sons of the Forty. No doubt they were calling Vic to give him hope and offer their services. Her heart ached for this courageous man who protected everyone else. Now it was time everyone came to *his* rescue. Inwardly, Claire was leading the charge.

While he was occupied, she went out back to the barn to check on the horses and make sure they had enough food and water. She moved to Comet's stall. "Hey, Comet." She patted his neck. "I know you've been looking for Jeremy. Sorry you didn't get your exercise today. We've all been looking for him." In a flood of emotion she rested her head against him. "He has to come home. He *has* to, or I don't know what I'll do."

While she hung on to Comet, she felt a hand cup her shoulder. She didn't realize Vic had come out to the barn. He'd probably heard her talking to the pony. His touch triggered her tears. She started sobbing and before she realized it, he'd pulled her into his arms. They clung to each other, seeking comfort while the tears gushed down her face, wetting his Western shirt.

As his body heaved with unshed tears, tearing her apart, she was aware of the warm smell of the horses combined with the soap he used in the shower. The heady combination plus the feel of his hard body reminded her he was a man as well as her employer. A beautiful man. A loving father. The ultimate protector. One who was utterly desirable and had been utterly devastated.

Shaken by the feelings coming from deep inside her while he was suffering unimaginable pain, she slowly eased herself out of his arms and stepped away. Since she'd been hired, she'd experienced too many emotions toward Jeremy and his father, and her emotions were now taking over. *Consuming her.* Tonight it was impossible to separate her feelings for Jeremy from the man who'd fathered him.

"Thank you for looking after the horses, Claire. Let's go back inside." He closed the barn doors behind them and they walked toward the house. Night had fallen. She shuddered to think of Jeremy out there somewhere, alone and terrified. Her mind wouldn't let her entertain the possibility that he wasn't alive. She could only imagine Vic's thoughts right now.

"What else can we do? Give me a job, any job, and I'll do it."

"It's a waiting game at the moment," Vic said as they went into the den, where he kept his computer. "Kit phoned back to let me know that no school district trucks were missing. It has to mean Leroy hid my son in the back of his truck, but where he took him is anyone's guess. If—"

"Don't say it, Vic. You'll find him alive. I *know* you will."

"You're right. I'm expecting a phone call from headquarters to keep me briefed on any results from the Amber Alert. And before long, I should hear from Kit, who's getting a warrant from the judge to search Bennett's apartment."

"Do you want me to keep you company, or would you rather be alone?"

His eyes swerved to her. "I'm thankful you're here."

Secretly glad he didn't mind her presence, she sat down in one of the leather chairs. "Have you told your sister-in-law?"

"No."

"What about Clint?" He was close to his second cousin.

He sat in the chair at his desk. "I'll give them both a call right now. The Amber Alert will shock them if they see it first. Thank you for—"

Just then his phone rang again. He wasn't on for long before he clicked off and jumped to his feet. "I'm heading over to Leroy's apartment. Kit got the warrant. Don't worry about your safety. The surveillance team will be watching you on a constant basis. I don't know when I'll be back. Take care, Claire."

She got up and walked him to the front door. "I'm sure you'll find something that will help."

"We've got to!" he called over his shoulder on the way to his car.

Her heart ached for him. His baby boy was missing. No parent was ever prepared for news like that, but if anyone could solve this case, Vic could. He was Jeremy's superhero.

Once Vic's car disappeared from view, she went to her bedroom to check her email. Claire had been on several job interviews already, but didn't think she would hear back from anyone this soon. But she needed something— *anything*—to do to keep busy until she heard from Vic.

He'd set up a desk for her in her bedroom, where she could study on her laptop. Since the day he'd hired her, no one could have been more thoughtful and considerate than Vic. The single-floor ranch style house was spacious with four bedrooms, a large kitchen, dining room and a den, where Vic kept an office. A family room off the vaulted living room contained an entertainment center with comfy couches and chairs. She'd fallen in love with the house, but tonight there was no Jeremy inside, and the place felt like a tomb.

Through bleary eyes she checked her inbox for new messages. To her surprise, two of the companies she'd applied to *had* responded to her. She opened the first one.

Dear Ms. Ames:
We would like you to come in for a second interview for the toxicologist/analytical chemist position at the new reference lab in the Houston–Sugar Land–Baytown area. As explained to you earlier, the lab is seeking a candidate for the day shift with experience in developing methods for urine toxicology drug testing on a wide menu of analytes. We have set up an interview with you on Friday, May 27, at 1:00 p.m. with the head

of the new lab. The salary range of $75,000–$110,000 is negotiable based on experience. Please respond ASAP.

She closed it and scrolled down to the email from Landry Scientific in Houston.

Dear Ms. Ames:
A staff member from Landry Scientific will be meeting with you on Thursday, May 26, at 11:00 a.m. for your second interview. The thrust of your work will be to conduct research, analysis, synthesis and experimentation on polymeric substances, for such purposes as product and process development and application, quantitative and qualitative analysis, and improvement of analytical methodologies. We are offering further incentives in terms of paying for additional schooling. The salary of $70,000 is negotiable based on experience and education. Please let us know if the meeting date and time are not convenient for you.

Claire buried her face in her hands. Pleased as she was at receiving this news, with Jeremy missing she couldn't think about more interviews right now. She could hardly breathe for the pain.

Too distraught to focus on anything, she closed her email and got ready for bed. While Vic was out actively pursuing the criminal who was responsible for Jeremy's disappearance, she was home, dying inside and unable to help.

Vic expected her to stay here. What if, by some miracle, the lowlife dropped Jeremy off somewhere and he was able to contact her? She had to stay put, but it was going to be the longest, most agonizing night of her life.

WITH KIT HELPING VIC, they scoured Leroy's empty apartment for clues, but there was nothing, not even a waste basket. After seeing the warrant, the manager had let them in.

"Does Bennett owe you money?" Vic asked.

"No, sir. He paid me cash up front for two months."

Vic exchanged glances with his partner. "So you knew he was leaving today?"

"That's right."

"Did you require a cleaning deposit?"

"Yes. He covered that, too."

"You knew he'd been in prison?"

"A lot of guys have served time. He said he had a job at a school as a custodian. As long as they pay me, I don't care."

"Did he tell you anything about where he might be going?"

"I asked, but he said it was none of my damn business."

"The woman across the hall said he drove an older blue pickup truck."

"Yeah."

"Anything you noticed about it besides the dents?

"Like what?"

"Anything that would make it different from another truck just like it."

"Um, I do remember one thing. There was an oval

decal on the back window with a crazy word like *duda* printed on it. Are you through with me? I've got to get back to my apartment. I've got dinner on the stove."

"Go ahead."

The second he walked away, Vic phoned headquarters to report the decal. After he hung up, Kit said, "I've learned that Jamison Lowell was the person who hired Leroy. He's no longer working for the school district office, but I have the guy's address."

Vic clenched his jaw. "Let's go find him."

Kit followed him to East Austin and they pulled up in front of a rambler home with a tidy yard. After walking to the front door, Vic rang the bell and they waited. When no one answered, he rang it again. This was like déjà vu.

"Stay there and keep trying. I'll run next door to the neighbor's house and find out what I can." Kit took off. Vic walked around the house and used his flashlight to look in the windows. The place was empty.

When he could hear voices from next door, he hurried over to join Kit, who introduced him to an older couple.

"These people here say that the Lowells moved last week. They don't know where, but figure they wanted to be near their only daughter, who's married and lives in Colorado."

"Do you know where in Colorado?" Vic pressed.

The woman pondered the question. "I'm pretty sure the daughter and her husband live in Vail. They do a lot of skiing."

"Do you know their last name?"

"I think it might be Preston," the husband said.

"Do you know what kind of car the Prestons have? Maybe from when they visited the Lowells?"

"A blue, four-door Passat."

"Thank you. You've been very helpful."

"I hope the Lowells aren't in any trouble. They're such nice people. He worked with the school district you know. We hated to see them move."

"Sudden, was it?" Vic stared at both of them.

The man nodded. "Yes, but then we didn't know that much about their family."

"I don't see a for sale sign on the lawn."

"Not yet."

Vic reached for his wallet and handed them his business card. "Please call my office when you find out the name of the Realtor selling the house."

"We will. Good night."

Once they were back at their cars, Vic pounded his fist against his windshield. "This has been organized for several months, Kit. I never saw this coming. Jeremy could be anywhere. He—"

"We'll find him," Kit broke in. "I'll follow you home and contact the Vail police. They'll do a search for a family with the last name Preston. We've got the make of the car. As for you, you need to get some rest. When we get to your place we'll talk strategy until you're too tired to think and can sleep."

"I'll never be able to sleep, not while my son is missing."

"Then take a sleeping pill—otherwise you won't be good for anything. Take a shower first. It'll help you relax."

Once at Vic's house, Vic told Kit to help himself to some coffee and started down the hall. He stopped at Jeremy's bedroom. It was unearthly still. Jeremy was gone. Pain attacked Vic's whole body. He sagged against the doorjamb for a minute and let out the sobs that kept coming.

God in heaven, preserve his life. Help me find him.

Brushing a hand across his face, he straightened and began to walk toward his room at the end of the hall. As he passed Claire's room, he noticed that she'd left the door open and her bedside lamp was on.

"Claire?"

"I'm here." She opened the door wider. "I heard you come in."

Her feminine silhouette was framed by the soft light. The gold strands in her hair gleamed among the copper. She wore the same kind of pajamas Jeremy wore with superheroes on them. A fragrance like peaches wafted past him. She must have washed her hair while he'd been gone. Jeremy loved this woman.

He cleared his throat. "Kit came home with me. I'm going to shower, and then we're going to work out a plan to find Jeremy."

"I'm glad Kit is with you. I'll make you both something to eat."

Grateful she was here, he headed for his bedroom. When he emerged ten minutes later, he found her in the kitchen wearing a navy blue bathrobe over her pajamas. She'd made waffles and sausage. Kit was putting food away like he'd never had a meal before.

Vic walked over to the kitchen table and sat down. "I owe you big time, Kit."

He looked up. "I'm still trying to pay you back for all the times you had my back. Your nanny is taking great care of me. These waffles are the best. Don't tell me you can't eat. You have to eat. Jeremy needs you."

"He does," Claire's voice echoed. Vic raised his eyes to hers. She was a beautiful woman even without makeup. Those gray eyes of hers begged him to eat and take care of himself.

Making up his mind he said, "I'll take whatever Kit is having."

A smile broke out on her face. "Coming right up." They ate every waffle she put on their plates. "If you're full, why not go in the living room so you can lie down on the couch."

Claire smiled at Kit, who got up first and urged Vic to follow him. He'd refused to take a sleeping pill. She was hoping that with some good food inside him, fatigue would take over and he'd fall asleep.

"I'm going to stretch out, too." Kit sat down in one of the fat leather chairs and put his feet up on the ottoman.

Vic had come to the table barefoot. She could see his eyelids drooping when he lay down on the couch wearing sweats and a T-shirt. He had to be exhausted.

Before long, both men were asleep. She took her cell

phone out of her pocket and snapped a picture of them. If she had it blown up and framed, the plaque beneath would say "Two of the Famous Four Texas Rangers at rest."

When Jeremy was found—and he *would* be found, Claire had made up her mind about that—she'd present this precious gift for him to treasure. She'd tell him this was the shape his father was in after searching for him nonstop all day and night. That was how much he loved him.

Claire sat in the chair matching the one Kit occupied and looped her arms around her raised knees to watch over them. She didn't know when she fell asleep, but the ringing of someone's cell phone woke her up. Her watch said ten after six in the morning.

Vic jackknifed into a sitting position and answered his phone. At this point Kit had awakened and stood up. She overheard Vic say the name TJ. He was talking to the head of the Rangers.

When he disconnected, he sprang to his feet. "The police caught up with Leroy at an all-night bar in Buda."

"Buda? It's not that far away. Thank heaven!" she cried.

"Amen to that. Leroy's truck was parked outside. The logo the apartment building manager told us about helped find him fast. That clue saved the day. He thought it said 'duda' or something close. The officers have taken him into custody at the jail downtown. Guess who was with him?"

"The two guys who got in the fight with him at the park."

"You're right on the money, Kit. They were hauled in for questioning, too. Let's go. I'll get changed and meet you outside."

After he disappeared, Claire turned to Kit. "Can I come with you?"

"I know how much you love Jeremy, but this is a police matter."

"But I feel responsible."

"In what way?"

"The second I didn't see Jeremy, I should have run right in the school instead of waiting in the car for a few more minutes."

"That wouldn't have made any difference, Claire. This kidnapping was planned down to the second. You shouldn't feel any guilt, but I guess it's human nature."

"It is," she said. "I can't stay here and just wait and wait."

He studied her for a moment. "Maybe you can't come with us, but if you drive down to the city jail, I'll tell them to let you in. You can talk to Vic after he's through vetting Leroy."

"Thank you, Kit." She smiled at him gratefully and raced to her bedroom to get dressed.

It took her only a minute to pull on some jeans and a knit top. She slipped on her walking sandals. After brushing her hair, she grabbed her purse and ran through the house to the door behind the kitchen. It led to the garage.

After she'd activated the remote, she backed out and took off for downtown Austin. Out of the corner of her eye, she saw a van parked a few houses away and knew it was the surveillance team. Before long she realized they were following her. Those were Vic's instructions.

I love him. I love his son.

She knew where to find the jail. One day several months ago, she'd humored Jeremy by driving him to see it. Claire had so many memories of him.

After making sure her car door was locked, she walked to the entrance, where an officer met her.

"Can I see some ID?"

She pulled her license from her wallet and showed it to him.

"You're Ms. Ames. Ranger Saunders said to let you in. You can sit in the lounge to wait for him." He checked the contents of her purse and gave it back to her.

"Thank you."

When she opened the door, the cold blast of A/C was welcome. Vic probably wouldn't like it that she'd come, but she couldn't stand to sit in the house and do nothing. Kit understood that. A dozen or so others were also waiting in the lounge. But they were here to visit inmates and had to wait until it was their turn.

It was a whole other world down here. Claire shuddered. This was the dark side of life Vic had to deal with day in and day out. But to face the man who'd kidnapped Jeremy had to be something else altogether. She'd never seen Vic's dark side. She didn't believe he had one. But this morning he was going to be tested.

Claire decided it was a good thing she wasn't the one in that jail cell with Leroy. The urge to strangle that monster with her bare hands was so strong she wasn't sure she'd be able to contain it.

Chapter Three

Vic stood in the corner while two guards brought Leroy into the room, his arms behind his back, hands and ankles shackled. His attorney walked in behind them. Kit stood in the hall on the other side of the one-way glass to watch what was going on. Later he'd interrogate Leroy's friends one at a time.

The school custodian had been put in a black-and-white-striped shirt and pants. The guards pulled out a chair in front of the small table in the bare room and helped him into it. Vic nodded to them and they left. The attorney took a seat in the chair next to him. Vic didn't recognize him.

Curious, he walked around behind Leroy and peeked at the green eye tattooed to his inner left arm. It was ghoulish. Leroy sat there with his head down. White-hot fury was building inside of Vic and threatening to take over, but he had to remember that this wreck of a human being was his only route to Jeremy. Vic went back to the other side of the table.

"Is my son still alive?"

No answer.

"I want to know who paid you money to kidnap my son. You've committed a federal crime. If you tell me where you've hidden him and I find him alive, then you'll only have to serve twenty-five years in prison instead of life." He stared at the attorney. "Tell him what I just said so he'll believe it."

"We've already talked. My client wants a jury trial, no plea bargain."

Someone was paying big dollars for Leroy's defense. Had they bought the judge, too? "If you're going for a verdict of insanity, it won't stick. Otherwise you wouldn't have been hired at the school." Vic leaned over the table with his hands on the top. "A jury will convict you and throw away the key."

"My client will take his chances."

His jaw hardened. "Even if you know my son's friend is going to be put on the stand? He'll testify that you tried to entice him and Jeremy into the custodian's closet outside his classroom to see your *other* tattoos." Vic's anger was kindled. "Speak up now while I'm still in the mood to listen."

Leroy sat there like a vegetable, infuriating Vic until he saw red. He lunged across the table and grabbed his shoulders. "Talk to me you worthless coward—"

"Ranger Malone?" He heard Kit's voice, but he was still so livid, he couldn't think. "Can I talk to you for a minute?"

The interruption got through to Vic, forcing him to release Leroy. On legs that felt as heavy as water, he moved past Kit into the hall.

His friend shut the door. "Hey, bud. I want to beat

the crap out of him, too, but when you grabbed the prisoner, you gave his attorney ammunition against you. I wager he'll inform the captain what happened in there and he won't sugarcoat it. Come on. Let's get you out of here. You need to go home. Claire's outside in the waiting room. She'll follow you."

His head jerked around. "What's she doing here?"

"She wants answers badly, too. Before we left the house she told me she felt guilty because she waited too long to go inside the school when Jeremy didn't come out right away."

"That's absurd."

"It is, but like I told her, it's a human reaction to an impossible situation. I'm still waiting to interrogate the two guys brought in with Leroy. When I find out anything, I'll phone you. Now do what you have to do to stay out of trouble and *go home*."

"I can't do that."

"You *have* to."

He raked a hand through his hair. "If it were your son…"

"If it were my son, then you'd be the one telling me to get a grip and go home."

"But I'm heading up this case!"

Kit shook his head. "Before I left headquarters the captain told me to keep an eye on you. He's asking someone else to take over the investigation. You're too close to it. Get out of here before the attorney sees you and files battery charges against you."

Vic knew his friend was speaking the truth, but his agony over what had happened to his son had affected his ability to control himself. If he'd had time alone in there with that creep, there'd be nothing left of Leroy. This was a living nightmare.

"Are you ready?" Kit murmured.

No. He'd never be ready while Jeremy was out there suffering, but this was one time when he needed to follow someone else's counsel. There was no one he trusted more than Kit.

After taking a deep breath, he followed him down the hall to the door that led to the lounge.

Claire saw him immediately and hurried over to him. The worry lines on her lovely face reminded him he wasn't the only one in pain over Jeremy's disappearance. "I wish I had any new information, Claire. For now all we can do is go home. Kit's going to call me after he's questioned the other two prisoners brought in with Leroy. We're investigating several leads I'll tell you about after we get back to the house."

They left the jail and he walked her to her car. "Drive safely. I'll see you in a few minutes."

"Is there anything I can do for you? Any shopping?" Her heart was in her eyes.

"If there is, I can't think of what."

"Then I'll see you at home."

He watched her drive away before he strode over to his car and got in. He put his head back against the headrest and closed his eyes for a minute. Never in his life had he come close to feeling like he did when he put his hands on Leroy. For a few seconds he'd lost complete awareness of his surroundings. If it hadn't been for Kit watching his back, he'd have beaten that lowlife to a pulp before realizing what he'd done.

Temporary insanity. That's what the defense called momentary madness. Never in his wildest dreams would he have thought he could be capable of forgetting the oath he'd taken to uphold the law. He ached for his son. But he'd compounded that ache by trying to take vengeance into his own hands. No jury, no trial. He'd been the executioner while his prisoner couldn't fight back.

What he'd done would never bring his son home. It would take him a long time to forgive himself for what had almost happened. He heard a horn honk and sat forward. It was Kit, waving to him before he drove off.

Humbled by the other Ranger's friendship during the darkest time of Vic's despair, he started the engine and left for home. As he pulled into the driveway, his cell phone rang. He checked the caller ID. It was TJ.

Vic dreaded the phone conversation they were about to have, but he had to answer it.

He clicked On. "TJ?"

"It's a damn shame about your son, but I still have to do my job. I just got off the phone with the DA who's going to prosecute Leroy's case. You overstepped your bounds at the jail. Though I've taken you off the case, I haven't suspended you. As for now, you're on vacation. I suggest you get some counseling with the department psychiatrist."

He knew the captain was cutting him slack by not suspending him, but he'd never felt so helpless in his life. "Yes, sir. Have you put Kit in charge?"

"Kit's too close to you. I've put Ranger Rodriguez on it. He'll be objective."

Vic groaned.

"I'm a father and can only imagine how I would feel and react if my son or daughter had been kidnapped. But there are still consequences to pay. After some therapy you can report for duty. I need you back on the force ASAP. I want you to call the psychiatric unit today and set up some appointments with the doctor you used before."

TJ meant Dr. Marshall, the psychiatrist who'd helped Vic deal with his grief after the tornado struck.

"We need you, Vic. You're one of our best and that's not lip service. We're all sending up prayers that your son will be returned to you soon."

Vic knew that. "Thanks, TJ."

Rodriguez was a good Ranger, but his instincts weren't quick like Vic's closest buddies. TJ's choice to head up this case was made on purpose because like Kit, he knew that Vic's other friends, Cy and Luckey, were too close to Vic to be objective. Vic got it, but he didn't like it.

After saying goodbye he left for home. It was ten o'clock in the morning. Jeremy should be at school and Vic should be on the job chasing down leads. How in the hell was he going to make it? But a nagging voice inside said *Because Jeremy needs you.*

Vic needed his son more.

Letting out a tortured sigh, he parked in the drive-way and climbed out of the car. Claire stood waiting for him at the front door. She had a way of making everyone feel good.

"Hi, Claire. How would you like to go for a horseback ride?"

She blinked. "Right now?"

"Right now. I'll change into my cowboy boots. The horses need exercise. It's time you and I had a talk."

That sounded ominous to Claire. "I'll put on my boots," she said, wondering what he had to say.

They walked out to the barn together. He brought their equipment out of the tack room so they could saddle and bridle their horses. Vic put a lead on Comet. Once they were mounted, they left the barn. Comet walked by Midnight's side with Claire and Marshmallow on the other.

For a little while they rode around the five acres in silence. Vic was deep in thought. When they'd gone the full distance, he dismounted near the fencing and let the horses graze. Claire followed suit, troubled by the lines of grief carved in his rugged features. "What did you want to talk to me about?"

He walked over to the fence and leaned back against it. "A little bit of everything. First off, Kit told me you're feeling guilty for the part you've played in Jeremy's disappearance. You did nothing wrong. Neither did anyone else. Some evil men planned this kidnapping with expert precision."

"I realize that."

"Today I lost my cool at the jail and came close to strangling Leroy Bennett."

"That's all I've been able to think about doing," she admitted.

"Well, I went too far when I grabbed him by the shoulders. Leroy's attorney was there and witnessed my actions. Kit saw it, too, and stopped me before I did something terrible. I was supposed to interrogate Leroy, nothing else. Because I crossed the line, I've been told to take a vacation from work while I get counseling." His black eyes glittered. "Does that alarm you?"

"No."

"It should."

"I may not be Jeremy's mother, but my grief is so real that I can't honestly say what I'd do if I had the chance to get that custodian alone. I'd slap him so hard he'd cry out for mercy." Her voice shook.

A sad smile broke out on Vic's face. "In my case, the captain feels someone else needs to head up this investigation while I get therapy."

Her spirits sank lower. "I'm so sorry, Vic. Is Kit going to be in charge?"

"No. He's putting another Ranger named Rodriguez in charge, and my hands are tied. I'm afraid that none of the four Sons of the Forty will be dealing with this case any longer. It's the right thing to do. Today my judgment went to hell when that criminal was sitting in front of me. It would probably go to hell again were I to be in charge any longer."

"That's because your son is missing and you're too close to the situation. I couldn't be objective, either."

"Which leads me to the next topic I wanted to discuss with you. Have you had any responses since your last two interviews?"

"I have. Actually, they both want me to come in for another interview. But I can't think about that right now. Like you, my judgment is totally impaired. How can I make smart decisions about my future when every minute I'm waiting for the phone to ring with the news that Jeremy has been found? This is no way for either of us to live, Vic. So I have an idea."

He moved away from the fence and put his hands on his hips in a way that was all male. When he did that, she couldn't help but feast her eyes on him. "What's that?"

"Since you're on vacation, what's to stop you and me from looking for leads on our own time? While Ranger Rodriguez conducts an official investigation, we can do our own thing behind the scenes and work around your therapy sessions. You have creative genius. That's what Kit tells me, and I've seen it for myself. So why don't we follow some of your hunches and see what we can come up with undercover, so to speak? Otherwise I'll go crazy, too."

"It's no wonder Jeremy loves you so much. He says you're more fun than any of his friends."

"That's high praise." She laughed sadly.

"It is. The only trouble with your suggestion is we won't be playing for fun. What we do could be very dangerous."

"More dangerous than what has happened to Jeremy?" she challenged. "We've got to find him, Vic, and I know you couldn't possibly let this case go. Jeremy needs us." She moved closer to him. "Will you think about it?"

"*Claire*—Damn it. Your tears get to me every time."

"So do yours," she whispered. "Call that psychiatrist and set up your therapy schedule. We'll plan each day according to your appointment and then follow a different lead until your son comes home. No one has to know what we're doing. We'll fly under the radar."

"You watch too many *Law and Order* shows."

"I've learned a few things, but there's no better teacher than you. Jeremy idolizes the ground you walk on."

He smoothed a tendril of hair away from her eyes. "Today I came home feeling like I was dying. But your idea has given me some new energy. You're good for me, Claire." He pressed a brief kiss to her mouth. The first he'd ever given her. "My greatest fear is that I won't be good for you. If anything happened to you because of me…"

"Nothing's going to happen to either one of us." Her whole body tingled from the kiss he'd just given her. She knew he was seeking comfort and didn't look at it in any other way. "Let's get back to the house. While you call to arrange your therapy sessions, I'll fix us lunch and we'll plan our strategy. After we've eaten, we'll get started."

"Sounds like a plan."

They mounted their horses. This time she grabbed Comet's lead and he walked next to her and Marshmallow. Vic took off in a gallop to give his horse a workout. Then he galloped back and walked with them the rest of the way to the barn.

While he took care of the horses and fed them, she went in the house. After washing her hands, she made tuna fish sandwiches, a Malone family favorite. She added a bowl of potato chips and some sodas. He made the call to set up his therapy appointments, then sat down at the kitchen table with her to eat.

She pushed the bowl in front of him. "What's the verdict?"

"I'm going to see Dr. Marshall every weekday starting tomorrow. He's aware of why the captain has given me vacation time. Fortunately for me, he's willing to accommodate me so I won't lose too much time before getting back to work. I'm supposed to report to him in the mornings at nine. The sessions are usually an hour."

"Do you know this doctor?"

"Yes. He gave me counseling after the tornado happened. That was such a black period—I try to block it from my mind. But I swear this experience is worse. Jeremy is so young with his whole life ahead of him…"

"Children and animals," she murmured. "They're so helpless." She finished her sandwich. "I'm glad you'll be seeing someone who knows your history."

"He's a good man."

"Vic? What's the first thing you would do if you were still in charge?"

"I'd drive to Buda and talk to someone in the bar." Claire recognized that with his razor-sharp brain, he'd already known what his next move would be. "It's only a half hour drive from here. I want to find out if anyone there knew Leroy. Was he a regular? What was the draw when he could have gone anywhere else?"

"I've been wondering the same thing. When he joined the military, where was his home?"

"The rap sheet listed his home as Austin."

"Buda's considered to be on the outskirts of the metro area. Maybe he's from there, Vic, or he has a relative there and that's why he had a decal on his truck. People don't put things like that on their cars or trucks unless it's meaningful for them."

"Agreed."

"We could check local auto body shops to find out if his truck was ever worked on there. I was also wondering where he got his tattoos."

Vic nodded. "We'll check out the local tattoo parlors."

"I've never been in one."

"It can be an illuminating experience."

She got up from the table. "I'll hurry and clean up the kitchen so we can leave."

"I'll help."

Claire eyed him for a moment. "Are you going to tell anyone what we're doing?"

"Not unless it becomes necessary. I suggest you don't tell your family, either."

"I won't. They're worried sick over Jeremy as it is."

A shadow passed over his face. "I need to find a connection to the person who got Leroy released from prison early. But we're going to have to do it the hard way because I can't let anyone know I'm a Ranger."

"Maybe we're private investigators working on a

case for an insurance company. You're Jim and I'm Elaine. We'll wear sunglasses."

Low laughter escaped his throat. "When I hired you to work for me, I had no idea how amazing you are."

She looked away. "Not amazing, just desperate to find Jeremy." Being his father, Vic knew all about that.

They cleaned up together. "Thanks for fixing lunch. It hit the spot."

"I'm glad. Give me a second to find my sunglasses and I'll meet you at the car."

"I'll run off a picture of Leroy for both of us. If I crop them, no one will know it came from his prison mug shot. While I do that, I'll tell the guys in the surveillance van they can leave until further notice because I'm on vacation."

"It's a good thing you're the Ranger," she said. "The thought wouldn't have occurred to me until after we reached Buda."

It wasn't long before they were driving away from the house wearing their disguises. He turned to her and smiled. With his thick, black hair and handsome features, Claire thought Vic was much better looking than any movie star or celebrity. She smiled back, trying to quell the rapid pounding of her heart.

They couldn't see each other's eyes. This was fun. In spite of the agonizing pain they were both suffering, it *was* fun to be doing something so important together.

"I need you to be my navigator." He reached in the glove compartment and handed her his iPad. "It's charged. Let's visit some tattoo places first. We don't want to go to the bar until evening."

Claire was thrilled to be given something to do. She started looking up addresses. "There are thirty listings throughout Austin. Buda has two shops."

"That'll make our job easy."

Buda was only fifteen miles south of downtown along the I-35 corridor. They found the first parlor using the GPS in his car. When they went inside, it reminded her of a beauty salon with the workers' individual areas. Two guys were getting tattoos.

"Hi!" An employee walked up to them. "Which one of you wants a tattoo?" He eyed Claire. "I can match a tattoo to the beautiful copper tint of your hair. It would look amazing."

"Thanks, but we're not here to get tattoos. My name's Elaine. This is Jim. We're private investigators working for an insurance company and wonder if you've ever seen this man in your shop." She pulled out the picture and showed it to him. "He has a green eye tattoo on the inside of his left wrist, and two snakes tattooed on his chest."

The guy shook his head. "Nope. I've done snakes and some eyes, but this dude isn't familiar."

"Maybe the other employees would recognize him?" Vic suggested.

"No. I run this shop and know everyone who comes in to get a tattoo."

"Okay, then. Thanks for your time," Claire said.

He flicked her another glance. "Sure I can't give you one?"

"Positive." She smiled.

Vic held the door open for her and they walked out

to his car. When they got in, he eyed her speculatively. "You're such a natural at this, it's spooky. I guess you realize that guy was checking you out."

"Hey, honey—I'm a hard-boiled private eye, so I don't mind as long as there's no touching," she teased.

He burst into unexpected laughter. When it subsided he said, "Where's the second shop? I want you to take the lead again. You're a pro."

With that compliment she took a quick breath before giving him the next address. Vic had no idea how much she wanted to be of help.

The next parlor was very modern and had a myriad of designs mounted on the walls. She saw a pink eye and a whole slew of snake tattoos. This time a woman covered in tattoos with ruby red hair approached them. Her gaze fastened on Vic. "Hi, I'm Zena and I run this shop. What can I do for you?"

No question this was Vic's turn.

"Sorry to bother you. My name's Jim. This is Elaine. We're private investigators working on a case for an insurance company. Have you ever seen this man in your shop?" He pulled the picture of Leroy from the pocket of his sport shirt. "He has a green eye tattoo on his inside wrist and two snakes on his chest."

She studied the picture for a minute and shook her head. "Never seen him before."

"Do you think one of your employees might have worked on him?"

"I know everyone who gets a tattoo here. Sorry I can't help."

"So am I," Vic said. Claire could hear the disappointment in his voice.

"If *you* ever want a tattoo—"

"I'll keep you in mind," he said before she could finish her sentence.

Claire followed him outside to the car, wishing she could do something to boost his spirits. "Let's go to Buda Graphic Design for autos and trucks next. I looked it up. They sell stickers and logos for cars. Maybe we'll get lucky."

"Maybe," he said without much conviction.

When he pulled up in front of the store, he turned to her. "I'll run in. Be back in a minute."

Since he wanted to be alone, she looked up the name of the local high school and found out there were two of them. On a whim, she called the office of the first school and got the secretary on the phone.

"Hi. I'm only in Buda for the day and wondered if I could speak to the librarian please."

"I'll see if Mrs. Marchant is available. Just a moment."

While Claire watched for Vic, she waited.

"Hello?"

"Hello. My name's Elaine Jarvis. I live in Austin, but I'm in Buda for the day, and I'm trying to find out if a friend of mine from long ago attended the high school here. His name is Leroy Bennett. I've lost track of him. He served in Iraq and probably would have been a student here twenty years ago. Maybe he was in the ROTC?"

"Oh, my goodness. I wouldn't have any idea."

"What I was hoping was that you could pull out a couple of yearbooks from nineteen or twenty years ago to see if his name was listed as one of the students."

"I'm afraid I don't have that kind of time. If you come to the library, I could show you where to look."

"Would that be all right?"

"Yes. You'll have to report to the office first and they'll give you a pass."

"I have a friend with me. Could he come, too?"

"I don't see why not."

"Thank you very much, Mrs. Marchant. We'll be there soon."

Vic would probably think it was a waste of time, but she kept thinking about the decal on Leroy's truck. Of course she could be way off track if that logo had been put there by a previous owner. There were so many ifs to do with this case, she was driving herself crazy. But the heartsick expression on Vic's face when he came out to the car made her more determined than ever to find the smoking gun that would bring Jeremy home.

He got in behind the wheel. "No one recognized him or remembered selling him a sticker like that. It's an old one."

That was what she'd been afraid of. "While you were inside, I made a call to one of the local high schools." He flicked a questioning glance at her. "I thought we'd look through a couple of old yearbooks in the library and see if he happened to be a student here at one time."

"Your brain astounds me."

"Now you have an idea of how I feel about yours,"

she said. When she looked over at him he was smiling. "Are you laughing at me?"

"No. I'm seeing what my son has seen in you from the moment you came into our lives. To be honest, I'm awed by your brilliant mind."

"If it's brilliant, it's because I love Jeremy so much and intend to help you find him." *He's a part of you, Vic. Don't you know that?*

Chapter Four

Since Claire had come to work for Vic as Jeremy's nanny, they had developed a natural camaraderie that made what they were doing easy. She really did have an inquisitive mind and thought outside the box.

"The science of chemistry suits your investigative skills, Claire. I don't need another Ranger with me to track down fresh leads when I have you."

"I could be completely wrong about this."

"I don't know. So far your intuition has been spot on."

He drove to the high school. After being given a pass, they went upstairs to the library. The librarian was holding class, but she showed them the shelves where they could find the yearbooks. Before long they'd pulled out three yearbooks for the years Leroy might have been a student there and took them to an empty table.

But after scanning each book, they came up empty-handed. While Vic reshelved the books, Claire thanked the librarian, then they left the school. "I found out this is the newer high school. The older one is on the other side of town. Before we give up on this idea, why don't we drive over there? The librarian gave me the address."

Why not? Vic trusted Claire's instincts. "Let's go," he said.

On the drive, Kit texted him. When they reached the school parking lot, he found a spot to park and turned off the engine. Along with the text were the mug shots of the two men arrested with Leroy.

Vic—I'm no longer officially on the case either, but from a friend who works at the jail, I learned the names of the two men who were arrested with Leroy outside the bar last night. Fidel Flores, 39, Austin, mechanic at Angelo's Body Shop was let go because he got to work late and left early too many times. Armando Varena, 38, Austin, laid off construction worker. I checked with Meyer's Construction. They said Varena had a drinking problem.

Ranger Rodriguez is still holding both men for questioning. I also learned another piece of information from my source. Leroy worked as a mechanic at the same body shop as Fidel after he returned from Iraq, but they had to let him go because of his problems with PTSD.

Good old Kit. Vic texted him back. My debt to you keeps growing. I'll keep digging around on my own. Hang in there. We'll find Jeremy.

I have to find him.

Once Vic had clicked Send, he handed Claire his phone so she could read the text.

"Couldn't Kit get into trouble for this?"

"Yes."

"Bless him." Her voice trembled. "If both men had access to other cars and trucks, maybe that's where Leroy picked up the blue truck. We could drive to Angelo's tomorrow and do some questioning on our own. That logo has to be on the window for a reason. Maybe someone who works there will know."

He nodded. "Once again we're on the same wavelength. Shall we go check out the library first and see if we can find anything?"

"Yes, and this time we've got three names to look up."

Vic squeezed her hand before they left the car. After they received permission to visit the library, he cupped her elbow as they climbed a flight of stairs to the second floor. They'd arrived during a change of classes and had to battle the crowds of noisy, boisterous students. She flashed him a smile. "I'm so glad I'm not in high school anymore."

He chuckled as they entered the library and were shown where to find the yearbooks. They ended up with three volumes to check. "This is a long shot, but I believe you know what you're doing, Claire. I have to admit that if I were with Kit, neither one of us would have thought of checking old yearbooks."

She lifted her head, smoothing some of the coppery gold strands from her forehead. "You'd have probably gotten around to it, but with your heartache it would be almost impossible to think as clearly as you do with other cases." Claire went right back to her search. It reminded him of all the times she'd worked on her studies after Jeremy had gone to bed.

He'd see her in the family room, sitting on the couch with her laptop. Her hard work and dedication had resulted in Claire's earning her master's degree with honors, yet she ran the household and took wonderful care of Jeremy at the same time. Not only was Vic proud of her, he'd learned to admire her. Jeremy adored her. *Jeremy*...

A sudden sharp pain stabbed him right between the ribs, and Vic picked up another yearbook. As he was looking up names in the index at the back, he heard a small cry escape Claire's lips.

"What did you find?"

"Look at this!" She handed him the yearbook. "Fidel Flores has one listing. It's his junior class picture."

Vic grabbed the yearbook for the next year and tried to find Flores as a senior, but he wasn't included. His gaze fused with Claire's. "This could be the tie to Buda that brought Leroy here! Maybe Jeremy is here, somewhere... I've decided you're my lucky charm, Claire. Let's find out if Fidel's parents or family still live here."

"How can you do that without using your sources at the Bureau?"

"Let's go out to the car and start making phone calls to every Flores who lives here. If we don't turn up any info, I'll phone Clint. My cousin might be able to help us with a more thorough search because of his police connections."

After Vic took a picture of Flores with his camera, they reshelved the yearbooks and hurried out to the car.

Claire pulled out her phone. "I'll do a statewide search on the various search engines."

He nodded. "While you do that, I'll call information for Buda." To his frustration, there was no Flores listed. After he hung up, he looked at Claire. "Anything from your end?"

"There are 100 listings for Flores in the state of Texas on Instant Checkmate. It's a daunting task if we decide to go through them one by one."

"Why don't we check out any auto mechanic shops while we're here and show them Fidel's picture? Maybe he's been seen around. You never know. First, I'll drive us back to the Buda Graphic Design shop. Even if they didn't recognize Leroy, they may know Flores."

Claire nodded and started looking up addresses. "There are eight listings for mechanics on this site. We can investigate one at a time."

"After we're finished, let's head to that steak house we passed a minute ago and eat dinner before we head on over to the bar."

"That sounds good."

Within an hour they'd canvased the area, but no one they spoke with knew or recognized Fidel Flores or Leroy Bennett. Frustrated, Vic drove them to the restaurant. They both ordered steak and salad. After the waitress walked away, Claire said, "I think that when we visit the bar where Leroy was arrested, we should go in separately."

Vic shook his head. "There's no way I'd let you go in there alone."

"But you'll be there keeping an eye on me. If we're

both alone, our chances of picking up information will increase."

"A woman like you walking in there alone is asking for trouble."

"But if I sit at the bar, then—"

"Then nothing! We'll go in as Jim and Elaine, insurance investigators trying to find a missing person."

"Was Leroy arrested inside or outside the bar?"

"Outside, according to what Kit told me before they impounded the truck."

She shook her head. "To think they'd gone there to drink when he'd just kidnapped Jeremy… It's incomprehensible. To be honest, I don't know how you're holding up, Vic."

"I wouldn't be functioning if it weren't for you." Every time he gave her credit, she came closer to breaking down. "Come on. Let's go."

He put some bills on the table and they walked out to his car. After finding the address for Shorty's Bar on the GPS, they drove there in silence. "It's a crummy-looking establishment," she murmured. "There aren't very many cars parked out here."

"It's only five to eight. The hard-core night crowd won't show up for a few hours. This is the perfect time for us to go in and ask some questions. Follow my lead. Maybe we'll get lucky and the bartender will be in a good mood."

She nodded before they got out of the car and walked into the darkened room. The small place reeked of smoke and old age. Canned country music poured out of the speakers. A middle-aged guy sat at the bar. There were other men sitting in the booths lining the walls. Claire stood out in the sleazy atmosphere, not only because she was the only woman there, but because she was too attractive for her own good.

After they found two stools at the end of the bar, Vic nodded to the barrel-chested bartender who'd been pouring a drink for the man sitting by himself. He walked toward them. "What can I get you?"

Vic put down a twenty dollar bill and the picture of Flores. "Two colas and some information about this guy. This is a high school photo from twenty years ago when he lived here in Buda with his family. Have you ever seen him? We work for an insurance company that wants to ask him some questions."

The bartender put two glasses in front of them and poured them their sodas. Then he held the picture closer. "Yeah. This guy's been in here before."

"When did you last see him?"

"Last night. He was hauled off by the police. You can find him in jail."

"Do you know if he still has family around here?"

"I don't know. Shorty owns this place and has done for thirty years, but he won't be in for about a half hour. He knows everyone in the area. Maybe he'll be able to tell you something."

"Thank you."

Vic's eyes slid to Claire. "Let's find us a booth while we wait." They carried their drinks to an empty one. He sat across from her.

"Why didn't you show him Leroy's picture?" she asked.

"If I'd done that, he'd start to wonder who I really am. In case Ranger Rodriguez decides to investigate here further, we're better off sticking with Flores on an insurance matter so it won't send up any red flags."

"Of course. How could I forget you've been ordered to stay away from the case. Maybe I should go out to the car and let you be the one to talk to Shorty. You know…in case Ranger Rodriguez shows up."

"It's too late now. The bartender has seen you with me, but I'm not counting on Rodriguez taking the time to drive out here now that Leroy's been arrested. He investigates by the book, so I think I'm safe."

"What if you're not?"

Claire sounded so worried. He covered her hand with his. She was trembling. "It'll be all right."

"If you say so," she whispered.

Reluctantly, he let go of her hand and finished his drink. "After I've talked to the owner of this place, we'll drive back to the house and look in on the horses before bed."

"I've been thinking about them. They've been abandoned today. While we're waiting, I'll give my mom a call. I promised to keep her informed. Please don't worry. I won't tell her what we've been doing."

While Claire was making her phone call, Vic saw a man who looked to be in his sixties show up behind the bar. He left the booth and walked over to the counter.

The older man stared at him. "I hear you've been waiting for me."

"That's right. I'm trying to locate the family of Fidel Flores. He went to high school here in Buda about twenty years ago. Your employee said he was taken to jail last night, but I won't be able to get into the jail to visit him. That's why I'd like to find someone in his family to answer a few questions for an insurance investigation."

The owner squinted at him. "There was a Flores family here years ago, but they all went back to Mexico."

"If that's true, why do you think Fidel came here last night?"

"He's hooked up with a Hispanic girl who lives here."

Adrenaline raced through Vic's body. "Can you give me a name?"

He shook his head. "Hey, Mick? Come over here." The other bartender approached them. "Got a name for the woman who started hanging out with Fidel?"

"You talking about Castillo's wife?"

"If she's the bottled blonde."

"Yeah. Eva. She shacked up with him after Castillo was sent to the clink."

Vic didn't need any more information. "I'm much obliged for your help." After handing him a ten dollar bill, he eyed Claire, who then followed him out of the bar to the car.

"Ooh, I'm glad we left. What a horrible place. Did you learn anything?"

"Yes. Fidel has been living with a woman named Eva, who lives around here somewhere. Before him she was married to a guy named Castillo, who's now serving time. I'm going to phone Clint to get me a police report on Castillo. Hopefully it will reveal a Buda address. I'm positive Leroy came to Buda because Fidel was staying here with Eva. They have a history."

"Vic—what if those three men brought Jeremy here and they've hidden him at her house?"

"Anything's possible." His jaw hardened. "I've got to stay here and find out."

"Phone Clint right now," she urged. "If your son is in Buda…"

"Whatever I do, I need to do it alone, so I'm taking you home first."

"Home?" she cried. "I'm not going anywhere if there's even the slightest chance Jeremy is here."

"This could get very dangerous if I'm right."

"I'm not leaving you," she declared with such intensity, he realized just how much she loved his son.

He let out a tortured sigh. "All right."

Vic got on the phone with Clint and brought him up to speed about his situation and the new clues that had come to light. Clint said he'd ask a friend at the station to search for the information on Castillo, but it might be an hour before he could get back to Vic.

He thanked him profusely and hung up, only to discover that Claire was doing her own search for Castillo on the Web. "I found eight possible matches, but only four are in or close to the Austin area. None mention Buda. Shall I call these four numbers? I could pretend I'm looking for a friend. I'll ask if Amalia is there. If a woman answers with a Spanish accent, at least we'd know a woman who could be Eva is at that address."

Claire was so clever, Vic was astonished. "If you do that, put your phone on speaker."

"Okay." She started calling. Three of the four calls were answered by a man on the other end. Each time Claire asked if she could speak to Amalia. All three of them answered with a Spanish accent and said she had the wrong number before hanging up.

On the fourth call a woman with an accent answered. "Amalia? Is that you?"

"No!" Following that angry sounding no, the woman on the other end hung up. Claire looked at Vic. "Did you notice she answered after the first ring? Like she was waiting for a call?"

"I noticed everything, and you did it perfectly. What's the address on that listing?"

"It's in Kyle, but there's no street address listed."

"Kyle's only ten or so miles from here. By the time we get there, maybe Clint will have more information for me." Vic started the car and drove to the I-35 corridor headed southwest. "Once we get an address, I've got a plan, and I hope it works."

ON THE WAY to Kyle, Claire prayed with all her might that they were on the right track. When they reached the outskirts of town, Vic pulled into a gas station to fill his tank. His phone rang before he got out of the car. After he greeted Clint, they talked for a minute before he hung up.

He turned to Claire. "Castillo's last known address was Bernie's Mobile Home Park in the north end of Kyle."

Claire quickly looked it up to find the exact location. After Vic filled the tank, he got in behind the wheel and they drove to the park in question. Like the bar they'd just left, the park was out of the way and run-down. The place looked old with shabby rectangular mobile units and only a few shade trees here and there.

Vic parked near the first trailer. "I'll find out where she lives. Lock the door while I'm gone."

She nodded as he got out and strode toward the end of the unit with the weathered white siding. An older woman answered his knock. A second later she pointed in the direction of the other units. Vic walked back to the car. Claire unlocked the doors so he could get in. "What did you learn?"

"I told her I was an insurance agent looking for Eva. She told me she lives in the end unit, but she's behind in her rent since her husband went to prison. If she doesn't pay it by tomorrow, she'll be evicted."

"So she's here?" Claire asked.

"Maybe. The manager says she hasn't seen her for a couple of days."

Claire could barely breathe. "This could be it. Jeremy could really be here." Her voice shook.

"God willing."

"What are you going to do, Vic?"

She heard his sharp intake of breath. "If Eva's keeping Jeremy here, then she's waiting for further orders. That could be the reason she answered her phone so quickly. I'll pretend I've come to take him to a secure place because she's being evicted tomorrow. I'll tell her that if the police find her with the boy, she'll be charged with kidnapping. That should scare her to death and she'll cooperate."

It was a brilliant idea, but dangerous for so many reasons. "How can I help?"

"I want you to stay in the car with the doors locked. She'll have a gun. If there's trouble and I don't come out, drive to the other end of the park and stay there while you call Kit. He'll know what to do. I'll leave the key in the ignition. Give me your phone and I'll program his number for you."

Her fingers shook as she handed him her cell. "Please be careful."

After he'd punched in the number, he gave it back, eyeing her with his jet black eyes. "I'll do whatever I have to do to find my son."

"So will I."

His lips brushed her cheek before getting out of the car.

Please, please, please be in there, Jeremy.

Vic walked up to the mobile home entrance and knocked hard with his fist. "Open up, Eva. Fidel got word to me from a friend at the jail where Leroy and Armando have also been arrested. The police confiscated Leroy's truck containing evidence, so I've come for the boy. I have to get him out of here before the police show up."

"Police?"

So she *was* here. The fear in her voice convinced him she had Jeremy with her. That meant whoever had planned this kidnapping would be coming for Jeremy. Every second counted. Vic had to move fast.

"The manager is going to evict you tomorrow. If you're caught with the boy, they'll force you to tell who's behind this and you'll go to prison for kidnapping. No one will save you. Fidel told me to bring you money to pay the rent. Just hand the boy over, Eva."

"How do I know you're working with Fidel?"

Vic took a chance. "Shorty from the bar in Buda is our go-between. Now it's my turn. I need proof before I hand over the money. How do I know the boy is alive?"

"Claro que si!" she rapped out in Spanish.

Joy swept through Vic at her declaration that his son was inside. "Then open the door and I'll take him out to the car."

"First the money!" She opened the door, but it was a mere slit because of the chain guard.

Vic reached for his wallet and pulled out four one-hundred-dollar bills. "This is all I could come up with on such short notice."

Her fingers took it from him. "It's not enough."

"There's more coming, but the manager won't call the police if you give her that amount tonight. Now hand over the boy."

"He's tied up in the back room."

Cringing with rage, Vic said, "I'll carry him out. Now open the damn door before I kick it in."

Suddenly it opened and he charged past Eva to the other end of the unit. The second he opened the door, he saw his precious son lying in a fetal position on the twin bed facing the wall. They'd gagged him with a scarf and tied his ankles with rope. He wasn't wearing shoes or socks.

Terrified he was unconscious, Vic hurried over to the bed and gathered him in his arms. Eva kept her distance as he carried his son through the unit. Once out the door he headed for the car.

He could see Claire behind the wheel. She undid the locks and he opened the back door and got in, taking Jeremy with him. He looked at Claire. "Drive us home," he said.

NEARLY OVERCOME WITH JOY, Claire started the engine and drove the car out to the road that led to the highway. Through the rearview mirror she was able to watch Vic undo Jeremy's restraints.

"Son? It's your dad. Can you hear me?"

"Dad?"

His dear voice was the sweetest sound she'd ever heard.

"You're safe now, sport. Thank God."

Claire saw Jeremy throw his arms around Vic's neck. They hugged each other so hard, she didn't know how either of them could breathe. "I knew you'd come, Dad," Jeremy said. Then he broke down sobbing.

"You've been so brave, Jeremy. Do you have any idea how proud I am of you? How much I've missed you?"

"I missed you, too. Did you find my magnet? I dropped it in the bucket before the janitor put something over my nose. It smelled awful and I fainted."

Tears rolled down Claire's cheeks as she listened.

"Was he waiting for you after class?"

"Yes. Right by the door. He grabbed my arm before I could get away from him and dragged me into the closet before anyone saw him. I screamed but he put a rag in my mouth. I don't remember anything else until I woke up in that room where you found me."

"Did that lady take care of you?"

"Yeah. She gave me some drinks and peanut butter sandwiches, and she let me go to the bathroom. But then she would put that scarf around my mouth and tie up my ankles."

"Are you hurt anywhere? Do you feel sick?"

"No. I just want to go home and see Claire." Jeremy sobbed again.

"Guess what, sport? She's driving our car."

"*Claire* is?"

"I'm right here, honey," she said over her shoulder. "I'm so happy your father found you, I could croak. Should we stop and get you a frosted root beer on the way home?"

"Can we?"

"Of course. This is a celebration!"

Jeremy had grown animated. "I bet Comet has missed me."

"We've taken him for walks, but I can tell he's been looking for you."

"Does Nate know what happened?"

"He knows you didn't make it home from school. And he told us that last week the janitor tried to show you his tattoos."

"I wish he never worked at my school."

"I wish he never did either, but now he's in jail," Vic said, reassuring his son. "After he's found guilty in court, he'll be sent to prison for life, and you'll never see him again."

"Good."

"How did you get so smart to put that magnet in the bucket? If I hadn't found it, I wouldn't have known what the janitor did to you."

"You've always said that if I'm ever in trouble, I should leave clues."

"Well, that was a big one. When I asked Claire if any of your magnets were missing, she looked and told me two were gone. Sabretooth and Wolverine. I didn't know the two of you had a secret word."

"Yeah. We like to play spy."

"Because of that clue, Claire and I were able to find you."

"Our plan really worked, huh, Claire?"

"It worked so well, you'll need to write all about it in your spy journal. One day when you're married and have kids of your own, you can show them the journal and let them read what happened to you in your own words. As far as I'm concerned, you're a superhero already."

Jeremy giggled, the first giggle she'd heard come out of him tonight.

They arrived at a fast food place and Claire pulled up to the drive-through speaker. "We'd like three frosted root beers, please. Anything else, guys?"

"Nope," Jeremy and Vic said at the same time.

She drove to the window to pay and passed back the drinks. On the way to the house, she drank hers, savoring the root beer and this moment. When he'd first gone missing, she'd feared she might never see Jeremy again.

"Dad? Can I say hello to Comet before I go to bed?"

"I think that's a terrific idea. It'll make your pony so happy, he'll be able to go to sleep."

He finished his drink. "Do horses sleep?"

Both Claire and Vic chuckled. "Yes, but most of the time they do it standing up."

"But *I* can't sleep doing that."

"Your legs don't lock like a horse when they sleep. But sometimes they lie down if there's no danger. Otherwise they need to be standing in case they have to get away from a threat really fast."

"I fought as hard as I could, but I couldn't get away from that janitor."

Claire saw his father hug him close. "He's a human predator, but he's been put away where he can never hurt anyone again."

"Dad—" he blurted. "Do you know where my backpack is?"

"I'm not sure yet."

"Maybe it's still in the closet at school."

"No, I checked there."

"I hope you can find it. I took my spy kit to school to show my friends. It has all my stuff."

"Even your Sabretooth magnet?"

"No. It's in my pocket."

"Tell you what, sport. I'll see what I can do to track it down."

"Can I sleep with you tonight?"

"You sure can."

"Do you have to go to work tomorrow?"

Claire looked at Vic through the rearview mirror,

and he flashed her a silent message. "No. Tomorrow we'll spend the whole day together."

"And Claire, too?"

"All of us."

"Hooray."

As soon as they got home, Jeremy flew to the bedroom to put on his cowboy boots. Then he came running down the hall right into Claire's arms. He hugged her hard, then hugged his dad again. "I'm going out to the barn."

"We'll be right there."

They watched his progress from the back door, not letting him out of their sight. Claire started to follow, but Vic trapped her in his arms and pulled her against him from behind. He'd never done anything like that before. It showed the degree of his happiness, but the contact aroused her desire for him, desire she had to tamp down.

"Thank God for you, Claire. He wouldn't be home with us now if it weren't for you. Your inspiration led us to him."

She turned in his arms and stared straight into his eyes. "We both know that inspiration came from a higher source. It wasn't meant for you to lose your son. That would have been too cruel after losing the rest of your family. One thing is very certain. The next nanny you hire needs to guard him with her life."

His hands squeezed her upper arms a little tighter before letting her go. "I'd rather not think about that on this of all nights."

Maybe *he* didn't want to, but when he'd hugged her

to him just now, she'd found herself wishing this could go on forever. In truth she'd become way too attached to Jeremy and his father.

She started for the barn ahead of Vic. Naturally he was so grateful for her help, he had to express it in the only way he could. But this moment wouldn't have happened if his son hadn't been kidnapped. From here on out, things were going to change in the Malone household.

For one thing, Jeremy would need counseling, too. For another, Vic needed to find a new nanny right away. Now that Jeremy had been found, Claire had to go in for those second interviews that had been set up for her.

The sooner she left their home, the sooner she could carve out a new life for herself. Vic had made his a long time ago. Now it was her turn to get her own life started and ignore the pain in her heart at the thought of leaving them.

After a visit to the horses, they walked back to the house. Jeremy took a bath, and then cuddled next to his father on the couch in the family room. Claire made popcorn, a snack they all loved, while Jeremy talked about his experience. He'd heard male voices once he'd awakened, but he'd been blindfolded. The poor dear had been through a terrible ordeal.

She sat in the chair on the other side of the coffee table. Finally the talking stopped. It was close to midnight when Jeremy fell asleep, safe in his father's arms. The picture of the two of them looking so relieved to be together brought tears to her eyes. Claire pulled out her phone and took another picture in order to remember this incredible night.

Vic's eyes opened. "Sorry I fell asleep on you."

"You need it. Would you like me to cancel your appointment with Dr. Marshall?"

"Thanks, but I'll do it. I need to make several calls before morning. First, I've got to let TJ know he can call off the search for Jeremy."

Claire nodded. "I'm going to phone my parents and tell them Jeremy's back home. Before I go to bed, is there anything I can do for you?"

"Get a good sleep. Tomorrow we'll load the horses in the trailer and drive to Luckenbach."

"Where your cousin lives?"

"That's right. Their place is adjacent to the equestrian park, which makes for a fun ride. It'll be good for Jeremy to be with family."

"I agree."

Vic needed his family, too. Clint had given him the address that had led them to Jeremy. She knew he wanted to thank his cousin personally and discuss the case with him. But Claire wasn't family.

She got up from the chair and started to leave the room. "Claire?" She looked back at him. "I owe you my life and Jeremy's. I don't know how to repay you." His deep voice throbbed.

"I have all the payment I want, seeing the two of you back together. Good night."

FINDING JEREMY ALIVE this soon after being kidnapped constituted a true miracle. Claire had been the instrument. The knowledge filled Vic with wonder. If he'd hired any of the other nanny applicants, this case wouldn't have had the same ending.

He was convinced she'd come into their lives for this very reason. Tomorrow during their ride, he would ask her to stay with them for another year. She could name her fee because he couldn't lose her. More than ever, Jeremy needed the stability she helped provide.

Vic looked down at his son, whose head rested on his lap with his legs extended. Carefully he slid out from under him and carried him to his bedroom. He'd promised Jeremy he could sleep with him.

After tucking him in, he walked over to a chair and pulled out his phone. He left a voice mail saying he had to cancel his appointment with Dr. Marshall, and then phoned his boss. Though he hated bothering him at night, this was important.

"Vic?" said a voice that sounded more asleep than awake.

"Sorry to disturb you, TJ, but I have wonderful news. Claire and I found Jeremy on our own tonight and he's home with us right now."

"What?"

"It's a shock to me, too."

"Thank God you found him!"

"Agreed. Ranger Rodriguez can call off the search."

"Okay. Now that I'm wide awake, tell me everything all over again."

Vic filled him in. "If you want to suspend me because I found Jeremy on my own, you have a right to do so."

"What in the hell are you talking about? I figured you would do something on your own. I just didn't expect results this fast. Are you sure your nanny isn't working undercover for the CIA?"

A smile broke out on Vic's face. "She's a chemist with a brilliant, inquiring mind. I'll email you all the details so Rodriguez can follow up on everything. And just so you know, I've arranged to see Dr. Marshall and will follow through."

"Good. You do that and call me at the end of next week. Then we'll talk about you coming back. I'll have Ranger Rodriguez follow up on the kidnapping case. I'm glad you have some time off to spend with your son. Enjoy it."

"I intend to."

"Vic? Do me a favor and watch your back. You're a target."

"I know. Thanks for understanding, TJ. Good night."

"Hey, Dad? Can we show Claire the miniature horse farm before we drive home?"

They'd just finished a picnic with Clint and his family in Luckenbach and had said goodbye to them. Though Claire knew Vic wanted to leave before nightfall, how could he refuse when he saw the excitement and pleading in his son's eyes?

Jeremy had been acting so natural all day, you would never know he'd been through such a harrowing ordeal. Then again, he'd had his father's and Claire's undivided attention.

"Tell you what. Let's finish loading the horses in the

trailer, and then we'll drive over there before heading for home. But we won't be able to stay long."

"You'll love them, Claire."

"I can't wait. I've never seen a miniature horse."

After the horses were loaded, she got in the back of the black Dodge Ram truck so Jeremy could sit in front with his father.

"Dad met Mom there."

"Really?"

"Yeah. She worked for the owner. Someone stole one of the owner's horses, and Dad went there to find out who took it."

Claire happened to meet Vic's glance when he looked at her through the rearview mirror, prompting her to ask, "Did you catch the guy?"

"Yup," Jeremy answered for his father.

"I'll have to hear about that."

"Tell her, Dad."

"It wasn't hard to track down the horse thief. He carried the new foal off in his truck in the middle of the night, but the tires left track marks. All I had to do was find out what kind of tires were mounted on that truck. I checked around at all the tire stores until I found out who'd bought tires like that. It led me to the man's house in Fredericksburg, where I made the arrest."

"Yup," Jeremy cried with animation. "He said Mom was so happy when Dad brought the horse back, she started crying."

Claire smiled. "I can understand that. And I bet he kept going over there to check on the horse. I've seen all those pictures of your mom. She was so pretty."

Jeremy jerked his head around to eye his father. "You thought she was pretty, huh?"

"I sure did and made up my mind to marry her."

Sharp pain attacked Claire's heart with the realization that he would always love his wife. As far as Claire knew, he'd never been with another woman during the nine months she'd been working for him. No other woman stood a chance. "You look like her, Jeremy."

"Aunt Carol says I look like both my parents."

"Well, you certainly got your dad's height, and you walk like him."

He looked back at her. "I do?"

"Yes. The first time I met you, I noticed the similarity. It's a father and son thing that made me smile. The next time you get out the family videos, you'll see what I mean." Those old family videos that showed the love Vic and Laura had for each other.

Five minutes later they arrived at Hershel's Miniature Horse Farm. Jeremy got out of the truck first. "Come on, Claire. The corral where you can watch them is around the back."

She ran to catch up with him. There were three tiny horses playing inside the fencing of the small outside enclosure. A man walked out and shook their hands. "Hi. I'm Mr. Hershel. Do you like what you see, son?"

"Yeah."

"They were born in the past three weeks. Take all the time you want to look."

"Oh, Jeremy—they're so adorable!"

"I wish I had one. Dad?" He turned to his father, who leaned against the fencing. "Do they cost a lot?"

"That depends."

After the kidnapping, Claire could imagine it would be next to impossible for Vic to deny Jeremy anything.

"I like that brown one with the white markings. Which pony is your favorite, Claire?"

"It's hard to decide." She studied each one. "That creamy palomino with the faint café au lait spots is a beauty."

"Which one do you like, Dad?"

"The black one with that big white spot in the middle of his back."

"Do you think we could buy all three of them? Then they wouldn't miss each other."

Vic broke into the deep laugh Claire had missed since his son had gone missing. She smiled at Jeremy. "They're cute all right, but they're a lot of work. Don't you think it might make Comet feel neglected if you started to spend all your time with them?"

"But we could all be together all the time."

She could see where this was leading. Vic was vulnerable right now. If he gave in to his son's desire, it would mean taking on a whole new project. Since she would be leaving soon, she hoped he didn't make a decision until after a new nanny had been hired. Preferably one who'd grown up around horses and could handle taking care of yet another animal in the Malone household.

Claire was also against the idea for selfish reasons. If Vic did buy a miniature horse for Jeremy right away, she would have to be involved in helping take care of it. Of course she'd become too attached. Combine that with her love for Jeremy—*and her love for Vic*—heaven help her, and she'd be swayed to stay on as Jeremy's nanny and pass up one good job offer after another.

The owner walked over to Jeremy. "Do you want to go inside the corral and talk to the horses?"

He turned to Vic. "Would that be okay, Dad?"

"Sure. Go ahead."

"Come with me." Jeremy followed the man around to the entrance and they walked over to each little horse so he could pet them. The sounds of delight coming from the boy caused her eyes to tear up. Twenty-four hours earlier he'd still been missing. She and Vic had been running on sheer faith that he was still alive and could be found. Again she was reminded that a miracle had happened.

Vic had moved closer and caught her brushing away the moisture from her cheeks. "I'm still having trouble believing we found him. Claire—" His voice sounded thick. "If it hadn't been for you…"

"We made a good team, *Jim*." She hoped that reminder would produce a smile, but his expression remained sober. "This has been the end to a perfect day, but Jeremy has school in the morning and you're rescheduled for an appointment with your therapist, so I'll see you two back at the car."

Without waiting for a response she headed for his truck. She'd love nothing more than to stay there all day, but it was time to wean herself from Jeremy and his father. Tomorrow and Friday she had final interviews for two different jobs. With Vic being on vacation, he'd have time to find the right nanny.

They had an hour and a half drive back to Vic's house. During the first part Jeremy chattered nonstop about the horses. But by the time they pulled around the side of the house to the barn, he'd fallen asleep against the seat. Vic carried him in the back door of the house to his bedroom. At that point Claire took over getting Jeremy ready for bed so Vic could unload the horses.

Jeremy woke up long enough to brush his teeth and get into his pajamas. After he got in bed, she drew the covers over him and sat on the end of the bed until he'd fallen asleep again. Vic came into the bedroom while she was deep in thought. "Claire?" She looked over at him in the semidarkness.

"He went right back to sleep. But I'm worried that when he has to go to school in the morning, he won't want to go."

Vic moved closer and sat down on one of the chairs. "Did he say anything?"

"No. But I've been trying to put myself in his shoes and know I'd be afraid after what happened."

"I've been worrying about that, too."

"Do you think when you visit Dr. Marshall tomorrow you could ask him to recommend someone who works with children? Jeremy probably needs to talk to a therapist."

"I'm way ahead of you. Until then, when you drive him to school in the morning, would you walk him inside and see how he reacts when you tell him you're going home? If he's anxious, phone me. My first therapy session starts at nine and will be over at ten, but I'll answer the phone in case there's a problem."

"Okay. I just thought I should remind you that I have a job interview tomorrow at eleven." At the mention of it, a grimace marred his handsome features. "It's downtown and shouldn't take more than an hour. If Jeremy doesn't want to stay at school, I'll drive him home and wait until you get there."

All of a sudden he got to his feet. "We need to talk, but not in here. Let's go in the family room. I'll leave his door open."

Sensing his tension, Claire left the bedroom and headed for the family room. She sat in one of the leather chairs. He remained standing. "I didn't realize your interview is in the morning."

"The other one is on Friday. I hadn't really thought about them until tonight." Earlier tonight she'd discovered an important truth. Feeling the way she did about Jeremy and his father, it would be painful to stay with them any longer than was absolutely necessary.

He rubbed the back of his neck. "Do either of the jobs look promising?"

"They both offer excellent salaries, but that's just on paper."

"Do either of them involve a change of location?"

"Both of them would be in Houston."

Vic shifted his weight. "How many applications have you submitted so far?"

"Ten, but these two sound the most promising."

He raised a black brow. "Do you mind my asking what salaries they're offering?"

Nervous because she knew this was upsetting him,

she moistened her lips. "For starting salaries, one said $70,000, and the other said $75,000."

She heard a strange sound come out of him. "Either position pays more than double what I pay you. Would you consider working for me another year if I offered you $70,000?"

Stunned by his offer, Claire could only look at the floor. "I wouldn't let you pay me that much."

"That's *my* decision, surely," he said in what she thought of as his Ranger Malone voice.

"Another nanny would be more than happy to make the money you've been paying me."

"But I don't want another nanny, and I promise you that Jeremy doesn't want another one, either."

Claire had expected a strong reaction from Jeremy, but not his father.

"Vic—Jeremy will be out of school next week. You're off work this week—now's the perfect time for you to find a new nanny. I'll help you pick the right person. You knew I would only be working for you until my graduation."

His eyes blazed like black fire. "But circumstances in our household have changed. The kidnapping was traumatic for Jeremy."

Our household? She swallowed hard. "I *do* know. That's why you need to get him to a therapist as soon as possible and hire a new nanny. The right set of people will make it easier for him to detach from me."

"You think he can shut off his feelings with a simple snap of the fingers?" He'd never been this short with her.

"No." She shook her head. "Of course not, but *you're* the rock he clings to. Other people, women, will come in and out of his life, but he has *you*, and he'll be fine. Now, if it's all right, I'm tired and need to get to bed. I'm sure you do, too."

Claire's pain went beyond tears. She hurried down the hall to her bedroom. Vic wanted her to stay on for another year and was willing to pay any price to make that happen. There was just one huge thing wrong with that scenario. She loved his son like her own. As for Vic, she was in love with him. Deeply in love.

But he wasn't in love with her.

Over the past nine months he'd never made any physical overtures. Not once. The only time he'd ever given her a kiss had been when he was at his most vulnerable, fearing that his son had disappeared forever. When they'd recovered Jeremy, he'd caught her from behind because he was euphoric to have his son back. Having lost his parents, he'd needed someone to hold on to and had derived comfort by being with her because she loved Jeremy, too.

But if the kidnapping had never happened, they'd still be stuck in the same place. Claire wasn't foolish enough to live with him for another year, hoping he'd develop feelings for her. If he hadn't been attracted to her from the very beginning, then waiting for it to happen was futile.

She was honest enough with herself to admit she'd fallen hard for him from the first day she'd met him. Over the months her feelings for him had grown until she was ready to burst. That was why she needed to leave him and Jeremy ASAP.

VIC STARED AT Dr. Marshall. "I couldn't believe I lunged for Leroy like that. I've never done anything even close to that in my life."

"It's understandable. You'd lost your wife and your parents. To think you might have lost Jeremy, too, sent you over the edge. If your colleague Kit hadn't come in right then, what do you think you would have done?"

He sucked in his breath. "I don't really know. The table separated me from Leroy. I presume I would have tried to shake an answer out of him before I realized what I was doing. To beat him unconscious when he was my only lead to Jeremy wouldn't have made any sense."

"That's an honest answer. Now tell me something else. How has your son behaved since you brought him home?"

"He acts like nothing happened, sleeps through the night. But this is his first day back at school. I have no idea how he's handling it, but the nanny will call me if there's a problem."

"Your boy will need therapy, too."

"I agree. Jeremy's nanny said the same thing. I wanted to ask if you could recommend a child psychiatrist for him."

"Dr. Andrea King. She has her own clinic in this hospital. I'll give her a call and explain the circumstances. I'm sure she'll fit Jeremy in. Just phone the main number and have the operator ring her office."

"I will."

"Our time is up for today. What I want you to do is think about the other reason why you came close to losing control. We'll talk about it tomorrow."

Vic frowned. "There wasn't any other reason."

"But there is. That's why your captain told you to see me. You have some unresolved issues in your life. As we explore them and you understand what part they played in that moment when you gripped the perp's shoulders, you'll be able to see why the incident happened. With understanding you'll be able to control your emotions in the future. See you in the morning."

Vic thanked him and left his office. But he was troubled by Dr. Marshall's remarks as he drove home. *Unresolved issues?*

His frustration level rose when he saw Claire sitting behind the wheel of her car in the driveway. She was on her way to her interview, but had waited until he returned. He parked alongside her and got out of the car to talk to her.

She lowered the window at his approach. He noticed she was wearing a white short-sleeved jacket with a navy tank top underneath. The outfit looked great with her coppery hair. Then again, everything she wore looked great. Her gray eyes showed concern. "Hi. How did your appointment go?"

The simple, normal question set him off, forcing him to take a quick breath. "He gave me the name of a psychiatrist for Jeremy."

"I'm happy to hear that. Was it helpful to talk to him?"

Good question. It would probably alarm her if he told

her he'd left the doctor's office unsettled, angry even. "Today I had to walk him through the facts. There wasn't time for anything else. Tomorrow we'll get started."

"It'll be good for you to have someone to talk to. I don't know what I'd do if I couldn't talk to my parents during an ordeal like you've just been through."

"You're very lucky to have them. How did it go at school?"

"Jeremy walked straight into his classroom. I stayed in the doorway and told him I'd be standing right there after school. He waved to me with a smile. I took it that he was giving me permission to leave, so I came home. So far, so good."

Vic nodded. "I shouldn't keep you from your interview." He stepped away from her door.

"I'll hurry home after. Oh—I made a fresh pot of coffee. I also wrapped up some roast beef sandwiches for you. They're in the fridge."

"Thank you. Take the rest of the day off. I'll pick up Jeremy. We'll see you at dinner."

"You're sure?"

"Positive. Good luck today."

Though he'd said the words, the selfish part of him hoped she'd turn the job down flat if it was offered to her. He'd offered her a matching salary, but she hadn't wanted it. Why would she when the nanny job was only a means to an end?

After she drove away, he went inside the house and poured himself a cup of coffee. Now that the crisis was over and he had his boy back, he should be feeling on top of the world. Instead his life seemed to have taken a new twist that left him anxious and dissatisfied.

Feeling totally out of sorts, he phoned Kit, who'd been assigned to a new case. Vic reached his friend's voice mail, but decided not to leave a message and hung up. Luckey and Cy were busy on other cases, too.

Vic realized he would quickly go out of his mind with no work to do. He'd like to take Jeremy out of school today and go on vacation. But he couldn't, not when he had therapy and needed to get Jeremy's therapy started. They could vacation later.

He grabbed a sandwich from the fridge and called Mercy Hospital to set up an appointment for Jeremy with Dr. King. The therapist had been told about Jeremy and made arrangements for him to come in tomorrow at four thirty in the afternoon. Tomorrow was his son's last day of school. There was going to be a classroom party.

Much as Vic dreaded it, he called the employment agency where he'd found both nannies before. They had his history in the files and were delighted to help him out again. After waiting a minute, he was told there were six women of different ages who'd applied for a nanny position. When did he want to meet them?

After some hesitation, he arranged for them to come at staggered times Monday and Tuesday after lunch. He'd be back from his therapy sessions and Jeremy would be home to meet the applicants. Claire had promised she'd be there, too, in order to help them make the final decision.

For the next while he went outside to wash his truck and car. Then he called his sister-in-law, Carol, and brought her up to date. Following that conversation, he phoned forensics to find out if they had found Jeremy's backpack in Leroy's truck when it had been confiscated. He was told they had it and he could come by for it at any time. He needed some good news about now and went to get it before any more time lapsed.

By the time Vic had showered and dressed, it was time to pick up Jeremy. He drove to the school and went inside to wait for him outside his classroom. The kids were finishing a math assignment. In another minute the bell would ring. His son sat at his desk with his notebook closed. If he'd finished his work, he had to be the only one.

All of a sudden he turned his head toward the door. When he saw Vic, he got up from the table and quietly walked toward him with his notebook. His teacher waved to Vic as if to say "it's okay."

Jeremy didn't say anything until they were at the car. "Where's Claire?"

"She's out doing some shopping." It was probably the truth, just not all of it. The time for explanation would come when they got home.

Vic knew his son was being very careful not to display emotion in front of the other kids at school, but he remained just as quiet on the way home. "Do you wish I hadn't come to get you?" he asked.

"Kind of."

"Because it isn't what dads do?"

"I don't want the kids to think I'm a sissy."

"I get it, sport. Sorry if I embarrassed you."

"That's okay."

He frowned. "Jeremy? Was it hard to be at school today?"

"Dad? Do we have to talk about it?"

Vic blinked. "Nope. What would you like to do?"

"Go home and ride Comet."

"Want to stop and get a treat first?"

"I'm not hungry. Claire said she was going to make tacos for dinner."

"That sounds good."

"How come you came to get me?"

Whoa. "I'm taking a vacation from work."

"I bet it's because Claire is going to leave. She said she would after she graduated. Did she get a new job yet?"

His son had been doing a lot of thinking during his ordeal. What to say… "She's being interviewed by several companies looking for a chemist." Vic looked over at him. Tears glistened on his boy's pale cheeks.

"I don't want another nanny. Aunt Carol said I could live with her."

If Vic had been shot through the heart, the shock couldn't have been any greater.

When they reached the house, Jeremy spotted Claire's car parked in the driveway. "She's home!" That was joy he heard in his son's voice. Vic followed him through the living room to the kitchen. Claire was cooking the ground beef for their dinner.

She smiled at the two of them. "I'm glad you're home. I've been waiting for you. If we eat an early dinner, then we can go riding after." She opened the fridge and handed Jeremy a cold bottle of Fanta Orange, his favorite drink. "Would you like a cola, Vic?"

"Not right now, thanks."

Jeremy unscrewed the cap and started drinking.

"How was school?"

"It was okay. Nate is still sick."

"Boy, he really does have the flu. I'm glad you haven't caught it."

"I know."

"After you wash your hands, come and help me chop up the tomatoes and onions."

"Okay. Be right back."

Vic walked over to the sink to wash his hands. "Give me a job and I'll do it."

Without looking at him she said, "How about shredding the cheese while I cook the tortillas?"

Their little picture of domestic bliss didn't fool anyone, particularly not Jeremy, who returned in a nanosecond and got busy dicing the vegetables on the bread board. He was good at it. Claire had taught him well.

She set the table and put out some sour cream and salsa. After slicing the avocados, she made a fruit salad and announced that dinner was ready. Vic put the bowl of cheese on the table, and then slipped out of the house to the car to retrieve Jeremy's backpack.

"Surprise!"

They both looked up as Vic entered the kitchen.

"My backpack! Thanks, Dad!" He ran over to give Vic the hug he'd been waiting for since the end of school. "My spy kit is in here, Claire."

"I know. Why don't we eat first? Then you can get it out."

"Okay."

When everyone was seated, Jeremy looked at Vic. "Where did you find it?"

"The police got it out of the back of Leroy's truck, where he'd hidden you."

"I'm glad he didn't throw it away."

I'm overjoyed you're still alive, son.

The dinner tasted good and everything seemed to be all right until Jeremy blurted, "Dad says he's on vacation. Does that mean you've got a new job, Claire?"

Chapter Five

Oh, help.

The time had come for honesty, but Jeremy had to be in a precarious frame of mind. Still, Claire couldn't lie to him. "I met some people today and I have another interview tomorrow, but I haven't made a decision yet."

"Will you still work in Austin?"

"No. Both positions are in Houston."

He crumpled his paper napkin. "I can't eat anymore." In the next instant he slid off the chair and ran through the house.

Sick at heart, she got up to go after him, but Vic beat her to it. "I'll talk to him. Thank you for the dinner. If you want to visit your folks, feel free. Jeremy and I need time together. He can help me do the dishes."

In the politest way possible Vic had asked her to leave. She understood. "I'll do that."

Claire had left her purse on the kitchen counter when she'd brought in the groceries. She reached for it and left the house through the back door. After walking around to the front, she got in her car and took off for her parents' modest home five miles away.

Her father worked in the accounting department at a local college, and her mom was a part-time dental receptionist. They'd been frugal all their lives in order to make ends meet. Claire's two older sisters were married and struggling financially. That was the reason why she'd wanted to get her master's degree and make a promising career for herself.

Today happened to be one of her mother's days off. Claire's dad wasn't home yet.

"I'm glad you're here." She gave her mom a hug and they sat down in the living room.

"How did that second interview go today?"

"Really well. The job sounds great and so does the salary. Even better, if I'm hired, they'll pay part of my tuition to get my PhD. Then I'd have to promise to work for them five years. With a PhD I'd have the credentials necessary to go almost anywhere."

"You'll be living in Houston?"

"Yes. It's only an hour and a half drive, Mom."

But Claire would never forget the pain on Jeremy's face when she told him where she'd be working if she took the position. He'd dashed from the dinner table. It had been an awful moment for her and his father.

"Did they offer you the position?"

"Yes."

"That's wonderful!"

"I agree. I told them I'd have to let them know sometime next week. I have a second interview with the other company tomorrow. If they offer me a position, too, then I'll have to weigh everything carefully before making my choice."

"It's a big one. Does Ranger Malone know you're this close to making a decision?"

"Yes. He told me he'd pay me the starting salary these jobs offered if I'd stay and be a nanny to Jeremy for another year."

Her mother looked incredulous. "You mean he would pay you $70,000?"

"Yes. Of course he couldn't have meant it. I told him I would never take that kind of money for caring for his son. This horrible kidnapping experience has caused him to overreact because he was so terrified he'd never see Jeremy again."

"Does Jeremy know how close you are to taking a new job?"

Claire jumped up from the couch. "Yes. His father has been given vacation time and Jeremy figured out he's home to find a new nanny. Tonight when the subject came up, he ran from the table while we were eating dinner. His father got up to follow him. Before leaving the kitchen he told me that if I wanted to visit you I should go. He and Jeremy would do the dishes. That's why I left and came over here."

"I see. It's time we had a talk, Claire. Sit down, honey."

She stared at her mom. "We *are* talking."

"Why have you turned this into an either-or situation?"

"What do you mean?"

"You know exactly what I'm saying. I know your love for Jeremy goes beyond what most nannies feel for their charges. When you've brought him over here other times, it's been clear that he adores you. His father knows that. That's why he's offered you more money so you'll stay."

"He hasn't been himself since the kidnapping, Mom."

"Naturally. His son loves you. It's obvious he doesn't want you to leave and is probably hoping you'll consider staying on longer than you'd originally planned. Would that be so terrible? I have the feeling you don't want to leave either, even if you've been offered a good position with that lab. Other offers will come along later. Tell me what's at the bottom of this."

Claire stopped pacing. "I *have* to leave."

"Because?" she prompted.

"Because I've fallen in love with Vic."

She smiled. "He's so attractive and remarkable, what woman wouldn't?"

"But it wasn't supposed to happen. I was hired to take care of his son."

"Which you've done so admirably, he's willing to pay a great deal of money to keep you on for another year."

Claire shook her head. "I couldn't. He's not in love with me, Mom."

"How do you know that?"

"What more proof do I need? You don't offer the woman you love $70,000 to stay, and I wouldn't take it." It hurt. It hurt so badly she couldn't stand it.

"He recognizes your worth, honey. I think the offer is quite revealing."

"No, Mom. He's so desperate to keep his son happy, he's willing to throw money at me, but I can't live this way any longer. We've been living in the same house for over nine months and he's never given me any indication that he has romantic feelings for me."

"Not ever?"

"While we were looking for Jeremy we had a few moments where we tried to comfort each other, but that ended the moment we found him. He's already made plans for us to interview some new nanny applicants on Monday and Tuesday of next week."

"But that was after you turned down his offer. With you leaving, he has to find someone to take care of Jeremy."

"If he has feelings for me, then I don't understand why he's never acted on them."

"Maybe he's been afraid of scaring you off in case you didn't feel the same way about him. Because you're a lovely young woman living in his household, he's been forced to draw a line to keep things professional. But you've taken such wonderful care of Jeremy, he realizes he doesn't want to lose you. Has he been seeing other women?"

"No, at least not that I can tell. Whenever he has any free time, he spends it with Jeremy."

"And you," her mother added. "It appears he'd rather be home with you and Jeremy than out with another woman. The man could be with any woman he wanted. Doesn't that tell you something?"

"No. Jeremy is his whole life! I was hired because he knew I'd be there for his son no matter what because I'd broken up with Bryce and wasn't in a relationship."

"You haven't dated at all since then."

"I wanted to honor my commitment to him."

"You did it so well, he wants you to stay."

Claire had grown restless. "But not as his wife!"

"You don't know what's on his mind, honey."

"Mom—he's already made arrangements to find someone to take my place."

"Not because he wants to. Your plan to get a job has forced him to act. Think about it before you rush into a decision you might regret."

I'll regret it if I don't. I love them both too much to be a nanny any longer.

"Thanks for the talk. I've got to go."

"Not like this. Wait for your father to come home. He had a staff meeting after work, but he should be here soon. Maybe a talk with him will help you."

"I'll call him later."

She reached for her purse. Her mother followed her to the door and hugged her before Claire hurried out to the car. Talking to her mom had only made her heartache worse. Vic needed time alone with his son, so she took a long drive, not planning to return to his house until she knew Jeremy would be in bed asleep.

THE EVENING ALONE with Jeremy had turned into a nightmare. After cleaning up the kitchen together, Vic's son had sobbed so long and hard, he looked pale lying in bed with his head against the pillow.

"Where's Claire?"

"I'm pretty sure she's still at her parents' house."

"When is she coming back?"

"I don't know. She hasn't seen them for a while."

Jeremy had turned on his side, looking into space with puffy eyes. "I thought she liked living with us."

Vic didn't know how much more of this he could take. "She's loved it here. I've heard her tell you that so many times. But she's been in college for a long time to become a chemist. It's what she's been planning on doing since high school."

"You mean she'd rather do that than stay here with us?"

"It's been her dream, Jeremy. She has an exceptional brain. I've told you how she helped me find you because she's so smart."

"She thinks I'm smart, too, and every day she tells me she loves me. But she couldn't love me if she wants to go work for some dumb company."

Jeremy wasn't listening to Vic. He couldn't get through to his son and prayed the therapist would be able to help. The room fell quiet. Just when Vic thought Jeremy had finally fallen asleep from sheer exhaustion, he turned over on his back.

"I don't want to live here anymore, Dad. Can't we move back to Blanco?"

Vic groaned inwardly. Not that again.

"If we live right by Aunt Carol, she'll let me come to her house every day and play until you get home from work."

"Jeremy? Your aunt Carol and uncle Dennis have their own family. You and I are our own family. We moved here to be close to my work and you've made friends. This is our home now, son."

"Can't you make Claire stay with us?"

Oh, boy. What was he supposed to say to that? "You can't force someone to do what they don't want to do."

He suddenly sat up in the bed. "You could if you scared her."

"What do you mean?" Vic was dumbfounded.

"You could tell her that if she doesn't stay with us, I'll run away and she'll never see me again."

The threat sounded bloodcurdlingly real. It had come out of his child who was still traumatized by the kidnapping and devastated that Claire would be leaving.

"Son…" Vic wrapped his arms around him and rocked him until Jeremy broke down once more and sobbed. "I love you. We're going to get through this."

Twenty minutes later his boy finally fell asleep. Vic lowered him to the pillow carefully and stretched out next to him. Amazing how he thought he'd already lived through all the grief possible in the past three years…

When Vic opened his eyes next, it was seven in the morning. Jeremy was still asleep. Vic rolled off the bed and hurried into his bedroom to shower and shave. When he'd dressed, he went back to Jeremy's room to wake him up, but his son wasn't there. Fear that he might have run away had him dashing through the house until he found him in the kitchen with Claire.

"Hey, Dad? Claire says to come and eat."

He breathed slowly in the hope of bringing down his heart rate. His gaze met Claire's. Vic hadn't heard her come home last night. "Mmm. It smells good."

"We're having pancakes and little pig sausages."

Those were Jeremy's favorites. The normal way he

was behaving right now made it hard to believe he'd had a meltdown last night.

"It's the last day of school. I thought we ought to celebrate the occasion," Claire commented and brought coffee and food to the table.

"Claire said she'd drive me to school, Dad."

"How about we both take you?" Vic could still make his appointment with Dr. Marshall on time.

"No. That's okay. She's going to pick me up, too."

Which meant Claire's one o'clock interview would have to be over in time to pick him up. After what happened at school yesterday when Vic had stood in the doorway of the classroom, his son clearly did not want his father anywhere around today. Something was going on inside him. Vic knew better than to argue with him. After Claire brought him home from school, Vic would drive him to the appointment at the hospital.

Claire had gone over to the stove. "Do you want another pancake, Jeremy?"

"No. I'm full."

"Okay. Then brush your teeth and we'll go."

He ran out of the kitchen. Vic cleared the table and walked over to Claire, who'd dressed in jeans and a lavender lace blouse that did wonders for her figure. "Will you be back here by ten thirty? I need to fill you in on a few things. We didn't get a chance to talk after you came home last night."

Her eyes flicked to his. "I know. When I went to his room, I saw you asleep on the bed next to him. It was very sweet the way he was cuddled up next to you."

"If you'd come in earlier, you would have heard him

sobbing because you're going to leave us. Do you want to know what he said to me? You could scare her, Dad, and tell her that if she doesn't stay, I'll run away."

Vic watched her eyes film over before she looked down in distress. "I—I'm glad he has an appointment with the therapist today," she stammered.

"Me, too. I have a plan for tomorrow and I want to know what you think about it. Meet me out at the barn after my appointment."

She nodded. "I've been worrying about this weekend, too."

Before he could say anything more, Jeremy appeared in the kitchen. "I'm ready, Claire. Let's go."

"Okay." She grabbed her purse and they started for the door leading to the garage.

"How about a hug first?"

Jeremy ran over and gave Vic one before following Claire out the door. Vic walked through the house to the front door and waved to them as they backed out on to the street and drove off.

Once they were out of sight, he locked up the house and left for the hospital. Dr. Marshall expected Vic to be punctual. He arrived with no time to spare, wondering what would be accomplished in this session.

"Good morning, Vic. Come on in."

"Thank you." He took a seat in front of the doctor's desk.

Dr. Marshall cocked his head. "How hard has it been not going to work?"

Vic rubbed the back of his neck. "To be honest, my son is going through such a terrible time, all my thoughts have been on him. He knows Claire is leaving us soon, and he's not handling it well at all. Last night he cried for so long I got worried. He's threatened to run away, or else go live with my sister-in-law and her husband. I'm hoping Dr. King can help me deal with him. We have an appointment this afternoon after Jeremy's school."

"Good. I believe he's suffering from the same anger issues you have, but he handles them differently."

"What do you mean exactly?"

"Like you, he feels as if his life is spinning out of control and he's angry. Dr. King will supply some strategies. But this morning you and I need to explore the reasons for the anger that caused you to step over the line in the course of your work."

"I was terrified I'd never see my son again."

"Because…"

Vic's brows furrowed. "Because he was the only person who could tell me if Jeremy was alive, let alone where I could find him."

"You were angry for another reason, too. Can you think what it would be?"

"I suppose it's because my wife and parents were wiped out three years ago and I couldn't do a thing to save them."

"That's one of the reasons. You were at work when the tornado struck and you were helpless to change the outcome. When faced with the possibility of your son being wiped out, you again felt helpless, and that anger caused you to make a mistake you would never normally make."

Vic nodded.

"But you're battling another fear that contributed to that mistake. The nanny who has endeared herself to your son is going to leave your employ. How long have you known she wouldn't be permanent?"

"She was perfectly clear with me about her future plans before I hired her. Her goal was to get a job in her chosen field of chemistry after graduating from the university."

"So none of this is a surprise to you."

"No."

"Yet you're acting as if she suddenly threw this at you. Has your son known about it all this time?"

"Yes."

"How long has she been with you?"

"Nine months."

"So from the moment she started working for you, your anxiety has been building because she's been a good nanny and you don't want to lose her. I think because your life has been running well with her on board, you've been in denial about her future plans. Then suddenly you were hit with the kidnapping and her imminent departure from your household."

"Yes." Dr. Marshall was good. Very good.

"It's obvious how your son feels about it, but the question is how do *you* feel about it?"

He sat forward with his hands clasped between his legs. "I wish she weren't leaving."

"You had another nanny before her. Was it difficult for you when she left?"

"Not in the same way."

"What way is that?"

Vic got to his feet, unable to remain seated. "Our first nanny was an older woman with family who needed her. Jeremy accepted it."

"As did you."

"Yes."

"So why is Claire's leaving so different?"

"For one thing she's…young and hits it off with Jeremy in ways I wouldn't have imagined."

"And she's a free agent, right? Still unmarried?"

"Yes."

"Have you asked her to stay on and put off getting another job yet?"

"Yes. I've even offered her a salary to match the one several companies are offering, but she turned it down because her mind is made up."

"How does that make you feel? Think hard to give me the right word."

Vic didn't have to think. "Helpless."

"Like this is another situation out of control?"

"Yes."

"So when you were interrogating the man who took Jeremy, you were feeling helpless for three distinct reasons, and that helpless feeling turned to anger you weren't aware had been roiling inside of you. At that moment you lost control."

Vic was floored. Dr. Marshall had nailed what was going on inside him. How did he do that?

"Our time is up for this session. Monday we'll get into why losing Claire represents such a personal loss to you. It's key to the underlying reason why you lost control in the interrogation room."

Vic left the hospital feeling uncomfortable and all wound up. He needed to channel his energy into something physical. As soon as he got home, he went out to the barn. By the time he'd mucked out the stalls and put the horses in the paddock, Claire had returned. He saw her coming toward him wearing her cowboy boots.

She hung her arms over the fencing. Marshmallow wandered over so she could rub her forelock. Claire had propped one of her shapely legs on the lower rung of the fence, and she made a beautiful picture, all coppery gold and lavender.

"How did it go with Jeremy this morning?"

"He saw Nate and Cory out on the playground and ran to them before the bell rang. I'm glad Nate's back today."

"Jeremy's going to need his friends now more than ever."

"I have no doubt he'll have lots of play dates this summer."

Vic leaned against the fencing. "I have to do something to help him right away. Do you think it would be crazy if I bought him the brown-and-white miniature horse he saw the other day?"

Her eyes lit up. "Oh Vic, he'd love that more than anything!"

"We could drive there tomorrow and make a day of it. If I tell him he has to take total responsibility for it, I'm hoping it might help him deal with the pain of you leaving."

She pressed her lips together as if she was having difficulty with that concept, too. "You couldn't have come up with a more perfect plan. He associates those little horses with his mom. Not that he has the memory. But he's heard you talk about it and it will have more meaning for him than if you bought him a puppy or a kitty."

"He has Comet, but I'm thinking he needs a pet."

"That miniature horse will be perfect! He can join a 4-H club when he turns eight. Austin's 4-H petting zoo was always one of my favorite places to visit when I was little. I bet Jeremy would just love to show off his adorable horse."

When you gave Claire an idea, she ran with it. Jeremy always said Claire was awesome. That word described her best. "I guess I have my answer."

Her smile captivated him. "Are you going to tell him tonight?"

"I'll wait until he's had his appointment with Dr. King. I'd like to run the idea by her first." She'd told him the session with his son would be private, but he could email her with any questions or concerns he had.

"I'm sure she'll think it's fabulous."

Not wanting Claire to find an excuse to go in the house, he said, "Why don't we saddle up the horses and exercise them?"

"I have time to ride for a little while before I leave." It wasn't a *no*, but her usual burst of enthusiasm was missing.

They set out with Vic holding Comet's lead. He was in a better mood having shared his idea with Claire. She'd turned into a real cowgirl and could saddle Marshmallow herself. He marveled that when she'd first started to take care of Jeremy, she'd only ridden a horse a couple of times.

As she broke into a gallop, her shoulder-length hair floated behind her like a shimmering red-gold pennant in the sun. He longed to bunch it in his hands. He longed to hold her again like he'd done the other night. Astride the horse, she had a stunning natural beauty. It was more and more unthinkable to him that she'd be leaving them soon.

"I'd better take Marshmallow back to the barn and get ready, or I'm going to be late for my interview."

He'd been so deep in thought about her that her comment jarred him. They'd been riding for almost an hour. "Let's go. I'll take care of your horse."

"Thanks. Come on, Marshmallow. Let's have one more run." The horse galloped all the way to the barn. Claire dismounted and hurried toward the house without waiting for him. She was always pleasant and friendly, but since they'd found Jeremy, he could feel her distancing herself from him.

Pondering her troubling behavior, Vic watered and fed the horses. Once inside the house, he phoned Hershel's about the miniature horse. If it was still for sale, he was interested. There was one extra stall in the barn. They could fit it out for the tiny horse. He'd let Jeremy plan how he wanted it to be. All he could hope was that his son would be so excited about the horse that he would be consumed with taking care of it.

While he was washing his hands at the kitchen sink,

the phone rang. When he saw the caller ID, he lunged for it. "Kit—what's up?"

"Plenty, but I only have a few minutes. Can you talk, or is this a bad time?"

"It couldn't be better. I'm home alone and thankful you called."

"How soon will you be back on the job?"

"When TJ tells me I can go back. I have to go through some more therapy sessions."

"Are they helping?"

"They're more upsetting than anything." Dr. Marshall sure had a way of pressing all his buttons.

"That's good. It means it's got you thinking. How's Jeremy?"

"Not good. I'm taking him to a child therapist this afternoon."

"Nightmares?"

"No, he hasn't talked about the kidnapping at all, but he's so upset that Claire is leaving, he got hysterical last night. She's already had one job offer and will probably get another one today."

"That's tough. If you don't want to talk, I understand."

"No, no. Tell me your news."

"I just found out that Jamison Lowell, the school district guy who hired Leroy, was killed in a car accident outside Vail last night. He drove through a guard rail. The police found him dead in his car at the bottom of a ravine. He was alone. I don't know anything else yet, but I figure someone got to him before he could talk."

"Sounds like it. This case just keeps getting bigger and uglier."

"You've got to get back to work."

Vic expelled his breath. "Tell me about it."

"I'll try to find out if drugs or alcohol were involved when the autopsy's done. Sorry, Vic, but I've got to get going."

"Like I told you before, I couldn't do this without you. Talk to you soon."

Vic hung up, aware that he had time on his hands. He should send Dr. King an email about the advisability of getting a pet for his son. He went into the den and typed the email, hoping the therapist would receive it before she met with Jeremy.

Once he'd sent it, he got up from the chair and paced the floor. Vic's next challenge would be to tell Jeremy they were going to see a doctor about the experience he'd been through. His son wasn't going to like it.

Chapter Six

Claire parked at the side of Pinehurst Elementary to wait for Jeremy. She had a lot to think about. She'd been offered the position at the lab in the Houston–Sugar Land–Baytown area. Now she had two positions to choose from, and both companies needed an answer from her next week. She was finally on the brink of the career she'd worked so hard for.

She ought to be dancing on the ceiling, but when she saw Jeremy come running toward her with the animal life cycle diorama she'd helped him make for class, pain stabbed her in the chest, robbing her of breath.

How was she going to leave this precious boy? Something had happened to her during the kidnapping. She'd felt as if she'd lost her own child. When they'd found him, she'd wanted to clutch him in her arms and never let him go, but that was Vic's right, not hers.

At this point she couldn't comprehend leaving Vic or Jeremy. How would a career ever compensate for the loss?

But how could she accept Vic's offer to stay on another year, knowing it would only be putting off the inevitable? With her credentials, she could always find work in her field, but if she remained in his employ, a year from now Claire would be in the same position she was now, heartbroken and looking for a job.

Who knew the changes that could come in another year? Vic might meet someone and fall in love. Claire was surprised it hadn't happened before now. Then he'd get married and Claire would be let go. Her suffering would be so intolerable, she knew she had to make the break now or pay the price.

"Hi, Jeremy," she said as he opened the door and jumped in the backseat with his school project. "Did you have a fun party?"

"It was okay. Will you drive me to Nate's? If I can't play at his house, can he come over to our house with us? We'll give Comet a bath."

"That sounds like a fun idea, but your dad asked me to bring you home because he has plans to be with you." She pulled away from the curb and started down the street toward home.

"But Nate and I want to play."

Normally he couldn't wait to be with his father. She took a deep breath. "You can tell him that as soon as we get there."

"Please don't take me home."

Alarms bells went off. Jeremy was up to something. Claire could feel it. Maybe he was planning on using Nate as an excuse to run away. He'd told Vic he'd do it. Was that idea in the back of his mind?

"Jeremy? I promised your father he could always

count on me. You wouldn't want me to break my promise, would you?"

"He won't care."

Whoa. "But *I* care."

"No, you don't. You're going to leave."

She heard tears in his voice and it broke her heart. Thank heaven she could see Vic on the front porch waiting for them as she pulled into the driveway. It prevented her from having to say anything because he walked toward the car and opened the back door to reach for Jeremy.

"I've been anxious to see you, sport." He picked him up. "How was your last day of school?"

"Stupid. I wanted to go over to Nate's, but Claire said I had to come home first."

Vic exchanged a silent message with Claire. "She was right. You and I have plans for the rest of the afternoon."

"What are they?"

"After you go to the bathroom and wash your hands, come on out to my car, and I'll tell you what we're going to do."

"Is Claire coming, too?"

"I can't," she spoke for Vic, saying the first thing that came into her mind. "My parents are expecting me. But I'll see you tonight before you go to bed."

His expression hardened like stone before he wiggled out of Vic's arms and ran inside the house. "Quick, before he comes back out, Claire. How did the interview go?"

She struggled to remain composed. "I was offered the position."

"That doesn't surprise me." He put his hands on the framework of her car while his black eyes studied her features. "Have you made a decision yet?"

Claire wished he wasn't standing so close and averted her eyes. She could smell the soap he'd used in the shower. He was such a gorgeous man. "No, but I'm leaning toward the company that will pay part of my tuition to get a PhD while I'm working."

"With a mind like yours, there's no telling how far you can go. How long did they give you?"

"I have to let both companies know by next week."

"That's a big decision. I'd better let you get going. Have a nice time at your folks'."

He moved away so she could leave. Her heart was splintering into little pieces. Vic could have no idea how much she wanted to throw her arms around his neck and blurt out how much she loved him. "Good luck at the appointment with Jeremy."

On that note she backed out and drove through the neighborhood to the main street leading to the freeway. Claire had no intention of going to her parents'. As long as she had this much time off, she'd take the more scenic route to Houston on 290 and see the layout of the two companies she could work for.

She'd been to Houston quite a few times over the years, but never dreamed she might be working there. While she was at it, she'd look at a couple of neighborhoods. She had to start paying down her student loan, but she still had enough money saved to put a down payment on a condo. Nothing fancy. Just livable and close to her work. Whichever company she chose, she probably wouldn't be with them for more than four or five years before looking for something more challenging.

If she went with the job that would pay for her to get her PhD, she'd need to find housing that was equidistant to the university and the company.

Once she reached Houston, she used the GPS to find the addresses and spent the next two hours driving around, making notes. But she couldn't summon even a modicum of enthusiasm for any of it. Her heart was too heavy.

At seven thirty she stopped for a hamburger and filled up with gas before driving back to Austin. The Friday night traffic was atrocious. By the time she entered the garage and saw Vic's car, it was ten after ten. Her pulse picked up speed because she didn't know what she was coming home to. Jeremy ought to be in bed, but today hadn't been an ordinary day for him.

She reached for the diorama, then locked the car and entered the kitchen through the door from the garage. The house sounded too quiet. Claire put the diorama on the counter and went to the sink for a glass of water. When she turned around, she discovered Vic had walked into the kitchen.

He picked up Jeremy's school project to inspect it. "I heard the garage door." Vic spoke in a low tone of voice.

"Did it disturb Jeremy?" she whispered.

"No. He had another long crying spell before falling asleep."

She bit her lip. "How did the session go?"

"I wasn't asked to join them, but I received an email from Dr. King after I got home with him."

Claire was almost afraid to hear what it said.

"She indicated that Jeremy wanted to talk about your leaving rather than the kidnapping incident. He's angry with me, but she believes that feeling will pass. She's made another appointment for next Friday, but she's not overly concerned and told me that getting him a pet might provide a good distraction."

"Did you tell him your plans for tomorrow?"

"Not yet. He was too upset to listen to me."

She put a hand to her throat. "Maybe she's not overly concerned, but I am." In the next breath she told him about her conversation in the car with Jeremy after school. "I got the strangest feeling that he had a motive for wanting to go over to Nate's house."

Vic's features looked bleak. "Explain."

"I wish I could. Twice now he's mentioned running away. We both know why, but maybe he's more serious about it than we realize. You'd think that after the horror of the kidnapping, it would be the last thing he'd want to do."

She felt his hard-muscled body stiffen even though they weren't touching. "If it were anyone but you, I might not take it as seriously. You think he has a plan?"

"I don't know, but I'm glad you want to buy him that miniature horse. Surely he wouldn't want to run away when he's got a new pet to take care of. Is it still for sale?"

He nodded. "I told them to expect us in the morning."

"I'll get up early to fix breakfast. Then you can tell him your surprise."

"Let's pray this works."

"I haven't stopped praying since the moment he didn't come running out to the car on Monday."

She looked away, consumed by guilt because the fact that she was leaving their household had brought on this latest crisis. But Vic had no intention of supplying the solution that would turn everything around. *Because he's not in love with you, Claire.*

Emotionally exhausted, she moved toward the hallway before looking back at him. "I can't believe that was only five days ago. So much has gone on, it seems like we've lived a nightmare that has gone on for a century. It's turned out for the best that your boss told you to take time off from work. Jeremy needs you desperately, as if you didn't already know. Good night, Vic."

Vic awoke before Jeremy. He'd slept in a sleeping bag on the floor near the door inside his son's room. The possibility that his boy might take it into his head to run away in order to punish Vic was a sobering thought that had kept him awake for a long time. Claire had uncanny instincts. For the next week Vic intended to stay vigilant.

He got to his feet and carried the bag into his bedroom. Once he'd showered and shaved, he pulled on jeans and a T-shirt. As he left his bedroom he could hear voices coming from the kitchen. When he saw what Claire had put on the table, he realized she'd gone all out for his son.

Jeremy sat there enjoying his favorite Lucky Charms cereal. It was a treat he didn't get to eat all the time, but today was a special day.

"That looks good."

"It is," Jeremy said and kept eating without looking at him.

Vic smiled at Claire before finding himself a big bowl from the cupboard. She was drinking coffee at the counter. He walked over to the table and poured out a portion of cereal and milk for himself before sitting next to Jeremy.

While he munched on his breakfast, he looked at his son. "Do you know what today is?"

"No," sounded the deflating, automatic response.

"It's someone's unbirthday."

He heard a laugh escape Claire.

Jeremy jerked his head around. *"Unbirthday?"*

"Yup. We're going to go get him and bring him back for an unbirthday party."

"Dad—are you crazy?"

"Wait till you see him."

"What's his name?"

At last Vic had garnered his son's attention. "I don't know."

"How come?"

"He was never given a name."

"I bet he's sad."

His son's compassion brought a lump to Vic's throat. "As soon as we finish breakfast, we'll go visit him."

"Can he eat cake?"

"Sure."

He turned to Claire. "Can we make him one and take it to him?"

"That's up to your father."

"Let's go see him and we'll worry about the cake later."

"Okay. I'm finished."

Vic ate his cereal down to the last spoonful. "So am I. You ready, Claire?"

"I sure am."

She sure was…all decked out in jeans and a kelly green top that looked incredible with her coloring.

Jeremy ran for the garage, but Vic called him back. "You're going the wrong way. Since we're taking the truck we'll leave through the back door." The trailer was still hooked up to it.

"How come?"

"I like to drive it when I don't have to go to work."

"I didn't know that."

Vic smiled sadly. There was a lot his son didn't know. "Let's go."

Claire left ahead of them, drawing his gaze to the feminine shape of her body. She waited by the truck for him to open the door and climbed into the back like she always did. Never once did she accidentally do anything in order to get closer to Vic.

For months now he'd waited for a sign that she saw him as more than an employer and Jeremy's father. But at this point the writing on the wall was clear that the miracle he longed for wasn't going to happen. Other women came on to him, but since she'd come to work for him, his thoughts had turned more and more to her until he couldn't see anyone else.

You're a fool, Malone.

He started the truck and circled around to the street.

"Hey, Dad—how come we're taking the horse trailer? I didn't know you loaded the horses."

"I didn't. I guess I forgot to unhitch it, but it's too late now."

"Oh."

"Why don't you turn on the radio and find some music you like?"

Jeremy crooked his head at Claire. "What's the kind of music I like again?"

"Do you mean reggae?"

"Yeah."

Vic learned something new every day. "I like that reggae, too."

His son's head whipped around. "You do?"

"Sure."

"When we go in the car, you always listen to the weather or the news."

Good grief. To prove he wasn't a grandfather yet, he turned on the radio and scanned for the right station. Austin radio played a lot of good reggae. Bob Marley's "Buffalo Soldier" was playing now, bringing back memories. For the most part he'd avoided listening to music since the tornado because it filled him with haunting pain. But for some reason it didn't bother him today. On the contrary.

Vic turned up the volume so it filled the interior of the truck. "Is this what you like?"

Jeremy's face lit up. "Yeah."

"It's cool music, huh?"

"Yeah. Did Mom like it?"

"She loved it. You must be her son."

His comment passed right over Jeremy, who said, "Claire likes it, too."

Of course Claire liked it. He flicked her a glance through the rearview mirror, but she was looking out the window. In fact, every time he'd tried to make eye contact with her during the drive, she'd been studying the landscape. Was it on purpose, or was he truly invisible to her as a flesh and blood man?

He smiled at his son. "I think everyone likes reggae. It's fun."

"I know. Claire told me it comes from Jamaica. We looked it up on the map. It's not that far away from Texas. We both want to go there someday. Have you ever been there?"

"Not yet."

For the moment his son's unhappy mood had lifted. The music *was* entertaining. *Don't fix it if it's working.* Vic left the station on and they were treated to reggae music all the way to Luckenbach.

"Are we going to Clint's house?"

Ah. It had just started clicking with him where they'd driven. "Not today. Remember we're going to see that someone and have an unbirthday party?"

"Does he know we're coming?"

"Nope. It'll be a surprise."

Vic took the turnoff for Hershel's. After they drove through the gate, Jeremy turned to him. "Who is it?"

"You've seen this guy before." He kept going until they reached the parking area near the corral. Only one tiny horse was outside this morning. Mr. Hershel waved to Vic from the fencing.

He got out of the truck while Jeremy got out the other side. Vic noticed Claire stayed in the truck. The two of them walked over to the owner.

Mr. Hershel smiled at Jeremy. "This little guy you met the other day has been waiting for you to come back."

Jeremy's eyes rounded in shock. He looked up at Vic. "Are we having an unbirthday party for *him*?"

"That depends on if you want him for your pet."

He blinked. "You mean you'll buy him for me?"

"Why don't you go get acquainted with him first and see what you think."

He scrambled around to the entrance of the enclosure without waiting for Mr. Hershel. While Vic watched his son, Claire joined him at the fence. His pulse raced. It seemed she hadn't been able to stay in the truck after all. What pleased him more was that she'd come to stand next to him.

"Have you ever seen Jeremy so excited?" His son had gone over to the little horse and sat down so it would come to him. The horse seemed fascinated and started sniffing him. A giggle came out of Jeremy when it licked his face.

"I *love* him, Dad!"

He felt Claire's hand on his arm. It sent curling warmth through his body. "Did you hear that, Dad?"

Vic's heart thundered in his chest. He studied her

lovely profile before facing her. "I heard," he whispered back, holding her gaze. "When love hits, you know it."

Her eyes grew a darker gray before she removed her hand and leaned over the fencing. "I think he likes you, too, Jeremy."

"I *know* he does."

"Put your arms around his neck and pull," Mr. Hershel suggested. "He'll lie down on you."

Jeremy did as he said and the horse climbed right into his lap and lay there like a baby. Vic's eyes smarted as he pulled out his phone and took picture after picture while his boy talked to the horse. Then he took a video. "Have you thought of a name for him?"

"Yeah. Daken! That's the name of Wolverine's mutant son."

Claire smiled at Vic, who'd lowered the phone. "You heard the man, Jim. Daken it is." Her eyes lingered on his face as if she couldn't look away. His breath caught. Vic knew she was remembering every single event that had happened from the moment Jeremy had disappeared. Their journey to find him had bonded them in a special way. He could feel it and her eyes didn't deny it.

"I think we should have a birthday party for him, Dad."

"But we don't know when he was born," he said while still looking at Claire. "That's why we're having an unbirthday party."

"You're funny, Dad. Let's play like today is his birthday! What do you think, Claire?"

"I think that's a perfect idea," she answered before

switching her gaze to Jeremy. Vic noticed new color in her cheeks. If he didn't know better…

She took some pictures with her cell phone.

The next half hour passed in a blur as Vic did business with Mr. Hershel and the little horse was loaded in the trailer.

"I want to ride with him, Dad."

"You can't."

"But he'll get scared."

"It's not a long ride. He'll be fine. You have to ride with Claire and me." They waved to Mr. Hershel and headed back to Austin.

"Do horses cry, Claire?"

"I don't think so."

"I bet he's afraid. I was afraid when I got taken away."

Finally he'd opened up about the kidnapping. Dr. King said he would when he was ready and she advised Vic to simply listen and support him.

Vic put a hand on Jeremy's shoulder. "I'm sure you were. We were afraid for you."

"But you found me."

"We sure did. That was the happiest moment of my life."

"Mine, too."

"Don't worry about Daken. We'll be home soon and he'll forget everything when you can spend all day with him. Just think of the things you have to do when we get home."

"Comet won't believe it!"

"Nope. You'll have to introduce them right off. Then

you can fix his stall to make him comfortable and do all that stuff."

"Do you think he can eat cake?"

"Probably a bite or two, but he'll prefer grass."

"Yeah."

"I heard Mr. Hershel say the horses like human treats," Claire interjected from the backseat.

"Hey—I could feed him some Lucky Charms!"

"Maybe a few," Vic cautioned. "You don't want to make him sick."

"What were those things Mr. Hershel gave us, Dad?"

"Some salt bricks and minerals to help keep him healthy. Remember Daken will need water, and he would love to be brushed every day."

"I love to do that! Comet loves it, too!"

Vic kept the reggae music going while Jeremy leafed through the small brochure Mr. Hershel had given him. There were pictures with directions on how to take care of a miniature horse. With his son's mind occupied, Vic could concentrate on Claire.

Something significant had happened between them at the farm. For the first time he felt he'd had a glimpse into her soul where her deepest feelings were revealed. She couldn't—wouldn't—have touched him, or looked at him like that with such longing otherwise. That was what it was. Longing… He'd swear to it.

He was in a completely different frame of mind than before they'd left Austin that morning. He felt excited, now, about the rest of the day. But after Claire had fixed them a birthday lunch and Jeremy had run out to the barn with some Lucky Charms treats, she informed him that her two married sisters were getting together at her parents' for a party. If Vic didn't need her, she was hoping to take the rest of the day off to spend with them.

What could he say? No—I want you to stay here? We need to talk about what happened this morning?

"By all means, be with your family."

"Thank you. I think it's good that you and Jeremy have the rest of the day by yourselves. I want him to defer to you. I'll be leaving next week, so the less I'm around, the better."

Vic couldn't have dreamed up what had happened earlier. This was a conscious effort on her part to keep them apart. Vic would let her get away with it this time, but at some point in the next few days he planned to force the truth from her.

She didn't want to leave him. He *knew* she didn't, and this had nothing to do with Jeremy. The days of behaving professionally were over. Vic had instincts, too, and before long he'd act on them.

CLAIRE LEFT HER parents' at nine thirty and headed back to Vic's house. It had been good to see her sisters, who both worked. They wanted to know which job she'd decided to take and envied her for having such great opportunities now that she'd received her degree. But she told them she was still thinking things over.

Kaye, particularly, couldn't understand how Claire had ever decided to be a nanny in the first place. Everyone wanted to talk about the kidnapping. Barbara kept asking about the dishy Texas Ranger she worked for. "He's a complete hunk, Claire."

She really didn't want to discuss him. "He's a wonderful father. Today he bought Jeremy a miniature horse."

"Oh…" both her sisters said at the same time.

"I have some pictures." She passed her phone around so they could see Jeremy playing with the horse. "He's named it Daken, son of Wolverine."

Everyone laughed. Her mom looked at her. "These pictures are priceless."

"I agree."

Her father studied the photos for a while. "When are you leaving them, honey?"

"As soon as he's hired a new nanny. Vic's interviewing some applicants on Monday and Tuesday. He wants me there, too. As soon as he's made a decision, then I can go. I went to Houston yesterday and found several condos for sale that are decently priced and in a good neighborhood."

"When the time comes we'll help you move."

"Thanks, Dad. I'd better go now. Love all of you."

When she got out to her car, she sat there for a minute, resting her forehead against the steering wheel. Wow. It was really going to happen. Talking with her family had made it a reality, but she'd never felt such pain in her life.

Before her family noticed she hadn't left yet, she pulled away from the curb and took off for the highway. The more she tried to deny her true feelings, the more she hated the thought of leaving Austin. Jeremy and his father had been her whole world for nine months. It ripped her heart out to think that next week this would all be over.

It didn't have to be over if she was willing to stay on. But was she really willing to hang on to a life that wasn't truly hers, living on the outskirts of a family without being a part of it? Without knowing Vic's love? For how long? Until he married someone and she had to leave?

Over and over Claire went through this thought process in her mind. Every time she ended up coming to the same conclusion. Nothing but marriage to him could ever satisfy her. She wanted Jeremy to be her little boy. If she never had another child, it wouldn't matter.

The way Vic had looked at her while they'd been at the farm today had set her on fire. She could still feel it, making her body tremble. Was she mistaken, or had she seen desire burning for her in the black depths of his eyes? Maybe she wanted him so much, she'd imagined those moments at the fence when she could hardly breathe.

When love hits, you know it.

He might have been talking about Jeremy and his new horse, but it seemed to her he'd meant it to mean something much more personal. Had it been his way of telling her how he felt about her? Did she dare think it? Believe it? If she didn't get an answer to those questions soon, she didn't know how she could go on living.

They'd both been so careful all these months to honor boundaries. In the beginning she knew he was still trying to put his grief behind him. Claire had been so careful not to intrude on his private thoughts. He was a man who kept things close to his chest, especially with the enormous responsibilities he carried as a Ranger.

She knew from the first day that she loved her job and wouldn't say or do anything that could jeopardize his faith in her. She could imagine the women who wished they had the inside track on him. But it would take a very special woman to penetrate the casing that guarded his heart.

He'd been so shattered over losing his wife and parents, it was a miracle he'd been able to carry on. Jeremy was the one responsible for giving Vic a reason to go on living. She'd learned that long before Jeremy had been kidnapped.

When she'd realized he wasn't coming out of school that day, her heart had almost died because she knew the news would tear Vic to pieces. If he'd been killed, then she knew Vic would want to die. They had to find him and find him fast. Someone upstairs had heard her prayers. His son was now home and safe and sound.

After parking the car in the garage, she entered the kitchen and tiptoed down the hall past the den. The door was closed, but she could see light shining through the crack. Vic didn't want to be disturbed. He was probably talking with his friends about the case he couldn't investigate further until his boss told him he could get back to work.

She peeked in Jeremy's room. He was asleep. The poor kid had to be worn out after such a huge day. To be truthful, Claire was exhausted, but it was the mental kind. After taking a shower she got ready for bed. She didn't know she'd fallen asleep until she heard Jeremy's voice. He'd come into her room and stood at the side of her bed in his pajamas.

Her watch said 2:00 a.m. Alarmed, she sat up. "Hi, honey. What's wrong? Did you have a bad dream?"

"No. Dad's in the den and the door is closed. Can I sleep with you?"

After the horror he'd lived through, how could she turn him away?

"Okay. Climb under the covers."

He scrambled onto the king-size bed. She gave him one of her pillows and turned on her side to look at him in the semidarkness.

Tears slid down his cheeks. "I don't want you to leave."

She leaned over and kissed his forehead. "Let's not worry about my leaving tonight. I want to hear about Daken."

"He follows me everywhere."

"You've got a friend for life. A horse can live a long time."

"That's what Dad said. Nate's mom let him come over this afternoon. He didn't want to leave when it was time to go home. Tomorrow we're going to teach Daken tricks."

"What a wonderful idea. I bet Nate wants a miniature horse, too."

"But they don't have a pasture or a barn."

"That's right, and your little horse has to eat grass."

"Claire? Do you like my dad?"

Wow. That was out of the blue. "Of course I do."

"But I mean do you really like him?"

Oh, Jeremy…

"Yes. I *really* do. He's the best Texas Ranger in the whole state and the best father I've ever seen. He found you when nobody else could. That's because he loves you so much." Suddenly she remembered something and reached for her phone. "I want to show you something."

"What?"

"That first day we'd been looking everywhere for you and had to come home to sleep. Your father and Ranger Saunders were so exhausted, they plopped down in the family room. Take a look. Your dad doesn't know I took this." She handed him the phone.

Jeremy laughed. "They look funny all sprawled out. Dad doesn't have his shoes on."

"I told him to take them off and lie down. He was so spent after worrying about you all evening, that he never moved the rest of the night. Neither did Ranger Saunders." She took the phone and put it back on the table.

"Claire?" Jeremy said. He sounded so sober.

"Yes?" Her heart was pounding.

"Do you love my dad?"

She needed to give him a safe answer. "Yes. Who wouldn't love him? He's what heroes are made of."

"I *knew* you did. Thanks for letting me talk to you. I'll go back to bed now."

That was a surprise. "Okay. See you in the morning. Sleep well."

Chapter Seven

Vic couldn't believe it when Jeremy climbed into his bed Sunday morning. He checked his watch through bleary eyes. It was only seven thirty. He hadn't left the den until three. Kit had sent him some information on the case. So far they hadn't been able to find a link to anyone higher up in the government who could've orchestrated the kidnapping plot.

Vic pored over the coroner's report on the crash in Colorado until long after he'd put his son to bed. No alcohol or drugs had been involved. Jamison Lowell had definitely been eliminated. Vic wanted to do a thorough background check on him, but it wouldn't happen until he was allowed back to work.

He'd heard the garage door open around ten and knew Claire had gotten home safely. Much as he'd wanted to intercept her, he needed to wait until they were alone. He didn't want Jeremy to hear them talking.

On Monday, after he got back from therapy, he'd make arrangements for his son to play at Nate's house for a few hours. Hopefully Nate's mom could bring him home when it was time for the nanny interviews. During the time they'd have alone, he hoped to get some answers from Claire before he made a decision that could change their lives.

"Dad—I've got something to tell you."

"Can it wait for a little while, sport? I haven't had enough sleep."

"But this is important."

"I know you love Daken, but you'll have to wait to play with him until after breakfast when I'm up and dressed."

"Claire let me get in bed with her last night."

That brought Vic to a sitting position in a hurry. He raked a hand through his hair. To his knowledge it had never happened before. His son had needed a mother's comfort. "If you had a nightmare, you should have come to my room."

"But you were in the den and the door was closed. You told me that when it's closed, I'm not supposed to go in because you're doing Ranger business."

Vic's eyes closed tightly. "That was a dumb rule. You can always come in. I'm sorry."

"That's okay. She was nice and didn't get mad or anything."

Claire would never be anything but loving to his son. He'd never seen her behave any other way.

"Did she tell you a story to help you get to sleep?"

"No. I asked her if she loved you, and guess what?"

Adrenaline surged through his body. "What?"

"She said she did! She showed me a picture of you she took on her phone when you were asleep."

"What?"

"It was really funny. You didn't have your shoes on and Kit was sound asleep, too."

Vic remembered that night all too well, but he didn't know she'd pulled out her phone while he and Kit were unconscious.

"She said you're a real superhero."

"She did, huh?"

"Yeah. She says you're the best Texas Ranger in the *whole* state."

The words were gratifying to hear, but there was a whole lot of difference between loving someone, and being *in* love. Jeremy didn't understand that distinction when it came to men and women.

"I bet if you told her you loved her, she'd stay with us."

He sucked in his breath. "You think?"

"Yes. You love her, don't you?"

"Yes. Everyone loves Claire."

"I mean the way you loved Mom."

Well, well. Maybe his boy understood a lot more than he'd given him credit for. "I think you're asking too many questions. Let me get showered and we'll talk later. Okay?"

No more sleep for him. The conversation with his son had him feeling wide awake. Later when he walked to the kitchen, he found everyone gone. Claire had left his breakfast on the stove.

Of course he knew where they were. He poured himself coffee and downed the eggs and bacon before heading for the barn. Before he reached it, he spotted three figures and a little horse out in the nearby pasture. Nate had already come over.

Vic stopped walking so he could take in the scene. Peals of laughter came from the boys as Daken followed them around. Like one of the kids, Claire sat in the green grass urging the horse to come to her. He yearned to get down in the grass with her and pull her into his arms.

Last Monday night he couldn't have imagined this scenario. With his son missing, his thoughts had gone so dark he'd come close to losing his mind. But Claire wouldn't let him sink into that black void. She loved Jeremy, too, and was determined they would find him. That woman never gave up. There was no one else like her.

Last year when she'd shown up to be interviewed for the nanny position, Jeremy had felt an immediate connection. Over the past nine months it had grown until the two of them had formed an unbreakable bond. Many times people thought she was his mother, and she had to tell them otherwise.

Vic had felt an immediate connection, too. Claire Ames was intelligent, vibrant and had a natural beauty no man would be immune to. In the beginning it had worried him because his attraction to her had been instantaneous. He'd feared he might not be able to keep his distance. But since she never overstepped her boundaries, they'd managed to live under the same roof and provide the stability Jeremy needed.

"Hey, Dad! Come and play with Daken!"

Jarred from his personal thoughts, he headed toward

them and gave Jeremy a hug. "Hey, Nate. How are you?" He tousled his head of blond hair.

"Good. That horse is so cute. I wish I had one."

"Well, you're welcome to come over here anytime and play with him."

The horse had walked over to Claire, who was still sitting. He kept butting his nose against her arm. She laughed and rubbed his head. Vic hunkered down to run a hand over Daken's back.

To his wonder a pair of crystalline gray eyes swept over Vic and lingered instead of looking away. She seemed to like what she saw. The feeling was mutual. Her wide smile, the lovely curves of her body were so enticing he was in danger of forgetting they weren't alone. Desire, swift and powerful, rushed through him.

To counteract her spell on him, he rolled over on his stomach. Pretty soon he could feel the horse's nose nudging him. The boys roared with laughter.

"Dad, Daken thinks you're playing a game."

Vic was glad that was what his son thought. He lay still while the horse continued to find ways to make him move. Claire broke into laughter. "You'd better do something soon, Jim, or that horse is going to walk on your back."

"Who's Jim?" Jeremy wanted to know.

"Didn't I tell you?" Claire answered him. "While your dad and I were looking for you, we pretended to be spies and wore sunglasses."

"You did? What was *your* name?" Vic's son was a quick study.

"It was Elaine," Vic stated and got to his feet. "Whenever we asked people questions, we told them we were Jim and Elaine from an insurance company investigating a case."

"That's awesome," both boys said in unison.

"Elaine was the awesome one. We were trying to find out why the man who kidnapped you had driven to Buda with his two friends. She got this idea to look up his name in an old high school year book at the high school to find out if his family lived there."

"Did he?" At this point Nate was as fascinated as Jeremy.

"No," Claire said, getting to her feet. "But we found a picture of one of his friends in the yearbook, and your dad tracked down his girlfriend, who was that lady at the house where they'd taken you. I wish you could have seen your father barge into that trailer and bring you out."

Nate's eyes had rounded. "Whoa."

She smiled. "Whoa is right."

"Then Elaine drove us home, and I bet she drove 100 miles an hour to get us there."

She darted Vic an amused glance. "Not quite that fast."

"Close," he countered with a grin.

"You'd make a good Texas Ranger, Claire." This from Nate.

"No, no. There's only one Ranger in thi—in the Malone family."

The near slip caused Vic's heart to skip a beat. The three of them *were* a family.

"Claire's a chemist," Jeremy muttered, not sounding

the least bit happy about it. He looked up at Vic. "Can women be Rangers?"

"You bet."

"I didn't know that."

"I have an idea," Claire spoke up before Jeremy could ask any more difficult questions. "Let's get Comet saddled so you and Nate can take turns riding. Maybe Daken will follow you."

"Yeah!"

Vic smiled into her eyes. She had a way… "Let's all go riding!"

Claire rode along while the boys took turns riding with Vic. Sure enough, Daken followed Jeremy wherever he went. It did the heart good to see his little horse's devotion this soon. Buying Daken had turned out to be therapeutic for Jeremy. For Vic, too.

It was almost one o'clock before the boys said they were hungry. Vic told them he'd take them out for lunch at their favorite drive-through. The boys voted for Short Stop. Claire called Nate's mom to see if it was all right.

After taking care of the horses, they took off for the restaurant. Because Nate was with them, Claire sat in front with Vic while the boys buckled up in back. He could get used to this in a hurry.

A big surprise greeted them when they got back to the house. Carol, his sister-in-law from Blanco, had come to Austin to do some shopping. She'd driven by to find out if Randy could play with Jeremy for a while. Vic always enjoyed seeing her, but wished it hadn't been today.

The three boys ran out to the barn. To Vic's chagrin, Claire excused herself so he could spend time alone with Carol. It was the last thing he wanted, but it couldn't be helped. No telling how long she'd stay away.

As he might have guessed, she didn't come home until late. It was almost eleven before he heard her car pull into the garage.

You escaped tonight, Claire, but tomorrow it's going to be a different story.

DR. MARSHALL STUDIED Vic as he walked into his office and sat down for their Monday session.

"You know what? You look rested. What's gone on at your house?"

Vic filled him in on the activities of the weekend. The psychiatrist smiled. "It used to be a boy and his dog."

"I know. Daken acts like a dog, but he can't sleep in the house, which is a good thing."

The doctor laughed. When it subsided he said, "Something else has changed."

"Yes. It has," Vic said definitively. "I know what you were getting at during our last session, and you were right. I've been upset for a long time by a situation that has been out of my control. Trying to hide it all these months from everyone turned my emotions into a volcano threatening to blow.

"The kidnapping was the catalyst that caused the eruption. When I confronted Leroy, who sat there knowing where my son was without saying anything, all my anger and frustration came together, and I exploded."

The older man smiled. "Good."

"I'm in love with my nanny, but all these months I've been afraid to do anything about it because I hired her to help me with my son, not to pursue her. I was afraid to reach out to her because she never gave me any sign that she might be interested in me that way.

"After the kidnapping happened, she helped me look for Jeremy. I loved her and my son so much, yet I couldn't do anything about either problem. What if I ended up losing both of them? The more Leroy sat there with his head bowed not saying a word, the angrier I got, until I couldn't take it another second."

"What do you think you've learned from this experience?"

"That there will always be times when certain situations are out of my control. That's when I need to identify them early enough to take a step back."

He nodded. "Are you planning to do something about your nanny?"

"Absolutely. When I leave here, I'm going to have it out with her."

"And if she doesn't give you the answer you want?"

"I'll have to deal with it, just like Jeremy. But I don't feel angry anymore."

"What *do* you feel?"

"Surprised that it took coming to you before I could see what I was doing by not admitting my feelings about her to myself. I was afraid that by owning up to them, I might lose her, so I kept putting it off, obviously to my own detriment."

"You've learned a lot. I thought we'd have to do more sessions for you to reach this point. Tell you what I'm going to do. I'll fax your boss a letter stating that you're ready to get back on the job with the proviso that you meet with me once a week for the next month. I want to see you next Monday and we'll talk some more."

Vic let out the breath he was holding. "Thank you, Dr. Marshall."

"Feel like you've been let out of jail?"

"You know it."

"Your boss will be happy to have you back."

They shook hands and he left with renewed excitement. He could get back to work, but right now all he could think about was Claire.

It was just ten o'clock. The session hadn't taken long. On the drive home he called Nate's mom. She informed him Claire had brought Jeremy over to play. She'd drop him off at one.

Vic thanked her and hung up before calling Kit to tell him the good news. His friend was out on a case, so he left the message on his voice mail. He'd probably hear from TJ before the day was out. He phoned Clint and had to leave the same message with him on his voice mail.

After that he left messages with his friends Cy and Luckey. No one was available, but it didn't matter. At the moment he was on his way home to Claire and couldn't think about anything else.

The cleaning service van was leaving just as Vic pulled into the driveway. He waved to them. After parking, he hurried into the house. "Claire?"

"In Jeremy's room!"

He headed in that direction. "What are you doing? I just saw the cleaners leave."

"They do a great job, but Jeremy left his spy stuff on the bed. I want the room to look tidy when you show the women around."

She'd dressed in an attractive, short-sleeved khaki dress with a rope belt. He could hardly take his eyes off her while she put Jeremy's stuff in the backpack.

"There. It's done." She lifted her eyes to him. "Are you hungry? I can fix you something."

"No, thanks. We need to talk."

"How was your session with Dr. Marshall?"

"First things first. Shall we go in the family room?"

His comment seemed to take her back. "Sure." She preceded him into the other room and sat down in one of the leather chairs.

Vic perched on the arm of the couch opposite her. "Jeremy told me he spent part of the night in your bed. Do you want to go first and tell me the thrust of the conversation? If not, I'll tell you what we talked about when he got in my bed."

Color seeped into her face. There was no mistaking the pinkish tinge. He waited. There was no response.

"According to Jeremy, you love me."

He heard a sharp intake of breath before she said, "My conversation with him was in the reverse of yours. He told me you loved me."

"During the night it appears my son decided to take the matter of your leaving into his own hands and fix everything."

"He's nothing if not straightforward," she muttered.

"Unlike his father when it comes to matters of the heart," Vic admitted.

"You lost your heart to your wife. Jeremy isn't old enough to understand the kind of pain you went through."

"I've been telling myself the same thing for quite a while, until he told me you took a picture of me the night Jeremy was missing. That's when I realized I've underestimated him. He gets everything."

She stirred restlessly. "What do you mean?"

"He figured out there was a reason why you took that picture when I didn't know about it."

"I took it so that when he saw it, he would know how exhausted you were while you were out trying to find him," she defended. "It proved your love for him."

"In his mind it proved something else, too."

"That I love you?" she fired. "I *have* learned to love you in my own way, Vic. You're a remarkable man and father, loved by your friends and family. What's there not to love about you?"

"I could say the same thing to you. I've loved you for a long time. After the way you helped me find Jeremy, I can't find the words."

She got up from the chair. "We made a good team."

He shook his head. "I despise that term. It doesn't begin t—"

"Claire?" a familiar voice cried out, interrupting what he was going to say. "Dad?"

Vic frowned. "In the family room, sport."

He came running into Vic's arm. They hugged hard. "How come you came home so soon?"

"I have a stomachache and told Nate's mom I didn't want to stay there."

Vic's glance met Claire's over Jeremy's dark head. "Then I'm glad you're here. Do you want to lie down in your room?"

"No. I want to stay in here with you and Claire." He curled up on the couch just as Vic's cell rang.

He pulled the phone from his pocket. It was Nate's mom. He clicked On. She started to apologize, but he cut her off. "No explanation is necessary. Thank you for letting him play there as long as you did and driving him home. He's fine now and will talk to Nate later." He clicked Off.

Jeremy lay there looking at both of them with his warm brown eyes. "Is everything okay?"

"Of course," Claire assured him. "Why wouldn't it be?"

He sat up. "Are you two going to get married?"

In an instant, Claire lost color. "You know what? While you two talk, I'm going in the kitchen to fix us some lunch. Maybe by the time it's ready, your tummy won't hurt so much."

His son's timing to come home couldn't have been worse. After she disappeared, Vic walked over and sat in the chair she'd vacated. Jeremy swung his legs to the floor. "Is Claire mad at me?"

"I don't think so."

"I bet she is."

"Why?"

"Because she wouldn't answer me."

"That's because she couldn't."

"How come?"

"A lady waits for the man to ask her to marry him."

"Oh. So you haven't asked her?"

"No."

"But you said you loved her, and she said she loved you."

Vic had to weigh what he was about to say with the greatest care. "Is that what you want? For us to get married?"

A smile broke out on his face. "Yeah. I wanted you to get married a long time ago."

Good grief. "Just because two people love each other, it doesn't always mean that they get married."

Jeremy slid off the couch. "Don't you want to marry her?"

"Maybe she doesn't want to marry me. Some women wouldn't like to be married to a lawman. You know Nate's dad?"

"Yeah."

"He works in hospital administration. He goes to work at eight in the morning and comes home at five every night. Nate's mom doesn't have to wonder where he is or how long he'll be gone."

"But Claire doesn't worry about you when you're gone on cases. She knows you have a job to do."

"That's true because she's your nanny. I hired her to watch out for you. But if I asked her to marry me, she might say that she doesn't want to be married to a Texas Ranger. Some women would be too afraid."

His son moved closer to him. "She wasn't afraid

when I got kidnapped. She helped you find me. She's awesome!"

Vic had no answer to counter Jeremy's faultless logic. "You're right."

"Why don't you ask her and find out?"

"I can't do it right now. We need to eat lunch first, and then those ladies who would like to be a nanny are coming over here to meet you."

His face scrunched up in a frown. "I don't want to meet them."

"We have to, but if you don't like any of them, we'll talk about it after they leave."

"Do you promise to ask Claire to marry you?"

"Tell you what. I promise to talk to her about everything tonight after you're in bed. Do we have a deal?"

It took him a minute to say yes. Then they walked to the kitchen together. Claire looked up at them. "Lunch is ready. Come and sit. Grilled cheese sandwiches and tomato soup."

"Yum."

She smiled at Jeremy. "Sounds like your tummy is feeling better."

"The pain's not so bad now."

"That's good."

ALL FOUR OF the women who showed up at the house were in their twenties. Claire found each one physically attractive in her own way. All four couldn't take their eyes off Vic. No doubt Claire had reacted the same way when she'd met him. Jaw-dropping gorgeous was a term Kaye had used in referring to Claire's employer.

After unloading the marriage bomb, Jeremy turned out to be a model of decorum during the interviews. His deed was done. That child…

Whatever he and his father had talked about before lunch had helped Jeremy to behave like the sweet boy he was. He took each nanny wannabe on a tour of the house and showed her his bedroom.

At the end of each interview, Vic and Jeremy would take the applicant out to the barn to show her the horses. Claire asked each of them a few questions and answered theirs. When Vic accompanied the last applicant to the front door, Claire and Jeremy waited for him in the family room so they could talk.

He walked in, but didn't sit. "They were all very nice. I know what I think, and I'm pretty sure Claire knows what she thinks. However the most important person here is you, Jeremy. We want to hear your impressions."

"They were okay I guess, but none of them wanted to pet Daken. The first one wore too much perfume. She asked me how come you weren't married, Dad."

His dark brows lifted. "Nothing about your favorite foods or what you liked to do after school?"

"Nope."

"Oh, yeah. She told me she's afraid of horses."

"Did you tell her she had to water and feed the horses sometimes?" Claire wanted to know.

"Yes, but she didn't say anything. Oh, and you know that one with the long black ponytail?"

Vic nodded. Claire thought she looked very exotic.

"She kept asking me how many girlfriends you had.

I showed her my picture album, but all she did was stare at *your* pictures."

By now Vic was looking frustrated.

"The one in those high heels stumbled in my room."

"Oh, no—" Claire exclaimed, trying to hold back a laugh.

"She fell on the bed. When I asked her if she was okay, she got mad and told me it was nothing. I didn't like her 'cause she wasn't nice. Oh yeah, and she's never heard of Wolverine, but she asked me a lot of questions about Mom."

"Dare I ask about the last applicant?" came the voice of ice. Claire couldn't look at Vic or she'd burst her seams.

"Well, she asked if I had an extra picture of you in your Ranger uniform she could have."

"What?"

"I told her the Rangers don't wear uniforms, but when you have to be in a parade you put on your white hat."

There was no holding back now. Claire burst into laughter that reverberated throughout the family room. Vic was clearly upset, but that didn't stop her from enjoying this moment.

"Jeremy Malone. You made all of that up."

"No, I didn't. Honest. They all asked me something else, too, but I'm not going to tell you what."

"How come? Why stop now?"

"It's a secret. Now that they're gone, can I go out to the barn and make sure Daken is all right?"

"Go on," Vic muttered. He was clearly in a foul mood.

Claire studied the face of the man she loved. "Honest, he wasn't lying, Vic. You are attractive and your picture has been in the paper and on TV several times in the past year. You're a Texas Ranger, a phenomenon, to these young women who'd love to take care of your son. They aren't shallow, they were just awestruck."

He took a deep breath. "*You* didn't act like that."

"You had no idea what I was thinking. I wanted to ask Jeremy dozens of questions about you, but I knew he'd tell you everything I said so I kept my mouth shut."

Amusement lurked in the depths of his gorgeous black eyes. "That's because you're too smart for your own good."

"I know a good thing when it comes along, and I wanted that job. My sisters were older and I always wished I'd had a brother, but it didn't happen. The minute I met Jeremy I thought he was exactly the kind of little brother I would have wanted. The perfect age. He's funny and creative and kind. After meeting you I thought, throw in the father, too, since his son is a chip off the old block."

He moved toward her. "So you thought of me as an old block?"

"Well, there are all kinds of blocks in all kinds of sizes and shapes, some more interesting than others. When Jeremy told me you could eat a whole box of Lucky Charms and a quart of milk out of the mixing bowl without stopping, I knew I wanted to be your son's nanny."

A heartbreaking smile broke out on his Vic's face.

"You mean that's what it took to get you to come to work for me?"

"That and the way the two of you walk. It's amazing, really. The way you hold yourselves, the set of your bodies, they're identical. It's fun to watch you when you're together side by side."

"I like to watch you, too, the way you walk, run, smile, laugh, the way your hair attracts the sunlight and turns the strands to gold, how good you always smell."

The words she'd only dreamed of him saying to her caused her heart to thud, but the moment was ruined when they heard the front doorbell. She couldn't believe the horrible timing. "Maybe one of the nanny applicants has come back for some reason. Do you want me to get it?"

"No, thanks. I'll do it and get rid of her quick." He charged out of the room while she stood there trembling.

A minute later she heard male voices, and before she knew it, Kit walked into the family room with Vic. The other Ranger wore an excited expression.

"It's nice to see you, Claire. What a difference from a few nights ago."

"I don't even want to think about it. How are you?"

"Great, now that Vic has been put back on the job. TJ has taken Rodriguez off the case and reassigned me to help Vic, since I was in on it from the start. I came straight here from headquarters. I've looked at the file and found something we ought to check out."

Claire knew what that kind of news meant to Vic. "That's great that you're back on the job, Vic!" She looked at Jeremy's father. "Did you know when you came home from your session this morning?"

"Dr. Marshall told me he was going to fax TJ and tell him I was ready to get back to work."

"Your boss works fast."

Vic nodded. "Now I need to tell Jeremy, but I'll wait until I put him to bed."

"I think that's a good idea. I'll start dinner for you. After we eat, you'll have to go out to the barn, Kit. Jeremy has acquired a new horse."

"You're kidding."

"I know how much you love horses. He'll want to show you himself."

"Of course. Why don't I go out there right now? Much as I'd like to stay for one of your delicious dinners, I can't because I'm meeting my half brother, Grady, for a meal. He's on the rodeo circuit and he's in town for the night, but I'll take a rain check."

"You've got it."

Claire shared a heart-stopping glance with Vic before the two men walked out the back door. It said he wasn't finished with her yet and set her pulse racing off the charts.

Chapter Eight

Kit was a horse lover and hunkered down to examine Daken. "I always wanted one of these when I was little. You're a lucky boy, Jeremy."

"I know."

"How are he and Comet getting along?"

"Good."

"I'm happy for you." He gave Jeremy a hug. "Glad you're back home safe and sound."

"Me, too. Claire told me you helped look for me. Thanks."

"You're welcome."

"She took a picture of you and Dad when you fell asleep at our house."

"She did?" Kit looked up at Vic, who understood it was something of a shock to hear.

"Claire will show it to you," Jeremy chattered.

"Well, I'll definitely have to ask her. And ask her to delete it," he mumbled, but Vic heard him and chuckled. Kit hated pictures of himself as much as Vic did.

"Don't stay out here too long, sport. Claire has started fixing dinner. You'll have to come in soon."

"Okay. Are more ladies going to come over tomorrow?"

Kit's brows lifted in silent query.

"No. I've already made my decision."

"Good," his son said.

He knew that was what Jeremy would say. Vic had made the decision a long time ago, but had been afraid to act until now. That little monkey knew exactly what was on Vic's mind. "I'll tell you about it later."

"Okay. See ya, Kit."

"You bet."

As soon as they got back to the house, Vic explained that he'd been interviewing nannies.

"How did that go?"

"The truth?"

Kit nodded.

"I'm going to phone the employment agency in a few minutes and ask them to cancel tomorrow's appointments. They'll also need to tell the women who already came to the house today that they don't need to wait for a call back—I've chosen someone else."

His friend grinned. "So you're keeping Claire on."

"Yup." One way or another.

"Walk me around to my car," Kit said. "I need to show you something I printed off for you to think about."

They approached his Silverado truck and Kit opened the door to reach for the printouts.

Vic looked at the heading at the top of the first page. "Jamison Lowell."

"Yup. These are his bank records. His salary at the

school district is public record. Name me a school employee who can deposit $20,000 at a time in his account, three different times in the past three months. Look at the dates of the deposits. That last one coincides with the day after he hired Leroy. Now, look at the date he withdrew all his money."

A low whistle sounded from Vic. "It all fits, Kit. He got his payoff in installments, then fled the state. Now he's dead." He looked at his friend. "Someone put out a hit on Jamison and had him killed once he'd hired Leroy."

"He was being blackmailed."

"No question about it. We've got to dig into Lowell's past. Because Jeremy was kidnapped after I was put on the gaming board, this has to mean Lowell was a gambler. Maybe he couldn't pay his debts and that's why he put his house up for sale. The first place to start tomorrow morning is the bank. I'll ask TJ to get a subpoena and meet you at headquarters. We'll need Lowell's bank records from Colorado, too."

"I read through Rodriguez's notes," Kit said. "There's nothing to indicate that Lowell's next-door neighbors ever got back to him about the name of the Realtor."

"In that case we'll swing by that house again. If it hasn't sold, we'll talk to the Realtor selling the property. There should be a sign up by now, or we need to find out why there isn't one."

"Let's check the casino near Luckenbach. Ask the captain for a subpoena to analyze the surveillance tapes. We'll get staff to go through them and see if they can identify Lowell in any of them."

"There's a ton of work to do."

Kit nodded. "Glad you're back. See you in the morning."

"Thanks for coming by. Before I left the doctor's office he said, 'Feel like you've been let out of jail?'"

"He understands all right."

Vic watched him drive away before he entered the house. Claire had to be cooking something Italian. They all loved three-cheese manicotti.

He went to the den first and made the phone call to the employment agency. Now that his duties were out of the way, he could concentrate on Claire. But once again he was thwarted because Jeremy had come back from the barn, regaling her with Daken's latest antics. She delighted in hearing about them. Their conversation sounded like mother and son. It warmed and filled the hole that had once done damage to his heart.

"Dad?" Jeremy poked his head in the door. "Dinner's ready. Guess what we're having."

"Manicotti."

"Nope. Guess again."

"Spaghetti."

"Nope. Have you ever had cannelloni?"

"Once, I think."

"Claire said it's made with veal. She let me taste it. I love it."

There wasn't anything about Claire Jeremy didn't like. As for Vic...

Jeremy's bedtime couldn't come soon enough for him. If the kidnapping hadn't happened, he would have made arrangements for his son to spend the night at his aunt Carol's. But Jeremy was still too fragile to be away from home yet. Vic needed to keep a constant guard on him and Claire. Until he put the people in prison who were trying to take Vic down for Quarls's arrest, no one was safe.

He needed to talk to TJ about putting surveillance on his family. *His family.* Claire *was* family and had been for a long time.

"Dad?"

His gaze flicked to Jeremy. "Let's go find out if Claire needs our help."

"When are you going to ask her?"

Vic had been waiting for that. "I have to talk to her about a few things first."

"But you promised."

He put a hand on his son's shoulder. "Give me time, and everything is going to come out right. Trust me."

His eyes grew dull before he turned away and hurried back to the kitchen. Vic hated that things were so complicated. Certain issues had to be straightened out until he could present Jeremy with a fait accompli. But that couldn't happen until he got a declaration out of her that she was in love with him.

When he reached the kitchen, Jeremy was already at the table. Claire's gray eyes lit on Vic. "Come on. The food's hot." She poured him coffee while he sat next to Jeremy. It was her way to serve them first and wait on them before joining them near the end of the meal. Before long that was all going to change.

"How come Kit came over?"

"He's going to be working with me again."

Jeremy put his fork down. "Is your vacation over?"

"Yes. I'm going in to the office tomorrow so I can clear up this latest case."

"Will *you* be here?" he asked Claire with anxiety in his voice.

"Of course."

Jeremy was showing signs of having a meltdown.

"Guess what, sport. After it's over, we're going to take a big vacation. I thought we might go to Jamaica and stop at Disney World on the way."

Claire look surprised before she smiled at Jeremy. "That sounds exciting, you lucky boy."

"But who will take care of our horses?"

"You remember John at the local stable?"

"Yeah."

"He'll come over every day to see to them."

"Oh."

Vic's gaze swerved to Claire. "This dinner is fabulous."

"Thanks. I thought we needed a change from the same old."

The same old suited Vic just fine, but Jeremy suddenly slid off the chair and ran out of the kitchen.

"He's loved having you home," Claire murmured.

"That's not what's wrong. I have to go to him. Please don't go anywhere. I'll find you after he goes to sleep."

Two hours later, that was exactly what he did.

Vic walked out to the barn and discovered she'd gone riding. He could see her silhouette in the darkness coming closer. "Claire?"

"Hi. It's a perfect night. I decided Marshmallow needed some exercise."

He walked up to the horse and rubbed her forelock. Claire stayed mounted. "You shouldn't be out here after dark."

"I couldn't help it tonight."

Vic couldn't help it either as he reached for her. "Come here, Claire."

"Oh—" A tiny cry escaped her lips when he put his hands on her hips and pulled her beautiful body down against his. She'd changed into jeans and a cream-colored Western shirt he hadn't seen before. Her fragrance intoxicated him.

"You're so beautiful. Do you have any idea how long I've dreamed of doing this? I'm going to kiss you. If you don't want me to, it's too late." Far too late to wonder about her feelings for him. He was on fire for her.

Without waiting for an answer, he lowered his mouth to hers. There was nothing tentative about his kiss. He'd held back his desire for her far too long. Now that he had her in his arms his passion had taken over.

Urging her mouth open, he kissed her deeply, reveling in the taste of her while his hands roved over her back, drawing her even closer so there was no air between them. She wrapped her arms around his neck and kissed him back with intense hunger. She'd been hiding her feelings, too, otherwise she wouldn't be caught up in this euphoria where nothing mattered but the two of them. Her response was more than he could ever have imagined.

He lost count of time and his surroundings as every

kiss grew into another one, leaving them breathless. The joy of loving and being loved again had quite literally taken his breath away. "I'm in love with you, Claire. I've loved you from the very beginning."

"I've waited so long to hear those words." Her confession almost gave him a heart attack. She kissed his face all over, starting with his eyelids. "I'm so in love with you, I've been bursting with it for months. If you hadn't said those words to me tonight, I don't know how I could have gone on living."

Their mouths met again in a frenzy of mutual need. "I've been so afraid you'd leave if I tried to get close to you too soon."

"I had the same fear," she admitted. "I didn't want to be the nanny who came on to you. All these months there've been so many times I almost stepped over the line I'd drawn. Today I saw myself in the four women who came to the house. They couldn't help their attraction to you any more than I could. I'm crazy about you, Vic."

"You never acted like them." He planted gentle kisses about her face before finding her lush mouth once more. "You stepped into the role of mother to Jeremy so naturally, it was like it was meant to be."

"I love him with all my heart. He's an extension of you in so many ways. I'm out of my mind in love with both of you. How could you not have known that all this time?"

"My fear blinded me to what I wanted more than life itself. I need you, Claire. More than you'll ever know."

He pressed his forehead against hers. "I know we have a lot to work out, but you can't leave me."

"You think I want to?" she cried. "Kiss me again so I'll know I'm not dreaming."

Heat licked through his body as she gave herself up to him, holding nothing back. Wanting so much more, he finally relinquished her mouth so they could both breathe. "Let's put Marshmallow to bed, then go back to the house. I need you with me all night long."

"Now that you've kissed me, I don't know if I can let you go long enough to reach the barn."

"Then we're both in the same condition." They kissed again, starving for each other.

Vic managed to find the reins and led Marshmallow into the barn while keeping Claire clamped at his side. He removed the saddle while she took care of the bridle. A quick trip to the tack room and they could close the barn doors for the night.

"At last," he whispered, catching her to him. He wrapped his arms around her, burying his face in the glory of her hair. "To have you where I want you is surreal."

Not liking any separation, he picked her up and carried her like a bride to the back door of the house, kissing her all the way. He held the world in his arms. But when he reached for the handle, the door opened, revealing his pajama-clad son in the light from the kitchen. His eyes were shining.

"Hi," was all he said.

Vic lowered Claire to the ground, but kept his arm around her waist. "Aren't you supposed to be in bed?"

"I woke up and couldn't find you."

"Sorry about that, sport."

"Did you…" He lowered his eyes. "You know…"

Yes, Vic knew. "Tell you what. Go back to bed and we'll come in to keep you company until you fall asleep again."

"Okay, but don't take too long."

The second he left them alone, Claire slid her hands up his chest to his face. She cradled it between her hands. Her eyes looked silver in the dim light. "I'm the luckiest woman on earth to be loved by a man like you. When I first met you, I thought such a love could never happen to me. I've gone to bed for so many months aching to get close to you. Being able to love your son has been the only thing keeping me sane."

"You don't know the half of it." Vic pressed a hot, hungry kiss to her mouth. "The thrill of coming home to you after work at night has been the mainstay of my existence. The guys have tried to line me up with other women, but I couldn't. You leave every other woman in the dust."

She kissed him hard and long. "My sisters got one look at you at my graduation and they knew why I never wanted to go out on dates. No other man measures up to you, Vic."

"Dad? Aren't you coming?"

"Give us a few minutes," Vic called back.

Claire gave him an impish smile. "Come on. You know he's not going to give up."

"There are times when he has to learn."

"Under ordinary circumstances that would be true,

Ranger Malone, but he's still recovering from the most frightening ordeal of his life."

"And ours," he said on a half groan. "While you were playing Elaine to my Jim, I knew you were the only woman I wanted in my life. I might never have found him if it weren't for you. I love you beyond belief." His throat had swollen with so much emotion he couldn't talk. Instead he drew her to him and rocked her for a long time.

"I love you more." He felt her body shake with happy sobs. She clung to him, wetting his shirt. With Claire in his life, he knew he could get through anything. "Don't *you* ever go missing on me," she warned him in a voice full of tears. "I wouldn't be able to function."

"I'm not planning on going anywhere without you. Shall we go help Jeremy fall asleep?"

"Yes. Just don't kiss me again or I won't be able to make it past the kitchen."

A deep chuckle escaped his throat as they moved inside. He locked the door and followed her trail to Jeremy's bedroom. He was sitting up in the middle of the double bed with his bedside lamp on. "I thought you were never coming."

Claire gave him a kiss on the cheek. "You know better than that. Love you." She removed her cowboy boots and sank down on one side of the bed.

Vic took off his boots. After turning off the light, he stretched out so he lay on the other side next to Jeremy. With Claire a body away, things were safer. Jeremy slid down and nestled under the covers.

"I love you, son. Now it's time to go to sleep. We're all tired."

A little sigh escaped Jeremy. "I love you, Dad. I love you, too, Claire."

It was just as well Vic couldn't be alone with her yet. He needed to calm his pounding heart and get himself under control. When he'd talked to Dr. Marshall about controlling his emotions, he hadn't been thinking about how it would be when he finally got her into his arms. There was no force greater or more powerful than love.

For the first time since Claire had come to live with them, Vic felt at peace. In a little while, when he knew Jeremy was asleep, he'd get up and take her with him so they could talk and make plans for the future.

LAST NIGHT HAD been the most thrilling moment of Claire's life. Vic had told her he loved and needed her. Lying there on the bed with him and his son, she'd felt complete. But she'd awakened this morning still on the bed wearing the same clothes, and both of them were gone.

Why hadn't Vic awakened her? Maybe he and Jeremy had gotten up early and had gone out to the barn. She'd never intended to sleep in there all night. Vic must have fallen asleep, too.

She picked up her boots and hurried out of the room to her bedroom. After setting her boots inside, she walked through the house and found Jeremy in the family room watching cartoons.

"Jeremy?"

"Hi! Dad had to go to work. He left you a message on the counter."

"Thanks." She rushed to the kitchen and saw the note.

Claire,

Kit called me at six this morning. We've decided to get an early start on this case. You'll be under surveillance to keep you safe. When I get home, you and I have a lot to talk about. Please tell me that last night wasn't just a dream. You did say you loved me, right?

Oh, Vic—she pressed the note to her chest, dying with love for him.

"Jeremy? I'm going to shower, and then I'll fix your breakfast. I thought it would be fun if we went to the library this morning and picked out some books to read."

"But I want to play with Daken."

"You can do both. Want to call Nate and see if he wants to go with us?" She bet his mom was trying to think up ways to entertain her children now that they were out of school.

Claire kept them busy all day. Since she hadn't heard from Vic by six in the evening, she took the boys to the Dairy Queen for Hungr-Buster burgers. They topped off dinner with chocolate chip ice cream Blizzard shakes for dessert.

Pretty soon it was time to take Nate home and get

Jeremy ready for bed. Her phone rang at ten o'clock. The second she saw the caller ID, she picked up.

"Vic?"

"Sorry I couldn't get back to you until now."

"I knew there had to be a reason."

"Kit and I are in Luckenbach. I'll explain everything later. All I need is the answer to one question. You're going to marry me, right?"

What a time to ask her. Joy that he'd asked her, plus pain that he might be gone a long time, buffeted her in waves. Tears trickled down her cheeks because he wasn't here to take her in his arms. "Yes. After last night, how could you think anything else?"

"Just making sure. Now I can breathe. We'll talk out all the details when this is over. But this much I can tell you. We got a break in the case while we were looking at a set of tapes. It has leapfrogged me to the higher-ups faster than I would have guessed. If I get the answers I want, then this case can be closed and we can celebrate."

She shuddered. She couldn't think about celebrations when he and Kit were in terrible danger. After the powers that be had arranged to kidnap Jeremy, they would definitely eliminate Vic if they could. But she needed to keep that concern to herself. He'd just asked her to be his wife. If she was to break down now and beg him not to do it, what kind of a fiancée would she be?

"This means you could be gone for a while."

"Hopefully not too long. You've got Carol's and Clint's help if you need it, plus twenty-four hour protection. Give Jeremy a kiss for me. I'll contact you as soon as I can. You won't be able to reach me by phone. If you have any questions, call headquarters. They'll keep you informed and convey any messages either way."

"Vic—please be careful and come back safe."

"When I do, I'm going to love you senseless. Are you ready for that?"

She fought the tears. "Hey, Jim—you're talking to Elaine. Remember?"

His deep chuckle came over the phone. "I love you, Claire."

"I love *you*. More than you'll ever know."

When she heard the click, she could hardly bear to be cut off from him. Last night he'd broken the silence and had let her know how he felt. How unfair was it that he was snatched away from her at the very moment he told her he wanted to marry her?

No way could she keep this news to herself. After she got ready for bed, she sat down to call her parents. Her mom answered.

"Hi, honey. How are you?"

"That's a good question. Is Dad there?"

"Yes. We're in the living room."

"Then put your phone on speaker. There's something exciting I have to tell you."

"Go ahead."

"Vic asked me to marry him!"

Her parents sounded overjoyed. They knew how much she loved him.

"We haven't made any plans because he's out on a case and might not be back for a while, but I had to tell you tonight. I guess it's no secret that I've loved him forever. He and Jeremy are my heart."

"We couldn't be happier," her dad told her. "What does this mean for you in terms of work?"

"Well, I won't be accepting either of the Houston job offers now. Vic's work is here in Austin. With it being summer and Jeremy out of school, I'll be taking care of him. In the fall I'm thinking I could get a part-time job as a chemist here in Austin. But it's all really up in the air. Are you two ready to be grandparents? He likes you both a lot already. Since Vic lost his parents, it's going to be especially important for Jeremy to bond with you."

Her father's voice broke when he said, "We can't wait to welcome that cute little fellow into the family."

"Your sisters are going to be thrilled for you," her mom chimed in.

"Just think. Jeremy's going to inherit two more aunts and uncles and some younger cousins. He's so cute. Did I tell you Vic bought him a miniature horse the other day?"

"You mentioned that," her father said.

"Yes. It's brown with white spots and so tiny it's absolutely adorable. Jeremy named it Daken. It follows him around everywhere when they go out to the pasture."

"Why don't you bring Jeremy over tomorrow?" her mother said.

"I will, but I'll call you first."

"Is he thrilled?"

"He doesn't know yet."

"When are you going to tell him?"

"In the morning. I can't wait. Now I'd better let you two get to bed. I love you."

"We love you. Good night and congratulations. We couldn't ask for a finer son-in-law-to-be, as if you didn't know."

There was no one like Vic. "Good night."

She'd barely hung up when Jeremy came into her bedroom. "Well, hi. Couldn't you go to sleep?"

"No. Can I get in bed with you?"

"Why don't we go back to your room and I'll stay with you until you fall asleep."

"Okay. Who were you talking to?"

"My mom and dad."

She followed him into his room. He climbed under the covers while she sat on the bed next to him. "Do you miss them?"

"I'll always love them, and I miss them if I haven't seen them for a while."

"They're nice."

"I'm glad you like them. They want us to go over there tomorrow. Would you like to do that?"

"Will Dad go with us?"

"No. He's out on a case and won't be home for a little while. He called earlier when I thought you were asleep. He told me to give you a kiss." She leaned over and pecked his cheek.

He was missing Vic. Hopefully her news would put a smile on his face. "Guess what?"

"What?"

"Tonight your dad asked me to marry him."

"He did?" Jeremy cried. His eyes shone with happiness.

"Yes, and I told him I wanted to be his wife more than anything in the world."

He shot up in bed and hugged her so hard he almost knocked her over. "Dad said a lady has to wait for the man to ask her. I've been waiting and waiting for him to ask you."

She laughed gently. "I've been waiting, too. Sometimes your father is slow as molasses before making up his mind about something."

"I know."

Jeremy sounded so adult just then, she melted with love for him.

"I always wanted my very own boy. I love you, Jeremy. If it's all right with you, I want to be a mother to you. No one can replace your own mother, but no one could love you more than I do."

He wiped his eyes. "I love you, too. Do you want to know a secret?"

"What is it, sweetheart?"

"I've wanted you to be my mother for a long time."

"Then aren't we lucky that we can be together as a family."

"Can I tell Nate?"

"You can tell everyone, even Comet and Daken."

He giggled. "You're funny, Claire."

She put an arm around his shoulders. "I'm the happiest woman in the world tonight."

"I'm happier." He looked at her with a loving expression.

"How come?"

"I never have to have a nanny again."

Chapter Nine

At 10:00 p.m. Vic got out of the Ford Super Duty F-350 Platinum crew cab truck he was using for his under-cover role. It had New Mexico plates and a decal of the Lipan Apache Nation on the back window. He locked it, looked around and then walked to a brown van parked two cars away in the packed casino parking area on the outskirts of Luckenbach.

Kit and two of the staff from the bureau running the surveillance van did a double take when Vic opened the door and climbed in.

"Good grief. When I look at you, I know it's you, but I don't recognize you at all. The Dream Tan really worked."

Vic grinned. "That's the idea. It's called red bronze. Clint's wife, Sandra, put it on me. She did my hands, too."

"It's a perfect job. Natural. Hey—take a look at the leather jacket." The guys whistled. "Nice. Expensive. The turquoise beading gives it an authentic air."

"It *is* an authentic Lipan design. One of my relatives lent it to me."

"The fit of the shoulders makes you appear bigger."

"He weighs fifty pounds more than I do. It's a good thing, considering I'm wearing a bulletproof vest underneath my plaid shirt."

"You're taller, too."

"I've got lifts in my cowboy boots."

"With that long black wig you closely resemble your Apache ancestor, minus the bandana. The touch of gray at the temples has aged you ten years."

"Sandra does a good job, don't you think?"

"I think you look scary as hell, in a classy, modern way. Claire and Jeremy need to see a picture of you dressed like this."

Before Vic could stop him, Kit took a couple of pictures with his camera phone. "I gotta tell you I wouldn't want to meet up with you in the dark. Do you know that spray tan makes your black eyes glitter?"

"Hopefully I look like a tribal elder from across the state line with means, ready to make some money at the roulette table and maybe something more." The casino came fully packed: slots, bingo, Texas Hold'em poker, blackjack, roulette, craps, baccarat. "From there I'll graduate to the backroom poker game. I've got my small dagger in case there's any trouble." He pulled it out from a sheath beneath his turquoise belt to show them, then put it back.

Kit squinted. "Like I said, I'm glad I'm on your side. Have you picked out a name?"

"Clint helped me. It's Eskaminzim. Don't worry about trying to pronounce it."

"I won't."

"It's authentic, but I go by the translation."

"Which is?"

"Big Mouth."

The guys chuckled.

"The Lipans speak English and Spanish now. I know enough to get by."

"I like your ring."

"Clint lent me all this ancestral turquoise jewelry. The listening/recording device is hidden in the necklace I'm wearing. You can't buy stuff like it nowadays."

"I believe you're having fun, Ranger Malone!"

"Aren't you?"

Kit nodded. "The top man needs to pay after kidnapping your son. Here's the cell phone you'll be using inside. It's programmed to reach us. That's it."

Vic put it in the front pocket of his jeans. "Well, gentlemen, I'm going hunting. See you later."

"Watch your back, Vic."

"Always."

He stepped down from the van and headed for the entrance to the casino. His plan was to get cozy with the management. Vic needed to mix with the casino personnel to find the man who'd been tapped to take over the money laundering scheme since Quarls's imprisonment. Given time, that man would divulge the author of the multimillion-dollar scam.

Vic had a hunch the corruption had been coming from the deputy secretary of the Department of the Interior, Fred Waters. He'd been overseeing Indian casino gaming interests throughout the United States for a long time. Waters *had* to be the one who'd orchestrated everything.

He was a millionaire many times over with accounts in the Caymans that law enforcement couldn't touch. He had the financial clout to order Leroy's early release from prison and put out a hit on Vic's son. Waters *had* to be the one who'd picked Quarls to launder money through this casino.

Vic had traced some fraud problems to Quarls and eventually made the arrest. The whole shady business with Jamison Lowell and the big sums of money in his bank account sent up a red flag. That kind of money came from drugs or gambling. Vic was prompted to take a look at the tapes pulled from the casino.

Yesterday, he and Kit had identified Jamison among the gamblers, and everything clicked into place. With Quarls taken out, Waters had picked another corruptible goon who carried out orders to play against Jamison. Once the district school administrator, who had a gambling addiction, was losing money, it was easy to blackmail him into setting up the kidnapping.

As soon as Jamison wasn't needed, they sent him to Colorado, where he was eliminated on the freeway near Vail. With the scent of coming victory in the air, a fresh surge of adrenaline filled Vic's body. He entered the casino and headed straight to the cage for chips. He pulled out his player's card linked to the hotel where he was staying in Luckenbach.

"Five thousand."

Once he had what he needed, he headed for the Mini Baccarat table. Earlier in the day, he and Kit had gone over the architectural drawings of the casino. Vic memorized every part of it for exits and rooms not open to the public. No expense had been spared to make it the most loaded casino in Texas.

All of it at the taxpayers' expense, with little of the proceeds benefitting the Indian nation.

The bulk of the money lined the pockets of the fat cats like Waters who believed they were untouchable and above the law. Eliminating a seven-year-old boy meant nothing to them. But Leroy hadn't finished the job. Claire had been the one who'd found Jeremy in time, thwarting Waters's plan to get even with Vic for the arrest. Now the tables had turned, and this was personal for him.

Despite the smoke, the place was well ventilated and attracted a cross section of people of every age and social class, many of whom were from out of state, judging by the license plates. Many people preferred a casino here in Texas to the ones in Las Vegas.

Vic joined the fast moving Mini Baccarat table and won fairly consistently for the next two hours. The house edge of 1.6 percent still allowed for him to build some earnings. When an African-American man, probably in his late twenties and wearing a tux, came by and whispered something to the dealer, Vic realized he'd been flagged. It was time to buy more chips at the cage.

"Three thousand."

After he moved on to the blackjack table, he knew he was being watched—which was the point. A half hour later, the same man came around again because

Vic was steadily winning. This time he struck up a conversation with him.

"We haven't seen you in here before."

"Some friends in New Mexico told me to come and check out this place. It's a good set up, but I was hoping for some action."

"Who are you?"

"My name is Eskaminzim. My people are thinking of putting up a casino near the Texas–New Mexico border. I'm visiting several casinos for ideas." Vic knew that Waters was always looking for another Indian tribe that wanted to build a casino. They were his cash cows.

"If you'll come with me to the back room, I'll introduce you to Mr. Ruban, the manager. He'll want to buy you a drink."

"No drinking while I'm on business."

"As you wish. Follow me."

Vic was led into another gaming room with two tables. One was empty, the other surrounded by some serious gamblers playing poker, some no doubt losing their shirts. A thin man of maybe forty came down the stairs in a tuxedo. He looked as if he could be Cuban with his three-inch-high El Yonki haircut.

"Mr. Ruban? This gentleman is taking a look at our casino in the hope of building one along the New Mexico border. He doesn't drink during business."

"Is that right? Thank you, Jori."

"Yes, sir."

After he disappeared Mr. Ruban told Vic to sit down at the empty table, but Vic preferred to remain standing. He stood two inches taller than the other man.

Ruban's speculative gaze swept over him. "You did well at our establishment so far this evening."

"I am pleased."

"What can I do for you?"

"I want to meet the person overseeing the casino."

"You can talk to me."

"You are the manager. Who is your boss? He's the one I came to see."

"He's not always here."

"Will you tell him I'll come by again tomorrow night to discuss business?"

"What's your name?"

"It's too difficult for you to pronounce. I'm known as Big Mouth."

"What tribe are you?"

"Lipan Apache."

"You must be an important member." His eyes were studying the jewelry.

"You like turquoise?"

"Yes. Yours is impossible to come by."

"That is true," Vic said with satisfaction. "I'm leaving now."

"If I can, I'll pass on your message."

Vic nodded and left the back room. After he stopped at the cage to claim his winnings, he walked outside and reached for his cell phone to call Kit.

"I'm almost to the truck. Meet me at the hotel as soon as you can. I'll call the kitchen for room service." Kit would be in disguise as an employee working the night shift.

On the drive to town, Vic kept an eye out for anyone following him. Ruban would send someone to tail him and check out his truck at the hotel. The front desk would verify he was registered there as the sole occupant of the room.

The Hill Country Inn displayed a no-vacancy sign. The casino had brought in new business. Vic got out, locked his truck and walked inside to the front desk to make sure they knew he was back.

"May I help you?" asked the pert young brunette woman behind the counter.

"Did someone leave a message for me? Room 220."

She went to check. "Sorry, sir."

"Thank you."

"Your jewelry is fantastic," she exclaimed, studying him.

"Family heirlooms."

"You're a lucky man."

His thoughts flew to Jeremy and Claire. *Lady—you have no idea how lucky I am.*

Vic turned away and caught the elevator to the next floor. After he'd reached his room, he phoned for room service and ordered enough food for two.

Kit would be sleeping in the second queen-size bed while they were on the case. The two other staff were sleeping in the van.

After removing the recording device, he took off his jewelry and removed the tan jacket. He peeled off his shirt, then the bulletproof vest. None of the guys liked to wear one, but it saved lives. Kit wore his firearm so they had protection.

Vic slipped on a T-shirt and pulled off his boots. In

a minute Kit arrived at the door with their food. Vic stayed out of sight as he opened the door. Kit came inside and put the tray on the table. On his way out he said, "You've shrunk, bud, but you still look intimidating. In case anyone is watching, I'll go back to the kitchen, then slip out and come back up in a minute."

"I'll leave the door unlocked."

"You sound like an ad on TV."

They both chuckled before he disappeared. Kit was always great to work with. At moments like this, he was thankful TJ hadn't suspended him. This was the only work he loved doing. He owed Dr. Marshall, too, for giving him a clean bill of mental health so fast. Before long Vic and Kit were going to nail Fred Waters.

Before any more time passed, he used his other phone and left a message at headquarters to be sent on to Claire and Jeremy that all was well and he would contact them soon."

He hung up just as Kit slipped inside and locked the door. After freshening up in the bathroom, he sat down at the table with Vic and picked up the device. "I'm curious to hear what went on inside there."

He turned it on and they listened to the recording while they ate club sandwiches and salad. Kit gave him a grin when the girl at the desk made a comment about the jewelry. "You scored a hit with Mr. Ruban and the ladies. We know what Ruban was attracted to, but she obviously loved your jewelry, too. You're a stud with this new persona. I'd love to see you try it out on Claire."

Vic shook his head and they listened to the digital recording again. "Let's hope the boss shows up tomorrow night. If he does, I'll try to shake a few more apples off the tree."

"It's going to happen. Now let's get some shut-eye. Are you going to sleep in that wig?"

"I have to. Sandra put me together and told me to leave it alone. I'm so tired I probably won't move."

"That's good, otherwise I'll have to put you back together tomorrow and it won't be pretty."

Before long they both headed for the sack.

AT TWELVE-THIRTY, VIC made his way downstairs for lunch in the hotel dining room. Kit had long since vacated the room, taking the tray of dishes back to the kitchen.

While he downed another meal, he had a visitor, not unexpected. He started his digital recorder. What did you know? It was Jori, right on schedule.

Vic looked up at him. "Don't you work at the casino?"

"Yes. Mr. Ruban asked me to deliver a message. He says the man you wish to meet is not available."

"Tonight? Or never."

"Never."

Interesting. So possibly the top man didn't want another casino infringing on the territory. "Tell him thank you for letting me know. You want some coffee before you go?"

"Sure. Why not?"

Vic signaled the waitress. "Two coffees, please."

She came right over and served them.

Jori was out of uniform and wore a nice crew neck

shirt and trousers. "You sure do have beautiful turquoises."

"I have lots more. It's made by my tribe."

"I bet you could get big money for that necklace."

"Many people have made offers. The last person was willing to give me one hundred thousand dollars. Since you work at the casino, maybe you make that kind of money?"

He shook his head. "Not that much."

"Casinos like that one make huge money. They should pay you more. Then I might be able to sell you some pieces I have that are similar to the necklace."

"If you build a new casino, would you give me a job for more money?"

"How much do you make?"

"Fifty thousand dollars a year."

"If I knew I could trust you, I might pay you as much as one hundred fifty thousand dollars. It's hard to find loyal employees like you who came all the way to the hotel to deliver a message for me. Mr. Ruban doesn't realize how lucky he is."

"Mr. Ruban isn't my boss. He's just the manager. Another man decides how much money I make."

Now was Vic's chance. "You mean Edgar Quarls? I heard he ran the whole Indian concession."

"No, no. Quarls is in prison. Now Mr. Fisher is in charge."

Bingo.

"I didn't know that. I'd like to meet him, but I guess it's not possible. Thank you for the message." He reached in his pocket for some loose turquoise he could use for a bribe. "Here." Three stones lay in the palm of his hand. "Pick the one you want. It is yours."

"Ah… You would do this for me?"

"You have done me a favor, so I don't waste any more time in this town. After I've finished my lunch, I'm moving on to the Kickapoo Casino in Eagle Pass."

The man blinked. "You would *give* it to me?"

"I have spoken. Any one of these would make a nice ring. I see you don't wear rings."

"I can't afford a good one."

"Well, you can now."

Jori hesitated before choosing the oblong stone. "I like this shape."

"So do I. It will look good on your long fingers. Mine are shorter."

The man laughed. "You're right."

"When you get it mounted, tell the person this is a genuine Lipan Apache turquoise."

"You are most kind." He plucked it from Vic's hand and studied it before putting it in his pocket. "Where will you build your casino?"

"Just across the Texas border outside Hobbs, New Mexico. When I get it built and you need a job, come and see me."

"What's your name?"

"People know me as Big Mouth."

Jori smiled. "*That* I will remember. The Apache with the big mouth and the short fingers."

After he left the restaurant, Vic couldn't get up to his hotel room fast enough. He pulled out the cell phone that connected him to the guys in the van. Kit answered. "What's up?"

"While I was eating lunch, I had a visit from Jori. He's the employee at the casino who introduced me to Mr. Ruban. I'm going to put the phone on speaker so you can hear our conversation on the digital recording. I'm starting it now."

The guys listened, but it was Kit's voice Vic heard loud and clear when the name Fisher was mentioned. The second the recording ended, Kit got on the line.

"You nailed it! Terrence Fisher is staff director of the House Administration Committee run by none other than Fred Waters. We've got the connection we've been looking for."

"Yup, and just as we thought, this has gone straight to the White House."

"Waters ordered Fisher to go after you. He did that by releasing Leroy early from prison, then hiring Jamison to set up Leroy in that custodial job."

"Mr. Ruban must have contacted Fisher and told him that I wanted to meet with him. By now they've tried to figure out who I really am, and Fisher smells a rat. I'm pretty sure I'm going to have company later on when I leave town. His thugs will probably try to gun me down on the highway."

"Do you trust Jori?"

"I don't know. If he's a good guy, then he's in danger because he sat and talked with me. He should have left immediately after delivering the message. Anyone watching the two of us at lunch would report back to Ruban, who's a sleazy character if I ever met one."

"Okay. Pack up and leave. TJ's coordinating everything with the highway patrol. They'll be covering you the second you head south of Luckenbach. There'll be more reinforcements farther along. Our van will be right on your tail. The boss is elated you found the missing link. This case is huge."

"We both knew it was. Talk to you in a minute."

Vic hung up and gathered his things. He put the recording device in his pocket. The next thing to do was pack all the jewelry, including the belt, into his suitcase. He laid the tan leather jacket over everything to protect the valuable items Clint had lent him before shutting the case. The last thing to do was leave the room key on the table. Then he was out of there and down to the truck in no time.

Someone had broken into it, but they wouldn't have found anything. Evidence of the break-in had to be all over the place, but he didn't have time to dust for fingerprints now. He put the small suitcase in the toolbox of the truck before getting behind the wheel.

It would take three hours to drive to Eagle Pass. If Jori had been a plant to find out Vic's next plan, Ruban would know it by now and would have passed the information on to Fisher. As he took off, he phoned Kit.

"Someone broke into the truck."

"That figures. We'll get prints later. In about three minutes, pull into the Tesoro gas station on the town loop. It'll be on the right. Go to the men's room. It's inside. An undercover cop wearing a Longhorn baseball cap will be coming out and pass you off a weapon."

"Copy that."

"You're wearing your vest, right?"

"Yes."

"Just checking."

He clicked Off and kept driving until he saw the station. Once he got out, he filled the tank, then went inside to use the bathroom. Twenty seconds later he saw the cop and started for the door, catching the gun to him before going inside. The Glock felt good in his hand. When he got back to the truck, he checked the clip to make certain it was loaded and put it under the seat.

Once he was on the road again, he phoned Kit. "Mission accomplished."

"That's a relief. I didn't like it that you went to the casino last night without your weapon."

"I couldn't take a chance."

"I know."

"I'm armed now. See anything suspicious yet?"

"No, but we'll be notified the second something doesn't look right."

Vic continued to drive south and chatted with Kit. An hour had passed. "Now that we know who's behind this, we can make another visit to Leroy at the jail. When we tell him we know everything, we can offer him one more plea deal if he'll spill the details. I want to know why he didn't kill my son."

"My thoughts exactly. Uh-oh—wait up. Something's coming through to the guys over the police band. Good grief."

"What's happened?"

"A few minutes ago an African-American male in a Toyota outside the casino near Luckenbach was found

slumped in the driver's seat with a bullet to the brain.
Some gamblers saw the body and reported it. No ID
yet."

"That was Jori."

"Informant or not, he's dead now."

"I liked him. This is a filthy business. When we arrest Ruban, then we've got Fisher and Waters."

"Hold on, Vic. I need to talk to TJ. I'll call you right
back."

Vic hung up and kept driving, knowing that at some
point between here and Eagle Pass, Fisher's cronies
were waiting for him. Another half hour went by without any action. Kit checked in now and then.

There was only an hour and a half to go until Vic
reached Eagle Pass. He'd just decided they were planning to ambush him there when he noted a helicopter
in the distance. It was probably an AirMed chopper.
But it didn't deviate from its course and was headed
in Vic's direction.

"Kit?"

"Yeah. I see it, too. Get off the road and run like
hell for the grove of trees on the right. We're going to
do the same thing."

"Doing it now!"

There was fencing running parallel to the highway.
He took his chances and rammed his truck straight
through it. He kept on driving until he could jump out
and take cover. He heard a bullet zing past his ear. The
Forest Service helicopter had swept in low, allowing the
sniper to get a good shot, but he'd missed Vic by inches.

He rolled in the underbrush beneath the trees and

heard return fire. When he looked up, he saw a police helicopter overhead. It was following the other one that was coming straight for the trees again. He heard a cacophony of police sirens getting louder. The sniper fired at him again, but missed. Vic rolled the other way to avoid the line of fire, not having enough time to shoot.

Then there was an explosion, and Vic saw the hostile helicopter lose control and come straight toward the trees. He got to his feet and started running for dear life. Before he reached the edge of the grove, something hit him on the back of his head. Dazed by the impact, he saw lights, and started to crumple.

"Vic—" Kit came running to him out of the smoke. Before he knew it, his friend was pulling him away from the trees that had caught fire. "Come on." He put Vic's arm around his shoulders. "Let's get you away from here." The air was black with smoke.

They were both coughing. "Where's the sniper?"

"Dead. The pilot, too."

"Add two more life sentences to those on Waters and Fisher. To be honest, I didn't think I was going to get out of there alive." They were headed for the highway.

"I knew you would. You're indestructible."

They could see several ambulances arriving. "I don't want an ambulance. Some debris hit the back of my head, but I'm fine now. The wig protected me." He removed his arm from Kit's shoulder, but neither of them could stop coughing. "Just give me a minute to catch my breath. I'll be fine as soon as I can take the vest off. Damn, it's hot out here."

"We're almost there. It's the boss's orders. You've

been through too many ordeals in the past ten days. He wants you checked out. I'll ride with you."

Vic eyed the scene of destruction. "The Forest Service lost a helicopter. I think I ruined the front end of the truck."

"When I saw you ram that fencing, my heart almost stopped."

"I decided it was all or nothing, so I went for it."

"Thank God you did. It bought you enough time for the sniper to miss his mark."

"Are the guys all right?"

"They're fine. One of them will drive the van back to Austin."

They kept hacking while they walked. "I should have warned Jori he was in danger."

"You didn't know what was going to happen."

"In my gut I did. He was young and vulnerable. You heard him on the recording."

"I'll listen to it again after we get in the ambulance."

"My suitcase is in the toolbox. The Glock is under the seat. Make sure we get everything back."

"I'll tell the sheriff right now."

One of the paramedics helped Vic into the ambulance, but he remained standing in order to remove his shirt and the vest. Kit climbed in and reached for the vest while Vic put the shirt back on. "Ah…that feels good. You like my tan?" he asked the medic. "It came out of a bottle, but it's washable." Another coughing spell ensued.

He reached up and removed the wig that had seen better days after his roll in the underbrush. Kit took it from him. The paramedic looked shocked. "I had no idea you weren't real."

"Oh, he's real," Kit declared. "What are you? One-eighth Apache?"

"Close. It appears my disguise worked, thanks to Sandra." He winked at Kit, who sat on the bench. Before he sat down, he pulled the recording device from his pocket. "Go ahead and listen."

Letting go with another cough, Kit pressed play then put it up to his ear to listen.

"Okay, now you can have at me," Vic told the medic. "The back of my head took a whack from something."

"You have a small lump, but it's not bleeding."

"It hardly hurts now." Vic watched Kit's expression while his vitals were taken.

"You're in amazingly good shape." On that note, the medic handed them both a bottle of water.

They both drank thirstily before Kit asked, "That stone you gave Jori—was it valuable?"

"No."

"I can see what you mean about him. He was just trying to make it in this world."

"We'll turn the recording over for evidence. TJ is going to be elated."

Kit looked excited. "We know someone on Waters's payroll commandeered the Forest Service chopper. With leads galore, there's going to be a huge investigation. Jori was the key that made it all happen. The sting paid off. Waters and Fisher never saw you coming until it was too late."

"Once again I lucked out," he said as the door of

the ambulance opened. Vic saw the sheriff deliver the suitcase.

"I'll return the gun to its owner. Great job you Rangers did today. The casino has been closed and the management is in custody pending a thorough investigation. A lot of shady business has gone on there."

That meant Ruban was no longer a threat. Vic couldn't wait to interrogate him. "That's music to our ears. We couldn't have done this without your department's help."

"You rest now. You're being driven back to the inn in Luckenbach to meet up with your crew."

"Thanks, Sheriff."

"Thank *you*."

Soon they were on their way. Vic sat on the side of the bed to talk strategy with Kit. So many loose ends to clean up kept them occupied until they reached the hotel. Vic thanked the paramedics and got out of the ambulance, taking his suitcase with him. Kit followed with the vest. The long wig dangled from his other hand. He started to head for the surveillance van when he heard a voice he'd know anywhere. "Dad!"

Vic swung around to see his son come running toward him. Claire was right behind him. What a glorious sight. But they both stopped short before reaching him.

"What did you do to your face?"

"You should see him in this wig. Here, Vic. Put it on and show them." Kit handed it to him.

At this point he was speechless and did as Kit said.

"Whoa, Dad—"

Kit was grinning. "Jeremy? Claire? Allow me to introduce you to Eskaminzim, a spokesman for the Lipan Apache tribe. He's better known as Big Mouth."

Claire walked all the way around him, eyeing him with stars in her eyes. "Big Mouth, huh? I think I like you even better than I liked Jim. You kind of resemble your famous ancestor Victorio Eskaminzim."

His heart was giving him fits. "How did you know to come here?"

"Your son makes a terrific spy. When we read your note and knew you'd gone undercover on a sting, he called Clint and found out you were in the other room with Sandra. When it was all over the news about a shooting outside the casino, we decided we couldn't wait, so we drove ninety miles an hour to get here and talk to Clint. And here you are…" Her voice cracked with emotion.

"Here I am." He rushed toward them and wrapped his arms around both of them, hugging them so hard Jeremy let out a yelp.

"What's the matter?"

"Your hair's in my face and I can't breathe."

Kit burst into laughter.

Claire looked up at Vic with those divine gray eyes pouring out her love for him. "You can get your hair in my face anytime," she whispered for his ears alone.

Chapter Ten

A night breeze coming from the open terrace doors wafted through the hotel room adjoining Jeremy's. Claire burned with love for Vic as she waited for him to come to bed. This was the fifth night of their honeymoon in Montego Bay. Tomorrow they'd be flying to Orlando.

Between the air filled with the scent of frangipani and the palm trees along the beach silhouetted in the moonlight, she understood the meaning of intoxication. Tonight they'd eaten around the pool and were entertained by a local reggae artist and band. Claire still felt the beat of the music in her veins. Jeremy had been in heaven and got to talk to the band members who let him try to play their instruments during the intermission.

He was so cute as he sat there sipping Shirley Temples with a girl his age named Trisha, who was there on vacation with her family from California. The family resort offered everything for children and adults, making their vacation a paradise. While the children had fun, Claire clung to her husband as they danced the night away.

Vic was a terrific dancer and had a sense of rhythm that made it exciting to follow his lead. He was full of surprises that thrilled her to the very core of her being. Though it had seemed as if she'd waited forever for him to tell her that he loved her, she wasn't sorry. They'd grown to be best friends first. Jeremy's kidnapping a month ago had swept them into the depths of agony, but their marriage had brought them ecstasy.

Vic slid into the bed after his shower and reached for her. "He's asleep."

"I'm not surprised. Jeremy has had the time of his life so far."

"What about you?" His lips roved over her face kissed by the Caribbean sun before finding her mouth.

"How can you even ask me that question?"

"I guess it's because I've wanted you for so long. Now that I can have my way with you, it's sort of hard to believe."

"I have the same problem. Make love to me, Vic. Again and again."

"As if you need to ask." He kissed the base of her throat, where she could feel the pulse of her heart against his lips. "I intend to satisfy your every whim."

Claire's breath caught. "Every time with you is like the first time."

She'd never had a lover, but she couldn't imagine making love with anyone but him. He took her to heights that made her feel immortal. The days here in paradise were spent with Jeremy, but the nights were for her and her husband. They took full advantage and slept little, before starting the whole heavenly process all over again several times during the nights they'd been here. The world would infringe again, but not for a while longer.

As the tint of dawn distilled over their love nest, Claire studied her gorgeous Texas Ranger, who'd fallen into a deep sleep. Their legs were intertwined, but his arm had relaxed, giving her a little room to enjoy his rugged features.

She could still see him in his disguise after Kit had told Vic to put on the wig. It amazed her that he had so many looks depending on the moment. Every so often he'd worn his white hat for some event honoring the Rangers. Then there was what she thought of as his PI persona with the sunglasses. And whenever they went riding, he looked the part of a genuine cowboy.

The memory of him standing at the altar of the church as her beloved bridegroom in a stunning dark blue suit always made her breath catch. In front of a small group, with both their families and the Famous Four in attendance, she'd pledged her love and devotion to him.

But his Lipan Apache look had to be her favorite. When he'd climbed out of the ambulance several inches taller due to the lifts in his cowboy boots, she had been blown away. Against his bronzed skin, his eyes glittered like black obsidian. Once the black wig was on, he became the warrior whose genes he naturally possessed on the inside.

There was a stature and magnificence about him that had astonished everyone that day, even Jeremy, who'd felt his imposing aura. Claire loved every part of this man, whether he was waking, sleeping, talking, eating, worrying or laughing. But she would never forget the night his son went missing. She'd felt and heard his deep sobs.

Yet there was still another part of Vic, the loving part she'd been introduced to on this unforgettable honeymoon. Her fate was sealed. She was now Mrs. Stephen Victorio Malone, and she loved her new role with a passion.

Once when she'd asked him about his first wife, he'd told her she'd called him Stephen because that was how they'd been introduced. But after his buddies in the field learned his middle name was Victorio, they'd nicknamed him Vic and it had stuck. She couldn't think of him as Stephen and was glad he could safeguard that special memory of him and his wife.

He was Vic to Claire. When she next came awake, she called out his name with longing. "I love you so much I don't know what to do about it."

Vic pulled her over on top of him. "Leave it to me to handle this, Elaine. I'm an expert."

She chuckled. "You certainly are."

"I love you, Claire. The last thing I want to do is leave today."

She groaned. "I don't want to leave either." She kissed him hungrily. "We'll have to come back here again soon."

"The captain would have given us another week off, but since I'd already taken one week to get my temper under control he—"

"I know." She shushed him with her lips. "He needs you back to finish up the Waters-gate case with Kit."

Vic chuckled. "That's what it is, a Watergate scandal, Texas style."

"You know what Sam Houston said about us. 'Texas has yet to learn submission to any oppression, come from what source it may.'"

"Ma'am, if you aren't speaking the truth." Another heart-stopping kiss followed his teasing.

She was finally able to catch her breath. "It appears Waters found that out the hard way when he went up against *you*, darling."

A knock sounded on the door to the adjoining room. "Dad? Claire? Are you up yet?"

They smiled at each other. "We kind of are," he called out to his son.

"Can I go for a swim?"

"Not without us. We'll be up in a minute."

"No, you won't."

"Jeremy Malone? What did you say?"

"It always takes you so long."

"I promise we'll hurry," Claire broke in.

"Promise?"

Vic shook his head no, but now that Jeremy was up, they had to hurry.

After saying "I promise," Claire rolled away and got off the bed on the other side, eluding the hand that tried to stop her.

He frowned. "Where are you going?"

"To the shower," she called over her shoulder. "This time I'm locking the door!"

"There'll be a price to pay for that," he growled.

"Goody. I'll be ready for any sentence you wish to pronounce once we're in the hotel in Orlando. And that's a promise I intend to keep."

"GOOD HEAVENS, JEREMY! You filled a whole pillow case with candy." Claire had spread out a quilt on the family room floor where he dumped his Halloween cache. Vic stood behind him grinning. She could tell her husband had enjoyed himself going trick-or-treating with Nate's dad and the boys. The two men wore identical Sabretooth masks.

"I know. You should see Nate's bag. His dad took most of his peanut butter cups."

"My dad always took my licorice candy."

"Yuck. I hate licorice."

Vic swooped down and picked up a couple of York Peppermint Pattie candies.

"Hey, Dad—those are my favorite!"

"I left some for you," he said after chomping down on them.

"What do *you* want, Claire?"

He was her thoughtful boy. "Hmm. I don't think anything right now. I ate too much stuff while I stayed here to give out candy to all the kids who came to the door. They were so cute, but no one was as cute as you are in your Wolverine costume. I'm glad I got some pictures of you before you left."

"I saw another kid with the same costume on."

"That doesn't surprise me, honey."

Vic darted her a loving glance. "There was a big crowd out tonight."

She nodded "You can say that again. All our candy is gone."

"That's okay," Jeremy said. "We have mine."

"You could open a store, sport."

Jeremy laughed. "No, I couldn't. You're funny."

"Remember the rule. You can eat one piece of candy now, and then you have to go to bed."

"Umm, I think I'll have a cinnamon gummy bear." He took off the wrapper and popped the jelly candy in his mouth.

"Okay. Now it's time to get this show on the road."

Claire loved it. Both she and Vic were dying to be alone. He was trying to hurry things along. "You'll need a quick bath first, honey. Don't forget to brush your teeth. I'll come in when you say your prayers."

"Do I have to go to bed right now?"

"Yes," they said at the same time. "It's late."

"Do you think Comet and Daken would like a Tootsie Roll?"

"I don't think so," Claire murmured. "Go on."

"Oh, heck."

While the boys were gone, Claire found a basket to put all the candy in and threw the pillow case in the washing machine. She could hardly wait until Jeremy was down for the night. After locking up and turning off the lights, she hurried to the bedroom and got dressed in a nightgown. She pulled on her navy toweling robe, the one with the pockets.

Pretty soon Jeremy called out that he was ready to

say his prayers. The three of them knelt at the side of the bed while he blessed everything and everyone, drawing things out to the nth degree. She peeked once at Vic and discovered he was watching her with a huge smile on his face. She had to admit this was a little bit of heaven.

"Amen."

In Claire's mind she could hear Vic saying a much louder amen. She struggled to hold the laughter inside.

Once Jeremy was under the covers, she and Vic gave him a kiss and said good-night. When they left the room, Vic reached for her in the hall and gave her a hungry kiss. "Good news. I don't have to go to work tomorrow. We can sleep in."

When they reached their bedroom, he untied her robe and threw it over the chair so he could feel her body. "Have you decided if you're going to take that part-time job at the lab in Austin? That offer has been out there for a few days. I'll support you in anything you want."

"I know that. You're wonderful, but I'm thinking I want to stay home for a while longer. Jeremy needs me."

"You're not just saying that because you think it will make me happy? Because honestly, Claire, I want you to be happy."

She put her hands on his chest and looked up at him. "I've never been so happy in my life. Tonight, watching Jeremy in his cute Halloween costume, made me realize that this time is precious while he's still growing. I don't want to miss any of it."

"If you're sure." His black eyes had a sheen that told her how thrilled he was by her decision. He started rubbing her arms as a prelude to making love.

"Oh, I am. In fact I've been so sure, I emailed them this afternoon that I was declining their offer. That's because of something else that happened today."

He cocked his head. "What do you mean?"

"Well, why don't you feel in the right pocket of my robe."

His brows met together before he picked it up and felt inside. He pulled out the home pregnancy test and stared at it. Vic was in shock, just as she was. His head reared. "This says positive!"

"Yes. I took the test this afternoon because I realized I'd missed my second period."

He dropped it on the chair and clasped her upper arms. "We're *pregnant*!"

"Yes, darling. Next year at this time we'll have to dress up our little warrior girl or boy in a genuine Lipan Apache costume. Can you believe it?"

"Sweetheart—" He picked her up and whirled her around. "We're going to have a baby!"

"I know. I'm so excited I think I'm still in shock."

He set her down gently. "How do you feel?"

"Fine."

"You mean it? You're not hiding anything from me? Cy's wife, Kellie, was so sick in the beginning she couldn't perform at the National Finals Rodeo in Las Vegas."

"I know. She told me while we were all at the picnic in Bandera over Labor Day."

He gathered Claire to his body and rocked her. "Jeremy's going to get a little brother or sister. It will be so good for him."

"I agree. That's why I want to be home and make him completely secure before our child comes into the world."

He buried his face in her hair. "What did I do to deserve a woman like you to come into my life? You saved me and Jeremy, and then you saved us again when you found him. I can't find the words to tell you what you mean to me. All I can do is show you."

"You keep doing that, my beloved Texas Ranger. You *are* my beloved."

* * * * *

MILLS & BOON®

Cherish™

EXPERIENCE THE ULTIMATE RUSH OF FALLING IN LOVE

A sneak peek at next month's titles...

In stores from 14th January 2016:

- **A Deal to Mend Their Marriage** – Michelle Douglas *and* **Fortune's Perfect Valentine** – Stella Bagwell
- **Dr. Forget-Me-Not** – Marie Ferrarella *and* **Saved by the CEO** – Barbara Wallace

In stores from 28th January 2016:

- **A Soldier's Promise** – Karen Templeton *and* **Tempted by Her Tycoon Boss** – Jennie Adams
- **Pregnant with a Royal Baby!** – Susan Meier *and* **The Would-Be Daddy** – Jacqueline Diamond

Available at WHSmith, Tesco, Asda, Eason, Amazon and Apple

Just can't wait?
Buy our books online a month before they hit the shops!
visit www.millsandboon.co.uk

These books are also available in eBook format!

'The perfect Christmas read!' - Julia Williams

Jewellery designer Skylar loves living London, but when a surprise proposal goes wrong, she finds herself fleeing home to remote Puffin Island.

Burned by a terrible divorce, TV historian Alec is dazzled by Sky's beauty and so cynical that he assumes that's a bad thing! Luckily she's on the verge of getting engaged to someone else, so she won't be a constant source of temptation... but this Christmas, can Alec and Sky realise that they are what each other was looking for all along?

Order yours today at
www.millsandboon.co.uk

MILLS & BOON®

Want to get more from Mills & Boon?

Here's what's available to you if you join the exclusive **Mills & Boon eBook Club** today:

✦ *Convenience – choose your books each month*

✦ *Exclusive – receive your books a month before anywhere else*

✦ *Flexibility – change your subscription at any time*

✦ *Variety – gain access to eBook-only series*

✦ *Value – subscriptions from just £3.99 a month*

So visit **www.millsandboon.co.uk/esubs** today to be a part of this exclusive eBook Club!